W9-CXP-321

WHERE IS MY SON?

When Audrey screamed, Richard spotted Merle immediately. The big man thought he was being cunning, but his clumsiness was almost laughable. Suddenly Richard was absolutely certain that Audrey had been right all along. He didn't understand how she knew or how Merle had pulled it off. But somehow this bastard had taken their son. He strode along the side of the house as though he had no idea that Merle was lurking in the shadows. When the bigger man leapt out in front of him, Richard surprised himself as much as Merle by rushing forward, gripping Merle by both shoulders, and powering him to the ground.

"What have you done with Zach, you bastard?" he screamed, slamming his fist into the man's face. *"Where is my son?"*

ALSO BY CHANDLER MCGREW

COLD HEART

"Incredible tension and suspense."
—*Mystery News*

"An engrossing reading experience."
—*Midwest Book Review*

"A tense and satisfying read."
—*I Love a Mystery*

NIGHT TERROR

Chandler McGrew

A DELL BOOK

Published by
Dell Publishing
a division of
Random House, Inc.
New York, New York

This is a work of fiction. Names, characters, places, and
incidents either are the product of the author's imagination or
are used fictitiously. Any resemblance to actual persons, living
or dead, events, or locales is entirely coincidental.

All rights reserved
Copyright © 2003 by Chandler McGrew
Cover photo copyright © 2003 by
Norman Owen Tomalin/Bruce Coleman, Inc.
Pavor Nocturnus definition copyright © 1996–2002
David W. Richards
www.nightterrors.org.

No part of this book may be reproduced or transmitted in any
form or by any means, electronic or mechanical, including
photocopying, recording, or by any information storage and
retrieval system, without the written permission of the
Publisher, except where permitted by law. For information
address: Dell Publishing, New York, New York.

If you purchased this book without a cover, you should be
aware that this book is stolen property. It was reported as
"unsold and destroyed" to the publisher, and neither the
author nor the publisher has received any payment for this
"stripped book."

Dell® is a registered trademark of Random House, Inc., and the
colophon is a trademark of Random House, Inc.

ISBN: 0-440-24122-7

Manufactured in the United States of America

Published simultaneously in Canada

March 2003

OPM 10 9 8 7 6 5 4 3 2 1

FOR CHARLI,
Night terrors are only dreams and I'll always
be there when you need me. I promise.
Daddy

Thanks to my wife, Rene, for the gift of time to write. Thanks to Deputy Harry Sims of the Oxford County Sheriff's Department and Chief Darren Tripp of the Bethel Police Department for making certain I didn't stumble over any procedural matters. Thanks as always to my agent, Irene Kraas, for hard work and constant faith. And last but *certainly* not least, thanks to my editor, Abby Zidle, for her understanding of my unconventional methods, which required her to edit not one but *numerous* drafts from start to finish. With all my heart, thanks, Abby.

NIGHT

Pavor Nocturnus (Night Terror): Sudden awakening from sleep, persistent fear or terror that occurs at night, screaming, sweating, confusion, rapid heart rate, inability to explain what happened, usually no recall of "bad dreams" or nightmares, may have a vague sense of frightening images. Many people see spiders, snakes, animals or people in the room, are unable to fully awake, difficult to comfort, with no memory of the event on awakening the next day.

—David W. Richards

www.nightterrors.org

1

SILENCE HUNG OVER THE DARKENED HOUSE like a shroud. Outside the window, the moon peered bleakly through the skeletal pines. Gray-black clouds scudded across the sky, rats deserting a sinking ship.

Audrey Bock screamed.

Her shriek resounded in the confines of the bedroom, and then away down the hall, like the caterwaul of a hell-bent train. Her husband, Richard, bolted upright, fumbling for the lamp. The alarm clock clattered to the floor.

Audrey screamed again. Beneath the fury of her gut-wrenching cry, other sounds struggled toward the surface in Richard's consciousness. His fingernails scratching the table-top. A thin breeze fluttering the curtains.

The light finally flicked on as Audrey screamed yet again.

She sat with her back pressed stiff against the head-board, staring straight ahead through unfocused blue eyes, her knees tucked tightly to her chest. Her short blond hair was tousled and her hands flapped wildly in front of her face, warding off some unseen menace.

Richard clutched her, following her gaze across the harsh shadows of their bedroom, into the empty hallway, barely lit by the bathroom night-light.

"Let him go!" she cried.

Richard shook her gently. "Honey, there's nobody there. It's just a bad dream. Wake up."

"She's got him!" Audrey shrieked, so loudly that Richard winced. "She's got him!"

"Honey, it's a nightmare. Wake up!"

"Leave him alone! Leave my baby alone!"

Richard tugged her back as she struggled feebly in his arms. "Audrey!"

"She's got him," she said in a voice suddenly far too calm. It seemed as though she'd taken a step back from whatever it was in her mind. As though her pounding heart had abruptly stilled, not because the terror was over, but because it had become too great to bear.

"You're asleep. You've got to wake up."

"She's going to kill him," she whispered, her words digging into his heart. "She's got my baby."

Richard couldn't understand how she could have her eyes wide open and still be sound asleep. This was nothing like the nightmares that had plagued her since Zach's disappearance. This was something different, more sinister. He couldn't reach her through the barricade of sleep, if she *was* asleep at all.

Without warning, her panic returned. "I've got to go!" She fought him, stronger this time, but still unable to break free.

He couldn't stand to see her this way. It summoned buried feelings of inadequacy and guilt. He stared at the ceiling, praying to find a revelation there, but none appeared. "Honey, if you don't wake up I'm going to put you in the shower." He wasn't sure that was such a good idea— he seemed to recall something about not shocking someone in the middle of a nightmare, or was that sleepwalking?— but he didn't know what else to do. Perhaps just the threat would work.

"Don't touch him!" she screamed. This time she broke free of his grasp, wobbling beside the bed, gesturing toward the shadows in the hall.

Richard slid across the bed, standing to wrap her in his arms again. Lifting her easily, he carried her out into the hall. Audrey pawed at the empty air, the terrible vision following her through the house. Richard lowered her gently into the tub, and she cringed in the far corner, quivering, as though the icy water had already been turned on.

"Audrey, please wake up," he pleaded.

Just as he feared, she gave no sign of hearing him. He turned on the tap, expecting another cry as the cold water struck her, but her silence was worse. She quailed in the farthest corner of the tub. The water plastered her hair to her head. Her chin rested between her knees and she shivered so violently her teeth chattered, but still she stared straight ahead at the nightmare visible only to her.

Richard knelt beside the tub, spray soaking his pajamas, stroking soggy hair out of her face. "Aud, it's a dream. It's just a bad dream. You have to wake up."

"It isn't a dream." Her voice was flat and mechanical again.

He lightly slapped her cheek. "It is."

She turned to glare into his eyes, and for the first time he thought she could see him, but the terrified expression that slowly slipped across her features told him she still wasn't back in the here and now.

"She's here!" she screamed.

He gripped her shoulders and shook her, barely feeling the icy spray on his back. "No one's here, Aud."

"She's got him." Her tone was hesitant again. Confused. Her emotional roller coaster frightened him as much as the crazy dream or his inability to reach her. What in the world could be going on inside her head? It was as if some mad scientist were alternately injecting her with uppers and downers, to test her reaction to the drugs. But he sensed a growing awareness of her surroundings in her eyes, in the way she jerked when the water hit her in the face again as he moved.

"Wake up, honey," he said. "You're almost awake. Come on. Stand up."

"I am standing up."

"No, you're not. Come on."

He lifted her to her feet, and she wrapped her arms around him, collapsing into his soaking embrace. They huddled together beneath the frigid shower for several minutes, until her breathing eased and her heart slowed again. She shook against him, sobbing into his shoulder.

"I want him back," she whimpered.

"I want him back, too, Aud." He held her at arm's length, peering into her eyes. "Are you with me now?"

She gave him a curious look.

"Are you awake?" he asked.

"Yes."

"Good. Let's get you dried off."

She stood compliantly as he removed her dripping nightgown and toweled her dry. Then he kicked off his own sodden pajamas and dried himself, tossing towels and pajamas into a damp pile in the corner.

"Let's go back to bed," he said, exhausted.

But she stood as still as a zombie and he realized that wherever she was, she still wasn't completely back yet. He lifted her again—like a child, because she wasn't much larger than one—and speaking calmly to her all the time, carried her ever so gently back to bed.

2

OUTSIDE THE OLD RED-BRICK COURTHOUSE with its one lit window, Arcos, Maine lay sleeping Friday night away. A freshening breeze stirred maples, oaks, birches, and balsams, wafting the scent of manure into town from outlying farms that were renewing their fertile black soil for spring. The easternmost reaches of the White Mountains shadowed the moon, and only starlight shimmered on the lakes and ponds that made the area a mecca for summer tourists. Arcos, seat of Ouachita County, lay at the foot of the slopes, as though ready to slide down into the water of Lake Arcos, hidden by a low ridge just behind the building. Flatlanders were always asking "Where's the lake?" and locals would point toward their backyards and say "right through there."

Inside the building, Sheriff Virgil Milche ran his fingers through his hair and gnawed on his monthly cigar, finally stubbing out the fat butt in a pristine ashtray on the windowsill to his left. Virgil's full head of ash-gray hair matched his eyes, and his face was fluted with sun-browned wrinkles. Although he was shorter than every deputy on the force, he was powerfully built with thick arms and broad shoulders.

His amber-shaded desk lamp gave the entire office a cozy feeling to which the rattling radiator in the corner contributed. But even this late in the season, with the warmth from the ancient heater threatening to put him to sleep, Virgil couldn't shake a chill. As he stared at the twin manila file folders on his otherwise bare desk, he heard the door open but didn't bother looking up. Deputy Birch was the only other officer on duty in Arcos that night.

"Want me to pick you up something to eat, Sheriff?"

Virgil shook his head, scraping at a small brown stain on one of the folders, residue from some long-forgotten fly he'd done in. Names were taped on the front of each file in plastic labels.

Timothy Merrill.

Zachary Bock.

Doodles of knives and pistols covered the flat manila space around the names. Virgil filled in a tiny bare spot beneath the second *a* in Zachary with a fountain pen.

"Virg?" Most times Birch was unfailingly correct, and he was one of the cops Virgil had never had to discipline. Not once. But alone in the office at night, Virgil didn't stand on protocol, and besides, Birch was more than just a deputy. Even though he was one of the least senior men on the force and thirty years Virgil's junior, he'd become a friend.

Birch padded closer to the desk. Virgil concentrated on not coloring outside the lines.

"Virg, are you all right?"

Virgil glanced up, wondering why Birch had never done anything about his hair. It was cut short enough to be regulation, but it always looked as though he'd accidentally dropped the blow-dryer in the tub with him. "What?"

"Are you okay?"

"Yeah, fine."

"Doris doing all right today?"

Virgil's eyes dropped back to the files. "Yeah. She's okay."

"Why don't you go home?"

"Later. What did you need, Birch?"

"Nothing, Virg. You just looked like maybe you didn't feel too good."

"I'm fine."

"Okay, then. I'll put those files away for you, if you like."

Out of the corner of his eye, Virgil saw Birch's hand

reaching, and he slapped down on the files a little harder than he had intended. When he looked up into Birch's eyes again, he saw surprise.

"Sorry," said Virgil, taking a deep breath. "I'll take care of the files."

Birch nodded, staring at the folders. "The Merrill boy disappeared before I started, but I was here when Zach Bock got taken."

Virgil nodded.

"I know it still bothers you a lot, Virg."

"Yeah, Birch. It bothers me a lot." He stared off into space, hoping that Birch would get the message. After a longer than average time, he did.

"I'm gonna run over to the Big Apple and grab an ice cream bar. You should go on home."

"I'm gonna do that."

"Tell Doris I said hi."

"I will."

Virgil watched through the glass panel of his office as the deputy exited the station. Doris liked that kid almost as much as he did. Birch was thoughtful, smart, a hard worker, and he knew when to get out of the way. Most of the time.

Virgil closed his eyes and rubbed his temples hard, but the pain he felt now wasn't the kind that could be massaged away. He opened his eyes and began flipping through Timmy Merrill's file. Black-and-white photographs slid across his desk and he gathered them up like a deck of cards. The woods across from the Merrills. Bicycle tracks in the dirt alongside the road. Timmy's cap, brought in later by a town roadworker who'd discovered it a mile from the Merrills' house.

Virgil set the photos aside and fingered through pages of depositions. Nobody had seen anything. That was one of only three things that tied the two disappearances, four years apart, together.

Nobody saw anything.

A lot of people thought Virgil was crazy when Zach Bock disappeared and he dug up Timmy Merrill's file. Timmy disappeared a mile from home while riding his bike. He lived a couple of miles outside of Arcos in a residential but still rural area. Zach Bock was kidnapped right off his front lawn. Zach lived with his parents on a five-acre wooded lot fifteen miles outside of town. His nearest neighbor was a quarter-mile down the road. Timmy was an average boy, not overly bright but not stupid. By all accounts, Zach was a prodigy. He could read and write by the time he was four. Timmy was large for his age, with blond hair and blue eyes. Zach was small, dark hair, and deep brown eyes like his father. Timmy was seven when he disappeared. Zach was nine. The kidnappings were four years and fifteen miles apart, and in the intervening years no other children had disappeared in the area and no similar abductions had occurred in the county. Yet Virgil remained convinced that the two events were related.

Both victims were young boys. Both were taken by someone in an automobile, since the dogs never found a trace of them in the woods, not a scent.

And no one saw a thing.

He slid the photos back into the file and closed it, stacking the pair. The swirl patterns danced before his eyes. He refused to believe that *two* monsters lived in his county.

He picked up the files and returned them to his top drawer. When he flipped off the desk light, the whole station went dark. He could hear Birch's car starting outside and the sound of a semi cruising up Route 26 where it merged with Main Street. But in his mind he could hear the sound of a madman laughing. A hideous, cackling, you-can't-catch-me-you-stupid-cop laughter that rankled and chilled at the same time.

There were monsters everywhere and Virgil had made a life out of making sure none of them came to live in Ouachita County. But it had been five years without one new clue since the first disappearance, and now he knew he wasn't likely to bring this one to justice.

He had other problems.

3

AUDREY AWAKENED THE NEXT MORNING to the smell of frying bacon. She stretched languorously, shocked by the feel of linen against her bare skin. Lifting the sheets, she stared at her nude body. She'd gone to bed in a nightie, no question about that. But that was the last thing she remembered, and forgetting things that she shouldn't have unsettled her. She grabbed her robe out of the closet and followed the smell of breakfast into the kitchen. Richard was a great cook. Better than her.

He glanced up from the electric griddle as she entered.

"How do you feel?" he asked.

"Sleepy. What time is it?"

He glanced at his watch. "Ten-thirty."

"Why'd you let me sleep so late?"

"It's Saturday. Besides, after last night, I thought you needed your rest."

She took the coffee he offered and dropped into a chair, frowning. "I slept like a log. But I woke up with nothing on."

"You don't remember anything?"

"Remember what? Did we have a wild night?"

"You had the worst nightmare you've ever had."

"Really?"

He set his coffee cup beside the griddle. "I had to carry you into the bathroom and put you in the shower to wake you up. That's why you were sleeping nude."

"You're kidding."

"I'm not kidding. It was awful. I couldn't get through to you. You just kept staring into space and screaming."

"Screaming?" She couldn't believe it. She was definitely tired—as though she hadn't really slept—but she didn't remember waking in the night, and she certainly didn't recall a shower.

"You kept shouting for *her* to let him go."

Neither of them questioned who the *him* was. Neither of them needed to mention that today was the first anniversary of Zach's disappearance. Suddenly the bacon didn't smell so appetizing.

She shook her head, staring into the black mirror of her coffee. "I can't believe I didn't wake up in the shower."

"You sort of woke up, after awhile. You talked to me, but it was like you were speaking through a wall. I carried you back to bed and you finally went to sleep again."

"I can't believe it. I don't remember any of it."

"You woke me a couple of times, and I thought you were going to do it again. I talked to you, and you fell back to sleep. But you were stiff as a board all night."

"I'm sorry."

"There's nothing to be sorry about. I wish I could have done something."

"You did something by being there."

He slid a plate of bacon and eggs in front of her and she picked at it.

"Maybe you should call Tara," he said.

"No." She didn't need Tara just because of one bad dream. Even though she knew Tara would probably be able to help, she couldn't call her. Being around Tara or speaking to her reminded Audrey of just how much she'd lost. Reminded her of *why* she was afraid of forgetting things. Tara had helped, once. But she couldn't help after Zach was taken. Audrey couldn't let her help the way she'd wanted to. She just couldn't.

"Then maybe we should call Doctor Burton."

"I don't need a doctor. It was just a bad dream."

"It was a heck of a lot more than just a dream."

"Can we talk about something else?"

"Like what? I'm on your side, Audrey. I just want to get you some help, that's all."

"What about you?"

"I'm okay." He carried the griddle to the sink and stood with his back to her, head bowed.

"I'm getting better," she whispered. She hadn't been weeping every day, standing in the front window staring out across the lawn. She hadn't awakened in the middle of the night to go tuck Zach into bed in what, six months?

She could see Richard taking a deep breath, working his way up to saying something, and she knew what it would be. She just didn't know how he would phrase it this time.

"I don't want another baby," she said.

His neck reddened.

"You can't replace my son," she said softly.

Richard turned slowly to face her. "Audrey, having another child doesn't mean we're replacing Zach."

"Then what the hell does it mean?"

"We can't keep on like this, Aud. It's killing us. It's killing me. He's gone. We both have to face that."

Audrey shoveled bits of egg around on her plate, staring at the swirling pattern in the yolk. The fork felt strange in her hand. Soft. Her entire body felt weird. What was happening, a panic attack? She willed her breathing to slow, concentrating on her pulse. Controlling it. Forcing herself to relax.

Richard sat down in the chair next to her. His dark eyes and high cheekbones reminded her of Zach. There were times now when she hated looking at him because of the resemblance. Hated *herself* for it.

"I loved Zach just as much as you did," he whispered.

She could tell by the startled look on his face that he realized his mistake immediately. Her voice was a heavy stone, poised to crush both of them. "I *still* love him."

"So do I, Audrey."

"Then why didn't you say so?"

"I only meant that we have to go on living."

"I'm living. You're living."

"No, we're not. We're just frozen in time. Waiting. Audrey, we've done all we could do."

"He's out there somewhere," she whispered, barely able to breathe. "He needs me and I can't find him. Someone took my son."

"Our son."

"I want him back."

"I want him back, too, but we have to face the fact that we may never get Zach back. There hasn't been one call. No one saw him taken. He could be anywhere."

She dropped the fork onto her plate. The handle was bent. "Why didn't they call? Why didn't we get a ransom note?"

"You know why, Aud. The police told you why. Zach wasn't kidnapped for ransom."

"Don't say that!"

"Honey, calm down."

She stared out through the open back door. "The bastard stole my son right here. From our home."

That burned. The fact that Zach had been taken from a place where he should have been safer than anywhere else in the world. When both she and Richard were home. That inflamed her guilt and her rage, but it also angered her that Richard was right. They had done everything there was to be done.

They had contacted the Ouachita County Sheriff's Department immediately. The Warden's Service coordinated the search. Rangers, deputies, even volunteer firemen searched the area with dogs for days. The woods surrounding the house were deep Maine forest, and farm-to-market roads spiderwebbed the mountains. She and Richard had run through the woods with the searchers, shouting Zach's name, searching for him beneath every deadfall pine, in every dry gully. But there was no hope, really. The dogs never got a scent.

The sheriff sent out a File 6 Missing Persons Report by teletype to all law enforcement agencies including the NCIC, the National Crime Information Center. Audrey and Richard had placed ads in local newspapers, paid for spots on radio stations, put professionally printed posters in stores and gas stations. And they would have spent most of their savings hiring a private investigator out of Lewiston, but the man had refused to accept any pay after informing them that there were no clues to be had. Zach had wandered into the front yard to play while Audrey worked in her back garden, and five minutes later he was gone.

One year ago today. How dare Richard think of another child.

"He's alive," she said.

Richard didn't respond.

"He's alive," she repeated.

4

AUDREY STOOD STARING OUT THE BACK door into her garden. She hadn't set foot in the backyard since the day of Zach's disappearance. Her perennials had survived but they were coming back wild, and the areas that would normally be planted with young annuals were filling with spring weeds. Everything about her life seemed to be going to seed, falling apart.

Since Zach's disappearance she and Richard had worn their love for one another like an old coat that had been slashed and ripped in some violent accident. The fabric could be repaired, but Audrey wasn't certain if it would ever fit the way it had before. After their argument, Richard had packed his briefcase and gone into Arcos to work on some client files—a CPA always had something to do. Whenever they fought about Zach, Richard went to work and Audrey brooded. Now it was time to stop brooding and get on with her life. That meant her garden.

Her aunt Tara had explained the rudiments of gardening to Audrey when Audrey was barely in her teens, bought horticulture books for her to study, worked with her until both their hands were callused, until finally Audrey outgrew her teacher and began to instruct Tara. In gardening, Audrey had found more than just a hobby to take her mind off her troubles; she had discovered solace and rebirth. She became so accomplished at it that three years after she and

Richard were married, she published a book on home flower gardening. *I Never Promised You a Rose Garden* became a hit. It was in its seventh printing now and Audrey had always been proud of the fact that she wasn't just a housewife, that she supplied more than her share of the family income.

The garden called to her now. She longed to smell the rich soil, to feel her fingers working through the damp earth, to hear the sound of crickets and birds. But when she rested her hand on the doorknob, it felt frigid to the touch, hostile, as though the house dreaded her departure. But what else could she do, spend the rest of her life inside, pacing from room to room in an old housecoat like some hag out of a Dickens novel?

Still, the door would not seem to open. An odd tingling tickled the very back of her mind, the first tiny signal of fear. But why should she be afraid of her own garden?

Then she realized that it wasn't her garden she feared. It was the door itself. It wasn't the place, but the passing into the place. It was that irretrievable step from the past year with Zach into this new one without him. Opening one door. Closing another.

She glanced around the kitchen. Sunlight glinted on the blue countertops and white vinyl floor. The dishes were washed and stacked. The laundry was dried and put away. The house was spotless. She could return to the manuscript for her new book and pretend to write, but she knew that was a game. She had to write the manuscript *out there* where it was lived. There was nothing more to be done indoors. No further living to be accomplished. If she remained in the house, it wouldn't be to live, but to die.

She clamped down hard on the knob and jerked the door open. Without hesitating on the stoop, she strode out into the backyard. The day was warm and golden, the air redolent with balsam fir and lilacs just beginning to flower. A pair of robins performed a mating dance on the lawn near her storage shed. One year ago she had been right over there, down on her knees in the dirt. A sudden, inexplicable sense of doom had overcome her, and she had risen to her feet and raced to the front of the house, calling Zach's name. On the grass at the edge of the lawn, where the ground dipped into the roadside drainage ditch, lay his bat. His baseball was never recovered.

She faked a confident stride over to her shed and found her tool bucket just inside the door. Toting it to the center of her garden, she slipped on her kneepads and knelt. The familiar position and the smell of damp earth slowly revitalized her. Removing her garden claw from the bucket, she scratched at the weeds that were making inroads into her carefully planted perennials. She stared at the tines of the tool as they traced finger patterns in the dark soil, as though the implement were guided by someone else's hand.

What am I doing here? How could I possibly come back to this place?

She bore down on the tool, burying it deeply, yanking it along. The rasping sound grated on her ears. She was here because she *had* to be, because if she *didn't* come out here and do this, then Zach's kidnapper would have won. He would have taken her son and her life. Wasn't Richard trying to beat Zach's kidnapper too? Beat him by burying himself in his work every day? Beat him by having another child?

Audrey couldn't bear that thought.

Even if another baby wasn't a betrayal of Zach, how could she possibly consider having another child? How would she ever keep him safe? She and Zach had been impossibly close, even for a mother and son. She always sensed when he needed her, when he awakened in the night. He never had to call—she was always there when he needed her.

Only that one time had she arrived too late.

She could picture it as though it was yesterday, Zach cavorting around her, more full of life than any nine-year-old should be, shouting and tumbling, grass stains on his T-shirt, sunlight glinting in his eyes. The yard barely contained his exuberance. One year ago today. The thought plunged into her, a knife to the heart. Zach would be ten now.

She tried to envision another life growing inside her. Tried to recall the feel of a tiny heart, beating in rhythm with her own. Suddenly the memory of another child flashed through her mind and she blinked in astonishment.

The image was gone as quickly as it appeared, but its shadow hung just behind her eyes, a picture of *herself* at the age of nine or ten. Bright blue eyes and a cockeyed smile. She was holding a small doll in her hands as though in offering. Only she didn't remember the doll.

Just as suddenly, another unfamiliar vision rolled across the screen of her mind, whirling past on fast forward. People and places she didn't remember, but people who stirred violent emotions nonetheless. The images aroused sadness, fear, and anger, and with these emotions came agony.

Jagged pain slashed through her abdomen, blazing outward in fingers of golden fire. Her teeth chattered as she clutched her belly. Her hands shook where they grasped her light cotton blouse. She struggled to get to her feet, but her kneepads merely dug deeper into the soft loam. The agony electrified every nerve ending in her body, sparked her synapses like strands of flickering lights on a Christmas tree. Minutes later, when the pain finally drained away, she knelt limply in the garden, clutching her arms tightly about her. Never in her life had she experienced such pain, not even during childbirth. And it had struck so suddenly, out of the blue. As she began to take note of her surroundings again, she noticed that her vision was still off. The day seemed dimmer, out of focus.

Just as her muscles began to relax, another wave of flame crashed down upon her. The agony was a chemical explosion that erupted inside her body, burning its way out through her skin. She glanced frantically at the unplanted earth, wondering if she should lie down and hope for the terrible seizures to pass.

But maybe something was horribly wrong inside. Maybe she was bleeding internally or some terrible tumor had just asserted itself. She needed help. Remembering the birthing techniques she had learned years before, she took short, shallow breaths, trying to relax. After what seemed an eternity, the second attack passed. She struggled to her feet and stumbled across the lawn toward the door, praying to get inside before another blast of pain struck.

She was halfway up the back stoop when the agony lashed her again. Worse than the first two. Much worse. She buried her fingernails in the wood bannister. The muscles in her arms tightened into steel bands as she doubled over, her cheek resting on the splintery stair rail. She had one foot on the landing, one on the top step. She eyed the door only two paces away.

Her body shook so violently she was afraid she might collapse into a boneless mass, but as the pain started to ease once more, she staggered into the house. She dragged a kitchen chair over to the wall phone, not wanting to be caught standing when the next attack struck. She knew more were coming. She imagined them, lined up in the distance, black horsemen, Tolkien ring-wraiths. She grabbed the phone and pressed the autodial button for Richard's office. He answered on the third ring.

"Help me. Oh, Jesus! It hurts so bad" was all she managed to say before the next wave of pain thundered over her and left her moaning into the receiver. She heard Richard, as though from a great distance, telling her he was on his way, he was calling the hospital.

The phone crashed to the floor.

The pain rose inside her, swelling like a molten rush of lava, burning its way through her. As the wave crested, she drifted away, deep down inside herself. Reality dissolved into thin echoes of sound and sunlight and the surflike pounding of her heart. She thought she heard, for just an instant, a child's frightened voice, and the sound of a child's feet, running.

She opened her eyes, but of course she was alone. She didn't know if she had been delirious for minutes or hours, but the sun hadn't moved and neither Richard nor the paramedics had arrived. And the pain didn't seem to have lessened all that much. She closed her eyes and clasped both hands again across her belly. She drew her knees up to her chest, her feet resting on the edge of the chair.

When she closed her eyes again, she heard pattering feet and then silence.

Audrey glanced groggily around the kitchen as Richard and the big paramedic lifted her onto the gurney. The pain had eased, but in its place a great sadness had settled. Something indefinable had cooled inside her along with the pain.

She felt empty.

As the gurney crunched across the gravel in their drive, Audrey lay back on the thin white pillow while Richard walked alongside, holding her hand. She needed to hear the child's voice again. Needed to remember it. She knew she had heard it before.

But it was gone.

The pain came again, but it was distant and dull. The spasms were farther apart, more controllable. Richard climbed into the back of the ambulance, never letting go of her hand, but she couldn't look at him. He wiped her cheek but the spot still burned, as though it were not a tear he had erased but acid. He whispered in her ear, consoling her, but all she heard was the dull drone of the engine.

And over it all, the frantic patter of a child's feet.

5

TWO HOURS BEFORE MONDAY'S dreary dawn, a lone delivery truck passed in front of Cartland Memorial Hospital in downtown Arcos. Tires hissed on pavement still wet from a late-night rain. A freight train moaned in the distance, heading for Montreal. A cigarette sizzled to its death in a glittering puddle, as a tall orderly with buckteeth turned to pass back through the sliding glass doors into the emergency room.

Two hallways over Audrey lay on her bed, sound asleep yet covered in a sheen of cool perspiration. The only sound in the room was Richard's light snore as he dozed in his chair. Then the curtain stirred against the window frame when a light breeze slipped down across the mountains. The open page of a book on the bedside table fluttered in reply. In the corridor outside, the soft padding of a nurse's shoes reached a low crescendo and died away.

Audrey's sudden shriek pierced the hospital quiet like a gunshot in church. Clutching at the sweat-soaked sheets that snared her, she bolted into a sitting position.

"The smell!" she gasped, gagging for breath. "The smell!"

She ripped at her head and face with frantic fingers, trying to strip the skin away from her skull.

Richard jerked upright in his chair, fighting his way out of the well of sleep. He wiped his eyes and squinted, then rushed to Audrey's side, grabbing her hands. The nurse's rubber soles sounded again.

The light from the lamp struggled to frighten away the demons of darkness, but they hung in the room like smoke. Weird shadows flittered—angular and harsh—as Audrey twisted on the bed. She shivered and Richard pulled her toward him, but she pushed him away.

"No!" she shrieked. "Let me go!"

He released her and she recoiled against the metal headboard. The nurse poked her head through the door.

"Get Doctor Burton!" shouted Richard, and the nurse disappeared.

Audrey reached toward her face again and he slid onto the bed, holding her tightly, binding her arms in his own. "It's all right, honey," he said. "There's nothing to be afraid of."

"No!" she screamed again. She rocked back and forth so hard the metal headboard rattled against the wall.

"Audrey!" said Richard, shaking her shoulders. "Audrey! Wake up! It's a bad dream."

He couldn't stand to see her so frightened. She seemed as terrified of his embrace as she was of the demons in her head. When she shoved him away again, he let her lurch out of bed. Then he raced in front of her, blocking her path. The door opened and Doctor Burton pushed in past the nurse. Burton wasn't much bigger than Audrey, but she was twenty years older, with gray hair and deep-set green eyes. She peered at Audrey over the top of thick-lensed bifocals, holding out her hand to Richard to freeze him in place.

"Audrey," she said calmly. "It's Doctor Burton. Can you hear me?"

The nurse leaned past Richard. "Are you going to prescribe a sedative, Doctor?"

Burton shook her head, never taking her attention off of Audrey. "It's Doctor Burton, Audrey. Can you hear me?" Burton reached out and laid both hands on Audrey's shoulders.

"I hear you!" Audrey shouted. "She's got him! I have to go to him! She's going to kill him!"

"Who's got him, Audrey? Has who?"

"She does! She has Zach!"

Burton brought her face closer to Audrey's. "Relax, Audrey. I want you to take a deep breath. Will you do that for me? Take a deep breath."

Audrey complied petulantly.

"Another," said Doctor Burton.

Audrey took another breath but stamped her foot like a small child, her face set, her eyes still glazed.

"That's good," said Burton, stroking Audrey's hair. "Can you see me?"

"I can see you!" screamed Audrey, stamping her foot again and trying to shake away from Burton, who held her shoulders lightly but firmly. "I have to go to him! He needs me!"

"You don't have to go anywhere," said Burton in a calm voice. "You're here in the hospital, Audrey. Here with Richard and me. Do you see Richard? Look at Richard."

She turned Audrey to face Richard and waited until Audrey nodded.

"We're here in a nice room and there's no one else here. I want you to go back to bed. Will you go to bed now?"

Audrey seemed confused, but when Burton asked her again, she nodded, and Burton led her slowly back to the bed, crooning softly that everything was all right. She placed Audrey back into it one limb at a time, as though Audrey were a mannequin. Then Burton raised the stainless side rail.

"Why is she like this?" asked Richard, hurrying to the other side of the bed. "Why would she listen to you and not to me?"

Burton shrugged, stroking Audrey's hair. "It's called a night terror. *Pavor Nocturnus.* To tell you the truth, we really have no idea what's going on inside *there.*" She nodded toward the point where her fingers massaged Audrey's temple. "The next time she might listen to you and not to me. Or to no one at all." She inspected the bright red welts where Audrey's fingernails had scratched her skin. Richard told her how they had occurred, and Burton shook her head again. "There's no telling what she thought she was doing," she said.

Audrey swayed from side to side, still staring into space.

"I don't get it," said Richard. "Her eyes are wide open."

"She probably won't even remember any of it when she wakes up."

"This is just like the one she had before," said Richard. He wanted answers, but he was afraid there weren't any. Doctor Burton had run enough tests on Audrey over the past twenty-four hours to find out something, surely. But she offered little hope as far as Richard was concerned.

"Honestly, Richard, we just don't know much about night terrors. All you can do is hold her. Talk to her. Try to comfort her."

"Talking to her when she's like this is like carrying on conversations with two different people."

"There's nothing wrong with her physically. My guess is that her pain episode was trauma-induced stress. I'd like Audrey to see a colleague of mine, Doctor Cates."

"A psychologist?"

"Psychiatrist."

"Audrey won't see him. I tried to get her to see *you* Saturday morning and she refused."

"You need to urge her to see him, Richard. This isn't going to get better without professional help and there's nothing more that I can do. I'm going to release her this morning."

"Can't you give her something?"

Burton shook her head. "I'm not a psychiatrist, Richard. I might be doing more harm than good."

"Audrey already has a psychiatrist."

Burton's eyebrows rose. "Oh? She never mentioned it."

"Her aunt Tara. But she hasn't treated Audrey in years. Audrey had a horrible childhood. It took a lot of therapy for her to work through it."

Doctor Burton nodded slowly before speaking. "I'm no specialist. But that might be what this is about. I really think it would be best if Audrey saw Doctor Cates. Being treated by a family member is highly unconventional."

"I'll talk to her."

Audrey reached toward her face again, but Richard snatched her hand. She was panting again too. Richard eyed Burton.

"All right," said Burton, pressing the nurse's buzzer. "I'll give her something so she can sleep tonight."

6

VIRGIL HAD AN UNDER-SHERIFF, a captain, and twelve deputies below him, scattered all over the county, but he had let it be known early in his first term that he was an *active* police officer. Unlike his predecessors, Virgil passed on most of the managerial and political tasks to his staff, preferring to work more closely with his deputies and to be seen around the jurisdiction he represented. He knew every inch of Ouachita County, every backroad, every logging trail, every hidden driveway. A day never went faster for Virgil than one spent cruising the countryside. But lately he found excuses to go out on patrol even more often and to stay out longer.

Now, with his first coffee still sloshing in his gut, he pulled the cruiser over on the shoulder along a deserted stretch of farm-to-market lane. Hitching up his gunbelt, he climbed the steep slope to a rusted wrought-iron fence winding through the woods around a cluster of gravestones. The little family cemetery sat back far enough from the road for solitude, and the view of the mountaintops over the trees was distant and peaceful. Many of the markers were so old the engraving had been worn away by time. Rosie Merrill's was not. To Virgil, it looked as fresh as an auto accident. He strode to the foot of her grave and bowed his head.

The morning was cool, filtered through thin wisps of

mist, and the surrounding woods seemed dreamlike and in-distinct. But something other than the everpresent guilt he felt when passing this place had drawn his eye through the trees to the old graveyard. He could have sworn he'd seen movement in the forest. His first thought was that it was Tom Merrill, come to visit Rosie's grave, but there were no other cars parked on the shoulder. Virgil wondered then if maybe he hadn't stumbled on someone vandalizing the graves.

He inspected the entire acre and a half of the cemetery, but other than one pickup that passed on the road below, the day was silent as death. And although gravestones had fallen or been pushed over in the past, there didn't seem to be any recent damage. There were no footprints other than his own in the dew-laden grass.

The more he studied the cemetery and the undulating waves of mist, the more he noticed how unusually quiet it was, even for a graveyard. Virgil had been a hunter since he was a child. The woods were seldom perfectly still. There should have been birds calling at the very least, insects buzzing. It was as though the forest itself were listening.

He spun slowly around, three hundred and sixty degrees, studying the trees. He supposed he was just getting hinky in his old age. That had to be it. Just nerves. He'd never been nervous alone in the woods before. He turned back to the gravestones and laughed at himself. He was acting like some kid in the cemetery on a dare. He shook it off and headed back down the hill through the graves. But he couldn't help but stop in front of Rosie's grave, couldn't pass her without notice like she was a stranger. And as he stood there, head bowed, one hand gripping the other, he was overcome by grief and guilt just as he knew he would be, swept up as he always was in the loneliness of this place where Rosie was now spending eternity. This was Rosie's world forever, a silent, misty place, and, for Virgil, it seemed filled with unanswered questions and silent accusations.

"I'm sorry, Rosie. I'm real sorry."

He began to sob. He leaned against a battered oak tree and wondered how tears could feel so good and still sting like hell coming out.

He hadn't cried on his earlier visits, but he'd always made a habit of talking to Rosie. He wanted to believe that she could hear him, but mostly he spoke to himself, because this was a sacred place and he had long ago made a pact with whatever inhabited this hallowed ground. Whether they were the ghosts of the dead or merely the memories of the living, he didn't care. This was a consecrated space to Virgil, a place in his life that he shared with no one. Not even Doris knew about his visits here, although he knew that Doris would have understood his need to come here better than anyone.

"I wanted to find him for you, Rosie. Find him and the man who did it. I've done everything I could. And now there's Doris to worry about. I guess it's just getting too much for me. And there haven't been any new clues since the last time I talked to you." He twisted the toe of his boot into the grass alongside the grave. "I got other problems now."

He turned and hurried to the cruiser without looking back, glad to be away from the reproachful faces he imagined in the shadowed trees. Hurrying to the cruiser, he was soothed by the throaty sound of the big engine carrying him far away, into sunlight. Into warmth. A couple miles farther up the road, he eased the car around a tractor and waved absentmindedly at the farmer driving the machine, but although the man's face was vivid in Virgil's memory, the fellow's name wouldn't come to him.

Once upon a time he'd had a mind and a memory like a steel trap. He'd known half the people in the county, memorized every state law, every county and town ordinance. Once upon a time he could spot a man breaking the law almost before the misdemeanor was committed. Once upon a time he'd been in on most of the major busts in the county. But for the past six months, Virgil hadn't issued so much as a warning.

Doris was dying.

Doctor Burton had referred her to a specialist, who referred her to more specialists in Boston. Somehow the doctors had diagnosed her cancer too late. Then, to try to rectify their mistake, they'd recommended chemo and radiation. But by that time, all the oncologists could promise was that the treatment might extend Doris's life by a couple of months. A couple of months of weak, nauseous, pain-filled hell. In and out of the hospital. On her back most of the time. Doris wouldn't have it. She wanted to do things her way. Always had. And Virgil couldn't argue with her.

But at least the quacks had been decent enough to refer her to a pain treatment center in New Jersey. The doctors there put her on a new, more powerful drug regimen, and the effect had been wonderful and terrible at the same time. Wonderful because the drugs masked the reality of her disease at first. She could function again, in a limited way, at least in the beginning, and, even now, the pain that had driven her screaming to the hospital in the first place was mostly controlled. The sight of Doris, doubled over in bed, screaming, had been more than he had thought he could bear. But he had learned a lot since then about what he could bear.

Doris had already worked her way through the denial steps. She didn't shriek at Virgil anymore or break down and bawl on the pillow beside him. She just smiled and nodded stoically and told him that everything was going to be all right, that she was at peace. And she wouldn't let him tell the kids.

Burt and Carole had their own busy lives out on the far coast. They called regularly and got home every year or so. It had been a hard decision, not seeing them one last time, but by the time Doris had accepted her fate, she didn't want either of the kids to see what the disease had done to her. Virgil wasn't sure that was the right way to handle things, but Doris was convinced that they would accept her decision in the end and that everything would be all right. Only everything wasn't going to be all right, because *Virgil* wasn't at peace. He hadn't planned for this. He couldn't eat. He couldn't sleep.

For thirty-eight years he'd been madly in love with Doris. He'd never once raised his voice in her presence, and he certainly couldn't even bring himself to argue with her. And all along, he'd known that one day they would part. Because, unlike Doris, Virgil didn't really believe in the hereafter. Virgil thought that anything he couldn't see and touch was bunkum. Of course, he never said that in front of Doris.

Well, only once. And that was right after they were married. Doris gave him a haughty, down-your-nose look. She'd dragged him off to the Congregational Church and plopped him down into a pew beside her, and his butt had warmed that same seat every Sunday for the past thirty-eight years until Doris had gotten too ill to go. Even though his church membership had undoubtedly brought him a lot of votes over the years, Virgil had resented being a hypocrite all that time. But he hated the thought of losing Doris a hell of a lot worse.

So Virgil had always had a plan. Well, not a plan, really. What he'd had was a thought, a hope. Someone else might have called it a prayer. Virgil had always figured on going before Doris. Because there was no way he could live without her.

Now he was scared shitless she was going to die before he did.

Doris had tried to talk to him about her *passing on,* but whenever she started conversation down that path, Virgil raised his voice on some other subject, and he kept raising it, louder and louder, pacing around and waving his hands, until Doris couldn't get a word in edgewise. She'd shoot him one of her *Oh, for Pete's sake, Virgil* looks and sigh and wait until he had wound down enough to shut up.

"All right, Virgil," she'd say. "All right. We won't talk about it right now, honeypie."

He'd drop down beside her on the bed then, and hold her and pretend that everything was going to be all right. But it wasn't going to be all right. She was getting weaker by the day. She was losing a lot of weight and her eyes were sinking into her head, and more and more the pain was getting stronger than the drugs.

People stopped by the house nearly every day with soup and home remedies. Doris kept telling *them* she'd beat this thing. But Virgil could see the worry in their friends' eyes. See the blame. Why aren't you doing more? they were thinking. All he could do was grit his teeth and turn away. Why *wasn't* he doing more? He was the goddamned sheriff for Gawd's sake.

He had pictured a hundred different ways of killing himself, but his children kept intruding on his thoughts. He saw them standing over his and Doris's graves, crying their eyes out, and he punished himself even more for what he would be doing to them, but he also knew that in the end that wouldn't matter to him. All that would matter would be the fact that he wouldn't have to face that empty house. He'd rather blow his brains out.

But not yet.

Not while Doris still needed him. He had to be strong for her. They'd made it through almost forty years of living together. That was why nowadays he didn't want to leave her alone in the morning and he was afraid to go home at night, afraid of what he might find. Why he sat for long hours after midnight staring at two case files he knew he was never going to solve.

With an effort, he dragged himself out of the darkness in his mind. This had always been one of his favorite parts of the county. Farmland gave way to foothills and only occasional homes dotted the roadside. Thick stands of maples fell into dense underbrush on either side of the road. Even with the sun clearing the sky of the few remaining clouds, the thick trees turned the day to soft twilight. Branches laced the road with crisscrossed shadow fingers. Virgil glanced to his left when a deer stuck its head out of the puckerbrush and he damn near ran over Cooder Reese.

"Shit!" Virgil jerked the wheel hard, pumping the brakes. Tires squealed and gravel flew. He was a hundred yards down the road before he could throw the cruiser into a looping turn and power back up the hill, his heart pounding in his chest. All that time Cooder stood frozen, one foot on the grass and one on the road.

Virgil whipped over onto the shoulder and took a moment turning off the ignition, waiting for his hands to stop shaking. He glared at Cooder, but he knew that wouldn't make any difference. Cooder gave Virgil the same sort of lopsided sneer he gave everybody, only Virgil knew there was no meanness in it. No contempt. Cooder wasn't like that. Cooder wasn't quite like anyone else except Cooder.

Virgil climbed out of the car and crossed the road with a purposeful stride. No one approached from either direction. The only time anyone was likely to travel this road was early morning or late afternoon, going to or from a mill job, maybe a housewife taking the scenic route into Arcos to shop.

"Where you heading, Cooder?" Virgil crossed his arms and locked his feet into a solid stance. He knew it would be a minute before Cooder answered. Things got into Cooder's head and then things had a way of working their way back out. But it took a while.

Cooder's T-shirt was greasy. His blue jeans looked as though they had been smeared with mud, or something far worse. But his blond hair looked freshly washed and combed, and though his expression made it seem as though he was concentrating, his eyes were dull, focused a million miles away.

"Walkin'," said Cooder.

"Yeah," said Virgil, spitting onto the pavement. "Why don't you and I move out of the road a little." Virgil walked over to stand on the grass and after a minute Cooder followed.

"Long time," said Cooder. His placid, dark brown eyes with their long-distance stare never left Virgil. A person who looked into Cooder's eyes long enough could get lost in them. A lot of girls had, back in the sixties, before the acid and heaven knew what else had turned Cooder into something not quite there.

Cooder had long since become a graduate of the defunct Perkins Mental Health Institute. Over the years he'd been in and out of the state-run facility so often that Virgil figured the institution must have kept an open file on him. But as government funding for mental health dried up and private health insurance became unattainable for all but the wealthy, more and more patients were shunted aside to make it on their own. Cooder was one of the first to go.

Virgil had never understood who had decided that Cooder could make it on his own. Every few years he managed to do something that required the state to lock him up again. Nothing terrible, mostly like the time he climbed up on the water tower and stayed there for two days *lookin'*, until four volunteer firemen risked life and limb to clamber up and get him down. But within a month or two he'd showed up on the streets again and Virgil had given up arguing with the state assholes.

"Long time," agreed Virgil. "Where you going, Cooder?"
Another wait.

"Walkin'," said Cooder at last.

The wind shifted. Virgil got a whiff and took a quick step back. Cooder smelled like the inside of a portable toilet.

"Walking where?" asked Virgil, though he knew it was useless. Cooder probably had no idea where he was headed. Or maybe he just wasn't going to give out the information. No way of telling.

"Walkin'."

Virgil stared back down the road, behind the cruiser. Cooder lived on the highway outside of Crowley, miles of quiet country lane away. He had a small house that his mother had left to him and he got by on social security and state aid. Virgil wondered for the thousandth time if there really *was* anything going on in Cooder's head.

"You want to be careful, Cooder. You can't be walking in the middle of the road like that. You're going to get your ass run over. You understand me?"

Another span of time.

Then a nod.

Virgil glanced at his watch. Going on ten-thirty already. Where the hell had the morning gone? "You had anything to eat today, Cooder?"

A slow frown signaled deep thought. "No."

"Right," muttered Virgil. He trotted back over to the cruiser. Leaning across the front seat, he pulled a sandwich out of the brown bag lunch he'd made for himself that morning, and brought it back to Cooder. Cooder accepted it as though it were his due and began chewing noisily.

"You're welcome," said Virgil.

Cooder nodded his thanks.

Virgil stared at him thoughtfully. He couldn't help the poor bastard. He couldn't help Rosie. How the hell was he going to help Doris or himself?

"Stay out of the road, Cooder," said Virgil as he climbed back into the cruiser and started the motor. Reaching for the gear-shift lever, he noticed Cooder waving the remains of the sandwich at him. Virgil rolled down his window.

When Cooder spoke, his voice was deep and resonant, like a country preacher laying some old friend to rest.

"Bad things, Virg."

Virgil's skin tingled as though lightning had struck. It wasn't so much what Cooder had said. It was the way he said it. Like some kind of pronouncement from God. Like a revelation. "What bad things, Cooder?"

Cooder took another hefty bite of the sandwich, chewing until he'd swallowed every last bit. But his eyes never left Virgil's, and Virgil couldn't look away.

Cooder wiped his lips with his tongue.

"I seen bad things, Virg."

"Jesus," muttered Virgil. No one he knew had carried on a meaningful conversation with Cooder Reese in over twenty years. But Cooder's voice and his words wouldn't let Virgil go.

"What bad things?" asked Virgil.

"Walkin'," said Cooder.

"Walkin'," repeated Virgil.

Cooder shoved the last of the sandwich into his mouth, and Virgil figured that he'd better stick around at least long enough to find out whether or not he needed to perform the Heimlich maneuver on the crazy bastard. Cooder chewed like a slow old milk cow, but there was no enjoyment in his eyes. They seemed even more distant than usual.

"Tell me what the hell you're talking about, Cooder, or I'm driving on out of here," said Virgil. "And you stay out of the road or I'll have one of the boys bring you in." *He* wasn't going to do it himself. No way. Let one of the young stallions ride twenty miles with Cooder smelling up their backseat. Cooder continued staring off down the road behind the cruiser, squinting as he worked his jaw slowly from side to side, chomping on an imaginary sandwich now.

"Bad things," muttered Cooder. Without further ado, he spun on his heel, and putting one ratty boot in front of the other, started his endless hike once again, headed in the same direction as Virgil's cruiser.

Virgil sat for a moment, watching Cooder's back. Cooder's blond hair glistened each time he passed from shadow to sunlight.

"How come you don't have any gray hair?" whispered Virgil, running his fingers through his own scalp. " 'Cause you got nothing to worry about?"

Bad things, Virg.

I seen bad things.

"Shit," said Virgil, shifting into drive.

7

THE ARGUMENT STARTED BEFORE AUDREY and Richard were out of the hospital parking lot, and it didn't end when Richard stalked off into their living room and turned on the television. But at least by then it seemed to have reached that stage of silent disagreement that married couples all understand. They weren't so much mad at each other. They were both angry at themselves because neither of them could bend.

Richard insisted that she see either Tara or the shrink Doctor Burton had recommended. Audrey was adamant against doing either. She hated the vague memory of her endless sessions with Tara. But she was equally afraid of another doctor opening the doors that she and Tara had worked so hard to close. And the last thing she wanted was for Tara to know that she was having visions or night terrors or whatever the hell they were. Tara would want her to come back, to stay with her, and surrender herself to the ordeal of closing those doors in her mind again. Audrey hated even the thought of the long sessions with Tara, although she couldn't explain why to Richard and, in fact, she didn't really *remember* why. Tara had never hurt her, she was sure of that. Never forced her to do anything she didn't want to do. It was just something about giving up control—if only for that briefest of times—that touched a raw nerve with Audrey.

All that was left to her of her childhood was unfocused flashes of horrible images, faceless monsters she *sensed* had performed terrible deeds that she couldn't quite remember. Under Tara's care, those old visions had gradually become fewer and less intense. There were months during her twelfth year when Audrey thought she was free of them forever. But then, without warning, they returned to savage her nights or torture the imagined safety of her days. Then she and Tara had to begin the endless sessions yet again. By the time Audrey met and fell in love with Richard, she thought she and Tara had the doors closed forever, her mind under control. The hateful images hadn't completely disappeared, but she no longer awakened in the night bathed in sweat. And when they came in the daylight, she could stare off into the distance and wait for them to pass without running screaming to Tara. Tara had taught her self-hypnosis so she'd have a weapon of her own against her mental demons, even if that weapon seemed to be losing its power lately.

The sound of a basketball game buzzed into the kitchen from the living room. Richard was a devoted fan, the type that followed pro, college, and high school ball, and in a pinch might stop to watch kids playing on the street, shouting encouragement from his car. Leaning over the kitchen sink, Audrey stared across the width of the backyard. The sun had lowered a little. A bright reflection glinted on the window in front of her. It obscured her view and she squinted. An errant shadow fell on the glass and with it came the terrible sense of despair that she had been fighting since her attack returned full force.

She cocked her head to make the reflection disappear, but no matter which way she turned, the image remained. In fact, it grew more and more distinct, until it was as clear as the image on a movie screen. She gasped, splashing both fists into the dishwater.

Zach peered through the glass, as if he were searching through a darkness that she could not see. She stared lovingly at his brown hair and dark eyes, but his face was marred by an expression of fear. He mouthed words but there was no sound. Instead, Audrey heard her own heart hammering in her chest.

His face was fuller, less rounded with baby fat, and his eyes were shinier and quicker than she remembered. His hair was cut shorter as well. He had grown in the intervening months and she took heart from the vision. Would she hallucinate an older Zach?

She traced the outlines of his face lovingly with soapy fingers, and he tilted his head as though accepting her caress. It was like touching the most fragile of blossoms. She wanted to feel his skin. Wanted the sense of human warmth to make the image real, but she was terrified of having the vision fade away beneath her tender touch.

She leaned so close to the window that her stomach pressed painfully into the countertop. Her nose brushed the glass. Their eyes met and the boy's eyes focused. Shock flashed across his face and hers. He panted heavily, as though he had been running, and perspiration glinted on his brow.

"Where are you?" Audrey whispered, tracing the outline of his face over and over in dishwashing detergent.

But even as she spoke, the image faded, shrank away from her. First there was a shadow on the glass, then a dusky hint, then daylight again, warming her garden. She recalled Tara crooning to her over and over years before. "It isn't real, Audrey. It's all just a dream."

"Honey," said Richard, shocking her with his presence so close behind her. She stiffened when his hands gripped her hips, pulling her back from the window. "I thought I heard you say something. Are you all right?"

There was nothing in the wet glass now but warm golden afternoon and a thin trickle of soapsuds. Richard wrapped his arms around her and drew her tightly to him.

"What is it, hon?" he whispered in her ear.

She closed her eyes, praying she wasn't going mad.

"Just woolgathering," she whispered.

8

AT ONE TIME VIRGIL HAD ENJOYED making the occasional meal for Doris and himself. Now it was a duty and the satisfaction he got from it was minimal because the ritual forced him to concentrate on the food and *that* caused him to realize just how little she ate. He stirred the bowl of chicken noodle soup before bringing the spoon to his lips. Just right—Doris hated food that was too hot. He set the bowl on the wooden tray along with crackers, napkin, a glass of cold milk, and the weekly paper, and stared at his handiwork.

Even as thin as it was, the spread looked pretty darn appetizing. But he didn't kid himself. He'd be happy to get Doris to eat half the soup and maybe take a few sips of milk. If he was lucky, he might finagle her into nibbling on one of the saltines.

He carried the tray into the bedroom, preparing himself for the thousandth time for the smell of sickness that waited like a wall, just inside the door. He could never quite figure the odor out. It wasn't antiseptic exactly, although Doris insisted on keeping a can of Pine-Sol beside the bed to spray on her tissues before tossing them into the trash. And it wasn't any kind of bodily odor. Doris would never have stood for that. It was just the smell of a person living in a room for too long without really living. Somehow the house and Doris's disease had meshed and Virgil knew that smell would never go away, no matter how much Pine-Sol the new owners sprayed after he and Doris were gone.

The bedroom itself rebelled against the dying it encompassed. Warm sunlight shone through the windows, reflecting off the dark wood floor and yellowing the curtains and old floral wallpaper. Fresh flowers in a tall vase by the door to the side porch needed watering, and Virgil reminded himself to bring a pitcher back from the kitchen.

Doris sat propped against thick pillows, wearing her old cotton nightshirt that seemed two sizes too big for her now. Her face was drained and her eyes were sunken, like black marbles in china cups. Her hair, always immaculate, was tucked back into a tight white bun, but it was thin and dull. Bony hands rested on either side of her like a pair of daddy longlegs. She looked eighty, not fifty-nine.

"Lunch," said Virgil, resting the tray on the bedside table and reaching for the remote. But Doris grabbed his hand.

"I'm watching this," she said, never taking her eyes off the set.

Virgil frowned.

A black woman in a bright orange shift sat facing the camera. She flipped tarot cards on the table in front of her and read someone's fortune in a fake Caribbean accent. A man off camera sounded amazed by the things the cards said about him. A toll number flashed at the bottom of the screen, along with a notice in tiny print that readings were done for entertainment purposes only.

"Why do you watch this bunk?" muttered Virgil.

Doris gave him a haughty shake of her head. Her thin neck looked as though it might snap. Virgil wanted desperately to look away, but guilt glued his eyes to her.

"You should watch, Virgil," said Doris. "Madame Zola has some real insights."

"You haven't been giving them your credit card number again, have you?"

"Not since you had your little tantrum."

Virgil didn't think he'd had a tantrum. He'd merely mentioned that they had bills to pay and spending dollars like there was no tomorrow on a television fortune-teller seemed silly to him. Doris had made him feel terrible by being contrite. It wasn't as though she had any hobbies, and most of her friends worked, so she was alone all day in front of the damned TV set. But the thought of a con artist taking her in galled Virgil.

"If you want to spend money on a fortune-teller, then spend ahead," he said. "You know I never meant to hurt your feelings."

"You didn't hurt my feelings. You were right. It was silly of me to waste money on a TV card-reader."

He stared at her, waiting for the other shoe to drop.

"Babs is coming by Tuesday night," she said.

Thump.

He slipped the napkin into her nightshirt top and placed a pillow on either side of her to hold the tray. Then he fed her the soup until she put her hands in front of her mouth to stop him. Her body quivered with every breath. She seemed fragile enough to shatter. Virgil suddenly pictured himself alone in this bed, holding his pistol in his lap.

"Tuesday," she said.

"That's tomorrow," he reminded her.

"We're going to hold a séance."

"A what?"

"You know. A séance. We're going to contact the other side."

He almost asked her the other side of what, but he was even more afraid of arguing with Doris these days than he had been in the past. Now, an argument would seem less of a breaking of some unspoken vow and more a potential murder weapon.

"Fine," he said.

"This is important."

"Why?"

"Because pretty soon I'll be over there."

"I saw Cooder today."

"Virgil, I will be. We need to talk about it."

"I damned near ran over him."

"I want to know what it's really like."

"He made me nervous."

Doris stared at him for a moment, then sighed. "Why on earth would Cooder Reese scare anyone? He's never been a danger to anyone other than himself. Has he?"

"Not that I know of."

"Then why were you nervous?"

He stared at the old inlaid headboard, trying to read something in the pattern of light and dark wood. Doris's mother had given them the bedroom suite as a wedding present. A lot of living had gone on in this room. Two kids had been conceived in this bed. The whole family had crowded in together on stormy nights, and Virgil remembered time after time carrying one or the other child back to bed sound asleep when he'd come in after a late-night patrol. Wedding suits and funeral suits had made their way out of the old dresser against the wall, and he had watched in the mirror of the matching vanity as Doris went from shy young girl to confident woman to beautiful matron.

Now it hurt to look into her eyes.

"I don't know. He said he'd seen bad things."

"Well, I can believe that."

"It wasn't so much what he said but the way he said it."

"What do you mean?"

"Nothing," he said, screwing up his lips. "It was just one of those funny things that gives you goose bumps. You know what I mean?"

"I want you to come to the séance."

"I'll probably be on patrol."

"Virgil. I want you to come."

He nodded, picking up the tray, wiping her chin gently with the napkin.

"Eight o'clock tomorrow night," she said, moving her mouth back and forth across the cloth. "We'll have it right here in the bedroom. Make some sandwiches."

"Sure."

He carried the tray back into the kitchen and washed the bowl and spoon, setting them in the strainer. What kind of sandwiches did you make for a séance? He pictured a bunch of old crones with snarled hair, sitting around waving wands over a boiling cauldron, but he was pretty sure that was something he'd dredged up from high school English class. Still, with Babs in charge, there was no telling.

The phone rang and he snatched it before it could ring again.

"Virgil," he said.

"Hi, Virg."

He smiled when he heard Marg's voice. He hadn't seen her in a couple of weeks, and he knew she was wondering why. Marg was his first cousin and his best friend. For fifty years they'd managed to make time for each other almost daily.

"Hi, Marg. How's things?"

"Missed you a lot lately."

"I been pretty busy."

"Yeah. I'm sure. Are you okay?"

"Good as can be expected."

"That's what I'm worried about. How's Doris holding up?"

"Not so good."

"Pain?"

"The pain isn't bad. But she's lost a lot more weight."

"You knew that was going to happen." Marg was head of the nursing staff at Cartland Memorial, just around the corner. Virgil had been forced to ask Marg about Doris's disease, after he realized that he'd blocked out most of what the specialists had told him. She hadn't pulled any punches.

"Knowing is one thing. Seeing is another," he said.

"Is there anything I can do?"

"Not that I can think of."

"You ought to stop by the hospital on your rounds. I'll buy you a cuppa."

"Soon."

"Mrs. Bock was here this weekend."

Marg knew about his feelings on the Bock case. But why keep him updated on the mother's health?

"What was she in for?" He knew Marg wasn't supposed to tell him. Knew that she would.

"She's having nightmares."

"That doesn't surprise me. Is she going to be all right?"

"Doctor Burton wants her to see a shrink."

"Of course." Virgil didn't think much more of head doctors than he did of people running séances. He figured neither one of them had any real idea what they were doing.

"What do you think happened to the Bock boy?" asked Marg.

Virgil stared out through the kitchen window into the neighbor's yard. Coincidentally, the Coglins' five-year-old was riding his toy tractor across the lawn. Virgil wondered why the Coglin boy was safe and sound at home and the Bocks' child was . . . somewhere else.

"Virgil?"

"I don't know."

"You have an idea."

"And so do you. Do I need to spell it out?"

"There's never been anything at all come up? Nothing?"

"Zilch. All I know for sure is that that boy didn't wander off into the woods."

"Neither did the Merrills' boy."

"You don't think Audrey Bock is going to do something to herself like Rosie Merrill, do you?"

"If Doctor Burton thought she was suicidal, she'd still be under observation."

"Rosie was never under observation."

"Rosie climbed in her car and drove off the bridge into the Androscoggin. She didn't even take the time to write a note."

"I don't want something like that to happen to Zach Bock's mother."

"You can't solve them all, Virg."

"Those are two that I'd really like to."

"I know. Maybe something will come up one of these days. You never know."

"What do you know about séances?"

"Are you serious?"

"Do you know anything about them?"

"I know you aren't about to find out what happened to the Bock or the Merrill boy at a séance."

"Doris is having one tomorrow night."

"Is Babs doing it?"

"How did you know that?"

"Come on. Babs St. Clair is the town weirdo, Virgil. Who the hell else would it be?"

"We have other weirdos," he said, thinking of Cooder.

"Not like Babs."

"You think it will be all right?"

"You mean, am I afraid that she might awaken a demon that will possess you or Doris? Or am I nervous that word will get around that my cousin is consorting with nuts?"

"Either," said Virgil, smiling.

"No to number one. Two, I don't care. But what about you? A sheriff holding séances might not be considered a good thing by a number of the locals. Have you consulted Pastor Donnelly?"

"No."

"Might not be a good way to get reelected."

"I'm not worried about that."

"No worries, then."

"I'll stop by for coffee."

"Do."

He started to hang up.

"Marg?" he said, at the last moment.

"Yeah?"

"Has Cooder been back in the hospital?"

"Not that I'm aware of. Why?"

"I almost ran over him this morning, on the back side of South Eden. He was walking in the middle of the road."

"That's nothing new for Cooder."

"I know. But he said something really strange. He said, 'I seen bad things.' It was more the way he said it than what he said. You know what I mean?"

"He wouldn't tell you what it was he saw?"

"You know how Cooder is."

"It's probably nothing, Virg. Between the psychedelics he fed himself, the tranks and antidepressants the doctors feasted him on, and a little electroshock for good measure, there's really no telling what goes on inside his head anymore."

"I know. It was just kind of eerie, the way he said it."

"Sounds to me like you need some time off, cuz."

"I'll let you go, Marg."

"Don't forget the coffee."

He hung up, still watching the Coglin boy.

9

AUDREY STOOD ON THE BACK PORCH staring out across the garden. Richard was taking an afternoon nap. She had halfheartedly tried to talk him into going to work, but he didn't want to leave her alone yet, and, to tell the truth, she wasn't ready to be.

Doctor Burton seemed certain the pain that had assaulted Audrey hadn't been caused by anything physical, but the memory of the unbearable agony frightened her, and in her mind the pain was tied to her garden. The memory of it was as powerful a deterrent as the grief it had replaced. But she had to face her fear somehow. She wasn't going to live the rest of her life afraid to cross her own backyard.

Steeling herself, she took two cautious steps onto the lawn. Her tools still lay beside her overturned bucket. If nothing else, she needed to put them away. That thought gave her a purpose, and she strode over and gathered up her claw and trowel. Turning full circle in the bright sunlight, she inhaled deeply. The smell of lilac relaxed her a little. No pain struck like a knife and slowly the tightness in her chest began to ease.

The day was as clear as sunlight could make it. A beetle crawled slowly across the leaves of a small rhododendron and high overhead a couple of ravens twirled in a springtime mating dance. There was nothing here for her to fear.

The ring-wraiths were gone. No demons in the alders.
There was only the age-old horror she carried with her like
a second skin.

A splash caught her attention.

A frog must have gotten into the small concrete fountain
that was the centerpiece of the back garden. Richard had
constructed the little pool for her two years before. He'd
run underground power to it and they could flip a switch in
the kitchen to turn on lights and pumps. Eventually it was
intended to feed a false stone-lined stream running the
length of the garden, but events had curtailed construction.

She set her bucket down and knelt beside the fountain
that was barely wider than a bathtub. A circular pattern of
ripples flattened back into its murky surface. If the splash
was caused by a frog, the creature had chosen a poor place
to live. The pool was scummy with algae and surely nothing
edible lived in its water. Audrey watched the greasy reflections of the maple trees. The foliage danced in seductive di-
amonds across the vanishing ripples.

The water seemed to deepen until Audrey stared, not
into the shallow pool, but into a bottomless darkness. She
felt as though she were sinking slowly into its dismal
depths, growing colder. The darkness was deathly silent
and a terrible sense of loneliness and abandonment per-
vaded the space she had entered. Suddenly Zach's face appeared in front of her and she thought she screamed his
name, but if she did, she didn't hear it. The darkness around
her seemed to absorb sound as well as light, and Zach's doe
eyes implored her to come to him, to find him.

To bring him home.

She reached out for him but her hands passed into the
water and through him, as though *she* were the apparition.
Just as with the vision in the window, it was maddening to
be able to see him so clearly, to be so close to him, and yet
not to be able to touch him, to hold him, to carry him in her
loving arms to safety.

As she watched, two large male hands dropped over
Zach's shoulders and dragged him away, fading into the
inky darkness. She began to sense the suffocating closeness
of the black water all around her. She felt herself struggling
to rise back out of the depths of the vision, but she was

locked inside it, unable to quite break the surface. She wanted desperately to get out of that terrible darkness, but at the same time she longed to be close to Zach once more, if only in a vision.

"Where are you!" she moaned.

Finally, still half-caught in the imagined depths, she struggled to her feet, stumbling blindly into the house.

10

RICHARD AWAKENED to a barely audible whimpering sound. Climbing groggily from bed, he glanced at his watch. Five in the afternoon. He stumbled down the hallway toward the kitchen, following the plaintive mewling noises. It sounded like Audrey, gasping for breath and crying, trying to be as quiet as possible, and it appeared to be coming from the hall closet.

With a quivering hand, he opened the door. She had burrowed her way into the farthest corner of the closet, her hands clasped tightly over her breasts. Her legs were scrunched up beneath her and she had lost one sneaker. She was shaking like a leaf. Richard dropped onto his knees in the pile of scattered clothes and touched her gently on the shoulder.

She quivered as though he had struck her. A squeal replaced her whimper.

"Audrey," he croaked. "Audrey, honey, what is it? What's wrong?"

She tunneled like a rabbit with a fox on its heels. He dragged her out of the corner and pulled her against him, until she melted into his chest. Her heart pounded beneath his palm as though it filled her entire torso, a huge pump, running wildly out of control. He wrestled her gently out of the closet and held her while he phoned the hospital.

It took forever for Doctor Burton's secretary to return

his call, but at least by that time he had managed to get
Audrey into bed. She stared at him over the top of the covers, her eyes wide and strange, as though she didn't really
see him at all. She was having another night terror, but he
couldn't understand how, unless she had fallen asleep in the
closet.

"Call the police," she said.

"You need a doctor, honey," said Richard, moving back
to the bed and sitting down beside her. He stroked her hair
back into place and tried to kiss her cheek, but she jerked
away.

"Call the police!" she screamed, her voice echoing down
the hall.

"Honey . . ."

"The police!" she wailed. "Call the fucking police!"

He rushed back to the phone. Her voice calmed a little
when she saw him lifting the receiver, but she didn't seem to
be looking at him. "He's got Zach," she said, again in that
awful, melancholy tone.

"Who, honey?"

"I don't know," she said, staring through him. She kept
running her fingers across her face, reminding him of the
night in the hospital, and he watched her closely lest he
have to drop the phone and rush back to her side. "He's in
a little room in the ground. It's so dark."

"That's crazy, Aud."

She made a face, as though she was trying to see through
a wall of fog. "He's scared. He's just a little boy and he's so
scared and lonesome. He needs his mother!"

"Maybe you were just dreaming. One of your night terrors. That's all it was."

"I know what I saw, Richard!"

"Aud," he said, ever so gently. "What did you see?"

She shook her head, closing her eyes. "My baby," she
whimpered. "They've got my baby."

She slumped down in the bed and curled into a fetal position, drawing the covers up over her head.

Richard eased the phone back onto the hook.

11

RICHARD LEANED AGAINST THE REFRIGERATOR, staring at Doctor Burton's back. When she fumbled with something on the table, trying to fit it into her bag, he leaned around and flipped on the kitchen lights.

"I've given her a shot to help her sleep," said Doctor Burton, zipping the medical case and hefting it by the handle. "She'll be out like a light in three minutes and shouldn't wake up all night."

"Thank you for coming," said Richard. "I can't figure out what happened. I was napping and then I heard Audrey crying.... She must have fallen asleep. I mean, she had to be asleep to have a night terror, right?"

Burton shrugged. "If it's only night terrors, Richard. But we don't know that. I spoke to Doctor Cates at home. He'll fit Audrey in tomorrow morning at ten. Here, take this."

Richard stared at the business card as though it were a death certificate.

"She needs to see him, Richard," said Burton. "You have to make her go, for both your sakes."

He slipped the card into his shirt pocket. "What if he can't help her?"

"*I* can't help her, that's for sure. But Doctor Cates is the best. You and Audrey can get through this, but Audrey needs to see a specialist."

"I'll make her go."

"Good."

He opened the door for her and she turned to face him, a bare remnant of twilight haloed around her.

"I've never told you how sorry I was about Zach," she said.

Richard stared at the floor.

"I'm not a therapist, Richard," she said. "But I know that grief is an important part of living. We can't bury it or forget it or it will bubble up and hurt us even worse. Audrey needs to learn how to deal with the loss of her child. You need to learn to deal with it. Doctor Cates can help."

"I'll take her."

Burton nodded and left.

Richard was getting a glass of water from the sink when light outside the kitchen window caught his eye. He hadn't noticed before, but Audrey must have tripped the switches for the fountain. Water danced and eerie green and yellow light illuminated the trees from below. They looked like giant trolls, hovering over Audrey's garden with outstretched, grasping hands. He stood for a moment, transfixed by the vision, wondering how his mind could transform such mundane surroundings into something so macabre. The trees grew more and more threatening, not trolls anymore, but weird creatures with thin, wasted limbs and gnarly fingers sprouting innumerable ice-pick talons.

He shook himself away from the vision, realizing that that was exactly what was happening to Audrey. That was what her night terrors were like. He staggered back into the bedroom, more determined than ever to find a way to help her.

12

EIGHTY MILES AWAY, Tara Beals replaced the phone on her desk, staring at the bumps that called themselves hills outside of Augusta, Maine. The rolling horizon was slashed neatly by the mullions in her office windows, and the sun turned the clouds into cotton candy. Adler, her Doberman, sat obediently beside her, pretending to enjoy the scenery while Tara patted him distractedly.

"Richard says she needs me and she won't admit it," she muttered, mulling that morning's phone call in her mind. It seemed that Richard trusted her more than Audrey these days. He was a good man, good for Audrey, and Tara had been happy to see them married. But he was siding with Audrey against her now, and Tara feared that all of her and Audrey's work would be undone. A mind was a terribly delicate mechanism, and Tara knew that better than anyone.

With high cheekbones and deep brown eyes surrounded by short hair, Tara had been stunningly beautiful twenty years before. Now she was only disconcertingly so. At five foot six, barely over one hundred twenty pounds, she had that perfect balance of features and form that men found irresistible. Coupled with a mind that had sent university professors into apoplexy, she was a formidable woman.

"She'll change her mind, Adler," she said, scratching absentmindedly behind the dog's ears.

She stared out across the grounds that had once been

manicured to perfection, but now grew ragged and wild. Sometimes she felt as though the same thing was happening to her. She opened a large manila file, studying each sheet of paper in the voluminous pile. When the sun slipped behind a cloud, she flipped on the desk light and began glancing through the records. Finally, reaching the last page, she closed the binder and sat for a moment staring down the darkened hallway outside her office.

She knew that Audrey had always hated the sessions, even though Tara had done everything in her power to assure that Audrey remembered only *good* things. She also knew that calling Audrey would do no good—their last parting had been heated. If she was going to help Audrey, she desperately needed Richard on her side. Audrey had to come to *her*. She had to decide for herself that it was time.

Call me, Audrey.

For God's sake, call me.

Virgil crossed the old concrete bridge over No Name Creek and drove slowly past the spot where he had almost run over Cooder. The morning sun cast long shadows, turning the asphalt into a black river as dark as Virgil's thoughts.

I seen bad things, Virg.

What the hell was that supposed to mean? Virgil figured he was crazy to even be worrying about it. Cooder was so burnt out there was nothing left in his head to get lit again. But even so, Virgil couldn't help but wonder if maybe there *was* something to Cooder's utterances. What if Cooder *had* seen something, only he was so fried he didn't know how to explain it? He was all over the place, in more ways than one.

Cooder seemed a more likely candidate for a séance than Doris.

Recalling the upcoming séance, Virgil cringed. A sudden picture of Babs St. Clair, decked out like the Tarot Woman on the TV, flashed into his head and it tickled his funny bone. Now that would be worth seeing. And it wasn't out of the question. Babs's sense of fashion was famous around Arcos.

I wish to hell I could believe there *was* something after this life. Doris, I honest to God wish I could.

But no matter how hard he tried, he couldn't get the idea past a wall in the back of his head. He'd sat there on the church pew with Doris all those years like a good Christian. Hell, he tried to *act* like a good Christian anyway. *That much* he could believe in. But he'd seen too much death in his job. He didn't believe souls rose out of the dozens of bodies he'd witnessed during his career. He wasn't expecting to meet Doris or his little sister or any of the rest of his family after he had his appointment with his service pistol either.

His baby sister's death had been on his mind since Doris got sick. He never knew *why* her death had been so hard on him. But it had. Maybe it was because she was the first child he ever knew that died. But she was gone forever just like the rest.

He swallowed a large lump and stared directly into the sun, trying to burn some faith into himself. The idea that he could somehow be suddenly reformed reminded him of the story of Saul of Tarsus, going blind on the highway. But no revelation came to him. No angel was standing in the middle of the highway.

13

AUDREY CROSSED HER ARMS and stared at Richard without comment. He was standing in the middle of the kitchen floor with his back straight as a broomstick. He had his fists on his belt and that determined look on his face that had made Audrey laugh a thousand times in the past.

She wasn't laughing now.

"You're going to see Doctor Cates," said Richard. "He made a special opening for you this morning and we're going to be late."

No reply.

"Doctor Burton recommended him."

Still nothing.

"You're going."

"Am I?"

Richard let out a long breath, deflating. "Honey, please go. You hardly slept last night, even after Doctor Burton gave you the sedative. Please..."

Audrey softened a little too. Her lips eased off her teeth and her nostrils stopped flaring like a mad bull. She sat down at the table and toyed with a napkin.

Richard dropped into the chair next to her. "Audrey. Please. Either go see Doctor Cates or call Tara. She's worried about you."

Audrey stared at him. "You called her?"

Richard shrugged. "I was worried. I just told her about the night terrors. Audrey, she wants to help."

Audrey shook her head. "I'm not ready to see Tara again."

"She loves you. You two should make up."

"I know."

"So you'll see her?"

"No."

"Then it's Cates."

She turned back to the tabletop, squeezing the napkin in white-knuckled fists. "Can't you just leave it alone? Please?"

Richard placed his hand gently on her arm. "No, Aud. I can't. You don't know what it's like for me when you have one of these things. I'm afraid you're going to hurt yourself. Honey, you hid from me in the closet."

He gave her a look that said it all. People had looked at her like that before, when she was younger, before Tara taught her to control the images, when she'd scream and run and hide for no reason people could see. It was terrible to see that look on Richard's face. She had to turn away.

"Maybe later . . ."

"Not later, honey. You have an appointment with Doctor Cates."

"But not today. I'm not ready."

"Aud," he said, ever so quietly. "Aud, look at me."

She glanced shyly at him.

"Aud, I can't go on like this. We can't. I'm asking you. I'm begging you. Come with me to Doctor Cates's office."

She bit her lip. Her fingers tapped restlessly on the tabletop. When she spoke she turned away again, staring out across the backyard. "I'm afraid, Richard."

He wrapped his arm around her shoulders and drew her close. She rested her head against him. "I know that. I'm afraid too. But Doctor Cates just wants to help."

"What if he can't help?"

She felt him draw a deep breath against her, and there was a powerful decisiveness in his voice now. "Then there's always Tara."

Audrey shook her head just as decisively.

"Why not Tara?" asked Richard. "I don't understand

why you two fought so much when she was here. You never fought before."

Audrey sighed loudly. She and Richard had argued when she had asked Tara to leave, a week after Zach's disappearance. There'd been a nasty scene, with Richard trying to referee while two of Sheriff Milche's deputies stood in the corner looking like they wanted to be anywhere but in Audrey's living room. Richard couldn't understand then why Audrey felt smothered in Tara's presence, frightened of the solace that Tara offered, and she didn't know how she was going to explain it now. She had trouble understanding it herself.

"I can't breathe around Tara," she said. "You weren't there all those years during our sessions. You don't know what it's like for me. I can't do that right now. I can't."

Richard shook his head. "All she ever wanted to do was help you."

"I know that," she said, trying to control her rising defensive anger. "But she does it by controlling me. Controlling what I think, what I remember. You don't understand!"

"I'm trying to. All I want to do is help too. Don't shut me out."

"I'm not shutting you out. But please don't ask me to see Tara right now."

Tara was too close to her pain. Too close to her past. In Audrey's mind, that was almost like being a part of it. At least this Doctor Cates was a stranger. A nobody.

"Then you'll have to see Doctor Cates. We can't go on like this."

She closed her eyes, surrendering. "All right."

"You'll see him? This morning?"

She nodded.

He kissed her gently on the forehead. "It's going to be okay. I promise."

But she shook her head. "Even if he fixes the night terrors," she whispered. "It won't be okay."

14

DOCTOR CATES'S OFFICE was located in a new business park in South Portland, set back amid tall maple trees and gleaming lawns. Audrey studied the landscaping. Lots of perennials—delphiniums and asters—and shrubs bordered with bark mulch. Here and there an ornamental mountain ash broke up the monotony. It wasn't her style but it was pretty and would be economical for a business to maintain.

She stared at the two stories of glass and then over at Richard. He tried to smile but his face was strained. They had spoken little in the hour and a half they'd been driving, staring straight ahead, and their uneasy silence continued as Richard searched the registry in the lobby and led them down a wide airy hallway to Doctor Cates's door. It took every ounce of Audrey's stamina to follow him inside, to wait quietly in the chair while Richard checked them in at the desk, to smile as the doctor's young female assistant appeared and introduced herself, leading Audrey away from Richard like a lamb to slaughter.

Doctor Cates turned out to be a tall, birdlike man. His salt-and-pepper hair haloed a shiny bald dome and friendly eyes shone through thick glasses. His dark-paneled walls were covered with diplomas and awards, and the floor-to-ceiling bookshelves overflowed with volumes with titles as long as their spines.

Audrey sat in a comfortable armchair and Doctor Cates faced her in another. There was no desk in the room, although she did note the obligatory leather lounge chair. She wondered if anyone ever really used it.

Cates smiled, reading her thoughts. "Actually, my profession frowns on relics like that. But strangely enough, some people really do prefer to recline there to talk. I think they don't feel they're getting their money's worth from a shrink unless they get to lie on a couch."

Audrey laughed nervously. She wished that Richard were beside her and not out in the waiting room. She didn't know what she was supposed to say.

I'm going crazy. That would be a start.

But she couldn't bring herself to admit it.

"You've been depressed since your son's disappearance?" asked Cates.

Audrey nodded. She noticed that Cates had no pen or paper.

"Bad dreams?" asked Cates, steepling his long fingers and staring through them.

"They aren't just dreams. I have them when I'm awake too."

"What do you think they are?"

"I don't know."

"They seem real?"

"They are real," she said, fidgeting.

"Tell me about them."

"I don't know what to tell you."

"Just tell me whatever comes to mind. What happens? Do you remember anything about the dreams clearly?"

Cates wasn't going to be able to help. No one could help. Because they weren't dreams. With each passing moment she believed that more and more. If she *was* crazy, it was a horrible craziness beyond fixing with psychiatry. She was slipping over that deep end where she truly *believed* what she saw in her madness.

"I see Zach and he needs me."

"Your son Zach?"

"Yes."

"It's always a little boy? In the dreams?" asked Cates.

She started to say yes, then remembered the first waking

seizure. "It's Zach. But once there was a little girl mixed up in there too."

"Who's the little girl?"

"I don't know."

"You don't recognize her?"

"I don't see her. I hear her feet, running. Sometimes I hear her voice, crying. *That* seems familiar. I know I should know her. But I can't get a clear picture of her somehow. There's something horrible about her."

"Horrible how?"

"I think something terrible happened to her."

"But you don't know what?"

She shook her head.

"Are she and Zach together?"

She closed her eyes for a moment, concentrating, trying to remember. "No. I don't think so. Some of it seems to be memory and some of it is happening now."

"While you're watching."

"Yes."

"You believe you're witnessing actual events when that happens?"

"I know how that sounds."

"Don't worry how it sounds. I'm not here to judge you. I'm here to help."

"When it happens, sometimes there's pain. A lot of pain. I see Zach and he's in this terrible dark place that I really can't see but I can imagine. I know it's underground, like a basement or a cave."

"And how do you feel after? Once you've awakened."

"I'm not always asleep," she reminded him. She told him about the vision in the window and the one in the fountain, and he frowned. "I don't even remember the ones when I'm sleeping. I wouldn't call those *visions*. I'm not sure what happens then."

"Hallucinations can be extremely convincing, Audrey."

She shook her head. "They weren't hallucinations."

"Didn't they seem at all dreamlike? Unfocused? Weren't you disoriented?"

She didn't want to admit that she was. To admit that would be to deny Zach. "No. I could feel Zach's fear. I could smell the dampness all around him."

"Smell it?"

"Yes. I could smell the odor of mildew and his own scent. A mother knows that smell."

He nodded. "Actually, olfactory hallucinations are uncommon, but they're not unheard of. What do you think they mean?"

Audrey glanced around the room. Even here, right now, the vision of Zach held captive threatened to creep over her. Doctor Cates's eyes narrowed behind the Coke bottle glasses.

"You want me to say I think my son is alive."

"Do you?"

She stared into the thick lenses, seeing both his clear eyes and the rows of books reflected behind her. It seemed like some sort of message: Here I am, eminent doctor with my knowing expression and my years of study, I can help you. Only he couldn't. No more than Tara could.

"What did you want?" he said, breaking her train of thought.

"What?"

"A boy or a girl?" he said, smiling again.

"It didn't matter."

"What about Richard?"

"A boy, I suppose."

"You suppose?"

"I don't recall him ever saying one way or the other. He and Zach loved being together. They were so different in some ways and alike in others."

"Had you ever experienced dreams or . . . visions . . . like these before Zach's disappearance?"

She frowned. "No," she said. Not like these.

"Tell me about some of the dreams."

"They were about my childhood."

Cates wiggled his fingers. "What about your childhood?"

"I didn't have a happy childhood."

"Did you come from a dysfunctional family?"

She laughed dryly.

"You find the question amusing?" asked Cates.

"I find the term inadequate."

Cates nodded, his eyes narrowing like a cat's. "Tell me about your mother."

"I don't remember her." But the question about her mother bothered her more than the others.

"No memories at all?"

"No."

"How can that be?"

"It was all erased."

"Erased?"

"My aunt helped me to forget."

"Your aunt? How did she do that?"

"Hypnotherapy."

"Hypnotherapy is usually utilized to help someone remember. Your aunt is a psychologist?"

"Psychiatrist."

"Why didn't you go to her for help?"

"She's retired," said Audrey. She wasn't here to discuss her relationship with Tara.

Cates frowned. "Do you remember anything at all of your childhood? There must be something."

"Flashes. Images that probably aren't real. I remember hiding in darkness."

Cates nodded to himself. His lenses were prisms now—reflecting the low light of the Tiffany lamps, in rainbow colors—making him seem buglike. "What were you hiding from?"

"I've never talked to anyone about my childhood," said Audrey, shaking her head. "I honestly don't remember much before I moved in with Tara."

"Your aunt?"

Audrey nodded.

"How did you end up with your aunt?"

"She took me."

"Took you?"

"I was ten when she came and got me."

"She got a court order?"

"I don't think so."

"But she must have."

"Must she?"

"The state wouldn't allow someone to just take a child from their parents."

"Well, she did."

"Your aunt knew you were in danger and she came to get you?"

Audrey nodded again, frowning. There was something else tugging at her mind, something that she was missing. There was so much missing. For years it had seemed like a blessing, having only to deal with the filmy remains of her past, the occasional nightmare, the fleeting image or sound that recalled unknown terrors and might send a quick shiver up her spine and be gone. Tara would explain to her again and again that *yes*, the dreams were horrible, but she was getting better, that if she only knew how terrible it had been *before*, she would know just how much better she was. And the dreams had faded over the years until they were nothing but simple nightmares that Audrey had trained herself to deal with.

"Why didn't your aunt contact the authorities when she came to get you?"

"I don't know."

"Did you tell her what was happening to you?"

Audrey frowned. "I don't think so," she said.

"But if you didn't tell her, then how did she know you were in danger?"

Audrey's voice quavered. "I don't want to talk about this anymore, all right?"

Cates ignored her. "Tell me about the night she came and got you."

Of all the places she was afraid Cates might take her, Audrey *really* didn't want to go there. But once he'd conjured up the memory, she was unable to stop the flow of images. They slipped over and around her, flooded her senses with flickering pictures of that long-ago night.

"I had just gone to bed," she whispered. "But I knew she was coming...."

"Your aunt? How?"

"I just knew. I kept hearing her voice in my head. Telling me to be ready. That she was coming to take me away. It sounded like she was talking to herself, only I could hear her. I was frightened, because I knew if I was caught it would be bad."

"Did she visit you often?"

Audrey tried to remember. She didn't recall any visits. Not ever.

So how did I recognize her voice? How did I know who

it was speaking inside my head? She felt herself being cast adrift, sinking deep into that long-ago night. The sensation was so much like the feeling of slipping into the depths of darkness in her fountain that she tucked her hands between her thighs to warm them.

"I heard a car door closing a long way away. But I knew it was her. I could feel her."

"Feel her?"

Audrey ignored the question. "I lay there with my eyes closed and I could see her creeping across the lawn in the moonlight. She was dressed in blue jeans and a T-shirt and white tennis shoes and she had a baseball cap pulled down over her eyes."

"You must have remembered *that*. You couldn't see it with your eyes closed."

Audrey frowned. "The memory is weird. It just ends there like a movie that's cut off in midscene."

"And that's all you remember? Your aunt came to save you, but you don't remember from what?"

The memory faded and Audrey was ever so glad to be back in the light of Cates's office. "It was a long time ago. I don't want to talk about it anymore."

But the unknown something kept scratching at her mind. That memory wasn't right. Part of the healing forgetfulness she and Tara had forged, had wiped away something in that terrible night—something that wanted badly to be remembered.

Cates tried several different tacks, but Audrey wouldn't open up again. Finally he glanced at his watch and sighed.

"Mrs. Bock," he said, "you're suffering from stress-related anxiety and depression. The causes? Your son's disappearance. Your history of childhood abuse. Issues that you have never fully dealt with that are now building up and coming back to haunt you. It's also possible that you're suffering either from a mild form of bipolar disorder or even a very slight case of schizophrenia, but we won't know that without further work together. My suggestion for now is relaxation, and I'm going to prescribe a sedative to help you do that. I would also like to schedule you for regular appointments for a while, to try to get these issues out where you can deal with them. What do you say?"

What could she say? That she didn't want *him* to deal with them? That she and Tara had spent years burying them so that she wouldn't have to face them? But they weren't going away, and she felt an increasing urgency to do something, *anything*. More than just the need to help herself before it became too late for her and Richard. A tiny voice inside her head kept insisting that she wasn't crazy. That Zach was alive. And if there was even the slightest chance that that was true, she knew instinctively that to help him she had to find the answer within her own head. She needed Doctor Cates.

She nodded and Cates smiled, taking her hand and walking her to the waiting room, where Richard waited nervously.

"Would you mind if I speak to your husband privately, Mrs. Bock?" asked Cates, taking Richard's arm. Audrey frowned but shook her head and took a seat.

Cates closed the door and Richard allowed himself to be ushered to a chair. As he sat, forearms resting on his thighs, waiting for Doctor Cates to speak, he felt like a small child awaiting a parent's verdict.

"Is Audrey going to be all right?" he asked.

Cates gave Richard the same diagnosis he had recited for Audrey.

"What are you going to do?" asked Richard.

"I suspect more than anything that her aunt did Audrey a grave disservice by suppressing her past. Audrey has never had a chance to face her traumas and deal with them in her own way."

"Tara loves Audrey like she was her own child."

"I'm sure that's true, Mister Bock, but I believe that the stress from the loss of your son and the anniversary of that loss has worked its way into Audrey's subconscious. That and her memories that have never been allowed to surface are responsible for these night terrors and visions."

"What can I do?"

"Be supportive. But not so supportive that you allow her to convince herself that her hallucinations are real. I'm going to prescribe Halcion, a mild sedative that works well in these cases. See that she takes it, and have my assistant set up another appointment for next week."

"All right." Richard assumed that the interview was over and he rose, shaking Cates's outstretched hand.

"Audrey believes that she was able to communicate with her aunt telepathically. Or at least she could hear her and see her aunt at a distance, through the walls of a house. Were you aware of that?" asked Cates.

Richard frowned. "She never told me that. Is that bad?"

Cates shook his head. "Not necessarily. Her memories are distorted. She doesn't really know *what* she recalls. More than likely that is just her mind's way of dealing with the jumble, of trying to make sense of what's left of her past. Audrey's problems didn't begin with your son's disappearance, Mister Bock."

"I know," said Richard. "I'll make sure she takes the medicine."

15

THE RIDE HOME FROM CATES'S OFFICE was as silent as the ride down, and all that time Audrey struggled under a heavy sense of depression. Things were stirring in the farthest reaches of her head that had lain dormant for years, like a storm brewing just over the horizon with only a distant black thunderhead to announce its arrival. On the one hand, she was certain that Richard was right. She did need Cates, did need *someone* to help her through this terrible time. On the other hand, her fear of reopening old unremembered wounds was so great she had trouble catching her breath.

They were almost home and she pictured herself there, using the image to try to relax, yet each *thwock* of the tires on the broken asphalt increased her feeling of despair. She adjusted her sunglasses, leaning back in the seat of the Camry as Richard eased the car around a sharp curve. Suddenly her throat tightened and the muscles in her legs cramped. She rubbed her hands together as though trying to feel the realness of her own body. Her palms were soaked in sweat.

Their driveway lay over the hill ahead and around a sharp bend. The landscape on both sides here opened into a low mountain meadow bordered by rusted barbed-wire fences. To Audrey's right, a stone wall disappeared into the tree line beside an unnamed creek. The forest was filled with the old rock relics, remnants of a time when the entire North-east was treeless farmland.

There was no reason for her to be experiencing the apprehension that beset her. Nothing except her loss. And yet she knew that was not it. She had a sense of being in two places at once, both inside the roomy, light confines of the moving car and yet locked within some dark, dank place that chilled her skin and sent waves of revulsion racing through her.

Dark.
I can't get out.
I want to go home.
I hate being alone.
I'm afraid.
Afraid of the darkness and of being buried down here.
I want my mother....

Audrey lifted her sunglasses onto her head and ran shaky fingers through her hair, struggling desperately to understand what was happening to her. Richard glanced over with an expression like a father reassuring a small child.

"It's all right, honey," he said. "We'll work through this."

She forced a half-smile, covering her fear.

"I love you. That's what's important," he said.

He gently squeezed her thigh and she slid her hand over his, praying for it to steady her.

"I want our baby back," she said, doing everything she could to block the strange thoughts from her mind, to still the terror drifting over her. The sense of disorientation was nauseating. It was all she could do to carry on the conversation.

"I want him back too," said Richard. "We've done everything we could. So, we deal with it."

"I can't deal with this," she gasped.

Against her will she drifted away. She no longer heard the thrum of the tires or the hum of the engine. Her ears were attuned to a strange humming sound like a giant fan, distant and ominous. Superimposed over the view through the windshield, like fog slipping over a windowsill, she saw darkness.

Shivering.
I'm so afraid.
Air surging through a narrow opening.
A sliver of light creeping from beneath an unseen door.
Something terribly familiar about this dark place.
Something in the silence.

She could barely breathe. With an effort of will, she focused on the dashboard as it fluctuated from a foggy gray mass to a hazy plastic that she reached out and touched. It felt wonderfully solid beneath her fingertips. She chanced a glance out the window. They were almost to the hill. A half-mile and they'd be home. To their right lay thick woodland. A big old rambling farmhouse and barn moldered in a wide expanse of fallow fields on their left. Although she must have driven this road a thousand times, Audrey had never really looked at it before.

The house was clapboard-sided, with steep gables. Black shingles were patched with odd-colored remnants. The paint was weathered and a half-dozen different coats peeked through the blisters. One porch post along the side of the house didn't quite reach the roof, leaving the entrance smiling gap-toothed, like a wooden jack-o'-lantern. The ancient structure meandered away from the road, winding back ninety feet, a square snake, built of boxes. It attached to the old barn like a chain to an anchor. The barn itself was sided with unstained cedar shingles, mildewed to the color of dark storm clouds. Broken windows peered out of the second floor of the barn, like black eyes, and, incongruously, a new satellite television dish capped the roof.

The window eyes of the house proper were unbroken, but displayed the same look of shabbiness, dust, and abandon. Here and there an old green shade drooped ominously, as though someone had ripped it from its mooring. Grass grew tall around the perimeter of the property, punctuated by the empty gravel driveway that ran past the porch to the barn. Except for the antenna, the place appeared abandoned, but it wasn't.

Audrey remembered seeing a big tractor-trailer parked there when she and Richard had last passed the place on the way into Arcos, and she was suddenly certain someone was watching her. She sank back, hiding behind the low dash, scrunching deep into the seat cushions. Her body tensed so that her toes crushed flat in the bottom of her sneakers. Her fingernails dug painfully into her palms. She couldn't breathe without whimpering.

"What the? . . ." sputtered Richard, hitting the brakes.

Audrey slapped at him. She grabbed the wheel and kicked out with her left foot toward the accelerator pedal at the same time.

"Get out of here," she rasped through a dry mouth, nodding ahead toward the hill. To the turnoff to their house. To safety.

"Go!" she screamed.

Richard bore down on the gas. The front end lifted and the Camry leapt ahead like a race horse bursting from the gate. As the house vanished behind them, Audrey's feelings of fear and dread slowly receded. Her arms and then her stomach began to relax, then finally her legs and feet as well.

But the knowledge that the decrepit old structure was now behind her, was unsettling.

Richard and Audrey stared at the white plastic bottle sitting ominously alone in the center of the kitchen table.

Halcion.

"I don't need medicine," she said.

"You need something," muttered Richard. "You should have seen yourself in the car."

She knew he thought she was going crazy. She had to admit that maybe she was. She wanted with all her heart to believe that Zach was alive. But was this about Zach? Or was it about something so terrible from her own past that Tara had been forced to bury the memory of it to keep her from going totally insane?

"I'm sorry," she said.

"You don't have anything to be sorry for," he said, coming around to sit beside her and place his arm around her shoulders. "I just want you to get better."

"I'm not crazy, Richard," she whispered.

"No one said you were. No one is ever going to say that."

"But you think I'm imagining things."

He stiffened against her. "Doctor Cates said it's just stress. The medicine will help."

When she sighed, it felt as though she had shrunk physically, as though all the air inside her and her sense of self were leaking out at the same time.

"What if I'm not imagining things?"

"Audrey, people don't see things like what you see, not in the real world. It's just stress. You've been under a lot of pressure."

"But what if it isn't stress?" she shouted. He drew back and she stared at him with frightened eyes. "What if it's real? What if Zach's locked up in some dark basement?"

"Do you really believe that? Is that what the thing in the car was about? Honey, the police interviewed all the neighbors. The old man who owns that house was out of town, remember?"

She nodded. She and Richard had followed every interview, read every report. Listened to the police discussing what *they* thought had happened, when they believed she and Richard were out of earshot. The general idea was that Zach was long gone, far away. Certainly not locked up in a basement next door. And she knew it was true. What she was thinking was crazy. She had to get hold of herself or else the next step Richard suggested might not be just a visit to the doctor. The next diagnosis might call for more than just medicine. She didn't even want to think about that. About being locked away somewhere in some small room.

"Honey," he said soothingly, "it isn't real. You need to take one of the pills and see if they help."

She nodded, her hands tight on the table. She was shaking. She saw fear in his eyes now as well as concern.

"I just want it to stop," she sobbed.

Richard hurried to the sink, returning with a glass of water. He opened the medicine bottle and dropped one of the pills into his palm. She could see him wondering if he should reach for another, but he closed the cap and held out both hands to her.

"This will make it stop," he said.

She stared at the pill and the glass. "And if it doesn't?"

"If it doesn't, then we'll do something else. We'll get through this. Whatever it takes, Aud. For as long as it takes. I'll be here."

"Promise?"

He nodded and she saw the determination in his eyes.

She took the pill, chasing it with the entire glass of water.

16

VIRGIL AND DORIS'S HOUSE was a comfortable 1940s two-story number with tall gables and a widow's walk over the front porch. He and Doris used to sit out there on summer nights, listening to the crickets and waving at neighbors passing by on the sidewalk. The house was a block off of Main Street, so it was farther from the lake, but sometimes you could get a cool breeze wafting over the water after sundown. Tall maple trees and high hedges separated most of the homes in this part of town, but many of the backyards were undivided, so that a couple who happened to be barbecuing up the street might end up with unexpected guests.

Virgil eased around a Honda Civic and a pickup truck in the driveway. Candlelight flickered in the bedroom window and he glanced around the neighborhood to see if anyone else had noticed. A few cars moved up and down the street, but no curious crowd gathered.

Reaching across the seat, he grabbed the bag of finger sandwiches he'd picked up from Patty's Bake Shop. He could hear women talking excitedly through the open window and he hoped to God nobody happened by for a walk while they were in the middle of the damned thing.

He really felt like putting his foot down this time. Of all the people he didn't care to have in his house, Babs topped the list. Virgil had known Babs ever since she'd moved to town ten years ago. Hell, it was impossible not to know Babs. She was constantly out on the street in her flowing robes or bandanas or some other ridiculous garb, regaling anyone who'd listen to her with half-baked ideas about how to save the world. Babs was into multivitamins, pyramids, crystals, aromatherapy, Buddhism, and who knew what else. It wouldn't have surprised Virgil to learn that she sacrificed chickens in her basement, and he didn't want her preying on Doris.

Doris had always been gullible. Pastor Donnelly had spoken to her a couple of times over the years about getting involved in what he called "heathen affairs." But Doris had stuck to mostly mundane pursuits: buying horoscope books, reading Shirley MacLaine. It wasn't until recently, after the disease, that she'd started getting serious. Virgil suspected that Doris was a little worried that maybe Pastor Donnelly didn't have all the answers and she was spreading her eggs around to different baskets.

"Let her do what the hell she wants," he muttered under his breath, closing the front door quietly behind him.

Opening the bag, he got down a serving dish from the cupboard, arranging the tuna- and chicken-salad sandwiches in what he thought was a nice pattern. He poured a large bag of chips into a bowl and placed the sandwiches and the bowl on a TV tray and carried them upstairs. He was hoping that Doris's visitors might coerce her into eating a bite. Maybe something good would come of the night after all.

There were candles on the floor in the downstairs hall and candles on each of the stair treads. He followed their wavering shadows up to the bedroom. The women were seated around the bed like biddies at a quilting bee, all of them staring solicitously at Doris and talking at once. Babs had on what looked like a sheet and she had a towel wrapped around her head like a turban. Virgil set the tray on a bedside table.

"Sit, sit," said Babs, pulling Virgil down into the chair beside her, at the head of the bed. He glanced around at what had to be one hundred candles of different shapes and sizes. They were on the windowsills, on the dresser, on the lamp table alongside the food tray, and on the threshold of the open door leading onto the side porch. One or more of them must have been scented, because the small room was immersed in the smell of jasmine.

"We'll eat later," whispered Babs, leaning uncomfortably close to Virgil's ear. "Doris is anxious to speak to the other side. She wants to get on with the sitting."

"The what?"

Babs gave Virgil an indulgent smile. "The sitting, dear. No one has called them séances in a hundred years, except Doris."

Doris chuckled.

"Is this really what you want?" asked Virgil.

"Yes," said Doris.

"All right," said Virgil, glancing around self-consciously. He knew each of the women present. Knew their husbands and families. Figured most if not all of them had voted for him. "What do I do?"

Babs got up and turned off the overhead fixture and the two bedside lamps. She reseated herself beside Virgil in the warm glow of the candle flames and slipped her palm into his. "Take Doris's hand," she said.

Virgil did as he was told and the group formed a circle of clasped hands. For a long time nothing happened. He glanced expectantly around and found that everyone else was peeking just as expectantly at Babs. Babs stared straight ahead, toward the wall with the framed picture of Doris on Salisbury Beach. Virgil had taken the photograph on their honeymoon, on the one day it didn't rain. It was a faded black-and-white, and although it held a lot of memories for him, he couldn't imagine Babs caring about it one way or the other.

After ten minutes of enduring cautionary glances from Doris, Virgil was about to ask if they could move things along when Babs's hand clinched his hand so hard a sharp pain shot up Virgil's arm. He turned to her and was shocked by what he saw.

Babs's cheeks were tight. Her eyes were rolled back in her head and the veins in her neck stood out like vines growing around an oak stump. Her hand quivered in his. Her breath rasped in her throat, panting through tight lips. As Almira Couvineau leaned across the bed toward them, Virgil smelled toilet water and brandy.

"Spirit?" she said, in her husky tobacco voice. "Are you there?"

"Who calls me?"

Virgil was shocked by the heavy masculine voice that emanated from Babs's lips.

"We call you in the name of our friend Doris Milche," said Almira.

Babs's chest heaved. "Why have you called me?"

Of course he was just imagining it. But the candles seemed to have dimmed.

"I want to know if I'm welcome...on your side," said Doris.

Babs seemed to flinch, and all the women gave Doris a funny look as though she'd broken some rule of the game.

"There is no welcome," growled the heavy voice out of Babs's throat. "If you come, you come."

Virgil glared at Babs. Nice. Way to make Doris feel better. Why couldn't she use a Sally Field voice and talk about Elysian fields and harps and the throne of God instead of frightening the shit out of her?

"But what about heaven?" asked Doris.

Silence. The women glanced nervously at one another, waiting.

"This is not heaven," said the voice.

"They're lost souls, Doris!" hissed Almira. "These spirits haven't passed over yet, for Christ's sake."

Virgil felt like Babs could have done a better job of indoctrinating the trainees before their first session. He wondered what the hell Doris had thought was going to happen.

"Well, then, I don't know what to ask," said Doris, frowning.

"Spirit," said Beckie Rossig, "can you tell me if my husband's cheating on me?"

A gasp came from somewhere. Virgil stared at Beckie, but she wouldn't meet his eyes. If nothing else, the entertainment value had picked up a notch. Virgil was about to tell Beckie that *he* could answer that question, but thought better of it.

"You can't ask questions like that!" hissed Almira.

"Well, I don't know why not," said Beckie. "No one else was asking."

"Because we're here for Doris," said Claudia Hermman, shaking her head. "Doris, you go ahead."

Babs's palm was becoming clammy. Virgil really wanted to slip his hand away and wipe it on his pants, but he didn't dare break the circle with Doris and the others watching.

"Now I don't know if this was a good idea or not," said Doris, catching Virgil's eye.

He smiled, trying to look encouraging.

The candles flickered. A breeze—far too cold for the season—stirred the curtains. A low rumbling started in Babs's chest, bubbling up her throat until it flowed from her mouth in a growl. "There is another here who would speak."

"Speak, spirit," said Almira.

"Who's there?"

Virgil glanced over at Babs, wondering again how she did the voices. It seemed like she switched from a professional wrestler to an adolescent boy in midstride.

"Answer!" said Almira, nodding feverishly around the table. All the women besides Babs quickly announced their presence. Then they turned expectantly to Virgil.

"Sheriff Milche here," said Virgil, feeling even sillier than before.

"I'm Timmy Merrill."

The marrow melted out of Virgil's bones. He didn't know whether to slap Babs or to just stand up and walk out. A more tasteless joke he couldn't imagine, but the women were staring at Babs spellbound and, God help him, something in the voice gripped Virgil as well. He didn't know what to do or to say.

"I'm scared," said the voice. For a second after the words died away, silence hung in the room like an ax over their heads. All the women continued staring at Virgil.

"What are you scared of?" asked Virgil at last. And what the hell was there for spirits to be scared of? Virgil shook his head, wondering if ghosts told people stories.

"I miss my folks," said the voice.

"They miss you too," said Virgil, playing along for Doris's sake. But he wanted to end this. It disgusted him. He hadn't had a lot of respect for Babs before. But *this*. This was too much.

"It's cold here. And dark."

Now that was just some more of what Doris needed to hear.

"My bike got thrown in the creek."

Virgil's skin went suddenly colder than the breeze, and he was sure that the candles were dimmer. No one had ever found Timmy Merrill's bike. It was assumed that the kidnapper kept it. He moved his head, trying to make contact with Babs's eyes, to figure out what kind of game she was playing at, but they were still rolled up in her head.

"Where, Timmy?" asked Virgil. "Where were you?"

Silence.

Babs's chest was really heaving, and Virgil could have sworn that the candlelight was growing dimmer. It was like Babs was sucking in part of the light.

"The old bridge. Down behind Haylands Mills."

Virgil couldn't believe what he was hearing. Had anyone ever searched there? Probably not. It was miles from the Merrill home. How in the world could Babs have ever thought of that spot? And how did she do those damned voices? Glancing at each of the women, he knew they expected him to play along to the end, even though the game was starting to give him the jitters. "Where are you, boy? What happened to you?"

"It hurt," said the voice. "It hurt bad."

There was the sound of genuine pain and betrayal in the voice. Just the way a young boy might sound who had been put in the position Virgil figured Timmy Merrill probably had. Babs was starting to make him as nervous as he was angry.

"What did, son? Who hurt you?"

Silence again.

More gasps from Babs. She wasn't looking too good. Her cheeks weren't red anymore; in fact, they were getting kind of pale.

"I don't know," said the voice. "It's dark here. And I'm scared."

All the women looked terrified now, but Virgil couldn't figure out how to end the farce. He couldn't very well tell the spirit to shut up. The women would have it all over town that he'd missed a chance to solve a terrible crime.

"Tell me what happened," said Virgil, frowning.

"I was riding my bike. Something hit me. When I woke up I was in a car and I was taped in."

"Taped?"

"Yeah. It's awful dark here."

"Did you see who it was?"

"No. There was tape on my eyes. It was dark. It's always dark."

"Where did they take you? Do you remember?"

"I think it's a basement."

Virgil could hear Cooder, reciting over and over in his head, *Bad things, Virg. I seen bad things.* Was it even remotely possible that Cooder's ramblings had anything to do with this? How? Virgil didn't think Cooder's house even had a basement, and no one in their right mind would let Cooder into theirs.

He shook his head. The stress of the two cases and Doris, and now this, was driving him crazy.

"I'm having trouble holding him," said Babs in her own voice. Her hand shook in Virgil's. She sounded weak as a kitten. "Come back, Timmy. We're here for you. Don't be afraid. We're here."

Virgil was twisted. On the one hand, he didn't believe in any of this bunkum. Everybody in town knew that Timmy had disappeared on his bike. On the other hand, the voice coming out of Babs's face frightened him. He couldn't for the life of him figure out how she was doing it.

"It's cold here," said the voice. But this time it sounded far away. "And there's so many of us."

"Who are the others?" asked Doris.

Silence.

"Do you know the others?" asked Babs.

"I can't see them. I just feel them."

The fear in the voice chilled Virgil. He imagined himself in total darkness, surrounded by people he didn't know, in some cold, tight space.

"I can't stay," said the voice, farther away than before.

"Timmy," said Babs. "We're here for you. Is there anything else you want to tell us?"

"There's bad people here."

The voice faded to nothing on the last word.

Babs tried to make contact with the boy again, clamping her eyes tight, calling his name. When that failed, she tried to contact the original voice. But again there was no answer, and finally the sitting broke up. The ladies left one by one, expressing their concern for Doris, their assurances that the other side wasn't so bad and that Doris wasn't going there anyway, and their pleas to Virgil to check out the bike. Babs stayed long enough to explain to Doris about the mix-up. She didn't claim to speak to heaven or hell and she didn't know any *authentic* medium who could. She could only contact those souls that were still on this plane and had not yet crossed over into eternity. When everyone else was gone, Virgil sat on the edge of the bed holding Doris's hand. He was shaken but didn't want to show it.

"That worked out pretty well," he said.

"It wasn't what I expected," said Doris. "Babs should have told me."

Doris looked exhausted, but when she spoke again, some of her old fire returned to her eyes. "You go out right now and look for that bike."

"Are you serious?"

"How could you not?"

For one thing, he'd feel stupid, wandering around in the dark down by that old bridge, on the word of a spirit out of the mouth of Babs St. Clair. "It's getting late. I'll go tomorrow."

"You go tonight or you won't get any sleep."

"You mean you won't let me get any."

"That's right."

"What do you want me to do? Drag the creek by myself?" He thought of the sodden woods and the raging streams the year Timmy had disappeared.

"It hasn't rained for diddly this spring. Likely that old creek is dry as a bone."

"Maybe."

"You heard that boy, Virgil. His soul can't rest until you find his killer."

"This is silly, Doris."

"You won't know until you look."

He sighed so loud she blinked. "Why am I arguing?"

He picked up the sandwich tray, then went around blowing out all the candles the breeze hadn't taken care of. He left the lamps out because, by the time he got back to the bedside, Doris was snoring lightly.

He kissed her forehead and left.

17

VIRGIL WONDERED WHAT KIND of coincidence it was that the road leading to the old bridge was the same one on which he'd narrowly missed killing Cooder. As he passed the spot where the accident had almost occurred, the moon broke through the trees and, for just an instant, Virgil imagined that the razor of golden light off to his right *was* Cooder, come back again to wait for him.

What if Timmy's bike was here?

No. That was too crazy to even contemplate. This was a fool's errand and a waste of time. But at least it had gotten him out of the house. He'd have just spent the next few hours pacing, pretending to watch TV in the room adjoining the bedroom, waiting for Doris to call out in the night when her pain needed its next feeding. Nowadays Virgil slept mostly in his recliner, when he slept at all. Still, he couldn't help but stare up the road, picturing Cooder there again, making his ominous pronouncement.

Crazy.

His headlights tunneled ahead as the trees flashed past, stoop-shouldered mourners along a funeral route. He spotted the outline of the bridge and pulled over, just short of the cracked and pitted old cement guardrail. When he slammed the car door shut, gunshot echoes slap-slapped away up the creek, and he pointed his flashlight toward the bridge.

The old structure was four car-lengths long, built during the Depression by government workers. Virgil hiked down the embankment through the tall grass, careful where he stepped. A rusted exhaust pipe slithered through the weeds like a jagged brown snake. Farther down toward the stream, a tire still clung to the rear axle from a long-forgotten vehicle. Virgil played the light over the creek bottom.

Doris was right. The creek bed was mostly dry. Only a narrow trickle of water flowed around widely spaced rocks. Virgil scrambled down the gravel banks of what would have been a roaring waterway during early spring runoff. He brushed off his pants legs and pointed the light back up under the bridge.

Time had sent cracks meandering across the cement face, and conspired with the elements to reveal ancient steel rebar where a few chunks of concrete had fallen away into the creek. But overall the old bridge was in good shape, considering the decades it had sat alone, uncared for, facing Maine winters and summers. It was a concrete monument to a breed of men who no longer existed.

The trees were thicker on the other side of the road and they grew closer to the creek. The arch of the bridge seemed to continue forever up the dark, wandering stream, creating an ominous-looking cavern, and Virgil's old aversion to shadowy, tight places sent a little surge of anxiety through him. This was stupid. If he was going to search the damned creek, he ought to at least do it in the daylight. How did Doris expect him to find anything in the dark?

He glanced back over his shoulder, deciding whether to go or to stay. It had been an easy slide down, but it would be a rough slog back up to his cruiser. Hell, he was here. Might as well look around.

He approached the bridge, shining the light on any place that might remotely have concealed a bike. There was plenty more refuse hidden up under the arch. There was even part of an old motorcycle frame, shoved way up tight where the concrete met the creek bank, but no bike, and he was glad to exit the other side of the bridge where at least the stars could break through. He really didn't care for the feeling of the dark hulk hovering over him. He'd already made it twenty yards up the creek on the other side of the bridge when it dawned on him that he was wasting his time going any farther.

The stream flowed the other way. If anyone had thrown anything into it, it would have been carried downstream. That was why there was less garbage the farther upstream he got from the bridge. He waded across the ankle-deep water and came back down the other side, shining the light up and down the slope. Of course, the bike might have been anywhere in the tall grass. If it was, the only hope of finding it was a long search in the daylight. He stopped for a moment, listening to the night sounds.

An owl hooted far off in the woods. To his left something rustled in the underbrush. Probably a raccoon or a porcupine. And of course there was the trickle of the tiny stream. He glanced overhead, but the stars were silent. Watching him on his fool's errand.

He glanced up toward the road, but the embankment on this side of the bridge was much steeper, studded with large outcroppings of granite. He hunched his shoulders and hiked back beneath the bridge. Once again he was struck by an odd sense of being *caught,* the bridge pressing down on him. He shone the light quickly around the arch to force the gloom away, and once again he was glad to be out from under the old structure when he reached the far side.

Virgil turned to scrabble up the loose gravel bank. The flashlight twisted sideways in his hand and he froze, leaning against the slope. Through the trees along the bank he could see that twenty feet downstream, back in the underbrush, a flood had washed a stretch of rusted chicken wire into a thick stand of yearling pines. It hung there like an old fishing net laid outside to dry. Tangled in its web he could just make out the curve of a black bicycle tire.

"Oh, shit," he whispered.

He pushed off from the bank, losing view of the wire, but never taking his eyes off the spot where he'd seen it. He approached the area with the trepidation of a hunter moving in close to a wounded animal's lair, afraid of what might leap out at him from the darkness. When he pulled back a snarled mass of brush, his flashlight illuminated the enclosed area like a spotlight in an oven.

Hidden in the bracken was a boy's bike. Virgil fought his

way through the undergrowth until he stood directly over the bicycle, staring down at it as though it was the first he had ever seen.

"Damn."

The cycle was in surprisingly good condition, except for a little rust and two flat tires. Obviously the wire had caught it on this higher ground during that first spring when the rivers were all running high, and it had lain here protected in the trees ever since. There wasn't a dented fender on it. The plastic grips on the handlebars still shone bright black in the light. No one had tossed this bike out because it was useless. Someone had thrown it in the creek so no one else would find it, just like Babs said.

Just like *someone* had said.

He trotted back to the cruiser and called the station. Birch answered.

"What's up, Sheriff?"

"I found Timmy Merrill's bike," he gasped, trying to catch his breath.

"No way."

"Yeah. I'm on Old High Road at the bridge over No Name Creek. I'm going to cordon off the area. I want you to start scavenging up a search party for tomorrow morning. Get hold of Martin over at Fish and Game and see if Bill Keens' dogs are available."

"You okay? You sound shook."

"Just winded. Find out about the dogs."

"You think the body is there somewhere?"

"No," said Virgil. "But we need to search anyway. Maybe we can turn up some more evidence."

"Right."

Virgil got the crime-scene tape from the trunk and returned to the bike. He considered running tape across from the upper edge of the bridge to the tree line, but decided that would draw too much attention. The idea was to protect the scene, not to attract gawkers before he'd even had a chance to figure out what he'd found. He crashed his way through the underbrush, laying out a large circle around the chicken wire and bike, wrapping the tape around trees and branches until he had the area completely encircled.

Then he stood for a moment with his eyes closed, listening to the woods.

"Are you here, boy?" he whispered.

For some reason he felt certain that he would know if Timmy's body lay close at hand, but he sensed nothing from the woods. Nothing except a growing heat in his chest every time he stared at the forlorn bike. It seemed like a deserted pet awaiting a master who would never return.

He climbed back to his cruiser and tossed the tape in the trunk, slamming the lid. Staring off up the road into the darkness, he began to wonder which promise he was going to keep: his promise to Doris, his promise to Rosie Merrill, or his promise to himself.

18

AS THE NIGHT WORE ON toward dawn, dew began to glisten on the blades of tall grass, reflecting blue starlight. Silver-lined clouds scudded across the moon, sending predatory shadows creeping through the forest all around. A lone cricket chirruped in the underbrush. A woman slipped into the alders like a breath of wind. No twig snapped beneath her bare feet. No branch rustled against her cotton skirt. Every step was measured and sure. Graceful as a deer or a wolf. But furtive as a weasel on the prowl.

She reached the top of the saddle in the hills and studied the Bock house sitting silent below, a thin light visible in the kitchen window. The bedroom was dark.

The woman surveyed the area. The road in front of the house was empty, as it was most times of the day or night. Nothing moved in the yard. She saw no one in the trees, but still she waited, uncertain. She didn't expect anyone to be awake at this hour, but she was stealthy by nature.

An owl hooted in the distance, a forlorn sound, full of portent. The woman carefully negotiated the steep slope, winding through the brush, stopping at the edge of the garden. She glanced at the fountain that sat still now, reflecting the intermittent starlight.

Then she slipped silently across the lawn like a mouse across a kitchen floor, hating the openness. She knelt beneath the bedroom window, her knees dug into the damp grass, waiting for her eyes to adjust to the deeper darkness. Then ever so slowly she raised them to the windowsill, peering into the dim confines of the house.

Richard had his arm draped across Audrey. She slept quietly beneath the sheet, curled with her back tight against him, facing the window. One faint ray from the hall lit her face in sharp relief, like a Rembrandt painting. Her hair was pulled back, and, wrapped in the embrace of sleep, she seemed childlike and unafraid. The woman could not pull her eyes away. She needed to remember every shadow, every texture, every pore. Her fingers tightened on the sill, as though she were about to burrow her way through the wall itself.

As the moon peeked from behind a cloud, it shone at a soft angle on the woman's face, erasing the wrinkles from her brow. In that instant, someone coming upon her in the backyard might have taken her for Audrey. Then the moon was gone again and age returned, along with grief. She glanced quickly around the bedroom.

Through the glass she heard a gasp and she jerked herself to her feet, scurrying across the backyard, ducking into the brush. Audrey's shrieks tightened the muscles of the woman's back as she rushed through the bracken to the top of the hill, turning just as the bedroom light flicked on.

She shouldn't have come. She knew better. But she couldn't stay away. It drove her mad being so close, being *almost* able to touch. She stood beside a tall spruce, invisible in the half-light, watching as first one and then two faces appeared at the window. They glanced in her direction, but she didn't budge and the searching eyes moved on. Then the back-porch light came on, sending long shadows racing across the lawn toward her. When Richard stepped out onto the back stoop in his bathrobe, the woman melted away into the forest.

The grass was cool beneath Richard's bare feet. He glanced around, but of course no one was in the yard. He was groggy from lack of sleep and trying to fight down his anger at Audrey for another night shattered. He didn't know how much more he could take. But as he approached

the window, he saw the fear in Audrey's face and his irritation melted. He waved at her and smiled, glancing around
in what he hoped didn't appear to be a comic rendition of a
man on guard. She lifted the window and leaned out.

"I saw a face," she said.

He nodded.

"I did," she insisted. "I woke up and she was staring
right at me."

"She?"

"Yes."

"What did she look like?" asked Richard.

Audrey bit her lip.

"Audrey?"

"Light hair. Gray, maybe. She was there and then she
was gone."

"Peeking in our bedroom window?" said Richard, trying
desperately not to sound condescending. Audrey sounded
confused, almost as though there was more she wanted to
say but was afraid to.

"I saw what I saw, Richard!"

He moved closer to the window, glancing once more
around the entire backyard, taking in the garden and the
dark forest beyond. "There's no one here now, Audrey. I'll
walk around the house just to be sure."

"Be careful," she said, closing the window and clicking
the latch.

Sure. I'll be on the lookout for some crazy gray-haired
woman who might be lurking in the shadows. But he nodded at Audrey and walked dutifully around the house anyway. When he reached the front yard he halted. His eyes
roved across the lawn toward the mailbox and suddenly a
pang tore at his heart. He'd stood in this same spot a year
before.

He'd rushed out of the house when he heard Audrey
shriek, and ended up here, listening to her cries disappearing through the trees, trying to make sense of them, to tell
where the hell she was or what she was doing. He knew instinctively it had to do with Zach. Only Zach could have
caused such terror in her cries. Finally he'd found her when
she broke out of the woods again, running up and down the
gravel lane, Zach's bat clutched to her breast, out of breath,

but still shrieking Zach's name. He'd caught up to her and held her, trying to get sense out of her. What had she seen? Where was Zach? When he began to understand that she hadn't *seen* anything, that she'd found the bat on the front lawn, some of the panic had eased and Richard had allowed himself a hint of hope. Maybe Zach had wandered into the woods. He was a boy. Boys did things like that. Only why wasn't he answering?

But Audrey's initial reaction had been the correct one. Someone had taken their son. And Zach wasn't coming back. Richard had finally accepted that.

He pulled himself away from that dark place in his mind and continued his halfhearted search. If a woman had been hanging around the house, she'd hiked in. There was no car down the road or in the drive. He'd completed his circle and started up the back stoop toward the open kitchen door when a glint on the grass froze him in place.

It had to be a trick of the light, but, from this angle, footprints shone like quicksilver where moonlight caressed the flattened turf. Richard cocked his head, trying to get a better perspective. He could make out five, maybe six clear imprints crossing the lawn directly toward their bedroom window.

He stepped slowly back down onto the lawn, never taking his eyes off the ephemeral tracks. The closer he approached, the more tenuous they seemed. He knelt beside the clearest example and touched the flattened grass with his fingertips. He couldn't believe it. Somebody *had* walked across the lawn. Someone with small feet, like a woman.

He stood and stared into the dark forest, squinting. The longer he watched the motionless woods, the less sure he became. He glanced back down at the flattened grass and wondered if he wasn't letting his mind run away with him. For all he knew, Audrey had made the tracks the day she had her last seizure in the garden. Lord knew how she might have run around on the lawn. He *really* wanted to believe that.

But then why were there no other tracks? Why wasn't the lawn covered with them? When he glanced back down at the tracks he noticed that the dew on the standing grass glistened, while the footprints seemed smudged dry. Was it possible that *he* was starting to imagine things? The tracks seemed so real.

He turned back toward the window. Audrey stared raptly at him and he smiled at her, wiping the tracks away with his foot and heading back into the house.

19

VIRGIL CLIMBED THE STAIRS toward the bedroom, too exhausted to keep his eyes open. He knew his lack of sleep and the fact that he wasn't eating good were wearing him down. With any luck, his lifestyle would take care of him long before he had to worry about another way out.

He placed his gunbelt on the side table in the hall beside the phone, where it had slept for thirty years, and tiptoed into the bedroom. To his surprise, Doris was wide-awake, watching television. A revival meeting was on and a preacher with an impossible head of wavy red hair was exhorting his viewers to send money so that he could continue in his mission. Virgil sat wearily on the bed, resting his head against the headboard and taking Doris's thin hand in his own. He closed his eyes and wished himself back twenty years before leaning down to kiss her cheek.

"You found Timmy Merrill's bike, didn't you?" she said.

"Now, how did you know that?"

She managed a chuckle as thin as her hand. "I've known you for thirty-eight years, Virgil Milche. Do you think you can keep secrets from me?"

He smiled. "Never have."

"That's right."

"It was there. Back in the brush. Gonna search the woods tomorrow."

"You won't find anything else."

"What makes you so sure?"

"Didn't you listen? Timmy said the bike was just dropped there. He isn't there. He's in some old basement." She shuddered. "Poor, poor boy."

"I heard what Babs said."

"What Timmy said."

"Whatever."

"But you don't believe it. How in the world could you not? None so blind, Virgil."

"I guess so."

She sighed, turning back to the television. In a minute her features softened again. She didn't even have the energy anymore to stay annoyed with him for more than a second or two. "You remember the week after we were married?"

He frowned. It had rained until he thought the second Flood was coming. He could never forget that. They'd planned the trip for over a year, saved like a couple of pack rats, and then the day they arrived the heavens opened.

"I was lying here thinking about those days," she said.

"About the rain?"

"About our first nights together. I was so scared I wouldn't please you. I'd never been with a man before."

He squeezed her hand gently. "You always pleased me."

She smiled and a light twinkle burned through the dullness in her eyes. "I figure you didn't mind all that rain, then."

He chuckled. "Now that I recall, I asked for and got some extra time off when we got back."

"You sure did. But I didn't get any."

They laughed together.

"Sometimes I know things," she said quietly.

"I wish I did."

"You do. You just don't *know* you know them."

"This conversation is getting strange."

"Uh-huh. You're not going to find that boy out there in the woods and you know it."

"Because Babs said so."

"I talked to her on the phone awhile ago. She was pretty upset."

"What about?"

"I'm not sure. She said ever since she left here Timmy

Merrill's been preying on her mind. But it wasn't only that. I think she's in a bad way somehow."

"I don't want Babs St. Clair calling and worrying you with her personal nightmares."

"She sounded scared, Virgil."

"So she called you? What did she think you were going to do for her?"

"Lend her moral support, maybe. Convince her that my husband isn't going to lay down and die just because I am. A lot of people depend on you, Virgil. They're going to need you when I'm passed on."

"Don't say that!"

"Promise me you'll stay on the case."

He sighed loudly. "I am on the case."

"Good."

"What do you expect me to do now?"

"Find those boys."

"Jesus."

"Don't take the Lord's name in vain, Virgil."

"I'm coming to bed," he said, unbuttoning his uniform. "I need a good night's sleep."

"Good. I'm tired too."

He got up and helped her down into a better sleeping position, kissing her brow again. "You need anything in the night, you just poke me."

But she was already asleep.

20

RICHARD RESTED HIS ARM on the car window and enjoyed the cool, wet morning air. Daylight was just rising over the distant hills, warming the sky but not the black-green rolling landscape. The wind was redolent with evergreen, and now and then he detected the smell of wood smoke.

Wood smoke in early June. Only in Maine.

He stared at the run-down farmhouse as he passed, thinking of Audrey's attack in the car, her sudden fear of the rickety old place. But no evil power emanated from it. No darkness overcame him, no sudden terror attack.

It did look dank and ghoulish though. If he were going to write a modern gothic novel, he might well use the house in it. A rusted tractor-trailer sat beside it like an ornery old watchdog, and he slowed, reading the sign on the side.

Merle Coonts Trucking.

And below that, in smaller lettering, with a cartoon picture of a smiling truck:

We Haul Anything!

Strange how you never noticed details. Until that moment he'd had no idea of his neighbor's name, although he must have passed the truck a hundred times. When he thought of it, he realized that he didn't know any of their neighbors at all. The closest one to their house was nearly an eighth of a mile up the road in the other direction.

Turning onto Route 26 into Arcos, he honked at Bill McDab

standing out front of the greenhouses that bore his name. Farther up the road he pulled into the Arcos Steak House parking lot, stared up at the sign, and smiled. The restaurant was Richard's biggest success story. He'd convinced Sam, the owner, to switch from the haute cuisine that had been slowly putting him out of business to more family-oriented fare. The steak house turned into a local institution overnight. Sam had become Richard's best friend and now it was Richard's policy to stop in for breakfast every morning.

Richard dropped into the booth that Bev kept cleared for him and glanced around at the chattering customers. The sound of clinking cups and saucers from the kitchen and the fast-moving waitresses gave the room an efficient air that would slow a little for the more relaxed lunch crowd.

Sam waddled through the louvered kitchen doors and dropped into the other side of the booth, handing Richard a coffee. Sam was in his seventies and, with each passing year, his growing success had revealed itself in his girth.

"How you been, buddy?" asked Sam in a husky voice.

"Good."

"And Aud?"

"She's good," said Richard. But he knew that Sam caught the hesitation in his voice. They'd known each other way too long.

"What's the matter?"

"Nothing probably. She's just having bad dreams."

"You can't blame her for that."

"We're going through a hard time. That's all."

Sam nodded. "I used to love seeing you three come in together."

The word *three* lit up pictures in Richard's mind that he didn't care to look at right then. "Audrey just hangs around the house. She doesn't garden. She doesn't read the way she used to. And she was writing another book, before. Now, I don't even know what she's done with the manuscript."

"She talked about it so much I thought it was already finished."

"It might be, for all I know. Whenever I ask her about it she says she's still working on it, but I know she's not."

"Maybe you just need to get her out of the house. Why don't the two of you go on a vacation?"

"I've suggested that. She won't go. She doesn't want to leave. Just in case."

"How about you? Are you still waiting for the call?"

"I guess I am, a little."

"You're looking better than you were six months ago."

"I'm doing all right, Sam. It's not something you just get over."

"No. Did I ever tell you about my boy?"

"I didn't know you had a son."

"I don't talk about Tony much anymore. It still hurts too much."

"I'm sorry."

"He'd be fifty now."

Richard didn't know what to say.

"He was killed in Vietnam," said Sam. "I used to keep all his pictures on top of the TV. But after we got word of what happened, I started going a little crazy. So did my wife. It was like we were worshiping those photos. You know what I mean?"

Richard glanced away, nodding.

"I began to sit in his room for hours on end," said Sam. "Sometimes I didn't even realize I'd gone in there or how long I stayed. My wife and I started drifting apart and we'd always been so close."

"What did you do?"

Sam took a long, deep breath, rubbing his jowls with one hand. "One day while Aggie was shopping, I took all the pictures and put them in a trunk in the attic. Then I packed Tony's stuff—his record albums, books, clothes, everything—and gave them to relatives with kids. When Aggie got home, I thought she was going to have a nervous breakdown. I won't kid you, it was bad. Real bad. And she didn't speak to me for days. Then it started to get a little better and a little better and finally we were all right."

"Like before."

"No. I can't say that. We were never like before. But we still loved each other, and did until the day she died."

They sipped their coffee in silence.

"You know," said Sam, at last, "sometimes I can still see all of Tony's stuff. It's like there's this shrine in my head. I try not to go there or I get lost. That's silly, isn't it?"

"Yeah," whispered Richard.

"No breakfast?" said Sam, glancing at the empty table.

"Not hungry," said Richard, rising.

Sam placed a fat hand over Richard's. "You two are too good for each other. Don't let this kill you and Audrey."

"I'm trying not to."

"Whatever help she needs, you get it for her, hear?"

"I will."

"You need anything, any money, whatever, you just call. Understand?"

"Thanks, Sam. We're all right."

Sam nodded, waddling along to the door. "Audrey's too sensitive. She feels things you and I don't. It's a mother thing. That can be a wonderful gift sometimes. At other times it can be the worst kind of hell. It'll drive a woman crazy. I know I watched it eating at Aggie."

"You got that right," said Richard, stepping out into sunlight that held no warmth.

21

THE BELL-LIKE BAYING of the hound shattered Virgil's thoughts. He glanced over the bridge railing, down toward the creek. The big black-and-tan bounced on the end of his thick leather leash like a puppy, but Bill Keens, the dog's trainer, glanced up at Virgil and shook his head.

"He's just excited," said Bill. "He gets frustrated when he can't find anything."

"Nothing?"

"If that boy was here, Sentry would have picked up something, even after all this time," said Bill. "This dog's got a nose like Jimmy Durante. I think the bastard just dumped the bike here."

"Give it a little more work," said Virgil.

"Okay," said Bill, turning reluctantly back toward the woods. "But I'm telling you it's a waste of time."

Virgil watched Bill and the dog disappear into the trees. He hadn't informed Tom Merrill about the bike yet, and he wasn't about to call for a full search if even Sentry couldn't find anything.

The bike was Timmy Merrill's all right. The boy had his name on a personalized plate underneath the seat. But the bike did nothing except lend credence to the voice out of Babs St. Clair's mouth, and Virgil meant to talk to her about that this very day. He didn't know if Babs was playing some kind of game or whether they'd all been the brunt of some weird coincidence. But someone was going to explain to him how he ended up finding the boy's bike right where Babs had said it would be.

Virgil had been up off and on all night, getting Doris water, cleaning her bedpan, feeding her pills. She was resting easier before he left, but he felt even more done in than usual and the day had just started. The only thing that kept him going was his desire to bring the kidnapper of Timmy Merrill and Zach Bock to justice before he died.

It was the same bastard both times. He felt it in his gut. Two different assholes hadn't come into his county and committed the same crime four years apart. If Babs knew something, by God, she was going to tell him.

He took the long way back to town, looping around by the Bock house to see if anything stirred in his head. Sometimes that happened, like he could hear a *click* and then things would fall together in his brain. Maybe passing by the scene of *that* crime would stir a recollection or tie two odd strands of information together in a new way.

He rounded a sharp curve and started to ease past a parked Buick sedan when he spotted Dan McNeil off on the shoulder, driving one of his real estate signs into the rocky ground with a small sledgehammer. Dan waved and Virgil pulled over in front of his car.

He sauntered across the shallow drainage ditch, smiling. Dan was one of Virgil's staunchest supporters on the Board of Selectmen, and Virgil figured he was about the most trustworthy real estate agent in the area. Virgil and Doris had bought their house from Dan when he'd first gotten his license.

"Catching any bad guys?" asked Dan, giving the sign a final whack and dropping the hammer onto the ground. He wiped sweat off his bald head with a light blue handkerchief that matched his shirt.

"Not lately."

"How's Doris?"

"About the same. You know."

"Yeah. You doing all right?"

Virgil glanced around at the thick forested area. "Yeah, fine. Living day to day. Whatcha selling, trees?"

"Five acres of prime property. Heavily timbered. Private. Water frontage."

"Water frontage?"

"There's a small stream back through the woods," said Dan, winking. "You look worn out, Virg."

"Bad night."

"Tell Doris our prayers are with her."

"Thanks. I'm sure that'll mean a lot to her."

"What are you doing out this way?"

"Just cruising. Say, you haven't seen Cooder around, have you?"

Dan frowned. "No. I haven't been looking for him. Are you?"

"Not really. I was just wondering."

"Why?"

"He said something strange the other day. You know Cooder. It probably didn't mean anything, but I still want to talk to him."

"Talking to Cooder is a waste of time."

"I know. But if you see him, give me a call. Okay?"

"Sure, Virg. Want me to detain him?" Dan gave Virgil a sly look and Virgil smirked in reply.

"A call will suffice."

"This doesn't have anything to do with the Bock boy, does it?"

Virgil stiffened. "Why would you say that?"

Dan shrugged. He gave the sign a shake to test it, then looked back at Virgil. "You're in the neighborhood, that's all. And I know that one bugs you."

"What do you mean?"

"Virg, everybody that knows you knows. Those two boys have been eating at you since they disappeared. You're the only one who never noticed how obsessed you are."

Virgil's voice rose a notch. "Obsessed?"

Dan put both hands out in front of him, shaking his head. "Don't get me wrong, Virg. Folks like having a sheriff they think really cares about them. But some of us worry that maybe you're getting hurt by it. You hear me?"

"Not that I don't appreciate your concern, but I'm just doing my job."

"Sure, Virg. I didn't mean anything by it. Hell, those two

disappearances tore up everybody in the community. My wife cried every night for a month after Rosie killed herself."

Virgil nodded.

"I get the creeps myself everytime I come around this area, to tell the truth," said Dan. "Can't see why anyone would want to live here." He glanced at the sign and changed his tune. "Not that it's a bad area. Just thinking out loud."

"Most folks up this way have lived here all their lives. Some for generations."

"Everybody but the Bocks and Merle Coonts."

"The Bocks' neighbor?"

"Yeah. The old farm just this side of Richard and Audrey's place. You know the one. Merle's semi is out front all the time. Merle bought the house two years ago."

"I didn't know Merle bought the place. I thought he must be in the family and had taken it over."

"Merle had me find the owners. I worked as a buyer's agent," said Dan.

"A buyer's agent?"

"Yeah. Sometimes people are looking for a particular property that might not be on the market, so they have an agent find one for them and they make an offer. That old farm had been sitting there for years. The owners got it in an estate and they lived in Florida. They didn't want to fix it up and they were tired of paying taxes, but they still stuck us."

"Why didn't you find another one? The county's loaded with run-down old houses."

"Merle didn't want another one. He wanted that one."

"Why?"

"Beats me. I told him the same thing. Hell, I could have had him a new home built on prime property for what he paid for that place."

"That doesn't make sense."

"Go figure. I don't argue with the customer. I closed the deal and it was fast and clean. Slam-bam and there's my commission."

"Where did Coonts come from?"

Dan frowned. "Out West, I think."

"And he moved all the way to the backwoods of Maine and couldn't live without that old farm?"

"Evidently."

"Who financed the house?" asked Virgil.

"He paid cash."

"How does a trucker end up with that kind of money?"

"I didn't ask, Virg. That's really not my business."

"You had to be curious."

"Curious, sure. Inquisitive, no. I'm a salesman. The wrong question in my business can queer a deal."

As Virgil climbed back into the cruiser, Dan tossed the hammer into the trunk of his Buick and walked up alongside Virgil's window.

"Merle Coonts is a nice enough old boy, Virg. Don't read too much into him buying that house. I mean, where was he the day Zach Bock disappeared? You questioned him, didn't you?"

"Yeah. I did."

"And?"

"He was out of state the day it happened. On a run to the West Coast."

"So he's clean."

"Yeah," said Virgil. Coonts had produced his logs and they had backed up his story. Virgil had gone so far as to call one of the delivery points. Merle had been there, just when he said he had.

Virgil drove away deep in thought. When he rounded the next curve he found himself staring at the Coonts place. Why would a man spend as much money as Merle had on the house and then leave it in such a state of disrepair? The corners were all out of plumb, boards were popping off the walls. The place looked like it would collapse in the next high wind.

He watched the farm disappearing in the rearview mirror, waiting for the *click,* but nothing happened. So he stopped at the end of the Bocks' driveway and stared at their nondescript little ranch house. Audrey had surrounded the place with sculptured hedges and shrubs. To Virgil, the place had a Hollywood feel, the way the shrubs blended into the gardens and the rock borders flowed around the trees, but he didn't know that much about landscaping. Richard was going to need to get out the lawn mower pretty soon, though, or he'd have a real job after the first good rainstorm.

Virgil pulled up near the side stoop, half-hoping that no one was home. But when Audrey's face appeared in the window, he smiled. She opened the door too quickly and Virgil shook his head and held up one hand. He should have known what she'd think. Her sudden frown darkened a face that was meant to shine. That saddened Virgil. What the devil was he doing here anyway?

"Hello, Sheriff," she said, stepping back into the kitchen as he climbed the stoop. "Can I get you some coffee?"

"Thanks."

"Sit," she said, bringing a carafe and cups to the table. "Richard's gone to work."

Virgil accepted a demitasse cup from Audrey, holding it self-consciously in his big hands. He and Audrey eyed each other, neither knowing what to say. Virgil figured the truth might be a start.

"I don't have any real news, Mrs. Bock," he said. "I'm not even sure why I'm here."

"Audrey," she said, nodding. "That's all right. I'm glad to see you."

She acted artificially calm to Virgil's mind. Her smile seemed glued on.

"How have you been?" he asked.

"Getting by. It's been a little more than a year."

"Yeah. I know."

"I was in the hospital."

"I heard."

"They gave me some medicine."

He followed her eyes to the bottle beside the salt and pepper shakers. "Does it help?"

"It makes me feel better. I don't have so many . . . night-mares."

"I guess it's good for you, then."

"I thought I saw Zach, you know," she said, staring straight through him.

She seemed hollow somehow, and Virgil thought of Doris, fading away before his eyes. But he and Doris had grown kids. Grandkids. He and Doris had had a life. Richard and

Audrey Bock's lives had been ravaged before they'd had a chance to start.

"In that window," she said, pointing across the sink.

Virgil stared at the sunlight glinting on the glass and, for just an instant, he, too, thought he saw something reflected there. "But you don't see it now? With your medicine?"

She shook her head. "I thought I saw him in the fountain out back too. But that was before I started taking the pills."

"How's Richard?"

"He's all right. He's at work now."

It didn't sound like she remembered telling him that already.

"I wish I had more to tell you, Audrey. I wish with all my heart I could have done more."

"You did everything you could, I guess. It wasn't you. It was me."

He frowned. "You didn't do anything wrong, Audrey. Don't ever think that. It was something that was going to happen and it did. There was nothing that you could have done. You couldn't be there with Zach all the time."

"It was me," she whispered. "I did it. We didn't close the door."

"What door, Audrey?"

"We didn't close it all the way and it got open again and now Zach's gone. It's my fault. I should have kept it closed."

Her voice was artificially calm, like her eyes. But the words were those of a mother crying alone in the dark, calling for her son, blaming herself because there was no one else to blame.

"What door?"

"The door to the basement. Where the little girl was."

"What little girl?"

"The other little girl."

"What *other* little girl?"

Audrey buried her face in her hands and shook her head. "I don't know!"

She seemed to have crossed over into someplace where Virgil couldn't reach her. But something about the conversation reminded him of the weird dialogue he'd had with Babs, the way he seemed to be talking to more than one person. He sensed that there might be *real* answers here if only he knew the right buttons to push.

"Who's the girl, Audrey?"

She squinted, as though trying to see down a long dark tunnel. "I don't know who she is."

She chewed her lip so hard Virgil was afraid she'd bite through it. He glanced at the bottle of pills, wondering if she needed another one or if she had taken one too many.

"She's locked up in the basement," she whispered. "She can't get out."

"Who, Audrey?" It all sounded so crazy. Virgil wondered if he should carry on with the conversation. Was it possible he was hurting her, driving her into madness? Playing with a person's mind was something a shrink could take responsibility for. Virgil didn't want to. But Audrey wouldn't stop now.

"She won't let the little girl go."

"Who has the little girl?"

"My mother."

That didn't sound like a hallucination. It sounded like a certainty. But the look in her eyes told him she had just discovered it. She stared at him as though waiting for confirmation.

"Your mother locked a child in her basement?"

When she spoke, he knew his reading of her was right. She *had* just realized what had happened. Or just remembered it. If it *had* really happened. "Yes," she said.

He stared at her face and tried to remember what Audrey had looked like during the search for Zach. Naturally she'd been distraught, wild-eyed, but now he had a sense that she was looking through some wall that he couldn't even make out. She looked as though she was exhausted, just the way she'd been exhausted on that day a year ago.

Was it true? Was her mother some kind of child abuser? Or was Audrey herself insane? And if she was, was it remotely possible that *she'd* had something to do with Zach's disappearance? He didn't want to believe that, but he knew mothers did sometimes get rid of their own children for whatever reasons.

"Why would your mother do that?" he asked, leaning closer.

"I don't know. I followed her into the basement. It was dark and cold. I could hear the little girl crying. The dog was barking outside and I followed the voices."

"Followed them where?"

"Into the room. Into the little room in the cellar."

Virgil glanced at the window and noticed that the glint of sunlight was gone from the glass. Shadows deepened in the woods outside and the kitchen was gloomy and chill.

"What happened there, Audrey? What happened in that little room?"

Her eyes flashed and her face tightened. "I don't know!" She clinched her fists and pounded her thighs until he gripped them and forced her to look him in the eye. Finally she focused on him and slowly her face softened. "I don't know," she repeated as he released her hands, both of them embarrassed by the intimacy.

She seemed to be back with him, but he had no idea of where she had gone. Could her mother have possibly done the things Audrey said? Or was it the drug talking? Could Audrey have been deranged all along?

"What did your mother do to you, Audrey?"

"Nothing," she said. She stared at him as though that remark, too, had been as much a revelation to her as it had to him. "She didn't do anything to *me.*"

"But she locked a little girl in her basement?"

Audrey frowned. "I think so."

"Did she know that you knew?"

"She found out that night. She saw me."

"What did she do?"

"I don't remember."

"Audrey . . . Do you think this has anything at all to do with Zach's disappearance?"

"Yes," she said slowly.

"How could it?" He was delving into completely unknown territory.

"She has him," she whispered. "I think she's going to make him disappear."

"Has who?"

"Zach. She's going to make him disappear. Then she'll say he's gone." The last words seemed forced from her lungs.

"Disappear?"

She shook her head, growing more agitated. "After she put the little girl in the basement, the little girl went away."

"Went away where?"

"I can't remember!" she screamed. "It's all gone!" She pounded her temples and Virgil reached out and took both of her tiny hands into his giant mitts again.

"Calm down, Audrey. Just tell me what you remember."

It took a moment for her to focus again. "Tara came and I went away."

"Went away where?"

"Home. With Tara."

"Your aunt Tara? The one who came to stay with you when Zach was taken?" Virgil remembered her. She'd been the kind of person that takes over quietly in a crisis and makes sure the bills get paid and the lights are on when it gets dark and everyone gets fed. She was a striking woman, a gray-haired, older copy of Audrey. But the deputies had told him that there was a ruckus later and the aunt left. Virgil figured the pressure had built up pretty high in the little house. No wonder.

"Yes. My aunt."

"She took you from your mother?"

"I told Doctor Cates."

"Your psychiatrist?"

She nodded.

"Tell me," said Virgil softly.

"I followed them down into the basement and I saw the little girl. It's all mixed up."

"How old was the little girl?"

Another confused look, peering into the past.

"My age."

"What did she look like?"

"I don't remember. I can't quite see her."

"Why would anyone do something like that?"

"The little girl fought her. She screamed and kicked and my mother kept telling her to be still. Telling her everything was going to be all right. The little girl's knees were bloody from the concrete. My mother was fighting with the girl. My mother looked up and saw me. She screamed at me."

"What did she say?"

"She screamed at me to go away."

"She didn't try to catch you?"

Audrey shook her head. "No. I don't think so."

"She just told you to go away?"

She nodded.

"What did you do?"

"I ran..."

"And *Tara* came for you?"

Audrey frowned. Virgil waited patiently.

"No," she said at last. "She didn't come for me that night.... Maybe it was later. I can't remember."

Audrey seemed hypnotized—and distant at the same time. "What's your aunt Tara's full name, Audrey?"

"Tara Beals."

"Spell it."

Audrey did.

Virgil took a small pad out of his shirt pocket and wrote down the name. "Where does she live?"

"North of Augusta."

He looked at her and she gave him the address, watching him write.

"What about your mother? Where's she now?"

"She's gone."

"She never tried to get in touch after Tara took you?"

"I thought I saw him in the glass," she said, glancing back mournfully over her shoulder toward the window.

"What about the memories, Audrey?" he said, ignoring her response to the previous question.

She stared at the bottle. "I haven't seen him so much since the pills."

"Well, that's a good thing, then."

"Is it?"

"Do the memories have anything to do with Zach disappearing?" he repeated, trying to get her to focus on his eyes again.

"I had a bad spell the other day by the old farm down the road."

"The Coonts place?" said Virgil. A nerve somewhere along the base of his spine twitched.

"The farm with the truck."

"What happened?"

"I thought Zach was locked up in their basement...." She looked into his eyes as though waiting for him to deny the possibility.

"I questioned Mister Coonts when he got back from his trip, Audrey. I told you what I found out."

She nodded. "The pills make it better. But now and then I get a glimpse of Zach. And he's still in a basement. I can feel it all around me. Dark and shadowy, with no windows."

"Did you see anything when you passed the house? I mean, really?"

He had the strong sense that Audrey believed every word she was telling him, even when all she could remember were shattered remnants of her past. He also believed that on some level, no matter what she said, she was still convinced Zach was held in the basement of the Coonts farm and that there was nothing she could do about it. But it would be just as easy to believe that Audrey was a victim of some horror in her childhood that had twisted her mind, turned her into a child-killer, and now that same warped psyche was covering up the crime by foisting suspicion off on an innocent neighbor.

You don't believe that. Look at her. She couldn't hurt a flea, certainly not her own son.

But stranger things had happened. What would that do to his one monster theory? Audrey surely hadn't kidnapped Timmy Merrill. But she *had* invited Virgil into the house. And she kept talking about a cellar....

"Audrey," he said, as calmly as possible. "Why don't you and I take a look around *your* basement?"

She squinted at him. "Why?"

If he found anything at all, a shyster defense attorney would probably say that she had given her permission for him to search under the influence of drugs, but that was a battle for a prosecutor to fight. Suddenly, more than anything, Virgil wanted to take a tour of the Bock cellar. He didn't really expect to find anything there. He *prayed* he wouldn't find anything there. But now it was one more item he needed to check off his list. "I'd just like to take a look, if it's all right with you."

Audrey shrugged. Virgil followed her to the cellar door

beside the pantry. When she flipped on the light and glanced back over her shoulder at Virgil, she seemed nervous.

"I don't want to go down there," she said, stepping aside.

Virgil peered down the bare wooden stairs toward the furnace, then back at Audrey. "What's the matter?"

"I never go down there."

"Never?"

"No. I don't like basements."

Well, neither did he. Virgil pulled the door wide open and stared down into the well-lighted cellar. "Looks pretty airy to me," he said in an encouraging tone.

Audrey shook her head and backed away, making Virgil just that much more determined to see the basement. But if there *was* something down there, he certainly didn't want to leave Audrey upstairs where he couldn't see her. If she was unstable, no telling what she'd do.

"Audrey," he said, "we *need* to do this. I'll be with you every step of the way. I promise." He tried to make it sound as official as possible, but he held out his hand reassuringly.

"Please don't make me go down there," she whispered.

Virgil stepped directly in front of her. "I'll be with you, Audrey." He took her hand and she followed him, but he noticed that her breathing was gaspy and her eyes darted around the kitchen.

Virgil stopped as a thought struck him. "Would you like to take one of your pills?"

Audrey shook her head. "I just took one."

Great.

"Come on, then," he said, backing down the stairs and tugging her gently along until they stood in the middle of the basement together.

The ceiling consisted of raw joists. White electrical wire fed porcelain light sockets loaded with bare bulbs. The walls were exposed concrete, as was the floor. A big green oil furnace took up the center of the room, sitting silent now like a sleeping guardian. The back wall was lined from floor to ceiling with cardboard file boxes. A row of them had been stacked to create a wing wall, blocking Virgil's view of the far corner.

He glanced around the open area, but nothing sinister caught his eye. If anything, the basement was too clean, too neat, but a CPA might have the neatness gene built right in. Still, people collected junk over time. Everyone did. Where was all the Bocks' junk?

"Mighty neat," he said.

"Richard doesn't like a mess," said Audrey. "He empties everything out of the basement once a year." Her voice was quaky. Virgil felt her hand shaking.

"What's the matter, Audrey? What is it?"

"Please," she said, trying to turn back to the stairs, but she was gazing at the wall of boxes and Virgil felt a shiver of doubt.

"Come on, now," he said, tugging her across the basement. "Just one quick look-see and we'll get out of here."

She didn't struggle. It was more like dragging a sack of sand. He rounded the barrier of files with Audrey in tow before he realized what he'd found. As he stared at the neat arrangement of clothing and toys, guilt tightened his throat.

There was no hidden cell here. No child had been kept down in this basement against their will, and there was no new rectangle of concrete in the floor where someone had disposed of a body. Instead, there was a bicycle that showed signs of frequent polishing. There were shelves of clean blue jeans and T-shirts and neat rolls of socks built into a pyramid. There was a large stack of board games topped with a Chinese checkers set. A telescope stood on a tripod, peeking out the cellar window high overhead. A dresser drawer backed against the files and the top was covered with rows of baseball cards and miscellaneous trinkets. A bookshelf was filled with books and comics. Virgil ran a finger along the top of the dresser. Not a dust mote.

"I'm sorry," he said, turning to Audrey.

Audrey turned away, staring down the length of the basement. "This is Richard's place. He comes down here when he thinks I don't notice. He stays down here for hours sometimes." She glanced back at the bicycle and then quickly away again.

"Come on," said Virgil, taking her arm. She jerked it away but followed him.

"Why are we here?" she asked.

"It was a mistake, Audrey. I'm sorry."

"You think I'm crazy."

"No, I don't. I think you've had a hell of a hard time. But I don't think you're crazy."

"Yes, you do. You're not going to help Zach, because you don't believe me. No one believes me. That's why I'm on the pills. Not to get rid of the nightmares. The pills help everyone live with me."

"Come on now, Audrey." He tried to shepherd her toward the stairs. First he hadn't been able to get her into the cellar, now he couldn't get her out.

She stepped around him into the center of the shrine, fingering the telescope, then the checker set. She opened the top drawer and lifted a white T-shirt to her face, sniffing the soft cotton, stroking it as though it were filled with a living, breathing, child.

"I can smell him," she whispered. "Doctor Cates told me mothers could. Did you know that?"

"Maybe I should go," said Virgil, but she ignored him.

"I didn't see it so much in Richard."

"It?"

"The pain," she said. "Pain hides sometimes. . . . I knew he was hurt. But he didn't show it like me. When he came down here I just thought he wanted to be away from me. Alone."

"Where did you think all this stuff was?"

She shrugged. "I thought it was gone."

"Gone?"

She nodded. "This is all *old* stuff. Zach's new bike is in my shed. His clothes are in his room." She lifted a T-shirt and Virgil realized it would have been too small for the boy. "He must have been saving all this *before* Zach was taken."

"Why don't we go on upstairs, Audrey."

"You wanted to come down here."

"That was a mistake," admitted Virgil.

"No. It was good I saw it," she said, patting the shirt back into place and gently closing the drawer. "Good I did." She closed the drawer slowly and perused the toys again. "He used to play with this telescope all the time when he was smaller. Knew all the planets. Then he got bored with it. He got into mathematics. Zach had a way with patterns. He could memorize them, figure things out."

"He was a smart kid," said Virgil.

"Richard bought him this because *he* loved astronomy when he was a kid," she said, stroking the telescope, leaving oily finger patterns on the shiny black surface. "Oh, Richard," she whispered, biting her lip.

"I'm sorry" was all Virgil could think of to say. He stopped and turned at the foot of the stairs. "If you get any information I can use just call." But Audrey never answered.

22

VIRGIL WAS HALFWAY BACK to town, still mulling over his meeting with Audrey, when Birch's voice on the radio shattered his thoughts.

"We got a situation here, Sheriff."

Virgil recognized Birch's voice on the radio immediately. He snatched the mike. "What's wrong?"

"Evan Johnson's holding a shotgun on Babs St. Clair and he looks like he's gonna use it."

"What's your twenty?"

"Right in front of Babs's place. She's sitting on her steps."

Virgil goosed the cruiser. It was only five minutes to downtown, but five minutes could be a long time. "Sitting?"

"Yeah. She's cool as a cucumber. But I don't like the look in Evan's eyes."

"Who's talking to him?"

"Steve." Steve Meyers was senior deputy. He'd been with Virgil for over twenty years. Steve had as much training as anyone on the force with hostage situations and negotiating with gunmen, which was about none.

"What's he doing?"

"Telling Evan that no one's gotten hurt and if everyone stays calm maybe no one has to go to jail."

"That's good. Reassure Evan that we aren't going to try to rush him or anything like that."

"Steve's doing that."

"You really think Evan's serious?"

"He's madder than I've ever seen him."

That was bad. Evan got into more fights than any other forty-year-old Virgil knew. Virgil had always wondered if Evan's keg might blow over one day and get him into something *real*. Virgil sure didn't want to see it turn into real homicide right on Main Street.

"I'll be there in two minutes. Tell Steve to keep doing what he's doing and everyone stay calm."

"Right."

Virgil slipped the mike back into place and blasted through the intersection onto Route 26 without slowing for the yield sign, lights flashing but no sirens. It was a straight shot from there into town and he made the last mile weaving in and out of traffic, slowing only as he neared the hill that led up Main Street.

It was a busy Wednesday morning. Every parking space was filled on both sides of the street and people milled along the shop fronts. Just ahead, the stores gave way to the small residential area between downtown and the hospital. Some people had noticed Birch's and Steve's flashing lights and were gawking or moving in that direction. Others could have cared less and were going about their shopping. That was an affected Maine attitude. Acting like it was none of their business. But Virgil knew they'd be the first ones to dig around for the real gossip.

He eased in between one of the cruisers and a pickup truck and parked on Babs's lawn. Babs gave him a look that said she didn't think that was necessary, but then she went back to staring at Evan. Virgil figured he would have paid closer attention if Evan had a shotgun pointed at him.

From behind, Evan looked like a bear in blue jeans. But Evan wasn't fat. He was broad muscled. The only loose flesh on the man was his beer gut. As Virgil eased around to stand a few feet to one side of Steve, he could see that the shotgun was actually *resting* across Evan's stomach, aimed directly at Babs as she sat casually on her front stoop.

"Don't try anything, Sheriff," said Evan. He sounded like someone who had decided on a course of action and was damned well going to follow through on it. "All it takes is two pounds of pressure on this trigger and this old bitch turns into ketchup."

Virgil glanced at Babs. She was more calm and collected than anyone else on the scene. The whole damned commotion was too weird. It seemed more like a comedy skit than a real *situation*. But the shotgun wasn't joking.

"Evan, how about we talk this over," said Virgil.

"Time for talking's done." Evan's finger twitched and he tensed, but there was no chance either Virgil or Steve could reach the gun before it blasted Babs into eternity.

"Why, Evan?" said Virgil, giving Steve a head shake to still him, edging a step closer himself. He glanced toward the road and saw Birch in a firing stance, his pistol leveled at Evan's back. If Evan fired, he'd be dead before he could pull the trigger again. Not that it mattered. One blast from the shotgun would finish Babs. "Why do you want to do something like this? Think of what it'll do to your family, to Janie."

Evan's mouth twisted and his hands shook. The muscles in his face looked as tight as barrel bands. "It's too late now."

"No, it isn't. It's never too late as long as you just put that gun down."

A siren sounded somewhere in the distance and Evan jerked his head toward Virgil. "Who's that?" said Evan, nodding over his shoulder toward the approaching car.

Virgil gave Birch a nasty look and Birch stepped out into the road, waving. In a second the siren went dead and Birch hurried quietly back to his position.

"Just another of the boys, Evan. Don't panic."

"I'm not panicking."

"No, you don't look like you are and that's good. We can work this out in a sensible way and go home."

"Don't think that's gonna happen."

"Why not?"

" 'Cause I'm gonna kill this bitch."

"Now, you don't want to do that. Your mother will be heartbroken, Evan. She's got a bad heart."

Evan nodded, sniffling. "I don't want to hurt Mama. That's for sure. But I've had it up to here with her!" He cocked his chin toward Babs and then spat tobacco into the grass.

"You just don't want to listen," said Babs.

"I've listened to enough of your shit!" shouted Evan. The shotgun shook in his hands, sending ripples across his belly. He glared at Virgil and yet Virgil didn't sense any danger to himself. "Kill me, Sheriff," he said. "Just kill me."

"No one's going to kill anyone. We're going to talk through this and work something out. Then everyone can go home in one piece."

"It's too late for that," said Evan, his finger tickling the trigger. "I can't go home now that Janie's gone."

So that was what precipitated this. Evan was a beater. But like most abusers, he *thought* he loved the girl. If Janie'd left him and he thought Babs was to blame, then there was gonna be hell to pay. Virgil was sure at that moment that Evan was about to do it.

"Evan!" he shouted. "Wait a minute! Take a breather. You don't have to do it *this minute.*"

Evan seemed to consider that. His chest swelled and his nostrils flared. He twisted his head from side to side, stretching. But his finger was still tight on the trigger. Virgil timed his move as Evan twisted his head again, and took another step closer.

"What is it Babs wants you to listen to?" said Virgil, grasping at straws.

"She talks bullshit. And she talks it over and over to my old lady until *she* believes it too. Tells her to leave me or something's going to happen to her. Now I ask you, should I put up with that kind of shit?"

"Well, no, Evan. I don't guess you need to have someone butting in," said Virgil. "Of course not. And you have a right to your privacy just like anyone else. You should come to me and let me handle it though. That's what I'm here for, you know."

"Like you'd do something."

"Well, I would. Now put down the gun and let's talk this out like peaceable people. No sense anyone getting hurt."

"*She* needs to die!"

Virgil nodded. "I don't want anyone to go to jail. I just want to straighten this out. Now put down the gun before something happens and everyone's sorry." Virgil thought that he'd seen the light of reason glinting in the corner of

Evan's eye. Evan was an asshole, but he doted on his aging mother and Virgil knew he didn't like being locked up.

"Janie's going to die if she stays with you," said Babs.

"You bitch!" The gun shook again.

Virgil took three sliding steps forward as Evan raised the gun from his belly with shaking hands. "Don't do it, Evan!"

"Gonna kill her! Gonna kill that old bitch now!"

Babs seemed to get the picture at last. Her eyes widened and she crabbed backward up onto the porch, but the hem of her dress caught on the splintery treads and she ended up lying back on her elbows with her knees up.

"Gonna blow you away, bitch!" screamed Evan, stepping closer, waving the shotgun at her.

"Evan!" shouted Virgil, trying desperately to get the man's attention. He knew it was now or never. With his heart pounding in his chest, he lurched forward. He shoved the shotgun upward just as Evan pulled the trigger. The roar seemed only inches from Virgil's ear. He continued forward, throwing all his weight against the bigger man, hoping that Steve was right behind him, because he knew he didn't stand a chance in a one-on-one fight with Evan.

But to his surprise, Evan was all done. He collapsed under Virgil and lay there, the shotgun fallen to his side. It was a second before Virgil realized that the bigger man was sobbing. Virgil shoved the shotgun aside and Steve took it away.

"Come on, Evan," said Virgil, rising to his feet and offering Evan a hand up.

Evan wiped his nose with the back of his sleeve and took Virgil's hand. Birch handcuffed Evan and led him to Steve's cruiser.

"Maybe you should use leg irons," said Babs, also standing.

Virgil sighed. "They'll do whatever needs to be done to keep him under control."

"You should have been keeping him under control all along."

"Janie wouldn't press charges," said Virgil. "Ever."

Babs nodded. "And so he just keeps beating her. Until one day he kills her. But it's going to be sooner than you think."

"Babs, you don't know that."

"I do know it. It's in the cards. I think he's going to kill her today."

Virgil shook his head, watching Birch protect Evan's head with his hand as Evan was pushed into the backseat of the cruiser. "He isn't going to kill anyone today and probably not for a while."

"The cards say different."

"The cards are wrong. Are you all right?"

"I'm fine."

Virgil turned toward his car. "We'll need a statement."

"How's Doris today?" asked Babs.

Virgil stopped and glanced back over his shoulder. "As well as can be expected."

"I pray for her every day."

"We appreciate that."

He couldn't believe how calm she was. She didn't even seem fazed by the crowd that was milling on her lawn.

"He really won't get out today?" said Babs. "There's no way he could get bond?"

Virgil shook his head. "By the time we get him booked, it'll probably be too late to catch a judge and it'll more than likely be a higher bond than Evan's mother can afford after this. It'll take them a while to come up with the money."

"We'd better go check on Janie right now, then," said Babs.

"I'll have one of my deputies run by their house."

"No. We have to do it."

Virgil sighed, frowning at her. "All right, Babs, if it means that much to you."

"We have to make sure she's okay." The way she said it made Virgil sure Babs didn't believe she was.

"Come on," he said wearily, waving her toward his cruiser.

23

VIRGIL PULLED ONTO MASON STREET, watching the manicured lawns of downtown turn to taller grass. The houses
here weren't any older, but they didn't receive the care their
brethren downtown did, and Arny's Quick Mart seemed to
be the boundary line where all sense of proprietorship went
out the window. The street ended in a gravel cul-de-sac
lined with twenty-year-old trailers. Virgil tried to remember
which one belonged to Evan and Janie.

He glanced across the seat. Babs's fixed gaze through the
windshield ahead reminded him of a drugged-out kid.

"You're going to have to press charges, you know," said
Virgil.

She shook her head. "I can't do that."

"Why not?"

"I don't want to take on the karmic debt."

Virgil blinked.

"It's that one," said Babs, pointing to a particularly seedy
double-wide with broken windows and two cans of over-
flowing garbage. The rusted hulk of a 1960s station wagon
glared at them from the back of the driveway. Virgil pulled
in beside the ramshackle stoop and climbed out of the
cruiser.

"Stay in the car," he said, but it was too late. She was
faster than she looked. Before Virgil could round the front
of the car, Babs was already heading for the front steps. He

caught up with her at the door. "I'll knock, if you don't mind," he said. Babs nodded, waiting.

The door sounded tinny and frail beneath his knuckles. Trailers were such pieces of trash. He thanked his lucky stars he and Doris had never had to live in one. Not that he was looking down on people who did. Not all of them.

"She isn't answering," said Babs, biting her lip.

Virgil tried the door but it was locked. He glanced toward the rear of the trailer. "I can see that."

"What are we going to do?"

Virgil frowned. "*We* aren't going to do anything. You're going to wait here while I check the windows. She may have gone for a walk."

"I have a bad feeling about this. It was all in the cards."

"Keep your feelings to yourself."

The windows were the old crank-out variety and they were all open, but not wide enough for Virgil to get his head under. So he was forced to shield his eyes from the sun and try to peer into the darkness through the dirty, angled glass and rusted screens. "Janie? Are you in there?"

He glanced back to make sure Babs was going to listen to him for a change, but the worry in her face irritated him all the more. There was no reason yet to think anything was wrong. No reason except that Evan was running around town with a shotgun threatening to shoot people, Janie didn't seem to be answering his knock, and Babs was worried about her karmic whatever-the-hell it was.

The last window was a few inches higher off the ground than the others and he had to stand on tiptoe to peek inside. As his eyes adjusted, he realized that this was the master bedroom. He could make out a double bed with ruffled covers, a dresser cluttered with papers and beer bottles, an open closet door with clothes hanging, and finally segments of his own face in diamond patterns. He stared at his reflection for a moment, trying to make out what it was he was looking at.

It was a mirror, blasted into a million fragments. There were odd patterns *on* the glass, liquid blotches tugged downward by gravity. He had a hard time looking away from the devastated piece of furniture, but as he did, more of the room came into focus. As his field of view widened, he saw more of the wet spots: on the paneling, one wide crimson splotch on the bed cover.

He spun on his heel and raced toward the front door, shoving Babs roughly aside. Adrenaline raced through him and he barely felt his arthritic knees as he kicked twice at the door, bursting it from its hinges.

As he rushed into the house, he noticed a wall phone to his right. "Call 911," he shouted at Babs. "Tell them to get an ambulance over here, now!"

He ran down the hallway to the open bedroom door ahead. He could already see a bare arm, lying on the floor. As he reached the door he placed his hand on the jamb for just an instant, steeling himself, taking a quick, deep breath.

Janie lay facedown on the lime-green carpet that was soaked in blood. She'd been shot from the front, because the remains of her nylon nightgown had been torn outward as was the flesh around the gaping hole between her shoulder blades. Virgil dropped to his knees, reflexively testing for a pulse at her neck, but of course there was no sign of life. Her body already felt a little cool to him.

"Tell the paramedics not to hurry," he said. "Tell 'em to send the medical examiner instead."

He knelt beside Janie, trying to remember the last time he'd spoken to her. He and Doris had known the girl all her life. She'd graduated with their son. But life hadn't been good to Janie. She'd begun to drink after her first marriage went wrong. Then she hooked up with Evan and went from bad to worse. Virgil had always wished there was something more he could do for her than just *threaten* Evan. Virgil gritted his teeth, hating the smell in the room. It was the same odor he'd had to suffer through at a thousand different locations. The salty-sweet smell of death. No, Janie would never press charges, and now it was too late. Seemed like it was just getting too damned late, period.

But he had to take care of the living now. Babs gasped behind him and he climbed shakily to his feet. She was biting her fist when he got to her, staring past him with wide, red-rimmed eyes.

"I told you to stay where you were," he said.

"Is she?"

He nodded.

"I knew it," she sobbed. "I tried to get her to leave him. I saw it coming in the cards. But she wouldn't listen to me. I knew he was going to do something today."

"There was nothing you could have done, Babs," he said, taking her by the shoulders and turning her back down the hall. "Come on. You shouldn't be in here."

He helped her to the cruiser, then called Birch on the radio. Birch didn't sound too surprised. Virgil supposed *he* should have seen it coming too. But over the span of his life, there were a lot of things Virgil should have seen coming.

"I came by today to warn her," said Babs. "Evan was asleep, but he woke up and threatened me."

"With the gun?"

Babs nodded. "I wasn't afraid of him. It's not my time and I told him so. There's nothing he can do to change that. Janie was scared, but I think she was more afraid for me. She came out onto the porch and asked me to leave."

"Why didn't you call us?"

"I did."

"You called the Sheriff's Department and told them that Evan threatened you with a shotgun?"

Babs frowned. "I don't think I mentioned that."

Virgil heard sirens winding up in the distance. There'd already been more of them sounding through town than Arcos had ever heard in one morning. "What *did* you mention?"

"I said that Janie was in terrible danger and someone needed to get over there before something happened to her."

"Who did you talk to?"

"Birch."

Virgil nodded. He'd get the real story out of Birch. Babs was having trouble catching her breath and her jaw was quivering.

"Things like this happen, Babs. They aren't right. But they happen."

"It picked her up like a leaf."

"What?"

"Blown in the wind. It was all in the cards, and there was nothing I could do. What good are they?"

The picture of Janie, tossed by the hurricane blast of the

shotgun flashed across Virgil's mind. He stared at Babs. But everyone knew a shotgun could do that.

The sirens were closer now, any second the sound of screeching tires would accompany them. "We all do what we can, Babs. Bad things happen and then things get better for a spell." But who was he to be preaching that philosophy? He didn't believe it. Things just seemed to be going from bad to worse.

Another cruiser pulled up beside Virgil's and Tod Smith, Virgil's under-sheriff, climbed out, brushing back an errant lock of brown hair before slipping his hat over his head. "What happened, Sheriff?"

Virgil gave him the rundown. "I'll leave you in charge, Tod. The medical examiner should be along any time. You know what to do."

Tod nodded, heading back to his car for his crime-scene kit.

Babs stared at the frowning face of the old station wagon, but she seemed to be reading Virgil's thoughts. "Things are going to get a lot worse, I think. You should let me do a reading for you."

Virgil forced a smile that looked more like a sneer. "Maybe I'll do that sometime."

24

BACK AT THE STATION, Virgil confronted Evan. The big lummox fell apart, weeping like a baby and swearing that he loved Janie more than anything in the world. He'd never *meant* to hurt her or anyone else. He confessed to everything, waiving a lawyer. Birch stood outside the door to the interrogation room, shaking his head.

"Put him back in his cell," growled Virgil. "And watch him."

Birch nodded. "You think he might do something to himself?"

Virgil glanced back over his shoulder, seeing Evan, picturing Janie. "No such luck, but watch him anyway."

"Right," said Birch. "You know Mac Douglass is here?"

"Mac? What's he up to?"

"Brought in Seth LeClerc."

"No kidding." Seth had run out on a warrant for driving without a license and been gone for over a year. He'd been stopped so many times without a license that he was legendary enough for the judge to award him a couple of years in Togus. Now it looked like he might really serve them.

"Tell Mac I'll be right down."

Birch nodded and left.

Mac Douglass was an old friend, a private detective from Lewiston. In a bigger metropolitan area, Mac might have made a better living. He had contacts all across the U.S. from his years on the force. But Mac was happy living in relative obscurity. He made a decent living off his retirement from the Maine State Troopers, part-time work chasing down deadbeat dads, and shadowing people trying to defraud the state on their workmen's comp. Over the years he and Virgil had scratched each other's back any number of times.

Virgil smiled when he spotted Mac.

"Had an interesting day, looks like," said Mac.

"I could do without interesting days."

"Amen. Guy's wife wouldn't ever press charges, right?" Virgil nodded and Mac shook his head.

"Maybe he'll kill himself," said Mac, his smile looking more like a grimace. "How's Doris?"

"Not good."

"Sorry."

Mac's eyes glinted and Virgil followed them to the pair of files still sitting on top of his desk. Mac read the names aloud.

"You still working on those?" he said, frowning.

"Until I die."

Mac shook his head again. "Any new evidence?"

"Not really," said Virgil. They had the bike, but it really told them nothing.

"Then why keep beating your head against a wall?"

Virgil shrugged. "They're my pet cases." He stared at Mac for a moment. "You want to do me a favor?"

"Name it."

"Use your contacts to get me some background information on Audrey Bock."

"The Bock boy's mother?"

"Yeah."

"Why?"

"Just a hunch."

He opened Zach's file and pulled up all the information he had on Audrey—address, phone number, social security—and made a copy for Mac.

Mac read through it all, shaking his head. "I wish you wouldn't do this, Virg."

"What do you mean?"

Mac held out the papers. "Pretend I'm a D.A. Tell me why I'm doing this."

Virgil sat down at the desk, staring out the window. "I want to know where she came from and how she got here. Most of all, I want to know if she's ever been put away for any reason."

"Put away?"

"Treated for mental problems."

"And if she has?"

"I don't know."

"You think maybe she did something to the kids?"

"I don't have any evidence that she did. I don't believe she could have had anything to do with Timmy Merrill's disappearance."

Mac nodded. "But you don't have any evidence that she didn't either. Is that it?"

"Yeah."

"As a D.A., I'd have to tell you you're wasting my time."

"So you won't do it?"

"I just want a little better reason why I should. The cases are old news, Virgil. Everyone around here knows it."

"Zach Bock disappeared just a few days over a year ago," said Virgil, glaring at his desktop. "That's not long for an investigation."

"Not if you have any evidence to go on. Do you?"

"Well, we found the Merrill boy's bike."

"What?" Mac sounded stunned and Virgil was happy that he had at least *something* to tell him, some tidbit of new information as an excuse for his continued scrutiny of the case. Mac wasn't stupid. He knew Virgil was fishing, clutching at straws. Virgil just hoped that he'd do what he could on the basis of their friendship and not question him too much on the whys. He certainly didn't want to explain about Babs St. Clair or Audrey's hallucinations about Merle Coonts's basement.

"I found it washed up in No Name Creek. It was in such good shape you could have aired up the tires and ridden it back to town."

"How did you know to look there?"

Virgil picked up the files and returned them to their favorite resting place in his cabinet. "I got a tip."

"From who?"

"What difference does it make?"

"I'm playing the D.A. again. You want me to work for you. Show me what you got."

Virgil sighed. "A woman named Babs St. Clair told me to look there."

"How did she know it would be there?"

"I don't know."

"You don't know? What the hell does that mean? What does she say?"

"If you must know, the information came out during a séance, all right? Will you check on Audrey Bock's background or not?"

"A séance? What were you doing at a séance?"

Virgil sighed. "Doris wanted it." He leaned back in his chair and rubbed the bridge of his nose, hard.

"That sounds pretty crazy, Virg."

"I know how it sounds. Will you check?"

Mac nodded. "Any ideas where I should start?"

"Start with a woman named Tara Beals."

Mac stared at him as though he had two heads.

"What?" said Virgil. "You know her?"

Mac took a moment answering. "I know *of* her. She's a shrink, right?"

"Yeah. Audrey Bock's her niece. Apparently Tara took Audrey away from her mother, so there was probably abuse at home when she was a child. I want to know if it could have caused Audrey to, you know, do something crazy."

"I don't know," said Mac. "I got to be careful, Virg, or they'll pull my license."

"I know that. Don't get yourself over a barrel. Just see what you can find out. Okay?"

"I'll see what I can do," said Mac, brightening. "You want I should bump off your killer before I leave?"

Virgil smiled. "No, thank-you. The state might not be too pleased with that."

Mac shrugged and left without saying good-bye. He was always doing that. Sometimes he just seemed to go off on a tangent. But he could lock onto a case like a bulldog. Virgil hoped something like that would happen now. He *needed* someone to lock onto something.

He watched through the window as Mac climbed into his blue sedan and drove away. Then he kicked his feet up onto his desk and tried to think of something, anything, that he'd missed over the past five years. He wanted the cases solved so bad he could taste it. So bad he was praying that Mac could speed things along, find another clue, anything to get the damned thing moving again before time ran out. But the more he cogitated about it, the less he thought he was going to live to see an end to it.

He got up from his desk like an old dog after a long nap, stretching every muscle in his body, trying to get the damned thing to work the way it should, the way it had twenty years before. Finally he shouted down the hall to Birch to tell him he had an errand to run.

There was nothing more to be found at No Name Creek, he knew that, but still Virgil was drawn back there. He pulled over on the shoulder, parking under the shade of a tall oak, sliding down the embankment and following the crushed grass trail the deputies had created during the search.

The bike was gone now, safely tucked away in the evidence locker after having been gone over by a forensic specialist from Augusta who told Virgil exactly what he'd expected to hear. Too late to find anything of any value. Still, as he trudged down the middle of the dry creekbed toward the spot where the bike had lain for five long years, he couldn't get the idea out of his head that the *place* was trying to tell him something. It kept calling to him in ways that he wouldn't have responded to a week before. Now he wasn't quite so quick to ignore a hunch, if that's what this was. Only it didn't feel like a hunch. It felt as though he was *supposed* to be here. Like he and the creek and the woods and the sky were all waiting for something to happen.

Timmy Merrill had been here. At least he had been as close as the old bridge. And his bike had washed up on that spot right there. It was as though the boy had left a residue of himself, and Virgil kept rubbing up against it.

You're getting too wrapped up in this again. You've got to ease off. Let it go.

Only he couldn't do that. Partly because the case had been eating at him for so long. Partly because of the nature of the two cases that he knew were connected. And partly because they were his only reason to keep on breathing when he was away from home. If he didn't focus on them, he focused on Doris, and he didn't want to go there right now.

He walked on past the crime tape, following the winding creek through the deep hardwood forest, listening to a rustling off to his right that he knew had to be another damned porcupine from the slow way it ambled through the brush. Porkies weren't afraid of anything. They didn't have much reason to be. Good thing it hadn't been here when the hounds came through. They'd have gotten a mouthful of quills for their trouble.

The sliver of water that meandered beside him was too small to be heard over the slight sound of the animal foraging, but Virgil could smell the clean dampness of it over the dusty dryness of the surrounding earth. It was good to get out of the cruiser for a while, even if it was on a wild-goose chase, and he wandered slowly another couple of hundred yards down the streambed.

He glanced over his shoulder when a twig snapped behind him. Porcupines weren't big enough to make noises like that. More likely a deer. He stopped in his tracks, waiting to see if it would slip out of the brush for a drink.

But what was a deer doing moving around at midday? They were mostly hunkered down about now, waiting till dusk to forage. And now that he thought about it, the porcupine was up early too. He turned back up the creek, cocking his head to see around an overhanging limb just as the sound of gravel sliding over gravel carried to him. Deer didn't make mistakes like that unless they were in one hell of a hurry.

"Anybody there?" he called.

More gravel, but no answer. He slid his hand over the butt of his pistol, unsnapping the strap. He thought he heard footsteps up the creek, but they were furtive sounds and he might have been mistaken.

"Hello!" he shouted.

Still no answer. It had to be his imagination running away with him. But just in case, he unholstered his pistol and took it off safety. Then he started—one silent step at a time—back the way he had come, staring up the creek but shooting glances to his left and right. He hadn't really been paying too much attention to his surroundings before, walking unimpeded down the dry bed. Now the creek seemed like an open sluice with no cover at all. He felt like a lone bowling pin at the end of an alley.

Why would anyone else be out here today? The investigation of the crime scene was officially ended. There was no equipment for anyone to return for. Maybe it was a gawker come to see what all the excitement had been about and they hadn't expected to run into him. But then why did they come out here while his cruiser was sitting big as daylight on the road? The thought that maybe someone had come out here for that very reason made him tighten his fingers around the pistol grip.

Virgil wasn't foolish enough to believe he had no enemies. Over the years he had put a number of people away. Some were still in. Many weren't. But it wasn't something that he lost sleep over, or no more sleep than most cops lost. Very few criminals were stupid enough to try to take revenge on a cop and the ones he could think of were still safely in the pen. As he eased around a sharp outcrop of exposed bedrock, he heard footsteps echoing away up the creek.

"Stop!" he shouted, breaking into a run.

Even though the creek wasn't steep here, it was still an uphill slog, and the loose gravel wasn't the best footing. To top it off, by the time he reached the next bend he realized for the thousandth time how out of shape he was. He hadn't run more than fifty yards and his face was already sheened with sweat and his throat burned. He slowed to a walk, clutching at a stitch in his side with his free hand. He was almost to the crime scene again when a car door slammed and a powerful engine roared off up the road. He tried to figure if he could make it out of the creek before the car disappeared, but he knew it was a hopeless race. Instead, he turned back, glancing around for footprints.

He retraced the entire length of his hike, but the dry gravel gave up nothing. On the way back out he stopped in front of the cruiser, staring off toward Arcos, the direction the car had taken, wondering what the hell had just happened.

He got home before five that day for a change and didn't get out of the house again for four days. But he didn't have much time to think about the missing boys or his mysterious visitor on the creek. Doris's drugs weren't dulling the pain the way they had and she was throwing up more than she was keeping down. Sometime in the middle of the first night, Doc Burton stopped by with a prescription, a shake of her head, a hug for Virgil, and then he was alone with Doris again.

Finally the spell broke like a fever, and she seemed to spring back a little. Enough that she insisted he get out and get some air. As usual, he hated to argue with her, but still he hid for a couple of hours downstairs—waiting to see if she'd call for him—before slipping out.

Birch had Monday off and Stan, the oldest man besides Virgil in the department, was holding down the fort. Stan glanced up at him from beneath wild gray paintbrush brows when Virgil walked in. "How you doin', Virg? Doris okay?"

Virgil nodded. "Yeah, Stan, she's feeling better. How're our prisoners?"

Stan chuckled. "Our license dodger is sleeping." He frowned. "Our local wife murderer requested a Bible. I didn't know he could read."

Virgil smirked. "Neither did I. Did you get him one?"

"Yeah. One of the Gideon Bibles from the back room." They couldn't leave them in the cells the way the Gideons wanted or the prisoners used the tissue-thin pages as rolling paper for cigarettes. As it was, there wasn't one complete Bible in the lot.

"Did Mac call while I've been gone?" asked Virgil.

"Mac Douglass?"

Virgil nodded and Stan glanced at a notepad, shaking his head.

"I'll be in my office," said Virgil.

He dropped into his chair and picked up the phone. The

secretary who answered told him Mac was out for the day, but she'd have him call as soon as she heard from him. Virgil tapped out a rhythm with his fingertips on the glass top of his desk. He picked up the phone and speed-dialed the state troopers in Augusta, asking to be put through to Charlie Southern, who was only as southern as the south side of what he called *Bahston*.

"You want the information when, Virg?" asked Charlie after Virgil gave him the lowdown. "Yesterday, probably?"

"If possible."

"We're kinda busy right now."

"I just need to know where she lived before Ouachita County and what her maiden name was. Any other info you can give me would be nice, though."

"I'm sure. Like what?"

"I'd like to know if she was ever diagnosed with any mental problems, maybe institutionalized. I asked Mac to check for me but I haven't heard back from him."

There was a moment of silence on the line. "Mac Douglass?"

"Yeah. What's the matter?"

"Nothing. It's just that Mac's had it kinda rough lately. I used to see him all the time. Now he don't come around that often."

"What happened?"

"You knew he and I were partners, back in the eighties, right."

"No, I didn't know that."

"Mmm. I never told anyone, but Mac *retired* because he was having problems."

"What kind of problems?"

Silence.

Virgil understood. Cops could have marital problems. They could have money problems. They could even have gambling problems. *Mental* problems they didn't talk about, because they didn't have them.

"What happened?"

"He started *going off* on people. His temper got very out of control. And then there were a couple of times when he just kind of shut down. Like nothing was getting in. I saw him like that once and it was kind of scary. I thought he'd had a stroke. Then he just kind of like clicked and he was the old Mac again. He saw someone about it, but that didn't work. They had to hospitalize him for a while. Not a regular hospital. You know," said Charlie. "He seemed okay and then he got worse again."

"Worse how?"

"Couldn't sleep, having nightmares, I don't know what else. He wouldn't talk to me or anyone else and he wouldn't go back for treatment, so finally he had to leave. There wasn't much choice. But I've always wondered if retiring was good for him."

"Mac once told me that retiring from the force was the best thing that ever happened to him."

"I could be wrong. Hang on, I'm going to put you on hold; one of our computer geeks just walked in. I can probably get a couple of answers for you from him."

Virgil listened to the dull buzz on the line. Apparently the state troopers couldn't afford canned music. When Charlie came back on the line, he had a number and name.

"Audrey Remont. She lived with her aunt, Tara Beals, outside of Augusta."

"What about her parents?"

"Mmm. Says here her aunt got custody in 1971. Mother's name was Martha Remont. Father deceased. Mother lived in Audesto, California. Sixty-one Pine Crest Drive. You want the phone number?"

"No. It must have passed through a dozen hands by now. Thanks. Do you have any record of charges against Audrey Remont or Audrey Bock?"

Charlie took a couple of minutes before coming back on the line. "Nothing here."

"Thanks again."

"If you see Mac, tell him I said hi."

Virgil hung up and got the number of the attorney general for California. After passing through a dozen different offices, he finally spoke to an assistant prosecutor, who told him that the information he was requesting was confidential and not available even to a law officer.

"Even if I could find out about the woman's medical history, I couldn't tell you," said the man.

Virgil had suspected as much, but brother officers were

prone to stretch the rules now and then. Anyway, he had other fish to fry. "Then maybe you can tell me if the lady in question was ever charged with any crimes in your state."

"That I can help you with."

"Great," said Virgil, before discovering that he was being routed to yet another office. The woman there took some time reestablishing his credentials before explaining that he had been connected to the wrong office and transferring him again. Finally a young voice—man or woman, Virgil couldn't tell—took the information about Audrey and returned in a matter of minutes to tell Virgil that there were no records of any charges ever being pressed against Audrey or Martha Remont.

Virgil had a hunch. "How about Tara Beals?"

"Who?"

"I don't have her social security. But could you run a check on just the name?"

"Is she any relation to the psychiatrist?"

Virgil stared at the phone. "She *is* the psychiatrist."

"Cool."

"You know who she is?"

"Yeah, dude. Tara Beals wrote the book on self-hypnosis. Man, it's the best. You really don't know who she is?"

"Not really. Could you check for me?"

"For charges? For Tara Beals? Man, are you serious? Was Martha Remont a patient of hers?"

"Sister. Check for me?"

"Yeah, okay. Give me a sec."

This time he got music. When the boy-slash-girl came back, he sounded surprised. "She was charged with trespassing, but then later the complainant dropped the charges."

"Who was that?"

"Weird."

"Who?"

"Martha Remont. Her sister."

It sounded like Martha was trying to keep Tara away from Audrey. Why? Because she didn't want the abuse exposed? Did she file the charges to protect Audrey's father or some unknown boyfriend who was doing the abusing?

"Tell me more about Tara Beals," said Virgil.

"A friend turned me on to her books two years ago," said the voice. "They changed my life. You should read them."

"But what about Tara herself?"

"I don't know. She's one of those recluses, you know. No picture on the cover, no bio except her credentials."

"And those are?"

"I can't remember them all. Seemed like she must have graduated from every highfalutin school in the East."

Virgil thanked the *person* and hung up. When he discovered that Tara's phone was unlisted, he called Charlie again.

"You're working overtime today," said Charlie.

"The number?"

Charlie gave it to him and he dialed the number, but before the second ring he hung up and pulled out his reverse reference phone book. Tara Beals, Old Route 137, Augusta. He called a friend at the post office who made some calls and got him instructions on how to find the house. It was a two-hour ride but he had no trouble finding the driveway, even though the name on the old mailbox was so weathered it was almost unreadable. *Beals* was emblazoned in brass letters on the wrought-iron gate. He wasn't too surprised to find a call box in the stone pilaster. Tara answered on the third ring with her name instead of "hello," and Virgil introduced himself.

"What can I do for you, Sheriff?" Her voice sounded like warm honey, and he remembered her from the first days after Zach's disappearance. She'd been a striking woman.

"I'd like to come up and talk, if you don't mind. I'm wondering what you can tell me about Audrey's past," he said.

"Nothing."

"Why is that?"

"I would think you'd understand. Audrey was my patient."

Virgil felt stupid, keying the intercom on and off like a radio. "This won't take too long. I don't want to know anything that happened when you were treating her, just what her childhood was like."

"You want to know more than that."

"Like what?"

"Like whether or not Audrey might be responsible for her own son's disappearance."

Virgil said nothing.

"She's not, Sheriff."

A pickup drove by and the two teenaged boys gave Virgil the once-over but he ignored them. "How can you be so sure?"

"Because I've known Audrey all her life *and* I've been her doctor. She isn't violent and she has none of the symptoms or background that would cause her to harm her own child."

"Can I just come up, please?"

The sound of the gate swinging back on its rubber hinges was like a sigh.

Virgil drove up the winding gravel drive, taking in the thick stands of oak and maple and the underbrush that protected the property like a hedge. The house was modern and well cared for but the grounds had been allowed to go wild, more like a field than a yard. He knocked on the door and Tara opened it wide to allow him to enter the foyer. She was shorter than he remembered, but just as stunning in a tight pair of jeans and western shirt.

"What can I possibly do to help you, Sheriff?" she asked. It was clear he was not going to be invited any further into the house.

"Are you aware that Audrey's being treated by another doctor now and that she's taking Halcion?"

Tara's voice was cold. "Yes. I knew that. I wasn't aware that you did."

"That's a drug to combat depression, isn't it?"

"It is prescribed for that among other things."

"Other things that I should know about?"

"You're being impertinent, Sheriff. Leave Audrey alone."

"I don't want to hurt Audrey. I'm just doing my job."

"And I'm trying to do mine."

"You have a fan in California."

"Excuse me?"

Virgil told her about the boy-slash-girl and Tara laughed. "I'm happy to know my book is accomplishing its purpose."

"When you treated Audrey, did you hypnotize her?"

"Again, that's confidential information."

But of course she had. Tara had written books on the subject. "When you hypnotized Audrey, did she ever tell you about another little girl?"

"What do you mean?"

"Audrey told me she kept seeing another little girl. Her mother—your sister—was holding the girl down in a basement, doing something horrible to her."

"Audrey has all kinds of terrible memories, Sheriff. Some are real. Some are figments of her imagination."

"And that one?"

"I'd say that one was a figment."

"But your sister did do something awful to Audrey or you wouldn't have gotten custody."

"It was a long time ago and it's really none of your business."

"I'm making it my business."

"I'm going to ask you to leave now, Sheriff."

"You did hypnotize her, right?"

"I did a lot of things during our sessions. Audrey's past was particularly traumatic. It took years to build the walls that protect her now. I beg you not to do anything that might bring them crashing down. Now I am asking you to leave. Will you, or must I call your superior officer?"

Virgil left. He was no closer to finding the boys' abductor than he had been before. And Doris was dying. It was like a clock ticking over the investigation.

None of it made any sense. He didn't really believe Audrey Bock had anything to do with Zach's disappearance. Maybe a mother might do something to her kid. But no way Virgil could believe she could *act* as distraught about it as Audrey did. She was going insane with worry and grief. And besides, if it *was* Audrey then that blew his one monster theory, because he just couldn't picture her, small as she was, hurling Timmy's bike over the high bridge rail and far enough out into the creek to have it wash up where it had. He wasn't even sure someone Audrey's size and build had the strength to completely overpower a child the size of Timmy Merrill.

But someone had killed those two boys and someone was going to pay for it.

25

BABS'S LIVING ROOM would have given Martha Stewart nightmares. Bead curtains blocked the opening to what looked like the kitchen. Woven straw mats covered most of the floor, and although the curtains seemed normal enough from outside the house, inside they were laced from floor to ceiling with a wild assortment of feathers, leaves, dried flowers, and what Virgil thought might be hair.

Most of the room was taken up with a wraparound sectional upholstered in faux leopard, offsetting the bright red Persian rug. Instead of a coffee table, a cut-down antique oak dinner table sat in the middle of the floor, covered entirely in half-melted candles of every size and description, all ablaze. A wagon-wheel chandelier, also filled with lighted candles, hung directly over the table and the walls were draped in a deep green fabric that Virgil thought might be silk. A large bookshelf standing between two windows was filled to bursting with leather-bound volumes bearing strange-sounding names like *Necronomicon* and *The Book of Changes*.

"Won't you sit down?" Babs waved toward the waiting leopard fur with a hand clad overwhelmingly in fake jewels. He sat uncomfortably on the edge of the giant sofa, leaning on his knees. "Can I get you anything? Tea, perhaps? I have green, and chamomile. You look like you could use some. It won't take but a minute."

"No, that's all right," said Virgil. But his outstretched

hand was too slow. She had already disappeared through the rattling, multicolored beads in a cloud of musk and jasmine. At least he'd waited until after dinnertime. Hopefully she wouldn't offer him anything to eat.

The entire house smelled of something, but the mixture was so overdone that it dulled the senses with its cloying sweetness, then drowned them completely beneath deep floral fumes. Virgil wondered if he'd ever be able to smell again. He fingered the upholstery gingerly, assuring himself that the fur wasn't real.

Babs rattled back into the living room with a steaming, man-sized mug in each hand. She handed one to Virgil and he took it politely.

"No cream or sugar, right?" said Babs.

Virgil's eyebrows furrowed. "How did you know that?"

Babs chuckled. It sounded more like the laughter of a logger than a woman only an inch taller than Virgil. But he discovered that he liked the honest sound of it. "No magic, Virg. I've seen you around town often enough to know you take your coffee black. Most people that take coffee straight, take tea the same way. Relax."

Virgil smiled self-consciously, sipping the odd brew. It tasted like boiled Band-Aids. But it gave him something to do with his hands, a way to organize his thoughts. He expected Babs to ask him why he'd come, but she seemed perfectly content to sip her tea and smile placidly at him until he got around to opening the conversation.

"Babs," he said, resting the cup on his knee. "Tell me what happened at the sitting."

Babs's smile was wide and toothy and her eyes lit up eagerly. "A new believer!"

Virgil shook his head emphatically. "Nothing of the sort. What I want to know is what really went on."

Babs's smile faltered and her eyes took on a questioning look. "I don't know what you mean."

"What I mean is, how did you do that? How did you make those voices? How did you know where Timmy Merrill's bike was?"

"It was there! I heard you found it."

"Yes, I found it. Now, what I want to know is how you knew it was there."

"I didn't. The spirits did. Of course Timmy would know where his own bike was."

"Come on, that's ridiculous and you know it."

"Know what?"

"There are no spirits. When you're dead, you're dead. You don't get up, put on sheets, and go around talking to the living. I don't believe that *you* really believe that."

"Well, you better believe it. Except for the sheets, I mean. I believe every word of it. Do you honestly think that I came over to your house and sat with poor Doris and *made all that up*?"

"I don't know what you did. That's why I'm here. To find out."

"No, you're not."

"What?"

"You're not here to find out what happened. You're here so I can tell you what you *want to hear* happened."

Virgil sighed into his cup and took another long sip of the now tasteless tea.

"I can talk to spirits, Virg, whether you want to believe it or not. Doesn't matter. They speak through me and they make contact with our side. It's a gift I have. Or sometimes it's a curse. But there's nothing that I can do about it. You heard what everyone else in that room can heard. And everyone else there believed they were hearing the voices of the dead. Except you. And you have more proof than any of them."

"You *sound* like you believe what you're saying—"

"Of course I believe it!"

"But there are other explanations."

"Such as?"

"The one that bothers me is that somewhere, sometime, you heard or saw something that gave you a clue about Timmy Merrill's disappearance. That information stewed around in your head until it came out at the sitting."

"Bull cookies, Virg! What other explanation you got?"

Virgil frowned. "One of them would be that you knew even more than that."

"That I was involved?"

"I don't believe that, Babs."

"Well, I hope the hell not."

"I'm a police officer. I'm trying to solve two cases that

are the worst I've ever worked on. I'm just looking for a little help. That's all."

Babs's eyes softened. She ran her fingers through her thick brush of hair. "I know that, Virgil. But you're locking out a whole world of help by refusing to believe."

Virgil turned back to his tea. "A man believes what he believes." He felt a soft hand on his shoulder but didn't look up.

"It's hard for you," said Babs. "Doris, I mean."

Virgil nodded, his throat tightening.

"I scared you at the sitting, didn't I? I didn't mean to. It was all a mistake, my coming. Doris told me she wanted to contact the other side. I thought she understood that she wanted to try to speak to someone she knew who hadn't crossed over."

"No, you didn't scare me," said Virgil, glancing at her, then away again.

"Yes, I did. It frightened you that Doris might end up there, in that darkness, with those lost souls."

"I don't believe in that malarkey. It angered me that you'd frightened Doris with that foo-fraw."

"You do believe, more than you even know. I can see it in your eyes. You believe in it just enough to be afraid of it, but you don't have to be."

"Why not? Why wouldn't anyone be scared to death after listening to you? Is that what you really think is waiting for us when we die, an eternity of darkness and fear? No thanks."

"But that's not what's waiting for us, Virg! Didn't you listen? I can't speak to heaven! I never said that I could. And I don't know any authentic medium who would ever make such a claim. I am able to make contact with souls who are still on this plane. Souls who have not yet crossed over. That's what a real medium does. We try to help those souls progress onward. I said it was a gift and a curse. It's a gift when I can help someone, alive here, or dead there. It's a curse when I can't. I'm just trying to help."

Virgil still doubted. But he didn't question her sincerity any longer. Babs believed every word she said. So where did that leave him?

"I found the bike, Babs. But it doesn't help much. All it

does is confirm that Timmy likely didn't get lost in the woods, but we already knew that."

"So what do you want from me? You want me to try to recontact him? Some I can, others I can't. It's not like picking up the phone. Think of it more like trying to catch the same minnow in a barrel with your bare hands in the dark. It happens. But there's no way of controlling it. If you want me to try now, though, I'll be happy to."

"No. No, I don't want you to do that." The last thing he wanted was to hear those voices coming out of Babs's mouth again. "I just thought if there was any way you could get me more information it would be helpful. After all, you did help find the bike."

"I know. And I've been thinking a lot about it since Timmy spoke. I wish he had given us more to go on. But the spirits are quite often circumspect in their speaking. It was surprising how forthright he was, to tell you the truth. But I want to give that boy peace. I want it very badly. Just as you must."

"Him and the Bock boy, both."

Babs shook her head. "I can't help you with the other boy yet."

"What do you mean *yet?*"

She stared at the cards in front of them. "I think his mother is coming to see me. I'll know more then."

Virgil let out a sigh that Babs couldn't help but hear. "You know Audrey?"

Babs shook her head. "No."

"Then why would Audrey Bock come to see you? You didn't call her, did you?"

"Of course not. Do you think I need to solicit customers?"

"I don't know that much about your business, to tell the truth."

"Well, I don't."

"Then why should Audrey come to see you?"

"I have no idea. But I was right about Earl and Janie, and I'm right about this. I dreamed that we met, so I know that we will."

Virgil shook his head. "Babs, I've dreamed about a thirty-pound bass I've been looking to catch since I was a kid. That's what dreams are, just dreams."

"To you," said Babs, snatching the stack of cards from the table. She was frowning now, muttering under her breath.

"What did you say?" said Virgil.

Babs shook her head. "Dreams are more than you think. And I've been having real nightmares lately. And more than nightmares. I've been having visions. That's never happened to me before."

Audrey Bock's words echoed in Virgil's head. He felt as though he'd stepped into a dryer and kept spinning around past the window, seeing the same room outside, but catching glimpses from a different angle with each spin. "Nightmares and visions about what?"

Babs sighed. "Just bad pictures. Horrible images. I keep running and running but I can't get away."

"Away from what?"

"I don't know. I never see what it is, but I know if it catches me it's going to kill me."

"Everyone has dreams like that, Babs."

"I keep having it over and over. It's getting so I don't want to go to sleep, then it happens when I'm awake."

"Maybe you should see someone."

"No!" she said, her eyes flashing.

"I didn't mean anything."

"I know you didn't," she said. She seemed surprised by her own outburst. "I believe in holistic healing. Not having my mind toyed with by some charlatan. I know what *they* are."

"What are you doing?" said Virgil, watching her shuffle the cards.

"A reading for you."

"I don't want a reading."

"You don't have to stay."

But he couldn't seem to make himself bow out of the room.

"Give me a question," said Babs.

"About what?"

She shrugged. "What's bothering you?"

What wasn't bothering him? He knew he wasn't going to escape gracefully, but he really didn't want to air his laundry for Babs. "My health," he said at last.

She stared at him as though wondering if he was joking,

then began flipping cards, mumbling to herself. The symbols made no sense to Virgil and he couldn't read the small print upside down and all, but he could tell from the look in Babs's eyes that she didn't like what she saw when she turned the last card. She seemed to take forever, glancing from card to card, her brow furrowed and her tongue slipping in and out nervously between her teeth.

"Well, give me the reading," said Virgil, "so I can get back to work. If I'm dying, just tell me."

Babs shook her head. "I don't see you dying," she said.

Virgil knew then that Babs and her cards were full of shit. "Well that's good, then," he said, rising.

She lowered him back into his seat with a glance.

"I said I didn't see *you* dying. Virgil, this is a bad reading. Real bad. I see people dying around you."

Virgil frowned. "Jesus, Babs, you don't have to be psychic to know that."

"Not Doris," she said. "Or not just Doris. . . . It's more than one person."

"There was Janie—"

"This isn't what's happened. It's what's gonna happen."

"Who is it?"

"I can't tell that."

"When's it gonna happen?"

"I don't know. Soon."

"That really isn't helpful information, Babs."

"I know. I'm sorry. I don't like giving readings like this, but sometimes I have to."

"Well, if that's the best you can do, that's the best you can do," said Virgil, rising at last and starting for the door. "I'm really more interested in anything you can dig up on Timmy Merrill."

"I'll see what I can do, Virg."

She followed him out onto the front porch.

"Quiet night," said Babs, glancing down the street.

Virgil followed her eyes. Both ambulances sat unattended in the hospital parking lot and Babs remarked on it.

"That's a good thing," said Virg.

"Good things have a way of being followed by bad," said Babs.

* * *

Marg was clicking a patient's chart into the stand behind the counter as the automatic glass doors parted for Virgil. He stood in the cool night, smelling the sudden outrush of medicinal odors that could send an eight-year-old into catatonia, wondering how much more his poor nose could stand.

"Virgil! You old dog! Come on over and give Marg a hug."

She managed, somehow, to slide her great bulk through the half door at the counter and out into the emergency waiting area. Virgil couldn't believe it, but it looked as though she'd gained another twenty pounds since he'd seen her last. He couldn't understand how the hospital could keep her on. She had to be hard on their group insurance. But she was a great nurse, a top-notch manager, and a wonderful people person. She wrapped him in a bear hug and he bussed her on the cheek.

"Missed you, you scoundrel!" she said, finally releasing him.

"Missed you too," he said, dropping into a plastic chair.

"Hold on five shakes and I'll get us some coffee."

"That would be great."

When she padded back down the hall toward him, she had two cups of very black coffee in her hands, and Virgil wondered what effect it would have when it hit the ground weeds-and-root concoction Babs had served him earlier. He sipped the bitter brew thankfully.

"You aren't looking too good, cuz," said Marg.

"Well, thanks for saying."

"I mean it. You look like you need to get more sleep."

"It's hard."

"I know. Have you thought anymore about hiring a nurse?"

"Doris won't have one. She doesn't want another woman running around in her house. You know how she is. Her home is her domain."

"What about a male nurse?"

"Have you lost your mind?"

Marg laughed. "Right. That probably would be worse, wouldn't it?"

"How have you been, Marg?"

"Same old, same old. My love life could be better. I don't know, you think it's my hair?" She cocked her head and patted the back of her tangled black hair with her hand.

"Could be. Considering a change?"

"Yeah. Been thinking of dying it green and getting spikes, checking out the butch scene down in Boston."

"Good luck."

"Nah. You know I'll never leave this town. Got too many dead family buried here, just like you. Somehow I just can't figure leaving them and living somewhere else."

"I understand."

"Where's Doris going to be buried?"

Virgil gasped as though she'd hit him in the gut with a baseball bat.

"Sorry, cuz," said Marg.

"It's all right."

"It is and it isn't, I guess. Sometimes my mouth gets ahead of my brain. I was just curious."

"We have a plot on High Street. The old church cemetery."

"Your ma and dad are there, right?"

"And Doris's mother."

"Not her father?"

"They were divorced."

"I didn't know that."

"Doris never talks about it."

Marg tapped his Styrofoam cup with her own. "You just cruising tonight?"

"Yeah. I stopped by to see Babs."

"What on earth for?"

"I'm not sure now." He told her about the sitting and about finding Timmy Merrill's bike.

"Wow. That's pretty weird, all right."

"What do you make of it?"

"Me? I don't know, Virg. I'm like you. I believe it when I see it, but then, you saw the bike. The question is, What do *you* make of it?"

"I can't make a damned thing of it, but I keep coming back to the idea that somewhere, somehow, Babs heard or saw something, something that didn't register with her at the time, but then it percolated inside her head and came out in Timmy Merrill's voice in my bedroom."

Marg nodded. "I think a lot of times that's all the super-natural is. You don't think Babs is pretending?"

"If she is, she's a better actor than anyone I've ever seen. No, I think she's telling the truth. She really believes it when these trances come over her."

"What did Doris think of the sitting?"

"Luckily I don't think she was too affected by it. I don't want her head filling up with mumbo jumbo that keeps her awake nights. She's awake enough as it is."

"If it gets to the point where you can't handle it any-more, give me a call. I know a couple of ladies that are real good, and if I explained the situation to them, they'd be as inconspicuous as kitchen mice."

"Thanks, Marg. But I'm okay."

"No problem. Everybody needs somebody sometime."

"I was gonna write a song about that at one time."

Marg's smile was as wide as her hips. "Me too! What a coincidence!"

"The other day you were talking about Audrey Bock."

Part of the smile faded. "She hasn't been back, but I gather that's because she's seeing a shrink now."

"I know. I went to see her."

"Busy little beaver."

"The doctor has her on Halcion."

"That's a standard drug for depression."

"Could it cause hallucinations?"

"It's probably supposed to keep her from having halluci-nations."

"That's what she said."

"Is she still having them?"

"She said she's getting better. But I'm not too sure. Could you find out who her shrink is?"

"I don't know. I guess I could if it was important enough. Is it?"

"Maybe it is. I don't know."

"He won't tell you anything, even if I do find out who he is."

"You mean he's not *supposed* to tell me anything. Some-times doctors can be helpful by the things they *won't* tell you."

Marg laughed again. "Okay. I'll ferret out the info. You can slide me a fin the next time you're in, gumshoe."

Virgil stared at her, seeing not the fat jowls or the double chin, but the same sweet face he'd been trusting with secrets since grade school. "Where are you going to be buried?"

"What?"

"You heard me."

"I haven't thought about it. Beside my parents, I suppose."

"You have thought about it or you wouldn't have asked *me.*"

"Maybe a little."

"I always kind of thought that you and I might be close. There's room on our plot."

"Are you serious? What would Doris say?"

"I mentioned it to her years ago. She said, 'Honeypie, I just always figured you and that cousin of yours would be together for eternity. As long as you're right there between us, it'll be all right.' "

"Well, I'll be damned."

"So?"

Marg's eyes were damp, and she sniffled as she spoke. "I can't think of anyplace I'd rather be. Sometime in the far future, I mean."

"Put it in your will, then, and don't forget. These things have a way of getting forgotten and then some klutz ends up getting power of attorney and they cremate you and drop your ashes over the Speedway."

"That wouldn't be so terrible. I know a lot of the guys in the pit crews."

"Let's don't go there."

They bantered like that for a few minutes until Marg's eyes dried up and the lump in Virgil's throat softened. Marg made a perfect three-point shot with her cup into the wastebasket beside the soda machine.

"I ought to be going," said Virgil, rising.

"What's your hurry?"

He glanced at his watch. "Need to make dinner for Doris."

"I forgot. I just figured Doris would be home cooking dinner. Isn't that stupid?"

"I do that too," he said, and without warning, in spite of his best intentions, he broke down.

Marg pulled him into her arms, rocking him back and forth like a baby. She stroked his back and murmured in his ear as he sobbed against her. Marg was the only person in the entire world that Virgil could open up to, other than Doris, and this was the first time he had let out all the pressure that had been building since the doctor's first diagnosis.

"Cry till you drop, big fella," Marg whispered in his ear. "You got this one coming."

A volcano of grief erupted outward, compressing his throat, spasming his stomach, and sending great rivers of tears pouring down his cheeks. The more he fought it, the weaker he became, until he had to give himself up to it wholeheartedly and let it go in a final all-encompassing wail that he buried in Marg's soft shoulder. Through it all, her hands never left him, and when he pulled back she nodded and smiled gently, reaching up to wipe his face with a tissue from her pocket.

"Glad you got that out?"

"I'm sorry, Marg."

"For what?"

"I didn't mean to crack up like that."

"That wasn't cracking up. Cracking up is what you do if you don't get the grief out. You can't walk around all the time with all that in the back of your head. It'll drive you crazy."

He made a shot with the tissue toward the can.

"Rim shot," said Marg. "But I'll give you two points."

"Distance was the same."

"Don't argue with the ref."

"Get me that info, would you?" he said, rising.

"Think it's important?"

"Now more than before," said Virgil as the automatic doors *whooshed* open again.

26

THE CROW HOPPED ACROSS Cooder's gravel back lawn,
clearing its throat. Cooder sat in his busted rocker that had
only one arm, and stared straight into the black eyes of the
animal. The bird had started out the morning in the top of
the tallest spruce, cawing loudly when Cooder stepped onto
the back porch. That had been six hours ago.

In all the time since, Cooder had barely blinked.

The bird danced slowly, ever closer, bobbing nervously,
then settling down. And each time it settled, it found
Cooder's eyes still fixed on it. It was a game Cooder loved
to play.

Of all the animals alive that Cooder knew, crows were
the hardest. They were smarter than anything and wild as
all get out. And ornery. Crows and ravens were hardheaded
to beat the band. It was a lot easier to do when you could
look them in the eye. But it was more than just the eyes.
You had to sit yourself just right. The animal had to *know*
that this big man-thing meant it no harm. Cooder's hands
were in his lap. His head leaned toward one shoulder. His
legs were crossed at the ankles. But it was a lot more than
just eyes and sitting right. Lord, yes. The bird had to
hear him.

Inside its head.

For six hours he'd been silently coaxing the skittish crow
forward, like a child clucking his tongue at a kitten.

Here, birdie. Here, birdie, birdie, birdie.

He could feel the bird's fear. He could see himself through its eyes. He liked that. It was a trick he had learned years before. In Perkins. When he'd sat for days on end gazing out through the tall barred windows into the sky. Sparrows would land on the old granite sills and beg for crumbs.

At first he'd amused himself by taming the tiny creatures to his hand. The nurses and staff were bored and underpaid. They enjoyed the show. They could care less if he was feeding wild animals. Or eating them raw for that matter.

But as time went on, he began to have weird flashes. Moments when he thought that he *was* the bird. Times when he seemed to be seeing everything through the bird's eyes. The first time it happened he had to stop when he fell down on the floor of his room. Hard to keep your balance two places at once!

It never really scared him though. Cooder was used to the flashbacks and blackouts and dead space in his head. He wasn't afraid of the things that his brain did. He tried to *enjoy* them the way he enjoyed everything else. So when he started seeing the grounds outside of Perkins from the air again, he just leaned back in his bunk, closed his eyes, and enjoyed the ride. He got so good at it that he began to be able to coax the sparrows to the window without the bread crumbs. And then, finally, he didn't even have to get the birds to come near. He could sit back, close his eyes, and slip right into their heads.

It was a strange trip, being inside the mind of an animal, but then Cooder's mind didn't work exactly the way other people's did anyway, and Cooder's whole life had been a strange trip. Cooder saw mostly pictures behind his eyes. He could work out the meaning of a sentence most times. If it wasn't too complicated. But then he had to figure out where the words fit in with the pictures in his head. Sometimes, before he could do that, he forgot the sentence. But he managed all right. He saw where he wanted to go and he went there. He saw what he wanted to eat and he ate it.

Of course, he never told a soul about his jaunts outside the grounds of the institute. He'd made the mistake of talking too much before and had been real sorry that he had.

He couldn't quite recall what his punishment had been, but he could still sense the horror of it.

The crow hopped up the back steps and now it bounced curiously along the edge of the porch, its head bobbing like a boxer. Cooder pictured the bird sitting on his knee and he transmitted that picture to the bird.

The bird's head tweaked nervously from side to side, gazing at Cooder first with one bright black eye and then the other.

Here, birdie, birdie, birdie.

Cooder knew he could force the animal up onto his leg if he wanted to. But he didn't like the feeling of fear animals gave off when he tried something like that. Their terror revolved right back into his own head and rattled him, and the bigger the animal, the harder they were to control. This was one big old black bird.

Here, birdie, birdie, birdie.

The crow took two quick hops nearer. Close enough to reach out and peck at Cooder's work boot. Testing.

Still Cooder didn't move. Instead, he concentrated on what the bird was seeing. He could see his own face, broad and dark from the sun, his blond hair greased back. He could make out the thick hairs on the backs of his fingers, draped between his knees. He looked like a giant to the bird, and he almost laughed out loud.

Here, birdie, birdie.

The crow crouched, tensing. Its wings started to spread. Its legs twitched. Cooder's dark eyes grew bright.

Here, birdie.

Virgil eased to a stop at the end of Cooder's driveway. He glanced at the name, painted in phosphorescent colors on the mailbox. The lettering was done freestyle in a flowing hand. Virgil wondered at the talent and steadiness required and tried to reconcile them with his picture of Cooder. Had Cooder done the painting? It would have surprised him if Cooder could still spell his name.

The house and grounds fit his image of the man better. The house was small, no more than one bedroom. Two windows flanked the entry, but the grass was overgrown and no one had blazed a path to the door. The asbestos siding was chipped and broken. Each window revealed different colored paint on its trim, as though whoever the painter was, he'd run out of material or changed his mind in the middle of the job. An electrical line dipped low across the yard and Virgil wondered if it was powered up. It would be like Cooder to have forgotten to pay his bill and never have the power restored. It wasn't as though he used electricity for hot baths.

Virgil pulled up alongside the house, feeling as though he had crossed some unseen boundary. While the front of the building was grassy and overgrown, the rear of the lot looked more like a gravel pit. The shells of two rusted automobiles faced each other like contestants in a perpetual game of chicken. An iron stove lay half-buried in the slope to Virgil's left, and scattered pieces of flaking metal scratched their way to the surface as far as he could see.

Without warning, a crow flapped angrily past him, then away into the deep woods, startling him out of his reverie. Virgil took a moment catching his breath after its sudden appearance.

"Cooder?" he called.

"Back here!" Cooder's voice echoed in the trees.

He rounded the corner and found Cooder sitting in a beat-up rocking chair. Virgil sauntered over and leaned on the rickety stair rail. Cooder seemed to be wearing the same clothes he'd seen him in last week. Virgil didn't know whether Cooder never took them off, had several sets, or washed and wore the same set of clothes over and over. Any one of those answers seemed problematic. But Cooder didn't smell as bad as before, so Virgil figured maybe he'd caught him at a good time.

"You see that crow?" asked Virgil.

Cooder smiled and nodded.

"Weird," said Virgil. "Damn thing nearly ran into me."

Cooder said nothing. His smile seemed stuck.

"You remember me almost running over you the other day, Cooder?" asked Virgil. He wasn't sure exactly what Cooder might remember. For all he knew, whatever had set Cooder off the other day was now vanished like mist.

Cooder stared and smiled. "He saw you," he said.

"Who?"

"The crow."

Now it was Virgil's turn to stare silently. Talking to Cooder was like trying to speak to someone over a bullhorn on a distant mountaintop. You always seemed to be getting echoes from a question you had asked sometime before.

"Yeah, well, he almost didn't see me in time. I thought I had a new hood ornament."

Cooder shook his head. "He heard you drive up."

It sounded as though Cooder thought he knew what the damned bird was thinking. "So why did he swoop around the corner like that?"

Cooder shrugged. "Long time, Virg."

"Not so long, Cooder," Virgil reminded him. "I damn near ran over you the other day. Don't you remember our little talk?"

Cooder frowned and Virgil could see that he didn't.

"You remember," said Virgil. "Over on the back side of South Eden? You were walking in the road. I gave you a sandwich."

Cooder smiled. "BLT!"

"Yeah, Cooder. Remember, I told you to stay out of the road?"

Another frown. "Bad things."

Now he was getting somewhere. "Yeah. That's what you said. You remember."

Cooder nodded.

"What did you mean you saw bad things, Cooder?"

"I seen bad things, Virg."

"Yeah," said Virgil, struggling to keep his frustration under control. "I know you did, Cooder. But you got to tell me what it was you saw. Did it have anything to do with No Name Creek?"

Cooder's frown spread all the way across his face. It hurt to watch him think. "Where's that?"

"The old concrete bridge. Right by where I almost hit you? Did you see something bad there?"

Silence.

Virgil stared around the backyard, wondering if Cooder had ever really *driven* any of the dead vehicles. Cooder had

had a driver's license at one time, back when he still had half a brain.

"Don't know nothing about no bridge, Virg."

Shit. There went another of his screwy ideas.

"Bad things," said Cooder, nodding to himself.

"But not at the bridge?"

"No."

Cooder's hands shook and he clenched them. But there was no violence in his face. Just worry, or maybe fear.

"Tell me what you saw, Cooder. What were the bad things?"

"Dark."

"What's dark?"

"In the dark place."

Virgil thought of Audrey's fragmented tale about the basement and Babs's recurring nightmares.

Cooder seemed to drift away without even moving. His eyes went blank and his body sagged. "It's awful dark. I don't want to go back there, Virg."

"Back where, Cooder?"

Another moment of silence.

"In the basement. It's dark. It's *real* dark. Don't make me go in there. I been there before."

The word *basement* tightened Virgil's gut. Why the hell did everyone keep mentioning basements, cellars, dark places? Coincidence was one thing, but this was more than Virgil's concept of coincidence could stand.

"You've been inside this basement? It's someplace you've really seen?"

Cooder nodded.

"Was the Bock boy in the basement, Cooder? The Merrill boy?"

Those questions seemed to bring Cooder back a little closer to what Virgil thought of as the surface. "Who?"

"Zach Bock," said Virgil. "The boy that disappeared last year."

Cooder looked at Virgil as though he hadn't seen him before. "Just me and the machine."

"What machine?"

"I think maybe he's alive, Virg," said Cooder.

"What? Who?"

"The little boy. Sometimes I feel him."

"Which little boy, Cooder?"

Cooder shook his head. Then he slapped his temple as though trying to loosen some stray memory clinging to his addled brain.

"It's dark," he said.

A little boy in a dark basement. Spirits finding bicycles. And a machine? What kind of machine? What the hell was that about?

"Where is he, Cooder? Where is the little boy?"

Cooder frowned and seemed to float away again. When he spoke again, even his voice sounded distant. It reminded Virgil of the sitting and he shivered in spite of the late-afternoon sun on his back.

An electrical charge seemed to jolt Cooder and when he spoke this time, his voice was harsh, raspy. "She's going to put the mask on him."

"What kind of mask?" asked Virgil, dreading the answer. "Why is she putting a mask on him?"

"Heavy."

What kind of mask was heavy? "Help me out, Cooder. Tell me where the little boy is."

Cooder shook his head. "I don't know, Virg." He focused on Virgil again, and Virgil found himself searching those impossibly dark eyes for more answers, but there were none there. He could see that Cooder wanted the visions out of his head as badly as Audrey Bock did.

"My medicine used to make it go away," said Cooder, staring off through the trees. "Now it doesn't help so much."

Again he sounded like Audrey.

"You think it's real, Cooder? The little boy? You understand what I mean by real?"

"Yeah, Virg. I know what real is."

"And is he?"

A space.

"Yeah. I think he's real."

"But you don't know where he is?"

"No."

"Cooder, do you remember me coming here after the Bock boy disappeared?"

Cooder frowned.

"A year ago, Cooder. Remember me asking you questions?"

"No."

"You said you didn't know anything. You hadn't been by the Bocks' house in awhile."

"I don't know, Virg."

"Cooder, do you remember Zach Bock? Do you remember what he looked like?"

Cooder shook his head slowly.

"Cooder, I need to ask you something."

"Okay, Virg."

"You didn't hurt that boy, did you?"

Cooder stared right through him.

"Cooder?"

"I don't think so."

"You don't think so?"

"No, Virg. I never hurt anybody. You know that."

"Yeah, Cooder. I do know."

"I didn't, did I?"

The pleading look in Cooder's eyes told Virgil all he needed to know. It would have killed Cooder to learn that he'd ever hurt *anyone*. He could no more have done anything to Zach Bock or Timmy Merrill than Virgil could. And even stretching his imagination, turning Cooder into an *accidental* killer, Virgil just couldn't see Cooder pulling it off. He'd have walked right up to the first passerby and confessed.

"You don't think I hurt him, do you, Virg?"

"No, Cooder. No. I don't think that."

"Okay."

"Do you know Merle Coonts?"

Hesitation.

"No."

"Never heard of him?"

Another hesitation.

"No."

Virgil explained as well as he could to Cooder where the Coonts place lay. Until he was reasonably certain Cooder had a picture of the location in his mind. "You must have been by there a hundred times."

Cooder nodded.

"Do you think the boy might be there?" asked Virgil. "Somewhere in that basement?"

Cooder shrugged.

"You never had bad feelings about that place?" asked Virgil.

Cooder frowned. "I don't know, Virg. I seen bad things."

"Yeah," said Virgil, fighting down his frustration yet again. "I know."

"There's no eyes in the mask," said Cooder. He seemed to be genuinely confused by that revelation.

"How long have you been seeing these bad things, Cooder?"

Cooder shrugged. Virgil hadn't really expected an answer. Cooder's version of time didn't match anyone else's. But Virgil had to try. He had to know what time frame he was up against. Maybe Cooder and Audrey and Babs really *were* experiencing some kind of communications that he couldn't understand. Maybe there really was a small boy locked up in someone's basement. If there really was a little boy, even if it wasn't Zach Bock, how much time did he have to find him?

"Do you have a phone, Cooder?" asked Virgil.

Cooder nodded.

"Good," said Virgil, making eye contact. "If you see anymore bad things, you call me, okay? All you have to do is dial 911. You understand 911?"

"Yeah, Virg. I know. 911."

"Good," said Virgil, heading back to the car. "Anything you think of, you call. You hear?"

Cooder followed Virgil to the cruiser like a curious bear.

"Sure, Virgil. I'll call."

"Good," said Virgil, leaning on the top of the cruiser.

"I'll call from Zeke's store."

Virgil frowned. Zeke's store was three miles up the road. "Just use your phone."

"Doesn't work."

Virgil sighed, shook his head, and climbed back into the car. As he pulled onto the highway, he glanced in his rearview mirror and noticed a dark Ford sedan about a half-mile back. But the car was driving slow and pretty soon it was lost from sight.

Virgil drove the long way back to town from Crowley along the route that would take him by the Bocks'. He drove slowly past their driveway, watching the hill ahead as the Coonts barn appeared like a snake rising out of a hole in the ground. As he passed by the front of the house, Merle stepped down from the old side stoop, headed for his truck. Without thinking, Virgil spun into the drive, cutting him off. Merle stood frozen in place, a big goofy mannequin. The way his bottom lip drooped, he reminded Virgil of Cooder. But Merle was bright enough to hire a real estate salesman as a buyer's agent. Bright enough to have the means to buy a place that wasn't even on the market.

Virgil climbed out of the cruiser and sauntered around to Merle's side. Merle looked like a kid meeting a cop for the first time. Not afraid, really, but maybe a little.

"Hello, Mister Coonts," said Virgil, both hands on his belt.

Merle nodded. He was in his fifties, six inches taller than Virgil, and outweighed him by a hefty margin. His work boots looked like giant clubs. He wore a frayed old flannel shirt and worn but clean khaki pants. You wouldn't be able to pick him out of the crowd in a truck stop, but standing in the middle of the gravel drive beside the cruiser, he looked somehow out of place.

"I talked to you a year ago," said Virgil, looking for recognition in Merle's eyes. Merle frowned, then nodded.

"The Bock boy," said Merle. "Yeah, I remember, Sheriff." His voice was deep and resonant, but hesitant.

"Yeah. The Bock boy. I was just wondering if you had come up with anymore information you could give me on that." Virgil didn't really think Merle would have anything more to say on the subject. But after the fiasco in Audrey Bock's cellar, he felt like he owed it to her to at least stop and ask. The sun glinted off glass and he glanced into the barn at a fairly new Chevy sedan. It seemed as out of place as the satellite dish on the barn's roof.

A dark sadness settled over Merle's dead brown eyes. "I don't know nothin'."

Virgil tried to spot anything fishy in Merle's body language, but the big man didn't move, no twitchy fingers, no odd angle to his head.

"Would you mind if I had a look around your house?"

"For what?" asked Merle. Now his big arms crossed in front of his chest.

"Just to take a look at your house and maybe your cellar."

"You got a warrant?"

"Do I need one?" asked Virgil, bluffing.

Merle stared at him. Suddenly the big man didn't seem so sluggish. His eyes appeared quicker, more alert. When he uncrossed his arms, his large hands fell away to his sides like a pair of baseball bats, and Virgil tightened. In that instant, he had been certain that Merle was about to strike him. But then the feeling disappeared as Merle shrugged and turned back toward the house. Merle chugged up the steps and into the tiny foyer, stopping to let Virgil pass. Virgil watched him like a hawk, but Merle made no overt moves, simply led him from room to room.

Virgil had seen a million old New England farmhouses. Every one was different and the same. They'd started out as one- or two-bedroom structures, with a brick chimney. Then the kids came and the owners would add on. Over the better part of a century, a house might grow from little more than six hundred to well over three thousand square feet. The homes ran the gamut from working farms that had been in families for generations to ramshackle abandoned structures in the middle of the woods to elegant renovations used in the summer by flatlanders escaping the city.

But Merle's house had the air of a building that had been used by transients. The messy kitchen and one back bedroom were the only rooms that had any feel of being lived in at all. One closet held three sets of pants, a few workshirts, and another set of boots. A TV sat on the dresser. Not one photo graced the walls. Why would a single man who lived like Merle insist on owning such a large old house?

"Come on," said Merle, hurrying from room to room as Virgil peeked into empty closets and under dusty mattresses. "Let's get this over with."

Virgil shrugged, his hand resting as casually as possible on the butt of his pistol. He was making sure he did not let Merle get behind him.

But the house itself got behind him. The walls were a dark presence, surrounding him, watching him. Waiting. But for what? He and Merle rounded a corner to face the cellar stairs and Virgil stopped, resting his hand on the wide molding.

"Go ahead," said Merle. "You want to see the cellar, don't you? Isn't that what you're really here for? You think I kidnapped Zach Bock and have him locked up in the basement or something."

"I'm not accusing you of anything, Mister Coonts," said Virgil, noting that Merle remembered the boy's first name.

"Yeah, right. Go on, check out the damned cellar."

"All right," said Virgil. He pulled the door open and waved Merle ahead of him, down into the dark, junk-filled cellar that was nothing like Audrey and Richard's.

The narrow, stone-walled space was low and cavelike. The floor was cold concrete and the entire space was filled, floor to joists, with old boxes and crates that seemed far too ancient for Merle to have brought them in. They were probably left by the previous owners, with only a narrow, winding passage through them. Virgil felt his fear of cramped places starting to act up. His palms got sweaty and his mouth went dry. But he wasn't going to show his unease to Merle.

The light through the one tiny window was almost nonexistent through the layers of grime, and Virgil wished he'd brought his flashlight with him. It made a good backup weapon as well as a light. He kept his eyes glued to Merle's back.

"Turn on a light," said Virgil, his words fluttering like moths through the cellar.

Merle shook his head without turning. "Burned out," he muttered, moving away. "Come on."

Virgil tried to catch up, but Merle knew the basement better than he. When Merle disappeared around a pile of boxes, an alarm sounded inside Virgil's head and he slowed. His fingers tightened on his pistol, and he used his free hand to touch a box here, shifting a pallet there with the toe of his boot.

Empty. They were all empty. Why would anyone keep so many boxes? A stray beam of light from the window allowed Virgil to read the label on one of the crates. Cattle feed. He could smell it now. The sweet odor of sorghum still clung to the old cardboard after all these years. At one time the boxes must have been filled with burlap bags of feed. So they had belonged to the original owners. Merle was just too lazy to haul them to the dump.

"You coming or what?" Merle's voice skittered through the maze, and Virgil was at once happy to know that the big bastard wasn't lurking around the corner, but also disconcerted to learn that Merle had gotten so far ahead of him. A rat stuck its head out from between two boxes right beside his left hand and he slapped at it.

Perfect.

Finally the claustrophobic confines of the basement opened out into wider gloom and Virgil was happy as hell to pass into it. But the size of the darkened space held its own dangers. He couldn't make out *anything* in the gloom and the echoing sound of Merle's boots on concrete told him the space was very large. His back tight, fingers taut, he searched for Merle. Realizing at the same time that he made a nice target framed in the doorway—even as dark as it was—he took a step to one side.

As his eyes grew accustomed to the shadows, he could just see the outline of run-down cattle stalls. That meant that somewhere the basement must stick out of the surrounding slope. There had to be another door. A way for the farmer to have brought his livestock in. But Virgil couldn't make out the far walls.

"So," said Merle, startling Virgil.

Merle sat ten feet to Virgil's left, atop what looked to Virgil to be an old steamer trunk resting against the wall. Merle's legs were crossed in front of him, and the bastard made a sweeping gesture across the wide-open expanse of the barn basement. He seemed to be pointing at one thin dusty ray of sunlight filtering through the back wall that Virgil could just make out now. As though Virgil might want to inspect *that*.

"Be my guest," said Merle.

As his eyes grew accustomed to the darkness, Virgil took the opportunity to search the entire perimeter of the barn, stopping to give the old barn door a shake, peering closely into each stall, sniffing, finding nothing. Even so, he had an odd certainty that there was something here, that Merle was hiding *something*. An unseen presence so deep-seated that it was part of the ground beneath his feet. It was as though the concrete, the foundation, the old cracked beams overhead were moaning at him, trying to tell him something in some language he couldn't understand. It raised the hairs on his arms. He ended his search standing in front of Merle, who still sat like a prim schoolgirl atop the old trunk. Virgil wondered that it could hold his weight. He also wondered if Merle always sat that way, with his legs tightly clenched.

"Seen enough?" asked Merle.

"What's in the trunk?" asked Virgil.

"Old clothes."

Old clothes? The one item that sat in this entire expanse of emptiness held old clothes? Virgil found himself wondering if the original owners *had* moved the boxes into the house basement. Or did Merle have some reason to want this huge expanse of hidden open area? What possible use could he put it to?

"Open it."

"You don't have a warrant."

"I can get one soon enough," said Virgil, stretching out his bluff.

Merle glared at him for a moment, but then he stood up grudgingly and lifted the shiny combination lock.

Why lock up a bunch of old clothes?

Merle spun the cylinder on the lock, placing his body between Virgil and the trunk. When the lock clicked open, Merle flipped the trunk lid back and stepped aside. Inside, just as Merle had said, was a pile of ratty clothes. Virgil rummaged all the way to the bottom, but there were nothing else inside. Why in the world would anyone lock up old clothes? Maybe his imagination was running away with him. Maybe Merle was just a harmless kook.

"Afraid someone will steal your shirts?"

Merle glared at him. "You want to see anything else?"

"Thanks for the tour," said Virgil, wondering what he could have missed.

"You know your way out," said Merle, nodding back toward the cellar door.

Virgil glanced over his shoulder and a chill shot through him. No way he was going to pass back through that long maze again. He squinted down the length of the barn.

"What's out back?" he said, nodding toward the barn door at the far end of the cellar.

Merle shrugged. "That way's out," he said, nodding once more toward the tight little cellarway.

Virgil shook his head. "I'm going out the back door."

Merle's frown became ugly, but he headed off across the floor. "Suit yourself."

Virgil followed, hating the sound of their footsteps echoing away in the darkness. The barn cellar was large enough, but the darkness made it seem tight nonetheless. Merle stood beside the door, sheltered in the shadows, and Virgil gripped the rusted handle and jerked. The door rattled but held in place and Virgil noticed another lock, this one a heavy brass, keyed number.

"Open it," said Virgil, now more than ever wanting to be outside the confines of the basement, the locked door seeming to make the darkness tighter still.

"Don't know where the key is," said Merle, petulantly. His pouting lips made him look like a fat, spoiled child. Virgil found himself wanting to slap the bastard. He thought that if he did, Merle might just run away crying, calling for his mother. He started to draw his pistol and Merle took a step backward.

"Hey!" said Merle, raising both hands.

"I'm going to shoot the lock off," said Virgil, jerking his gun out of the holster, waiting to see if Merle would produce a key.

"Fuck you," said Merle, moving aside and crossing his arms.

Virgil placed the pistol barrel within a hairsbreadth of the lock and pulled the trigger. The shot blasted through the brass, nearly blowing the lock through the rotten barnboards. The sound shook the floor overhead and dust that smelled of hundred-year-old hay drifted down over them like snow.

Virgil yanked the lock aside and slid the big door open wide enough to step through. Warm sunlight flooded over him and he breathed in deeply. "Thanks for the tour," he said, giving Merle a look that let him know he'd be back.

Merle followed him to his car, and once again Virgil wondered what it was he was missing. Merle was a strange one, no doubt, but there was no child hidden in his house, and he had no more to tie the man to Zach Bock's disappearance now than he had a year before.

Why had Merle acted like such an asshole, though, if he really had nothing to hide? Why egg a cop into shooting a lock off your door? One more question to add to the pile. He stared into Merle's eyes as he climbed into the cruiser, trying to get the man to back down. But Merle never looked away, and finally Virgil put the car in gear and eased down the drive using *that* as an excuse for losing the battle.

When he glanced toward the house again, Merle had disappeared inside.

Virgil was halfway back to town when he noticed the dark Ford sedan in the rearview mirror again. His first thought was that it was coincidental, the car stopping somewhere just as he had, and then taking off again at the same time. But after a couple of miles, his curiosity was aroused at just how far back it was staying, so he pulled over to the shoulder, eyeing the rearview mirror.

The car pulled over. Too far away for Virgil to read the plates, but they looked to be from Maine. Now he had no choice but to turn around and see what they were up to. He made a U-turn only to find that the sedan had beaten him to it. The sedan was around the curve ahead before Virgil could straighten out and floor the accelerator. He flipped on the siren and flashers and reached for the radio. Birch answered and Virgil gave his location and the make and color of the sedan. The closest deputy was ten miles away on a parallel road, but he might be able to cut the guy off up ahead. If Virgil could catch sight of him again before he disappeared down some side road.

The trouble was, the country was riddled with logging roads and backroads and roads that weren't even really roads anymore. Virgil slowed as he passed an intersection with a narrow lane that climbed away to disappear around another tree-lined bend. He had to make an educated guess and he *guessed* the guy hadn't taken that turn. So he gassed the car again and roared off down the hill, talking to Birch on the radio all the time, letting him know exactly where he was and what he was doing, so Birch could coordinate a roadblock if they could run the guy into it.

Virgil had no idea why the guy was running. It could have been a million things. He might have been wanted for any number of things. Maybe he was driving on a suspended license. He might not even be in trouble. Virgil had had experience with innocent people who just panicked around a police officer. But a little voice in the back of his head told him it was none of the above.

He blasted around a corner and up ahead he saw the tail end of the sedan dropping away again. He floored the cruiser, listening to the rumbling of the big engine, feeling the springs in the seat press into his lower back.

"Gotcha, you son of a bitch."

Up ahead the road opened into farmland again, straightening out for a long straightaway. The bastard wasn't going to lose him in the curves and there weren't but a handful more side roads between there and the highway. He topped the hill doing a hundred and ten, praying there was no old lady in a Honda Civic on the other side.

What there was was a dark Ford sedan parked sideways in the middle of the road, blocking both lanes. Virgil reacted instinctively, feathering the brakes, trying to squeeze by on the gravel shoulder as the car's speed dropped to ninety, then eighty. He missed clipping the tail of the sedan by a hairsbreadth, shooting past so fast that the driver—who sat nonchalantly behind the wheel—was just a blur, neither man nor woman to Virgil. The rear tires of the cruiser skidded on the loose surface, the back end of the car skewing until one tire caught the grass and nearly rolled the car. Virgil fought the skid, spinning the wheel, trying to will the heavy auto back up out of the ditch, but to no avail. The big cruiser shot down the embankment and through a barbed-wire fence, grumbling to a stop with its tires buried in the soft soil of a freshly planted cornfield.

Virgil shoved open his door, fumbled out of his seat belt, and cursed his way to his feet, drawing his sidearm. But the dark sedan was already just a memory.

27

RICHARD AWAKENED THE NEXT MORNING like a troll crawling out from under a bridge. He stretched his arms over his head, gripping the headboard, trying to work out the kinks in his back. Glancing over at Audrey, sound asleep beside him, he couldn't help but notice how much like an angel she looked. She hadn't cried out in the night since she'd been on the Halcion. Hadn't had a nightmare or one of her night terrors. But then last night, just after midnight, she had started to moan. He'd lain beside her, not wanting to touch her or even move lest he do something to shift her deeper into the dream. Finally she'd drifted off again and sometime around dawn he, too, had finally slept.

Now, as they drove into Arcos, he kept glancing over at her as she leaned back in the seat beside him. He hadn't wanted to go to work, but it was Friday, things were piling up, and he couldn't keep putting his accounts off if he wanted to retain his loyal clients. But he'd been surprised when Audrey offered to ride along. Surprised and pleased. Still, he kept checking on her. She seemed distracted, even more than she usually was by the Halcion.

He'd driven ten miles out of their way in order not to pass the Coonts place, but she hadn't even noticed—or if she had, she'd made no comment. When he tried to draw her into conversation, she answered in monosyllables. So as he pulled into the parking space in front of his office, he still had no idea what her plans were. He hoped they weren't going to get into an argument about her taking the car. He'd read the warning label on the pills, and if that wasn't enough to decide him, her attitude was. When the engine died she glanced around as though just realizing where they were, then smiled at him.

"We're here," he said, pocketing the keys and climbing out of the car.

His business was located one block off Main Street, in a group of houses that had been converted to office space. Two dentists had the white cottage to the left, a couple of attorneys—clients of Richard's—had the Victorian manse to his right. There were signs along the street for massage therapists, a couple of real estate companies, and Shay Martin, his friendly competitor in the numbers racket. Mister and Missus Reblette were the sole residential holdouts on the street, a nice old couple who didn't seem at all fazed by their uniqueness or lack of regular neighbors.

"What're your plans?" he asked, waiting for her on the sidewalk.

She squinted into the sun, drinking in the day and shaking her head.

"Come on in, then," said Richard. "I'll make a pot of coffee and you can watch TV in the back office while I work."

"I'm gonna go for a walk."

"You sure?" he said, studying her.

She smiled. "I'm okay," she said, touching him lightly on the arm. It seemed like she wanted him to kiss her, but he felt uncomfortable making the first move, like a teenager on a blind date.

"I'll be all right," she said.

"Sure you will." He leaned in and they bussed awkwardly. She tapped him on the shoulder and started off toward Main Street.

"Take you to lunch?" he called after her.

"Sure," she said, waving over her shoulder without looking back.

He watched her until she disappeared around the corner. Then he went inside, hoping that this was a new day after all, that Doctor Cates and his pills were going to give him back the old Audrey.

Audrey hadn't been alone in town since Zach's disappearance, and she almost felt like a tourist. It was amazing how much things had changed since she'd last walked the streets. You noticed things you didn't when driving past. Or maybe she just hadn't noticed *anything* for the last year.

The diner had a new neon sign in the shape of a crossed knife and fork. Not classy but effective, she decided. And she was surprised to find a pet store where the thrift shop used to be. She stopped for a few moments, entranced by the dark wet eyes of a yellow lab puppy that kept gooping up the glass with sopping puppy licks. She had to drag herself away.

The hardware store had all their spring and summer gear out. The sidewalk was lined with bright red lawn mowers and all manner of barbecue grills and gardening tools. She stopped to read the ingredients on a fifty-pound bag of lawn fertilizer and shook her head. Too much nitrogen in the mix for this altitude and climate, but you couldn't expect a hardware store to know that. She preferred to do her chemical shopping at the farmer's co-op.

Traffic seemed heavy for a weekday; most of the diagonal parking spots were filled and she said hello to a couple of people who knew her name, but whose faces she couldn't *quite* place. Thankfully none of them stopped to talk or saddled her with the one thing she feared most—their pity. Maybe they thought enough time had passed for her grief to have run its course. Or probably they were just too polite to chance awakening hurtful memories.

The stores gave way to another residential section, before Main Street ran out a couple of blocks ahead and turned back into Route 26 in front of the hospital. She didn't intend to go that far, afraid that someone there might recognize her and she *would* get drawn into conversation. This walk wasn't about connecting with people. It was about reconnecting herself with the outside world. But only a little at a time. She had come close to drowning, and was now taking her first tentative steps back into the tiny wavelets along the shore. She could see the breakers, but she wasn't ready to plunge into them.

When she reached the corner she stopped and glanced over the manicured lawn in front of the house she faced. The grass was cut close, like a golf course, but it was healthy and green. The owners hadn't bought *their* fertilizer from the local hardware. The walk was edged to perfection and thick lilies surrounded the wide front porch. The heavy floral curtains spoke of an older female and Audrey got the idea that the home was owned by a retired couple who had probably bought the place before she was born. He would be ex-military, or maybe an old millworker. She'd be a life-long housewife. They probably had a dozen kids and enough grandkids to flood across the lawn on holidays and other visits.

The thought of kids racing across the grass stabbed at her heart, and it took her a minute to catch her breath. As she stared at the front porch she noticed a small shingle sign beside the ornate glass door and realized she'd made a mistake. This wasn't a residence after all. More than likely the sign had a name with esquire after it. Some old attorney who worked only on cases that interested him, for people he knew. She tried to remember if she knew the names of any other attorneys in town besides Richard's neighbors. Frowning, she took a few paces up the walk to read the sign.

As she did so, the front door opened and a middle-aged woman with a bright blue scarf on her head reached out and emptied her mailbox, standing half-in, half-out of the house. Audrey stood frozen, hoping the woman would close the door and go back inside without noticing the stranger trespassing on her walk. But instead, she finished flipping envelopes and looked up, locking eyes with Audrey. When the woman smiled, Audrey was disarmed.

"I'm sorry," said Audrey, smiling back. "I was trying to read your sign."

"What's wrong with that? That's why I put it there," said the woman, tossing the mail back inside the house and stepping out onto the porch to greet her. "Come on up!"

Along with the scarf, the woman wore a thick, wool, knee-length skirt with bobby sox and tennis shoes. She looked like a bag lady with new clothes. But she seemed friendly enough, and Audrey decided this might be just the right time to ease a little farther out into the waves. Not knee high. Just up to her calves, maybe. She stepped up onto the porch and shook hands.

"I'm Audrey Bock," she said.

"Babs St. Clair," said the woman. She angled her head, studying Audrey's features, and Audrey noticed how hawk-like her eyes were, darting from Audrey's nose to her lips and down her torso.

The woman seemed familiar, but Audrey couldn't place her. "Have we met before?"

"Not in this life," said Babs. "But you were coming to see me, weren't you?"

Audrey glanced at the sign and hoped she didn't show her shock. The lettering was calligraphic, swirling gilt.

Babs St. Clair
Seer, Healer
The Universe is Large,
I am small.

"No," said Audrey, trying to look Babs right in the eye now and not be drawn to the sign again. "I was just passing by."

Babs laughed, tapping the sign. "Some people like it. Some think it's a little over the top. You a believer?"

"In what?"

"Anything. Whatcha got? There's not any right or wrong way to *believe.*" That thought seemed to dredge up a frown that looked out of place on Babs's face. "That's not exactly a fact, I suppose. You can believe the wrong way. Or rather you can follow the wrong path. But you're not."

"Excuse me?"

"Following the wrong path. That's not you. You're heading in the right direction."

"How do you know that?"

Babs laughed again, slapping Audrey on the shoulder hard enough to set her back on her heels, somehow doing it without hurting her. Babs acted like a jovial kid brother or a friendly bear. "Because you're here! Come on in." She turned and disappeared through the door before Audrey could reply.

"No! Really, I was just passing by."

"Come on," said Babs, throwing the door wide open.

For the first time, Audrey realized that the window in the frame had been cut in shapes of crosses and Stars of David and crescent moons and other shapes that she assumed were spiritual but which had no meaning to her.

"I'm not going to hurt you," said Babs. "And I never charge for the first consultation. What have you got to lose? Have you got an appointment somewhere?"

Audrey shook her head, unable to lie to the woman.

"Then come on in. You can pretend nothing I say means anything and it's all just hocus-pocus. Virgil does."

"Virgil?"

"Virgil Milche, the sheriff. He's one of those hard-to-convince characters. But he's coming around. I told him you'd be coming to see me. Wait till he hears you showed up."

"No!" said Audrey, shifting her feet. "Please don't tell him I was here."

"Why not?" said Babs. "It's nothing to be ashamed of."

"How could you have known I was coming?" said Audrey, as disconcerted by that as the possibility that her visit might become public knowledge.

Babs shrugged. "I know things like that. Come on, I'll do a quick reading."

"No, really. I'd rather not."

But Babs wasn't going to take no for an answer, Audrey could see it in her eyes.

"Come on, now. Don't be afraid. If nothing else, you'll have passed the time and I'll have kept in practice."

"Practice at what?" said Audrey, letting Babs close the door and shepherd her into the room. She sniffed at the candle smoke, taking in the wild decor. Strange how someone who kept her yard so immaculate would live in all this . . . chaos.

"Reading the cards!" said Babs, playfully shoving her into an armchair across the table from her.

Audrey stared at the stack of cards, alarm bells sounding in her mind. Her face felt suddenly hot and she shifted uneasily in the chair.

"What's the matter?" said Babs, the frown creasing her face again but not reaching her eyes. "You got questions, don't you? Everyone's got questions."

Audrey frowned all the way to her forehead before nodding. She had questions all right, but they weren't going to be answered by this woman. Maybe they were never going to get answered, but she didn't want to believe that.

"You been hurt pretty bad," said Babs. "Seems to me like maybe you think you been hurt worse than anyone else in the world."

"How do you know that?" gasped Audrey. "You don't know me. You don't know anything about me."

Babs shrugged. "I don't need the cards to read some things. I can just feel 'em. I know pain when it hits me. Let me read the cards. It can't hurt, can it?"

Audrey nodded slowly, glancing at the deck of cards facedown on the table, wondering if maybe it *could* hurt. But even the faintest possibility of an answer was enough to tempt her. "All right," she whispered.

Babs took the chair across from her and carefully shuffled the deck, laying out three cards in a line from her to Audrey, facedown. Then she lay a fourth card atop the one in the middle. Then one to each side, and finally another line of four to Audrey's left.

"Now let's see," said Babs, leaning back in her chair. "What would you like to ask?"

"What should I ask?" said Audrey, sitting up stiffly.

Babs shrugged. "Usually a person has some question they'd like answered. I read the cards and try to give it to 'em. Don't get me wrong. I can't give you the race results or the stock market quotes for tomorrow. But I can tell you if you should be planning a trip to Florida or whether a new man is right for you. You get it?"

Audrey nodded. "I don't have any questions like those," she said. "What I want to know is specific."

"I don't want to disappoint you."

"I've been disappointed for a long time."

Babs smiled reassuringly at her and turned over the middle card, underneath. Nodding to herself, she lay it back in place faceup.

"I'll just do an open-ended reading then and see what pops up."

The card read *Justice* and showed a hand-painted picture

of a scale. Audrey glanced up, surprised to see Babs frowning again.

"What's the matter?" said Audrey.

"Nothing," said Babs, flipping the card around so it was facing her. "If the card faces away from the reader, its meaning is reversed. But usually it's just a bad shuffle."

"Does that mean there isn't any justice for me?" Audrey didn't believe in the supernatural. But the card falling that way was not a coincidence, because she *believed* that. There hadn't been any justice for her and Richard. Certainly none for Zach.

"You can't read anything from just one card," said Babs. "Two tarot readers might have the same lay and come up with different interpretations altogether of what the *whole* meaning was. We have to wait. That first card is your present situation. But *Justice* can also be read as *balance* or *peace*."

Audrey shrugged. If two people couldn't agree on the meaning, what good was it? But either way, she figured the card had fallen right to begin with; she didn't have much balance or peace either.

Babs flipped the second card over and placed it sideways atop the first. It was a picture of a drunken man stumbling down the street and the caption read *The Fool*. Babs glanced at Audrey and Audrey was certain Babs had a question she was afraid to ask.

"What?" said Audrey.

"Does anyone in your family drink?"

Audrey shook her head. "Richard and I have a glass of wine occasionally. Not very often."

Babs bit her lip.

"Anyone do drugs or is anyone on medication?"

Audrey fought hard not to show her surprise. She shook her head. That wasn't a lie. She hadn't told Richard yet. But since this morning, there was no one in her family on medication.

Babs shrugged, turning over the center card nearest Audrey.

"What's that?" said Audrey, leaning to check out the picture of an old woman sitting in what looked to be the mouth of a cave.

"The Hermit," said Babs. "This card represents your goal or destiny. Something you're either fated to find or want to find. It can also be someone or something to guide you."

"Guide me where?"

"To a higher plane. Or maybe just to the grocery store." Babs laughed and Audrey shook her head.

Babs flipped the card in between the two lines of cards. It was a beautiful but somehow menacing woman in long flowing robes.

"The High Priestess," said Babs.

"What does she mean?"

"She represents your distant past. She could be the foundation of events that are happening now or in your recent past or in your future. She's a seeker. That can be good or bad. If she seeks enlightenment, that's good. If she seeks money or fame or something like that, that's bad."

Babs flipped the card nearest to her and frowned. Audrey cocked her head to see the bright red devil with a gleaming pitchfork. She looked Babs in the eye.

"This represents your recent past. I guess we already discussed that, eh?"

Audrey nodded.

Babs flipped the card sitting all alone to Audrey's right. A man in a peaked cap waved a wand over his head, and stars spun in a circle following its path.

"The Magician," said Babs. "This represents future influences."

"Magic?"

Babs shook her head. "It can mean something like resources. Or a person who magically appears in your life. Or who knows, maybe it *is* magic. You have to stay open."

One part of Audrey wanted to relax and enjoy the game. Babs was as entertaining as any carnival sideshow. But another part of her warned her to be on guard, that things were not as they seemed. She felt a strange affinity with Babs—though she was sure she'd never met the woman in her life—and an odd attraction for the cards as well. Although the pictures and names were in no way familiar, they stirred something deep in her memory. It seemed to be something about the cards themselves. Something in the way Babs shuffled them, slipping them in between one another like a riverboat gambler.

There was now only the line of four cards to Audrey's left. Babs flipped the one nearest herself. The image on the card stunned Audrey, and Babs noticed, cocking her head to look Audrey in the eye.

"What does that represent?" whispered Audrey, staring at the picture of a woman down on her knees, staring into a pool of water. She seemed to be looking at her own reflection, but the water was disturbed, or the image was untrue, not quite discernible. Though it didn't seem to match the picture in any way, the caption read *The Hanged Man*.

Babs frowned, shaking her head. "This is what we call a New Age deck. As you can see, there isn't any hanged man. That's because the card's meaning and the picture never seemed to go together in the old decks. But they kept the names since it came down from medieval times. This card represents visions, things that are real and unreal to you at this moment. It represents *who you are* right now. What do *you* see in it?"

Audrey shook her head, unable to peel her eyes away from the card. Even the tall grass behind the woman reminded her of her own overgrown lawn. The tiny pool could have been her fountain. The image in the water drew her steadily downward.

"Audrey," said Babs, reaching across to tap her on the arm.

Audrey shook her head, finally breaking the pull, staring hard at Babs. "I want to ask my question now."

"That isn't the way it works. We could start again, if you'd like."

The way she said it made Audrey certain that Babs would love to reshuffle the cards. The way they had fallen had made her at least as touchy as Audrey. Audrey shook her head.

"No," she said. "Now. I want to ask my question now." She stared at the woman on the card again but refused to be drawn into the water.

"All right," said Babs at last. "Ask."

Audrey nodded to herself, biting her lip. "Where is my son?"

When Babs didn't move to flip a card or answer, Audrey looked up at her. Babs's face had changed. She seemed to be almost in a trance, but Audrey could see her brain working behind her bright eyes. "Audrey, like I told you, the cards aren't specific. I didn't mean to upset you."

"I'm not upset," said Audrey, lying. "I want you to answer the question."

They locked eyes, but Babs turned away first, flipping the next card. It showed a turret, a tall crenellated tower made of stone, and overhead a lightning bolt hung ominously. The card read *The Tower*. Audrey stared at Babs.

"These are things that affect you now. The way your life is running. The tower represents revolution. Drastic change."

"Where is my son?" whispered Audrey.

Babs sighed, flipping the next card. It showed a Romanesque warrior in a chariot wielding two spears. It was titled *The Chariot*.

"These are your inner emotions," said Babs.

Audrey stared at the card, taking in the wicked-looking spear points, the determined look on the warrior's face. She nodded, staring her question back into Babs's eyes.

Babs flipped the last card.

Audrey knew what it represented without being told. The figure was as old as time. Babs glanced away from the faceless monk with the skeletal hands and the scythe, but again, Audrey caught her eye. The air in the room had gone deathly still. Audrey thought she could hear the candles flickering, but they didn't seem to be giving as much light as before.

"What does this represent?" hissed Audrey, barely able to catch her breath.

Babs shook her head. "You need to let me take in the entire feel of the lay. I have to have time to commune with the cards—"

"What does it represent?"

Babs sighed. "The last card is supposed to symbolize the final result. But you haven't let me work. You can't just read one card at a time."

Audrey stared at Babs, waiting. Babs refused to speak, pretending to study the cards.

"It represents death," said Audrey.

Babs nodded slowly.

"My son is going to die," whispered Audrey.

"What?" said Babs.

"I can feel him. So close. I can see his face. Almost touch him. I know he's alive. All I want to know is where he is."

"But your son was taken over a year ago."

Audrey glared at her. "So?"

Babs shook her head. "I only meant—"

"Meant what?"

"I'm sure you're right. I'm sure he's okay."

"I didn't say he was okay," said Audrey. "I said he was alive. Now you're telling me he's going to die. I don't believe it."

"The cards didn't say your son was going to die."

"What?" said Audrey, grasping for any other answer.

Babs shook her head. "The card signifies death, it's true, but it can mean the death of a relationship as well as other things. Or it might be someone else who dies. I need more time with the cards and I need to touch you again."

"Touch me?"

"I need to sense you in order to find out what the cards are trying to reveal."

Audrey held out her hand and Babs gently flipped it, laying her own palm across the back of Audrey's wrist. Babs closed her eyes and Audrey could have sworn she actually felt something pass between them, like a flittering electrical jolt. When Babs opened her eyes, she studied the cards with a new intensity, but Audrey didn't like the way she glanced nervously from card to card.

"What is it?" asked Audrey.

Babs shook her head. "Just as I suspected," she said at last. "You have to take in the fullness of the lay. I see you being reborn, Audrey. You're going to come out of this terrible time that has held you prisoner for so long and find the power within you to live again."

"And the death card?"

"We all die."

"That's all it means?"

Babs seemed to take longer than she should in answering. "That's all it means."

But Audrey knew she was lying. She and Babs had both discovered a deeper truth here today, but both truths might not be the same, and neither wanted to speak about them to the other. Audrey rose slowly to her feet, watching Babs's face closely. The woman seemed to have an inner pain of her own that she had not sensed before.

Finally Babs came around the table to guide Audrey to the door, but she pointedly never made contact with Audrey again. As Babs stood inside and Audrey outside the house, Audrey turned to look at Babs one last time.

"Do you know anything about the disappearance of my son?" she asked.

Babs stared past Audrey, as though trying to gather the daylight into the darkness behind her eyes. When she shook her head, Audrey knew that she was unsure of her answer.

"Not in the way that you mean. But everything happens for a reason, Audrey. You keep that in mind."

"What reason could there have been for my son to disappear?"

Babs stared at her with infinite sadness in her eyes. "Try to always remember the good," she said. "That's all we can do, really. Remember the good."

"If you know anything, please tell me."

"I'm sorry. I just read cards," said Babs, closing the door in Audrey's face.

Babs sat back down in front of the lay, her hands resting flat on the table to still their shaking. It wasn't just the terrible tale the cards had revealed for Audrey that rocked her. It was the strange sensation she had gotten when they had touched. It was as though she had suddenly made contact with a part of her own past. As though Audrey were not a real person standing in her living room, but some specter from Babs's subconscious, half-dream, half-nightmare.

Ghastly images had assailed her so fast she couldn't interpret them except as some kind of horrible montage. In a split second it had occurred to her that she was both reading Audrey's mind and remembering events from her own past. But how could that be? She didn't have any memory loss and, as far as she knew, she and Audrey had never met.

But how stupid a thought was that? Would she be aware of memory loss?

She stared at the cards, trying to wring more meaning from them. It was a truly terrible lay. Even worse than she had revealed to Audrey, since most of the cards had come up reversed and she had simply turned them over to face her without Audrey noticing. Reversed cards weren't just opposite in meaning, they were bad. Very bad.

Audrey's life was a shambles and it was going to get worse. Like everyone else who knew about the tragedy, Babs assumed that Audrey's son was dead. But whether or not that was true, more disaster and death was heading her way, and since there was nothing that Babs could see in the cards that could be done about it, she had chosen not to tell Audrey. Best to let life come as it would. She prayed that one of the deaths she foresaw at the end of the lay would not be Audrey's, but there was no way of telling. The lay was filled with horror. Babs had never read one like it.

But it wasn't even just the cards or the strange sense of kinship with Audrey that had her on edge. Babs's mind was churning. The more she stared at the picture of the high priestess, the more it seemed to speak to her. Sometimes Babs liked that card. Sometimes she didn't. The image could conjure pictures of a powerful, righteous Earth Mother. It could also elicit feelings of a conniving, venomous witch. It was the picture of the witch that Babs couldn't get out of her head now. The more she stared at the card, the more she didn't see it. Instead, she saw a vague semblance of a real person. Someone she should remember but couldn't quite.

Maybe she *did* have some memory loss.

She dragged all the cards together, getting a residual sense of gloom just from their touch, and stacked them neatly. She wiped her hands over and over on her skirt. Finally, she flipped the switch by the door, turning on the overhead light for the first time in years. She just couldn't seem to dispel the darkness.

28

AUDREY RETURNED TO RICHARD'S OFFICE in a daze. She didn't know what to make of the strange session with the St. Clair woman. She was disturbed and confused. But she wasn't crazy. She clung to that thought. Something was going on around her that was beyond her comprehension, and the woman and her tarot deck had barely touched upon it. Audrey bore herself as calmly as possible in front of Richard, explaining that she had a terrible headache and simply wanted to go home. He drove her there without comment, stopping in the kitchen to get her a glass of water and a couple of aspirin that she dutifully took. He also brought her the Halcion and wouldn't go back to the office until she swallowed one, hating the feel of the pill sliding down her throat, feeling *violated* by it. He didn't make her stick out her tongue to prove she'd taken the medicine. But she knew he wanted to.

Now she sat at the table trying to *think* the drug out of her head. She'd dutifully taken the pills every day since Doctor Cates had started her on them. But the Halcion hadn't gotten rid of the visions the way she'd hoped. Instead, it had turned them into hideous misty images that not only appeared on any shiny surface, but followed her through the house, playing on the back of her eyelids. Instead of feeling as though she were in contact with Zach, the drug was a barrier, allowing her to see but not touch. She no longer felt the sense of contact, the sense of immediacy. She knew the images *meant* something, but she couldn't seem to reason out what it was any longer. There was still a sense of horror in her silent dreams. But it was the distant horror of a scary movie, not the immediate terror of a mother watching her firstborn in peril. It frustrated her even through her haze.

Richard thought she was sleeping soundly each night. What she was doing was wandering through her dreams, crying out silently for Zach, searching for him, since he no longer appeared to her. She was more exhausted now than she had been during her night terrors. But she hid the fact from Richard that the medicine was worse than the cure, because she didn't have the strength or the presence of mind to face another argument over Tara with him. Not while she was under the influence of the drug. That was why she'd made up her mind the night before. She was getting off the pills and going to work with Doctor Cates to rip her demons out into the open once and for all.

But now Richard had tripped her up, forcing her to take one of the damned things again.

The pattern in the laminated tabletop writhed like a mass of black-and-white snakes, weaving in and out of itself. She listened to the scratchy sound of her own breathing and tried to focus on the hallucination in front of her rather than the picture that wanted to burn itself into the front of her brain. She couldn't do it. The picture of Richard's shrine in the basement kept torturing her.

Richard had hardly ever shown his pain. He'd never broken down in front of her. Even the shrine had been a way of hiding his hurt from her. He'd only taken things she hadn't remembered: old clothes, old toys. Zach's room upstairs was untouched. Richard's self-control and secrecy had led her to the reluctant conclusion that he didn't miss Zach the way she did. Didn't love him as much. She thought it was a guy thing.

But the memorial he'd constructed didn't fit her conception of Richard's grief. Every item of clothing, every toy, was clean, perfectly organized. Orderliness had always been the one point of contention between Richard and Zach. While Richard was neat to the point of obsession, Zach chose to

leave things where they fell. And no matter how much
Richard preached, no matter how much he tried to instill his
own pattern of living on Zach, it didn't take. Zach was going to grow up a free spirit.

Only now, Zach wasn't going to grow up.

As it always did, that thought stilled her breathing.

He's dead. My baby's dead. All the visions of Zach . . .
they're all just dreams. Insanity. Hallucinations.

She rested her head in her arms. Richard was right. They
weren't living. They were just existing in some kind of tortured limbo. She thought of him, alone in the cellar for
hours, dusting the bike, oiling the gears, polishing the lens
of the telescope. What was going on in his head all that
time?

She lifted the bottle of Halcion and stared at it, so light
in her hand. She shook it like a child's rattle. More like a
pacifier. Finally she took it to the counter and placed it in
the cupboard and closed the door. She stared at the kitchen
window, but it was just glass. Her neglected garden drew
her attention and she thought once again how it mirrored
her and Richard's relationship. She was killing that too. She
had to break out of this terrible trap somehow, and
she knew that Doctor Cates was only part of the answer. If
she and Richard were going to have any chance at a life,
then she had to start helping herself.

She *knew* instinctively that she'd made a mistake burying
her past. No matter what she said, Tara was wrong. Audrey
knew that Tara had done what she had out of love. But her
treatment had been a mistake. And the drug was only making
things worse, distancing her from the things she needed to remember. She knew the cure she envisioned was going to be
terrible. Her gut clenched with fear of the unknown. What if
she had done something that needed to be forgotten? That
was her worst concern. What if Tara had done what she had,
to bury not only horror but also guilt?

Whatever it was, she was determined now to face it. She
was not only ready to see Doctor Cates again, she was anxious. Anxious to get on with her life. With the decision
made, a great weight lifted off her shoulders.

She picked up the phone and autodialed Richard, leaving
a message.

"Take me out to dinner," she said. She smiled, knowing how surprised he'd be when he got back to his office and realized the call was from her. "I mean it. I'll be dressed when you get here. I love you." As she said it, she realized just how deeply she meant it, how much different her life would be without him. She wasn't going to lose him now. She was going to do everything in her power to restore the life they'd shared before. Everything.

When she hung up the phone, she felt freer than she had in months. Even though she still felt lethargic from the Halcion, she felt strong, almost lighthearted. She even took a couple of hours to sit at the desk in the living room and work on her long-ignored manuscript, compiling a list of plants that she needed to research so that she could begin a list of growing periods and fertilization requirements. The one thing she wasn't ready to do was enter her garden. But she did stand in the back doorway and give it fair warning.

"I'm coming back. Not today. Today, I'm taking off. Richard and I are going out to dinner tonight. We're going to come home, make love, and go to sleep. Tomorrow, I'm coming out there." She didn't feel in the least funny talking to the air outside. It gave her a sense of control over the inanimate world around her. The plants couldn't talk back. They couldn't mock her. They couldn't tell her she was going crazy.

At five o'clock sharp she decided to get ready. She felt like a young girl preparing for a first date, choosing an outfit she hadn't worn in ages—tight-fitting skirt, light spring sweater, and a pair of high boots. She thought the combination made her look like a tart, but she knew Richard would like it. She laid the clothes out on the bed and took a shower. When she returned, she put on the ensemble and sat on the edge of the bed, brushing her hair.

Glancing at the bedroom window, she recalled the face she had seen there.

I didn't see it. Richard said no one was there. It was all in my head. Just like the image in the kitchen window.

The face wouldn't leave her mind. She brushed harder, bearing down, scraping her scalp, but it wouldn't go away. She felt as though the face in the night had been more than just a frightful image. It had been meant as a *reminder.* Her mind was trying to tell her something.

She closed her eyes, and—steeling herself—for the first time ever, she tried to get a glimpse behind the doors that she and Tara had so laboriously constructed. She tried to relax, taking long slow breaths, picturing her thrumming heart easing to a stop. Slowly at first, images came to mind and, instead of recoiling from them, she let them come. Suddenly a picture of a hideous metal mask shimmered in front of her eyes and she shuddered, but she gritted her teeth and tried to see *beyond* the mask, to rip the rest of the weird memory out of its box in her mind. To open it and face it. Each subsequent flash seemed to reveal just a little more. But she couldn't quite get it. Couldn't meld the flood of images into a coherent whole.

Instead of memories from her early childhood, she caught weird glimpses of her years with Tara, as though she were standing outside herself, watching their therapy sessions. She had the odd sensation of hearing Tara's droning voice without being able to make out the words. Her own voice was unintelligible as well.

The trouble was that Audrey didn't have *any* clear memories of her childhood at all. Not the time spent with her mother or most of the early years with Tara. She seemed to have emerged at around seventeen like a butterfly from a chrysalis, unable to recall anything of her caterpillar youth.

She remembered Richard asking her about her childhood when she was eighteen, before Tara had warned him not to. It had shocked Audrey to learn that he remembered so much of his. By that time, it had become normal for Audrey to assume that childhood was a fog for everyone. Her therapy had progressed to the point at which she no longer wanted to know about her past. Her curiosity had been erased along with her memories and she had been left with an ingrained fear of disturbing them.

She had tried to help herself after Zach was taken, using the tools that Tara had given her, closing more doors, hiding away the hurt. Had she somehow buried feelings for Zach that she should have allowed their rightful time, their rightful place in her grief? Had she taken the easy way out and in doing so, stuck herself in Neverland? She lay back on the bed and spread her hands and feet, relaxing, taking longer, deeper breaths. First she imagined her feet going to sleep, growing so heavy they wanted to sink through the mattress, then her legs, her torso, finally her head. She couldn't move now if she'd wanted to. She began to count backward from one hundred, telling herself over and over that she was falling into a deep restful sleep. She blanked out her thoughts and pictured blackness.

With practiced slowness, she began to place herself into a trance.

29

A SMALL FLOWER ARRANGEMENT nestled on the seat beside Richard, filling the car with the smell of roses. The call from Audrey had been unexpected. She sounded happy and alert, almost like the old Audrey, the one he hadn't spoken to in over a year. Obviously the pill had relieved her headache as well as her depression, at least for the moment. Maybe they'd do a movie. They hadn't been out for a night together since he couldn't remember when.

He wondered why the drugs had worked, and Audrey's self-hypnosis seemed to be losing its power. Could it be that there was something wrong with her brain? Something chemical? Neither of the doctors had said so. But the thought nagged at him.

He pulled into the drive and turned off the car, forcing the worry from his mind. Stepping up to the door, he glanced across the lawn, and remembered the footprints. His eyes traced what would have been the path of the tracks. He could still picture them clearly in his mind, surrounded by glistening dew, and a heavy hand seemed to settle on his shoulder. He hadn't wanted to acknowledge their presence then and he certainly didn't want them intruding on his thoughts now. But as he stared across the empty lawn, he knew that he had been wrong to erase them with his foot, wrong not to at least mention them to Audrey.

Climbing slowly down off the side stoop, he strode over

to the bedroom window. Audrey was napping on the bed. The footprints were gone, of course, the grass risen back into place, but he remembered the location and direction close enough. He strode out across the lawn and, when he reached the edge of the garden, he picked his way through the mulch, careful not to disturb any of Audrey's perennials. Fifty yards above him lay a saddle in the hills, a dip like a rifle sight. He stared at the thick bracken and alders and then down at his suit and dress shoes. This was silly. He probably *had* imagined the footprints.

Only he was increasingly certain that he hadn't. Someone *had* been spying in their bedroom window.

If you believe that, then why don't you call the sheriff? Why don't you tell Audrey?

Tell them what? That there were footprints on the lawn, but now they were gone?

The saddle in the slope was in a direct line with their bedroom window and the lay of the footprints he had seen in the night, but it looked like easier going off to the right, making a wide sweep *around* the worst of the undergrowth. By the time he had clawed halfway up to the top of the hill, his face was scratched by branches and his hands were chafed and raw. Burrs clung to his pants and jacket, he was breathing heavily, and he considered turning back.

He glanced up at the notch in the ridge and then back toward the house. Equally far either way now. But the house was downhill. And what did he think he was looking for up here anyway? What did he hope to prove? Even if there had been a trespasser, no one was going to be up here now. He glanced back up the slope. What the hell, he was already halfway there and covered with debris. He grabbed a branch and dragged himself up another couple of steps.

The ground was loose beneath his feet. Twice he stumbled to his knees, catching himself on the thorny brush. By the time he forced his way through the last of the bracken and stumbled to the top of the ridge, his hands were bloody and his lungs stung. He stood there for a moment, hands fisted on his hips, chest heaving, staring across a grassy clearing at the backside of the Coonts farm.

He glanced at the old farm, then back down the slope behind him, to his and Audrey's bedroom, and a chill ran up his spine. He recalled Audrey's terror attack when they'd passed the farm. Like she knew something. Or *felt* something. But that was crazy.

It surprised him how close they actually lived to Merle Coonts. In the car it was a five-minute trip around the looping road to their drive. Yet he had traversed half the distance between them on foot in that time, by simply climbing the hill.

Could someone really be hiking over from the farm in the middle of the night to peek in their windows? But why in the hell would anyone in their right mind do that?

Maybe they *weren't* in their right mind. That thought chilled him almost as much as the one that followed tight on its heels.

Maybe it wasn't the neighbor's tracks he'd seen. Maybe they were Audrey's. He couldn't really tell, after all, which way the prints were coming from. They were just impressions in the damp grass.

Maybe *she* had climbed up the hill to see what was there. She'd seen the old house and it got into her subconscious. That and Zach's disappearance, coupled with God only knew what kind of leftovers from her past, had sizzled around in her head and pretty soon she'd invented some woman kidnapping Zach and keeping him in the basement next door. What better place to have it happen than an old beat-up farmhouse?

But Audrey would never have been so intrepid. Audrey was a home gardener, not a wilderness explorer. He glanced to his right and his heart caught in his throat.

There was a path.

Rather than straight down the slope, back the way he had come, it wound its way to the bottom. It hadn't been visible from below. From that vantage point, all he had seen was an impenetrable thicket. But looking down on the alders, he could make out the winding pattern of a trail. A trail that looked man-made.

No. He couldn't believe that. It had to be an animal path, or the natural growth pattern of the underbrush.

But following its sweep, he spotted the entrance to it a few yards to his right, and he hurried over, anxious to check it out, still more anxious to be back on familiar ground. He tried to lock the trail into his mind, lest he lose it halfway down.

By the time he reached the back side of Audrey's garden again, he felt as though he had completed a marathon. His suit was in shambles. His shoes were scratched beyond repair and his pants were torn. He climbed the back stoop and stood for a moment, glancing back up the hill, a terrible muddle of possibilities swirling in his brain.

 **30**

AUDREY, DEEP IN HER SELF-INDUCED TRANCE, had lost all sense of body and time.

She wandered down a dark hallway that she knew was not a part of her past or her present. It was simply a construct that existed in her mind. She dimly recalled helping Tara build it, piece by piece. Remembered the audible *click* of each of the doors closing, sealing off a part of herself, protecting Audrey from the past. But now she wondered if that was really what they had accomplished.

The walls of the corridor seemed solid as stone. And the doors were thick and strong. She remembered Tara's singsong voice in the dim distance. "These doors are thicker than they are wide, Audrey. The locks are made of a special steel that cannot be cut or melted. There is no key. When we close these doors, no power on earth will be able to open them again. No one must ever open these doors."

Audrey stared at the door in front of her and she shuddered. She glanced down the rest of the long hallway and hurried on past that door. She didn't want to be near it, much less touch it. She was after answers and something told her that behind that door lay answers. But they were answers that might destroy her. And there was something different about that door in other ways. She seemed to recall building it by *herself*. But it didn't have anything to do with Zach. She knew that.

It had to do with her alone.

The farther down the corridor she traveled, the darker it became, until she could hardly see her hand in front of her face. She was approaching the final door, the door to her earliest memories. And it was open. She floated inexorably toward it, like a leaf adrift on a river current. She reached for the walls, but they receded from her grasp and she was swept forward into the waiting darkness.

She heard laughter first. A sweet remembered sound. The laughter of a little girl. Exactly like her own laughter. Only Audrey knew immediately that it wasn't her. It was Paula.

Paula?

Why was that name so familiar? She didn't recall ever knowing anyone named Paula, and yet she knew her intuition was correct.

As the laughter swelled, the darkness diminished, and Audrey opened her eyes in another world. She was a small child again and she danced with childish abandon. A mirror image of herself held her by the hands, and the pair spun round and round until they collapsed into a dizzy huddle on the summer grass.

Audrey was stunned, staring at the little girl as though she were a ghost.

Paula. My twin. The girl in the mirror. How could I have forgotten her? Why was her memory so terrible that Tara had to lock it away behind this door? What happened to Paula?

But she knew. Or at least she sensed some of what was to come, and the horror dimmed the daylight around her. Paula was the faceless little girl in her visions. The girl behind the mask.

The girls—no more than five or six and clad in tan romper suits—laughed and rolled in the grass. This was the recorded memory of a brief, wonderful moment in her past and she tried to hold onto the joy of it, but the young Audrey—through whose eyes the older Audrey was now looking—was not concerned with remembering. Had no idea of the terrible events about to unfold. She glanced at Paula offhandedly, then slowly around the white-fenced backyard.

Tall oak trees shaded the lawn. A swing set with an attached slide sat near the fence. A brightly painted doghouse guarded the center of the yard and a half-grown German shepherd tugged playfully at the end of a leash attached to it, wanting to join in the fun.

Gidown.

Audrey had named the dog because he was always on the furniture. Her mother was constantly shouting at him, "Gidown!" and the dog would slink away with a canine grin, chastised but unrepentant. A small boy hid behind the doghouse, whistling through his teeth and teasing the dog. Her brother, Craig.

Forgotten. Just like Paula.

He was ten years old. Dark-haired, with dark eyes. Like Zach. A heavy weight suddenly settled on Audrey's heart. How could I have allowed myself to forget Craig and Paula? Why did I have to?

Audrey's vision followed the high white fence back to the house. The old building appeared giant from her child's perspective. The wide eaves two stories over her head hung from the cloudless sky. The house was as well cared for as the fence, freshly painted siding, double-hung windows gleaming in the sun. The back door opened and a small, dark-haired woman stepped out into the shade of the porch, searching the backyard.

Audrey's imagined breath caught in her throat. She thought the woman was Tara—a much younger Tara than she remembered. But realization struck her like a blow.

Not Tara. Mother.

Whenever Audrey had tried to picture her mother, the only image that appeared was that of an old crone. A snarl-haired witch with close-set black eyes and a warty face. A woman garbed in filthy clothing who lived in shadows. Audrey didn't know whether the picture she had of her mother was real or whether she had simply created it to fit the hateful half-memories that haunted her. The woman she envisioned dragging the little girl into the basement bore no resemblance to the woman she now saw standing in the light of that long-ago day.

How could this beautiful woman have changed in a few short years into the horrible monster that Audrey recalled?

Had she somehow caused her mother to metamorphose into the dark creature that she remembered? Was that the guilt that she was so terrified of discovering?

Her mother called for Craig, who argued. The dog spotted him at last and raced around its house to place his front feet on the boy's shoulders. Both girls stared at the boy and Audrey noticed that she could sense Paula's feelings toward Craig. Love, respect, awe.

Craig finally gave up the fight and disappeared inside the house with their mother, and for some time the girls played quietly together, swinging and skipping rope. But something had changed. A dark cloud seemed to have slipped over the sun. The day dimmed and Audrey knew that all was not right inside their home.

Paula was the first to notice. She stared at the still-open back door and her easy smile was now a straight-lipped look of concentration. She turned back to face Audrey and shook her head.

Time flashed. Clouds scudded eerily fast across the lowering sky before their mother returned to the back porch. She seemed to have shriveled, dropping down onto the top step and staring out across the yard with empty eyes. The girls ran to her and crowded near like ducklings fearing a storm. Their mother seemed not to notice them at first.

"He's gone," she said.

The words echoed down through the years and struck Audrey in the center of her heart.

He's gone.

They were words she'd heard in her childhood, and then words she had spoken herself. Words she hated more than any others she could think of. What could have possibly happened inside that house in that brief period of time?

Where had he gone?

Their mother shook her head, still staring blankly out across the fence into the distance.

"He's gone," she repeated. She turned to look at each of them in turn and drew them close. A mother duck, shielding her brood. But why hadn't she shielded Craig? What had happened to him? Had she taken him down into the cellar? Was that what this memory was about? Or was something else happening here? Was this even the same day that Craig had gone into the house with Mother?

Audrey wanted desperately to ask so many questions, but she was locked inside another body in another time and she could only relive events as they were revealed to her.

What have you done with him? she wanted to scream. As she looked into the tortured eyes and face of the woman before her now, she began to sense the madness that would become the greater part of her mother in the coming years.

"He's gone."

It struck Audrey again how much like Zach Craig had looked. Could it have been Craig's face she'd seen in the kitchen window? In the fountain? Was that what happened? Was the answer to Craig's disappearance locked away somewhere, back down that long corridor? Was the truth of his vanishing so terrible that it, too, had to be sealed tightly away from her conscious mind?

If she could open those doors and find out what had happened to Craig, then perhaps she could put the boy in her visions to rest. It would mean that she had been wrong about them, that there was no hope for Zach, but perhaps she would finally be able to say good-bye to him.

She jerked away from the memory of her siblings and her mother, now frozen like a photograph, and stepped back through the door into the long corridor again. There was a pressure change at the doorway, as though she were being sucked once more into the present from the vacuum of her past. A whispered voice skittered down the hallway, calling her name, and it took her a moment to recognize the source.

Richard.

As his voice grew more strident, she felt her body shake and she opened her eyes. Richard held her upright, gripping both her upper arms.

"Jesus, Audrey," he said, easing her back onto the bed. "Are you all right? Can you hear me?"

"Of course I can hear you," she said, sitting up and stretching. Even though she remembered everything she had just experienced, she felt better than she had in months. She was more confused than ever about her past, but now she knew that she *could* open the doors. Before, she had only wanted to.

"I was afraid you'd OD'd on those pills. You were out like a light."

He was wearing his bathrobe and his hair was still wet from the shower.

"I didn't hear you come in," she said, studying his face. "You've got a scratch."

He shook his head. "It's nothing. Tell you about it over dinner, okay?" He looked as though he had something more to say but didn't know how to say it.

"Sure," she said, sliding around him to get off the bed. She was surprised to see that it was already dark outside. "There are some things I need to tell you too."

He watched her straightening her blouse. "How about a nice candlelight dinner at home? I'll thaw out a couple of steaks."

"I thought you were going to take me out."

"I just thought it would be nice for us to be alone."

"Okay," she said, kissing his cheek. "That would be nice."

31

RICHARD WAS ENJOYING the silence in the house for a change, staring across the kitchen table at Audrey. She was so beautiful and so vulnerable that he wanted to take her in his arms and carry her away somewhere safe. She did seem better, but he still wasn't sure Doctor Cates had been the right decision. He wanted to call Tara, but Audrey didn't want to see her. Tara had explained to him why it was so hard for Audrey to have any kind of relationship with her anymore.

"She's been hurt, Richard. Hurt more than you can possibly imagine. We've had to lock away so much of her past that Audrey *has* no past, and a part of her blames me for that. And she's afraid that if I try to help her, she'll lose Zach the way she's had to lose her childhood."

"It wasn't *your* fault."

"No. And on some level Audrey knows that. But I was the one in the chair across from her all those years, making her forget."

"I'm sorry."

"I'm sorry too. But I'll always be here for Audrey. And for you. I want you to know that."

That was the day Tara had left their house; the last time he'd seen her. He leaned across the table now and took Audrey's hand. She smiled back at him shyly, as though the expression had faded from disuse.

"Are you sure you're all right?" he asked.

"Better than I've been in a long time," she said, but she frowned when she spoke. "I'm figuring some things out."

"You seem distracted."

"So what's new?"

"Did you take your medicine?"

She glanced through the glass doors, out across the backyard, and he squeezed her hand.

"Audrey?"

"We'll talk after dinner. Can't we have a nice dinner?"

"All right. I'm sorry."

Richard sipped his wine and pronounced it suitable. Audrey chuckled under her breath.

"What?" he said.

"You wouldn't know a good year from vinegar."

"I beg your pardon. I took a wine appreciation class at college."

"You did not!"

"I went to a lot of frat parties."

"That I can believe."

"I haven't seen you smile like that in over a year."

"You haven't smiled much either."

They chatted quietly, steering clear of Zach's disappearance, clear of children, clear of Audrey's night terrors. They spoke instead of gardening and accounting. Until Audrey felt the time had come. "I have something to tell you."

Richard shook his head, wiping his lips on his napkin. "Me first."

"All right."

He dropped the napkin onto the table and pushed back in his chair, staring at the white lace tablecloth as though reading cues from it. When he sighed loudly, Audrey knew he was having trouble with the words. She hadn't expected whatever he was going to say to be quite so important to him and a tiny twinge of fear surged through her.

"Whatever it is," she said, "just say it."

"I love you."

"I know that. I love you too. Was that so hard to say?"

He lowered his chin down onto his chest and stared her straight in the eyes. "I think maybe there *was* someone in our backyard. I think maybe you *did* see someone."

"What?"

He took a long time before answering, gathering his thoughts. "I should have told you, but I was afraid my imagination was running away with me. I found footprints under the window."

"Oh, my God!"

He shook his head. "It might not mean anything, Audrey. Maybe they were old prints."

"*Whose* old prints? Why would they be underneath our window?"

"I don't know. But I'm going to find out. I'll talk to the sheriff tomorrow."

"Call him tonight."

"I don't have anything to tell him. The prints are gone. Maybe it's just all in *both* our heads. We've both been under a lot of stress. You have to admit it *sounds* crazy."

"I don't care how it sounds anymore."

"I'll call Sheriff Milche tomorrow."

"Promise?"

He nodded.

"What if Zach's in that old house down the road?"

Richard sighed. "Audrey, *that's* crazy. The sheriff told you all about the investigation. He checked out *everyone*. Nobody around here was involved. And even if the guy is a Peeping Tom, that doesn't have anything to do with Zach. Don't let your imagination run away with you."

"I'm not letting my imagination run away with me. I can feel Zach! Or I could until I started taking those damned pills."

"The pills are helping you."

"No, they're not. I know you think they are. But they make things worse, not better. I'm doing what you wanted. I *want* to work with Doctor Cates now. But I'm not going to take the pills anymore."

He sighed again. "Are you sure about that?"

She nodded, determination set deep in her eyes.

He reached out and took her hand again. "Okay, then. As long as you think Doctor Cates can help. I'll be right beside you all the way."

She squeezed his hand.

"You seem like you have more to say," she said.

He took a deep breath and when he spoke he put all the sincerity he had in his words. "I don't want to have any-more children."

"But you said . . . After all our arguments?"

"I've thought about it a lot. I know what having more kids would mean to you."

"But—"

"Let me finish. I was being selfish and I realize that now. Our marriage means more to me than anything in the world."

"Richard—"

"I'm serious."

"Stop!"

He stared at her with the most guileless face she had ever seen in her life. If Richard had told her at that instant that he had signed up for the astronaut program and been ac-cepted, she would have believed him.

"I should have gone first," she said.

"Why?"

"Well, for one thing, I don't want you to give up on hav-ing another baby."

"Are you serious?"

"Yes. I mean, not yet. Not right now. But someday."

The relief in his eyes was so evident it was painful to look at. "That's fine, Audrey. Whenever you're ready will be fine."

"I just have some things to work through with Doctor Cates. Then we can think about the future."

"Fine. Whatever you say. It's just that, well, you know, Doctor Cates is going to dig things up. Are you absolutely sure that's what you want to do?"

She took a deep breath and closed her eyes. "Richard, there's something going on in my head, and it's going to drive me crazy if I don't find out what it is. Even if it's bad, I think I can face it. What I can't face is the not knowing. I had a twin sister, Richard."

"What? Are you sure?"

"Yes."

"What happened to her?"

"I'm not certain. But I know it was bad. It had to do with the mask I've been dreaming about."

"You never said anything about a mask."

"I didn't?" She shook her head and frowned. "I had a brother too."

"Audrey, are you sure these are real memories?"

"They aren't hallucinations."

"I didn't mean that. But sometimes our mind makes up things in our past. I forget what it's called, but I've read about it. That's why eyewitness testimony is so easy to beat in court."

Audrey shook her head. "These aren't fill-in-the-blanks memories, Richard. It's not a question of whether or not someone was wearing a red shirt or a green one. I know their faces. I remember playing with them."

"When did you remember that?"

"This afternoon. I was practicing self-hypnosis."

"*That's* why I couldn't wake you. Why didn't you tell me?"

"You startled me, that's all."

"Well, if you think Doctor Cates can help, honey, then I'm all for it."

She withdrew her hand, smiling to let him know he shouldn't read anything into the gesture. "I know you think I'm crazy. But I still think the man in that old farmhouse has something to do with my dreams."

"You never said anything about a *man* in your dreams."

"There isn't one."

"Then how—"

"I don't know how. But I know it's true. Please don't think I'm insane."

"I don't think you're insane."

"You'll call the sheriff?"

"I promise. First thing tomorrow."

32

THE MASSIVE MULLIONED WINDOW diced the moonlight spilling into the room. The vaulted ceiling was two stories overhead, shrouded in gloom. An iron catwalk surrounded the open space on three sides, girding high bookshelves and a spiral staircase. The massive building dwarfed the woman and dog silhouetted by the frigid light.

Tara stared out at the distant hills. She was tired and wanted to go to bed, but her work wouldn't let her. She was close. So damned close. Unconsciously she massaged the two small scars on her left bicep, inflicted years before by one of her patients. Her eyes gleamed in the yellow light, while her small form below the neck was obscured beneath a light blanket. Beside her leather armchair, Adler rested his jowls on crossed paws and stared out into the night with her.

Tara had been sitting in silent meditation for over three hours. She was perfectly capable of maintaining her present state until dawn, but she had no intention of doing so. The light trance was simply a way of recharging her batteries, relieving stress and focusing her mind. The dog noticed immediately when Tara began to return to her body. The merest blinking of her eyelids alerted Adler and he *woofed* gently. Tara stretched her neck, then her shoulders and arms, stopping to lean and pat the dog before rising and completing her postmeditation exercises.

She flipped on the lamp over her desk and fingered the two thick manila folders. Closing her eyes she could recite line for line, page after page, from the hundreds of miscellaneous reports, affidavits, and records. She could pull either patient's face into the front of her mind from a mental database that was as accurate and probably faster than any police computer on the planet. Her hard files were stored mostly for management and organizational purposes, but now there was little to manage.

Not that losing either her license or her government funding had ever really affected her. If anything, the newfound freedom had given a boost to her experimentation. Before, she'd had to operate within the constraints of the system. After she lost her legal facade, she became autonomous. True, there were no research grants, and no large institutions with their endless supplies of research material would hire her. But she had no monetary worries. By the time her license was revoked, she had already made a fortune on her book sales, and few people thought to connect her name with a little-known government program.

Thinking of her books reminded her of her meditation. Usually Tara would fall into a deep state of oblivion when she meditated. But occasionally something transpired in her subconscious, ideas jelled, memories synthesized into new insights, and she had discovered some incredible revelations upon returning to the present.

Like tonight.

Enough bits and pieces had wormed their way out of her subconscious mind for her to develop a picture. She could hardly believe the fatal line of coincidences that had occurred in order to turn her carefully constructed fortress into a house of cards, but believe it or not, she had to take action now.

She shuffled aside a chart marked 79B and picked up another, unlabeled. Laminated and taped to the folder was a color photo of a young girl, about ten, with straight blond hair and piercing eyes. The look on the girl's face was what the Marines called the thousand-yard stare. It was clear that the adolescent had witnessed more than her mind could assimilate. Anyone glancing at the photo might wonder if there was any hope at all for the child.

Failures.

79B and Audrey both.

The thought of Audrey as a failure bothered Tara deeply. Richard hadn't called back since informing her that Audrey had gone to see Cates. Why? He was supposed to call immediately anytime Audrey showed signs of dredging up her past. If she was starting to pry at the doors in her mind, something needed to be done. And she certainly shouldn't be talking to another psychiatrist.

And not only psychiatrists!

She stared at the phone on her desk, listening to the last call again in her head, word for word.

"She went to see Babs St. Clair."

Tara hadn't been able to believe what she was hearing. What insanity was that? Audrey had no connection to the St. Clair woman. Tara had never cared for the coincidence that had led Babs St. Clair to choose to live so close to Audrey. But the likelihood of the two of them ever meeting seemed remote and even if they did, what harm could it cause? But that had been before Babs started blurting out information on the Timothy Merrill case. *That* revelation had been a stunner. There was no way for Babs to know anything about the case. No way.

"Why?"

"I don't know."

"What did she do after?"

"Her husband drove her home."

"Keep doing as I told you." She held a ballpoint pen close to the receiver and clicked it once. "Portal," she said.

The phone had gone dead.

Tara strode across the hallway to the elevator. The bright lights inside forced her to squint, but she found the button without looking, just as Adler leapt in beside her. The lift dropped precipitously and came to a sudden stop, but rather than exiting through the open doors, she turned and reached beneath the rectangular metal bar that ran around the perimeter of the elevator at waist height. With a barely audible *click,* the rear wall swung outward, revealing a dank, brick-lined corridor with missing floor tiles.

The air was thick with mildew and disinfectant and something else, something almost nauseating. The soft *whoosh* of the door closing behind her harmonized with the circulation system struggling valiantly overhead. The dog's panting breath sounded like a metronome as he loped along beside Tara.

She turned down a dark side corridor and stopped in front of a white metal door. Slipping a key from a thin gold chain around her neck, she opened the door and stood for a moment, preparing herself. The smell that the corridor had only hinted at, hit her full in the face. She stepped into the laboratory and the door hissed closed behind her.

No matter how high the ventilators were turned on, no matter how often she cleaned her laboratory, the odor of death would not leave it. The noxious smell of feces, urine, blood, vomit, disinfectants, and formaldehyde saturated the floor, walls, and ceiling.

She knew that she was overly sensitized to it, when she should have been completely indifferent after all these years. It was because she was such a sensitive person that she had taken to her chosen field to begin with. Since childhood, Tara had been drawn to people with problems. She was a fixer by nature. And the one thing that she could not stand was other people telling her how to do things. She knew how things had been done in the past. Freud and Jung and all the others. She had named her dog Adler because she thought the Doberman exhibited more sense than the man.

Against one wall of the white, tiled room, a small boy, clad in a set of Barney boxer shorts, sat strapped tightly into a wheelchair. His head was encased in a metal helmet with red and gold electrical wires attached in a polka-dot pattern upon it. Bright adjustable lights circled him. The walls were hidden behind glass cabinets filled with bottles and jars, and strange electronic equipment in green and blue and gray stood around like a silent computerized audience.

Tara stood beside the chair and stared down into what would have been the child's face, willing him to focus on her. When she felt nothing, she reached out and twisted one of the myriad dials attached to the face of the machine. Voltage raced through bright electrical wires taped to the boy's shaved head, and the smell of ozone and singed flesh was added to the ghastly stench. Tara calmly watched read-outs on monitors placed strategically over the boy.

She had never wanted to hurt anyone. But she could when she had to. This was about her life's work. About the development of mankind. And she wasn't going to make any more mistakes.

From now on, the doors she closed would stay closed.

THE TERROR

All the things one has forgotten scream
for help in dreams.

—Elias Canetti,
The Human Province

33

COODER SCRUBBED THE DENTED SOUP POT, ignoring the nickel-sized pieces of Teflon that floated away into the big old slate sink, listening to a Grateful Dead song in his head, and enjoying the vibration of the steel wool in his hands. Cooder lived a frugal life, but to him it seemed full enough.

Gas was delivered monthly so his stove worked, and state checks and food stamps covered his basic needs. Since he wasn't particular about his clothes, he wore them for years. The phone and power had long since been turned off, but he kept a five-gallon can of kerosene beside his chair, to refill his three oil lamps, and they gave him all the light he needed. His water was gravity-fed from a spring in the hill out back, but it only came in cold. That was all right with Cooder. A sponge bath or a good splash now and then in the summer was all he needed, and besides, he got rained on enough on his endless walks.

The noonday sun bounced off the windshield of the Chevy half-buried in the backyard, splintering rainbow patterns across the kitchen window. Normally he would have been caught in the colors like a deer in a headlight, but ever since Virgil's visit, Cooder had been tickling at something hard and crusty in the dusty back side of his brain.

The pot clanged into the bottom of the wide stone trough and Cooder dropped into his sitter, a recliner so ancient it looked as though it had been reclaimed not once but twice from a Dumpster. He propped his feet on an apple crate and crossed both hands on his stomach. Then he closed his eyes and tried to remember what it was that had been gnawing at him.

I seen bad things, Virg.

Now why had he said that? What was he talking about? It was as though he had opened his mouth and a stranger's voice had spit out. Only it wasn't a stranger, it was his voice and his words and he knew right off, without being told, that they were true and he had wanted to say them. But as soon as Virgil had asked him what he was talking about, the thought had raced out of his sieve of a head.

He *had* seen bad things. He dreamed about them sometimes, and sometimes the pills didn't get rid of all of them the next day. They drifted through his mind like phantoms, turning his wake-up time into a nightmare. It was then that he went walking. Only outside, with the wind in his face and the open sky overhead and his feet *nick-nick-nicking* along on hard asphalt, could he get any relief.

He had awakened in the night with a flash so bright in his head that he was unable to breathe. Pain struck from all directions. Pain he'd felt before. He'd struggled to his feet, leaning against the wall with his fingernails digging into the decaying plaster, the sound of it falling to the floor like sand in an hourglass, dribbling away the minutes of his life. He hadn't been able to get back to sleep in bed, finally curling up in his sitter and drifting off again just before dawn.

He'd been thinking about the flash all through his oatmeal. All through his coffee. All through the ritual of washing dishes. He thought about it now in the semi-comfort of his recliner. He couldn't figure out what it meant. Where it had come from. But he knew he *should* know what it was. He *should* remember what had caused it. Whenever he was just about sure he had something, a distorted image would shimmer across his mind and then melt into something completely different. Something that made no sense at all.

He recalled Virgil's visit and he wondered if somehow the pain and the weird flashes and Virgil had anything to do with one another. Virgil was looking for a little boy. Did Virgil think *he* might have seen the kid on one of his walks?

He *had* seen children. In fact, he thought he might have seen a lot of children. But which one was Virgil looking for?

He slammed his hands together and the slap echoed through the tiny house. With unusual vigor, he fumbled to his feet and stomped out the back door, not pausing on the stoop. When he reached the road out front, he was so intent on his walk that he was very nearly run down by a speeding semi. The roar of the air horn blasted away through the trees, but that was only a momentary distraction to Cooder.

Somewhere along his route, on one of his countless walks, something had gotten into his head. Something he had had to tell Virgil. But the thought had raced out of his mouth with the sound, and if he ever wanted to recapture it, then the only way that he could think of was to go and find it. The sun warmed his back and the wind was in his face.

Somewhere ahead, there were bad things to see.

34

THE DINER WAS DESERTED late on Saturday morning, and Mac and Virgil had a booth near the windows. Virgil had politely made it clear to the waitress that they wouldn't be needing anything more.

"Audrey Bock's maiden name was Remont," said Virgil. "Her mother's name was Martha Remont. She filed charges against Tara for trespassing in California before Tara took Audrey from her."

Mac's coffee mug seemed too big for him and he gripped it in both hands. "Quite a family."

"I have no information at all on Audrey's father. I have a hunch he died before Audrey knew him, but it's just a hunch." Virgil read from a spiral notepad on the table. "I need more info on Martha."

"You want me to look for the mother?"

Virgil shrugged. "If you can find her. Looks like she disappeared completely. Couldn't find hide or hair of her after Audrey begins to show up on her aunt's tax returns."

"How did you get Tara's tax returns?" said Mac, frowning.

Virgil grinned. "You're not the only one with friends."

"You're going out on a limb, Virg. What are you trying to prove?"

"I want to know what's going on with Audrey Bock."

Mac shook his head. "What's going on? Virg, the woman lost her only child."

"I think she had a lot of problems before that. Her husband called me this morning. He thinks they have a Peeping Tom at their house, but Audrey's convinced it's their next-door neighbor and that her son is locked up in his basement."

"Did you check it out?"

"Yeah. There's a trail behind the house real enough. But I couldn't find any tracks on it other than the husband's, and Merle Coonts was out of town on a trucking run the night it happened."

Standing in that notch in the hills, Virgil and Richard had stared at the back of Merle Coonts's house in silence until Richard spoke.

"Why would he come over here and peek in our windows?" he said, never taking his eyes off of the farm.

Virgil frowned. "We don't know that he did, Mister Bock."

Richard shook his head. "You saw the trail. I wasn't mistaken about the prints."

"You said they were small. Audrey says it was a woman at the window. Merle Coonts lives alone and if you'd ever seen his feet, you'd know they aren't small."

Richard sighed loudly. "I know it doesn't make any sense. But Audrey's so sure."

"I'll talk to Merle Coonts again," said Virgil, staring back down the trail, with Richard close behind. "Close your drapes tonight and lock your windows and doors."

"You'll let me know what you find out?"

"Of course."

But Merle was just coming back from another cross-country trip, and once again his logs held up. When Virgil mentioned the trail through the alders, he just shook his head and denied any knowledge of it.

Virgil stared at Mac now, hoping for a break. "What about you? Haven't found out anything for me?"

Mac glanced out the window. "Sorry. I've been really busy on another case. Sounds like you're finding out plenty all by your lonesome." Mac turned back. "What have you got on the mother?"

"A kid in California ran her address through his computer and it gave me names and phone numbers up and down the block. I called. But in California, everybody moves every couple of years. There's no one left that lived there eighteen years ago. So that was a dead end."

"Who else did you talk to?"

"I spoke to Motor Vehicles. Martha Remont hasn't had a license there since Audrey split. I also called the county registrar. She sold the house that year too. It's like she disappeared off the face of the earth. No tax returns. No license in another state."

"Could have been a Jane Doe."

"Maybe. Or maybe she just wanted to disappear."

"That takes a little expertise. Do you think Martha Remont had it?"

"I have no way of knowing what she had. Don't even know what she did for a living, if she worked."

"Did you get any information on Tara's background?"

Virgil shook his head. "She's retired. Had a respectable career. Lives alone near Augusta."

"That all?"

"She's fifty-two. Wrote a couple of best-selling books on self-hypnosis."

Mac made a face. "Hypnosis?"

"Yeah. Kinda do-it-yourself home therapy. Forget the bad things. Get on with your life."

Virgil set his cup on the table and reached into his vest pocket for another crumpled sheet of paper. "Graduated top of her class from Columbia in the late sixties. Another degree from Stanford. Did independent research work under Timothy Leary, for God's sake. She also worked with James Reins. Know the name?"

"Should I?"

"No. Unless you're into ESP and such. Reins worked for the government for a while on a project to spy on the Soviets using something called long-distance viewing."

"The U.S. government paid for that?"

"I guess they paid for a lot of goofy stuff during the Cold War. She worked at several institutions over the years on grants. I can't find anyone who knows anymore detail than that, regarding what the grants were for or what she was trying to accomplish. In the early eighties her funding was pulled and evidently enough of her colleagues disagreed with her methods strongly enough to have her license to practice revoked. I got the idea that even the government guys started to feel antsy about the way she was conducting her research. But by that time it didn't matter, since she had two best-selling books and could retire in luxury to her secluded home."

"Virgil," said Mac, leaning across the table, "do you suspect Tara Beals?"

Virgil frowned. "No."

"Ah . . . You suspect the kid's mother."

"I didn't say that."

"You've already asked me to look into Audrey Bock's past, and you're only investigating women, Virg. How many other women have I mentioned? You don't think the grandmother suddenly appeared out of nowhere and kidnapped her own grandson?"

"According to Audrey, her mother was crazy."

"Do you have any evidence linking the old lady to the disappearance of her grandson?"

"No. Like I say, I'm not even sure she's alive."

"Just a gut feeling?"

"Not even that."

"Then what?"

"I don't have anything else!"

"Jesus, Virg. You need to take some time off."

"That's the last thing I need."

"Well, I'm sorry I couldn't be more help. I'll see if I can dig up anything on Martha Remont as soon as I get a chance."

Virgil shrugged, studying him. "Are you okay?"

"Yeah," said Mac. "I'm okay. Why wouldn't I be?"

"No reason. You just seem distracted lately."

Mac sighed. "I'm thinking about getting out of here for a while."

"Where you going?"

"I don't care. I just need a break."

"Then you ought to take one." Virgil stared out the window for a moment and both men held on to the silence. When Virgil spoke again, he turned to face Mac. "I like bouncing stuff off you. If I told Birch or anyone else some of the stuff I'm thinking . . . you know."

"They'd think you were obsessing again."

"At the least," said Virgil, smiling.

"Virg, have you ever considered the possibility that maybe you are?"

"There's something strange going on in this county, and I'm going to find out what it is."

"Something like *what*?" said Mac, frowning.

"For one thing, Tara Beals is covering something up about Audrey."

"You spoke to Tara?"

Virgil nodded. "She wouldn't tell me anything about Audrey's past. That's why all the digging."

"Well, she wouldn't, would she? I mean, she was the woman's doctor."

"That's what she said."

"Then maybe you ought to leave that end of it alone."

"These aren't dead cases. There's something going on," said Virgil. "I can feel it in my bones."

"You're starting to sound a little paranoid, Virg. Or are you psychic?"

Virgil shook his head. "No. But I'm starting to listen to one."

Mac's frown was worse than Virgil had expected.

35

RICHARD CHECKED THEM IN at Doctor Cates's front desk at two o'clock Monday afternoon. Right on time. Audrey sat on a love seat beneath a huge painting done all in shades of blue, wondering again if Cates would really be able to help her, and if she was prepared for the help he might offer.

Richard sat down beside her. "Are you sure you want to do this? You might not be able to separate the bad from the good."

She nodded. "I know this is the right thing. I thought you wanted me to do this."

He frowned. "I want you to be better."

"You don't think Doctor Cates can make me better?"

He tried a smile. "Sure. I'm just nervous, I guess."

"Me too."

Doctor Cates's office door opened and a pretty brunette woman of about thirty emerged with Cates behind her. She was smiling with tears in her eyes. Audrey felt trepidation building, but when Cates noticed her and opened the door wider, she strode through it without glancing back at Richard.

"I don't know where to start," said Audrey, taking a seat.

Cates shrugged, cleaning his glasses with a monogrammed handkerchief. "Just begin anywhere you like, then."

"I think I'm getting better," she said.

"That's good."

"I'm not taking the pills."

Cates frowned. "You stopped the Halcion? Why?"

"I didn't like the way it made me feel. Like I was out of control. Out of touch.... And I believe now that you were right. I need to confront my past and deal with it."

"I'm glad you've come to *that* decision. You have to face your past. I can only help you work through it."

Audrey nodded. "Where should we start, then?"

Cates steepled his fingers in front of his face. "What can you tell me about your aunt and your therapy sessions with her?"

"I told you about the hypnotherapy."

"Do you remember any of your past before that at all? Are any of the memories starting to work their way through to the surface?"

"Yes."

"Good memories or bad?"

"They're all mixed up."

Cates nodded.

"Will you be hypnotizing me?" she asked.

"How do you feel about being hypnotized?"

She shifted in her chair. "All right ... I guess."

"Well, then, maybe we will try to open some doors that way." Cates noticed Audrey's shocked expression. "What?" he asked.

"Doors. Why did you say doors?"

Cates seemed confused. "I don't know. It seemed like a fitting analogy. Why?"

"Tara called it closing doors."

"Interesting way of putting it. As though she thought of the past as compartmentalized. Rooms to be shut away where they couldn't be seen."

Suddenly a large lump formed in Audrey's throat, and a vision flashed before her eyes. A young girl screaming as a woman's hand slipped a heavy, eyeless mask over her head. Audrey could barely breathe. The room around her grew dim and she felt dizzy and cold. Just as her mind started to drift back to that long ago night, Cates started speaking again.

"Audrey, what can you remember of your sessions with your aunt? Anything at all?"

She shook her head, struggling to drag herself back into the room. "I can't remember much of anything. That was the point. To forget."

"To forget your terrible past."

"Yes."

"But doesn't it seem strange to you that you would forget the sessions too?"

"I never thought about it."

"Do you recall anything? Anything at all? Images?"

Audrey shook her head, staring at her hands, searching. "Tara saved me. If it wasn't for her, I'd be dead, like my sister and brother."

"Did Tara ever treat your sister or brother?"

She shook her head. "I don't remember them. Tara saved me."

"Yes, so you said. But we weren't discussing that. We were discussing the treatments. What do you remember?"

"I . . . Light. I remember bright lights. Tara saved me."

Cates stared at her until she looked into his eyes. "You keep saying that. But each time you repeat it, you seem less certain."

"Do I?" That thought shook her. Why would she be unsure? Tara's coming to save her from the terrors in her past was the very foundation of her existence. The one memory she clung to, however faint.

Cates nodded. "All right," he said, unsteepling his fingers. "Leave that for now. Tell me about the things you're starting to remember."

Audrey began to rock back and forth in her chair like a child. "I remember a twin sister and an older brother."

"Yes. What happened to them?"

Audrey stared at the floor between her legs. "I don't know. I think my mother did something terrible to them."

"Terrible? Like what?"

Audrey took a moment answering. "I think she killed them. But she did other things first."

"What other things?"

"I see my mother, then my brother goes away with her and never comes back. The same thing happens to my sister. But that time I remember being in a dark room. I think it was in our basement and my mother was putting this horrible mask on my sister and my sister was screaming bloody murder and then I never saw her again and then Tara came for me. Tara saved me."

"Audrey, the way you say that I sense that you *want* to believe it more than you actually do. It's almost like a programmed response."

Audrey glanced quickly around the room. "I do believe it."

"When you talk I hear you say one thing, but your eyes and expression seem unsure. Your body language tells me you're unclear on Tara's position in your past."

Audrey's frown spread. "Tara never hurt me. Tara never would hurt me."

"But she buried your past."

"To protect me from the bad memories. Why are we talking about Tara?"

"Tara seems to be central to this. She's the one who buried your memories to begin with."

"She had to. They were terrible. I couldn't live with them."

"But could *all* of them have been so terrible that they needed to be hidden?"

"I don't know." But she *did* know. Cates was touching on the same thoughts that had been gnawing at her for days. What good things had she lost when Tara erased her past like a giant hand swooping across a blackboard?

"Do you want to?" asked Cates. "Are you ready to try to find out?"

She nodded slowly. "What do you want me to do?"

"I think I'll let you tell me what *you* want to do first."

Audrey took a long, deep breath. The doors had been closed for so long and she'd gotten by. Tara had said her past was unimaginably horrible, but she sensed that somewhere in there Zach, or the truth about Zach, was hiding, and she'd face any horror imaginable if it meant even the slimmest chance of finding him. Even if it only meant finding out what had happened to him so she could put him to rest at last. She had to *know.*

"I'd like you to hypnotize me. I want to know what's behind *my* doors."

"All right. But have you *really* considered this? You of all people should know that regression has risks."

"Everything has risks. I want you to hypnotize me."

Cates steepled his fingers again. "All right, then. Lean back and try to relax. I want you to take slow, deep breaths and imagine yourself in the most peaceful place in the world."

She did as she was told, half-closing her eyes. Imagining herself in a beautiful garden. Not her own garden. She still wasn't quite ready to go back there after all. No, this was the garden of her dreams. Ever so slowly Cates began to speak and she felt the well-remembered sense of losing herself. She was surprised at how fast she started to go under. Cates's voice was full and throaty in the big office, then more distant, finally echoing down a long corridor. And then she was back in the recesses of her mind again. She didn't hear the voice commands now. It was as though *she* was directing this memory walk.

That long-ago day in her childhood began to replay for her, slowly at first. Her sister and brother were romping in the yard. Gidown bounced off the end of his chain. Her mother, her hair gleaming in the sun, called from the back porch. And then her brother disappeared and once more that door in Audrey's mind swung closed. She didn't need to remain here. She'd opened this door on her own. She knew where it led. With only the slightest hesitation, she turned to the next door. When it opened, she was faced with a terrible darkness, but as she entered—had she really *wanted* to enter?—the gloom was splashed with milky moonlight.

A child cried in the distance, and Audrey shook with fear. It was the same cry she had heard that day in the kitchen. She glanced at her hands and saw that they were the hands of an adolescent, unlined and free of the gardening calluses her fingers now sported. Across the floor, an arrangement of sofa and chairs faced a large bookshelf. She slipped behind an open door to get out of the moonlight. A dog barked wildly outside.

Was that Gidown?

She tried to remember the sound of Gidown's bark. But she wasn't sure. In any case, this wasn't the mournful howl of a pet left out of the game. The barking sounded more like a hunting animal, angered at not being able to reach its prey. The sound pressed Audrey farther back into the wedge of wood between the door and the wall, but there was another sound as well. Coming from the other side of the room. The sound of laughter.

Laughter that sounded like darkness.

That was a thought directly from her childhood, blurted into the present. She could no more help herself in this re-creation of her past than she could control events in that forgotten year. This was not a dream she might manipulate. It was a memory, cast in stone. She either had to exit into the white corridor in her mind or ride the recollection to whatever terrible end it revealed. She crept around the sofa and found herself staring down a long dark hallway, but she needed no light. The laughter was guide enough. She followed it through endless corridors of darkness. Then there was the strangest sense of dropping through space and she was in another corridor.

The smell of mildew and damp concrete hung in the air. Overhead, bare bulbs lit cold white concrete. The cellar seemed devoid of life. Still the insane laughter rattled Audrey's ears. She followed it along the winding brick-lined tunnel until she found herself in front of a heavy metal door.

Just like the ones in my mind. Only this one is real. This had to be our house. But how could it? The tunnels seemed endless. No one owned a house like that. There was something *wrong* with the picture. Something skewed, as though two memories were trying to assert themselves at the same time. Still she knew the place. And she knew the laughter as well. Because she had heard it often enough in her childhood that it was burned into her brain, and now she was re-calling it as though it had been there all along. Only it didn't always sound like that. Not dark, and sad, and crazy.

It had to be her mother's laughter.

She reached out with a childish hand and turned the knob. It wasn't locked and the door swung open as easily and silently as only a well-hung, well-oiled door can. The small room was better lit than the dusky basement, and it was lined from floor to ceiling with some gray metallic-looking sheeting supported by evenly spaced broad-headed nails. They were sheets of lead.

She rounded a corner and froze, staring at her mother's back. Mother was on her knees, struggling with Audrey's sister. The girl's feet kicked frantically between her mother's legs and she was screaming. But her screams were muffled. Sweat streaked her mother's raven hair and the lights glinted on the gray that had begun to appear in it. When Audrey gasped, her mother glanced over her shoulder and Audrey saw the glint of madness there.

And terror.

"I have to, Audrey," she said, in a breathless but gentle tone. "I have to do this. Please try to understand."

As Audrey backed away into the basement, biting the back of her hand, her mother rose to her feet and then Audrey could see her sister, clawing madly at the hideous eyeless monstrosity that was locked onto her head. There was a small hole at the mouth, but the rest of the heavy metal device covered the head like a helmet, strapped tightly beneath the chin and belted around the throat. A small brass lock clinked behind Paula's neck. Audrey could just see her blond braids beneath the horrid object as the girl rolled over and over across the cold, lead-lined floor.

"No!" Audrey whispered. "No!" Until the words became a scream echoing around her. "It's my fault! She did it because of me!"

Finally she could hear Cates's excited voice. "Come back, Audrey. Come back, now! Can you hear me? Come back, now! It's not your fault!"

His hands were tight on her wrists, pressing them down against the armrests of the chair, and his eyes were so close to hers that at first she had trouble focusing on his face. Her entire body was bathed in cold sweat, and the trembling that she had sensed before was barely subsiding.

Cates let out a loud sigh. "Are you all right?" he asked, his voice easing a bit as he relaxed back into his own chair, releasing her arms.

She nodded dumbly.

"I had to physically pick you up and put you back in your seat. I thought you might run screaming from my office."

"It was bad."

"I know. You were talking all the time."

"Really?" That was weird. She didn't recall that at all. She was accustomed to losing memory while she was under. But what else had she done *physically* while under hypnosis that she was unaware of?

"So your mother put the mask on your sister?" asked Cates.

"Yes."

"Why would she do something like that?"

"I have no idea. She was crazy."

Cates studied her for a long moment. "The way you describe it, it would seem to have taken some expertise to make such a mask. Was your mother some sort of craftsman?"

Audrey shook her head. "Not that I know of. I mean, I don't really know *what* she was. All I know is that she was evil!" Audrey rocked in the chair even more frenetically than before, now clutching her sides.

Cates nodded. "All right, Audrey. Try to relax. Would you like a Halcion now?"

Audrey shook her head firmly. "No."

"All right. Some water or juice?"

"Water, please."

Cates brought her a glass from a small bar in the corner, watching her closely as she sipped it. He set the glass on his desk and dropped back into his chair. As he did, he removed a deck of blue-backed cards from his jacket pocket. Audrey glanced at them curiously, but discovered to her surprise that she recognized them immediately. They weren't a tarot deck, but she felt the same sense of nerves she'd felt in Babs's house while watching her shuffle the cards.

Cates nodded, studying her face. "You've seen cards like this before."

"I think so."

"Do you mind?"

She took a minute answering and her voice was tentative. "No. . . ."

He held up a card, showing Audrey only the back, and she had the curious sensation of a glowing circle appearing behind her eyes. But a part of her rebelled, wanted away from the cards even more than she had wanted away from the door in the corridor. There was something about these cards that spelled *danger* to her in giant neon letters, but at the same time, she sensed a turning point here, a decision that had to be made, a nexus where some unseen forces crossed. "Circle," she said hesitantly.

Cates lifted the next card.

Audrey paused.

"Circle."

Another, and then more.

"Triangle."

"Square."

"Triangle."

"Squiggly lines."

They worked their way through the entire deck and then Cates replaced it in his pocket.

"How did I do?" she asked.

Cates was slow to answer. "I just wanted to see how accustomed you were to working with the cards. There was a little bit of early apprehension, but it quickly disappeared."

"You're saying I've been tested before."

"I think so. For one thing, you knew all the shapes that might come up without being told."

"There's something about the cards. Something I can't explain."

"What do you mean *something*?"

"I'm terrified of them," she said, frowning. "But it's more than that. It's almost as though I can *see* what's on the other side but I'm afraid to tell you."

Cates frowned, pulling the cards out of his pocket again and watching Audrey's face. "What exactly is it about them that frightens you? Why would you be afraid to tell me?"

"I don't know. But I was really scared to answer you when you first showed them to me."

"Why did you agree to the test, then?"

She shook her head. "I'm here to make a change in my life. Maybe my subconscious sensed that this was the way to start. I don't know. It felt right though. How did I do?"

"Not bad," said Cates. Without preamble, he started flashing cards again.

"Circle," said Audrey, staring intensely at the blue-back

of the card. Then, "Square, squiggly lines, square, triangle, straight lines, square..."

When the last card was done, Cates hid the deck in his pocket again and stared at his hands.

"What was my score? You didn't write down the correct answers."

"I didn't need to," murmured Cates.

"Why not?"

"Because there were no wrong answers. Not this time. Not last time. I've never even heard of anything like it."

"That's impossible." She stared at him, waiting for him to smile or laugh, but there was nothing in his face but amazement.

"I agree," said Cates. "But you must have known."

She looked at the top of the deck, barely visible in his breast pocket, shocked to discover that she was *certain* that the top card was now a triangle. "Known what? That I could do card tricks?"

"The cards only reveal the existence of psi power. Nobody really knows whether what's happening is a form of telepathy or something else altogether. Most subjects who do exhibit higher than average ratings have those scores drop to average figures when the person running the test is unaware of what's on the card. This would seem to show that telepathy exists."

"You're saying I'm telepathic?"

"I don't know how else to explain what you just did."

"Why did you think I might be?"

"To be honest, I don't believe in telepathy. Or... at least I didn't. I merely wanted to get your reaction to the cards."

"Why?"

Cates sighed. "I've done some research since I last saw you. Your aunt wasn't only known for her work on hypnotherapy."

"What do you mean?"

"She also studied the paranormal. That got me wondering whether *you* might have been tested."

Audrey felt the muscles in her throat tightening. Suddenly she had trouble breathing.

"Are you all right?" said Cates, leaning closer, resting his hand on hers.

She nodded, trying to catch her breath.

"Here," said Cates. "Take another sip of water."

Audrey waved the glass aside. "If I'm really telepathic, then Zach *is* alive."

Cates frowned. "Audrey, no one understands telepathy, if there even is such a thing."

"But you saw—"

"I saw an as yet unexplainable phenomenon. Amazing. But don't infer from that that you have really been in communication with your son."

"If it wasn't Zach, then I want to know what the hell it was."

"Slowly. Everything will come with time."

But Audrey refused to be dissuaded. "I don't have time. And I still haven't opened that last door."

"No. And I don't think you should just yet. You have a lot to deal with already. It's going to take us several sessions before you're ready to take that next big plunge. You've been extremely traumatized by your past. Your aunt Tara had that right. Reliving all of it at once would be too much."

"I have this fear now that you were right, that a lot of what I lost wasn't bad. That I needed to remember it!"

"What kind of childhood could it have been with a twin sister, and a brother, and a dog that didn't have *some* happiness, Audrey? You've erased it all. The good and the bad. You've been robbed. Robbed of your childhood and of the right to grow up as an adult with a past. Good, bad, indifferent, it's your past. It's what makes you who you are, and now you can't possibly know. Up until two minutes ago you didn't realize that you might have an incredible gift. I know researchers that would pay a king's ransom to have you in their program."

"Please! Don't do that. Don't tell anyone."

Cates held up both hands. "That's the last thing I'd do. I was simply saying that you are a phenomenon. Surely Tara knew that."

"No, she didn't."

"Are you sure?"

"I can't tell you *why* I'm sure. But I'm certain." She nodded to herself. "I think if Tara did know, I'd know it."

Cates's face sank. "I was so certain."

"What's the matter?"

He shook his head. "I had devised this theory that Tara was studying telepathy, and perhaps other psi powers, and that she was using hypnosis to either try to improve upon them or discover what caused them."

"So?"

"I figured perhaps Tara took you to live with her when she realized your potential."

Audrey shook her head. "No. She came to get me because something bad was going to happen to me."

Cates seemed to consider that. "In any case, I'd like you to come back in a week. I'll have my receptionist set up another appointment for you."

"All right."

Cates walked her to the door. Before he could open it, she spun to face him, her eyes bright.

"You don't believe in contact with the dead, do you?" she asked.

Cates frowned. "No. I don't believe that's possible."

She smiled, slipping past him. "Neither do I," she said.

"Audrey," he said, catching her arm, "you kept mentioning the sound of a child's feet. Running. Do you know what that was about?"

She frowned, thinking of the pain in her garden, the sound she'd heard echoing in the house. Suddenly she knew. "It was me," she said. "I was running away. I could hear the sound of my feet giving me away. I couldn't hide. And I couldn't run. I was trapped."

"By who? Your mother?"

She nodded. "I guess so," she said, shocked at the feeling of grief the admission caused her.

36

"AN OLD FRIEND who has access to medical records called me last night." Mac's voice was loud enough on Virgil's cell phone that he had to hold the receiver out at arm's length. "Martha Remont was in and out of mental institutions in California for nearly ten years."

"What for?"

"Some kind of child abuse. Let me see. Oh, this is good. She locked her kids in a room in the basement and didn't let them out. She had three kids they know. The state of California finally granted Tara Beals custody of Audrey, but it was a long, drawn-out affair and pretty messy evidently. Martha later claimed Tara kidnapped Audrey, but Tara got custody."

"Audrey says she did, basically, to save her from her mother."

"Good thing, probably."

"The state bust her?"

"It was the state that sent Martha to the mental institutions, yeah."

"What happened to the other kids?"

Mac was slow answering. "Disappeared."

"Think she killed them?"

"Probably, but the state didn't have enough evidence to charge her on that one. They searched the house but all they found was a lead-lined basement where she probably kept the kids locked up. They never found any bodies, so they didn't charge her. I guess they figured they had her locked away for life anyway."

"So where is Martha now? Have you got any more information?"

"Same thing happened in California that happened everywhere. The state kind of lost track of mental patients when they couldn't come up with the money to keep 'em locked up anymore. She got shuffled out in the early nineties. I tracked her to a residence in Sacramento. According to neighbors, she lived quietly there for five years. Two years ago she sold the house and disappeared."

"Did she live alone?"

"No. She had a man in the house."

"Anything on him?"

"Truck driver is all I got."

"You're kidding."

"No. Why?"

"Audrey Bock's neighbor drives a truck. He bought the house about two years ago."

"Well, that's a coincidence. But I'd say it's still pretty slender evidence. I don't have a name or anything on the guy. Neighbors didn't remember much. He was a long-distance trucker. Gone a lot."

"Could be Merle Coonts," said Virgil, shaking his head.

"Could be a lot of people. Have you got anything else on the guy?"

"No. He let me search the house and basement. But it wasn't a *thorough* search."

"Either he's real cocky or he's innocent."

"I didn't get the feeling of innocence. It was something else. The guy's a creep."

"What else can I do for you, Virg?"

"You've done a lot. Thanks, Mac."

"Guess that gets Tara off the hook, then."

"Sounds like it," said Virgil.

Arnold? Daniel? Ernest? Cooder had always liked the name Ernest. Liked the way it made a man sound. Like you could trust him. But was that the boy's name?

His old work boots sounded a tight rhythm on the pavement, but he ignored the sound, focusing on the gnawing in his brain. It wasn't just the names. Something else just as bothersome scratched at his mind like a bit of flotsam scraping against a dock piling, but was it something he knew, or something he felt?

A lot of times Cooder got the two mixed up. He was never sure if he knew a storm was blowing in because he'd overheard someone say it, caught a brief bit of weather reporting on someone's radio—at the diner, for instance—or if he just *knew* those kinds of things. But he was uncannily good at predicting the weather, so good that people often asked him his opinion of the long-term forecast. He could feel the pressure dropping now, like he'd just taken a long step off the edge of a tall building. It was going to be clear and seasonable for a little while, but there was one hell of a storm blowing in.

He never slowed his pace as he hiked down the back slope of the hill. The land opened out into a wide valley and a battered old farmstead sat moldering to his right. A satellite dish on top of the barn was silhouetted against the sky. Suddenly his mind seemed unusually clear. He breathed in clarity like thick air and the invisible substance flowed through his brain, opening synapses that had lain dormant for decades, leaving him standing on the side of the road, staring at the house but not knowing why. He was a receiver, waiting for a transmission.

After what seemed minutes, but might have been an eternity, some part of Cooder's brain registered the sound of an approaching automobile, and he recalled Virgil's warning, glancing down at his feet to ascertain that he was not in fact standing in the middle of the road again. The Camry rounded the far curve and then slowed slightly as it passed the farm. Squinting, Cooder could make out the dark-haired male driver and, as it drew alongside, he saw the pretty blonde passenger, and for just that instant the veil of syrup that had him locked in place parted. He felt as though somehow he and the woman had just been introduced. But the strange sensation was more than just recognition.

He and the woman had touched each other.

* * *

Audrey was stunned, breathless.

As they passed the old farmhouse now, she'd stared straight ahead, trying to find a quiet place in her mind. Trying to hold back her fear and reach out for Zach at the same time. If she wasn't insane, if he was there, in that house, she was going to find him. But to Audrey's dismay, Richard slowed and perused the old house curiously, and her terror began to overpower her sense of purpose. She wondered if Richard was just waiting for her to scream at him to hurry up, but the closer they got, the more intent Richard's gaze seemed.

Suddenly Audrey found herself drawn away from the presence of the old house toward the figure standing like a heavy-set mannequin off to her right. Sandy hair blew wildly about the man's vacant face. But as the car flashed by, their eyes met and Audrey gasped, not quite understanding why.

She hadn't been afraid of the man. Although he was weird-looking, like a vagabond, there was no menace in his face. Something strange and somehow wonderful had passed between them, some bond beneath the level of consciousness. Had it really happened? She glanced back but the hill was already behind them and Richard was turning up their driveway.

"Who was that?" she asked.

He glanced over at her. "The bum? I have no idea. I've seen him around. He walks a lot."

The sun was just setting as they entered the house and Richard flipped on the kitchen lights. He stared into Audrey's eyes for a moment and then sent a meaningful glance toward the cabinet where she had placed the Halcion.

She shook her head.

"Are you sure?" said Richard.

"Doctor Cates agreed," she said, stretching the truth. "I'm going to work through this with his help."

Richard tried not to frown.

"He's helping me, Richard. He really is."

"Okay," he said, kissing her lightly before wandering off into the living room. The sound of a basketball game rattled down the hall.

37

BABS FLIPPED THE TAROT CARDS with the expertise of a Vegas shark, snapping them onto the table between soft and runny candles. The flickering flames were numerous enough to summon a thin bead of sweat on her wrinkled brow.

She'd done a thousand readings over the years, but rarely for herself. She knew enough about the supernatural to realize that she didn't want to know her future. Others, half-believers, could take bad news and call it hocus-pocus. Of course they learned in the end, but then it was too late.

Babs, on the other hand, was a full believer—in the cards and other things—and she knew that the cards didn't lie. They might not be direct. They might reveal the truth in layers that were difficult for the ordinary mortal to understand. But they didn't lie. That was why she was performing this reading for herself for the fourth time in as many hours. Because sometimes they *were* direct.

The first time she had been shaken but not panicked. She'd stared at the cards for long moments, catching her breath, taking in the fullness of them. Tarot cards could not be interpreted correctly if the adept only read into them the separate meaning of each card. That was strictly for base amateurs. Each card played off the other, each lay revised the lay before, until with the final card, the complete reading could be revealed by a skilled professional.

But that first deal of the tarot had been even more uni-

formly ominous than the one she had done for Audrey
Bock, until with the fall of the last card, Babs could barely
breathe. Never in her years of working with the occult had
she seen anything remotely like it. She stared suspiciously at
the deck in her hand, but she had shuffled it herself before
the reading.

She brewed herself a large pot of tea and forced herself
to eat a healthy breakfast of sprouts and tofu. By the time
she finished she had almost convinced herself that perhaps
she *had* misread the cards both times. It was possible. After
all, a reading was just an *interpretation*. If she was depressed or distracted, it might have happened.

She did another reading. This time she used only the
twenty-two cards of the major arcana. She wasn't interested
in subtlety.

The cards fell differently this time, as of course they
would, but the conglomerate effect was the same. Death.
Horrible death in her future. Not just in the future, either.
Today. She dropped the rest of the deck as though it were a
hot iron and backed away from the table, pulling her eyes
away from the cards with great difficulty. Even as she
hurried into her bedroom, the picture of the reaper with
glowing eyes shining beneath his dark hood and his wicked-
long, sharp scythe wrapped in skeletal hands, flashed re-
peatedly on the front of her brain.

A walk. A nice brisk walk would clear her mind. But as
she strode purposefully out onto the porch that afternoon, clutching a thin cotton scarf around her shoulders,
she'd stopped in the pale sunlight. What if she was hit by
a car?

She'd glanced quickly up and down the street, lifting her
chin to peer farther along at the hospital parking lot. One
or two cars passed slowly, but they remained on the street.
None threatened to leap the curb and run her down, and
was that a horrible enough death to match the message in
the cards?

She thought not. No, the cards had foreseen something
peculiarly gruesome and painful for her and she couldn't
imagine what that might be. Babs was not a reader of
Stephen King or his ilk. She didn't follow the tabloids or
study every story on serial killers or watch those types of

movies. In fact Babs hadn't *been* to a movie since *The Sound of Music,* but she did have an ample imagination nonetheless, and it was working overtime as she stepped down onto the walk in front of her home and tried to decide what to do.

Doris. I'll go see Doris.

And so she did. By the time she reached the Milche house, she had managed to attain a certain level of calm. Enough to let herself in quietly—since Virgil wasn't home and she knew Doris was in no shape to answer the door—catch her breath and straighten her plaid skirt. She tiptoed up the stairs and found Doris watching a game show. Doris barely had the strength to register surprise when she saw someone unexpected standing on her threshold.

Babs was astonished at how fast Doris had slipped downhill. Had it really been only a couple of weeks since she'd last seen her? She looked like death itself. If it was possible, she seemed to have lost even more hair and her eyes, sunken before, were now positively entombed in the depths of their sockets. Her withered hand, as she lifted it to welcome Babs, shook like a leaf in a windstorm. For a moment Babs forgot all about her own problems and dropped onto the bed to comfort her old friend.

Doris's voice was raspy as a leaky radiator. "I missed you, Babs."

"I missed you, too, Doris. You're looking good."

"Don't give me that baloney." Doris forced a weak smile. "Won't be long now."

"Don't say that."

"True. But I don't worry about it. Pastor comes by every day now. I'm right with Jesus."

"Well, that's good."

"Are you right with him, Babs?"

Babs tried to be right with everyone. Buddha, Jesus, Mohammed, The Great Spirit, the entities that inhabited the earth. But when it came down to it, had she been wrong all along? Was there a final decision that had to be made? That thought bothered her. What if there *was* only one God and he was the jealous kind the pastor kept whining about?

"I think so."

"Don't think so. You got to know. 'Course you got a little more time than I got."

"I don't think so."

"What do you mean?"

So Babs told her. Doris's eyes seemed to slide to the front
of their sockets and when her jaw dropped, Babs had the
uncomfortable sensation of staring all the way down her inflamed and constricted throat. She wondered if that was
what the gateway to hell looked like.

"Need to tell Virgil," said Doris.

"Why? There's nothing that he can do about it, Doris.
And he wouldn't believe me anyway."

"You saying it's set in stone?"

"When the cards speak like they did today, it is."

"I don't believe that. Christ gives all of us choices in this
life."

"I can make all the choices I want as to how my soul is
set before I die. I can die a good woman or a bad one. But
the cards say I'll be dead before the next sun rises."

"Don't say that."

"I'm trying to make my peace with it."

"It's hard."

"How did *you* do it?"

Doris rubbed the back of her neck and closed her eyes
for just a second. "I prayed a lot. And I had Virgil. Much as
he thinks he's not a comfort to me, he is. I'd meant to ask
you to keep an eye on him after I was gone. . . ."

"Sorry."

Doris shrugged. "Marg will take care of him."

"That must be soothing for you to know."

"She's a good woman."

"I suppose. You know her better than me."

"Of course, she always thought you were a bit off."

"*Me?*"

"Well, not everyone takes to men. Marg is *different* in a
different way."

"You can say that again," said Babs, studying Doris's
face. "I'm wearing you out. I'll go."

"No," said Doris, gripping Babs's hand with the little
strength she possessed. "Stay long enough to pray with me."

"Sure."

They prayed aloud, both asking for forgiveness for their sins. Requesting eternal salvation in the sweet arms of Jesus Christ, our Lord and Savior, and when they were done Babs found that she did feel better.

"Thank-you, Doris," she said, leaning and kissing Doris lightly on the forehead. "We'll meet again very soon. I'm sure of it now."

"Me too."

"Give my love to Virgil."

The walk home went better than the walk over. The late afternoon sunlight no longer seemed filtered through a silken cloak of gloom. It had a nearly optimistic edge to it. Babs didn't doubt her coming demise any more than she had when leaving home, but Doris's unquestioning faith had shored up her own. Whatever was coming, she was ready to face it.

But stepping into the candlelit house once more, she felt her resolve bending just a little. It was one thing to accept your fate. It was another to move toward it blindly, waiting for a freight train roaring down the karmic path in your direction. She went straight to the cards and read them once again.

The cards told her that she was not going to be alone when she died. That bothered her. She couldn't be certain from the reading whether it meant she would have friends close by or that someone else would die with her. The final clue that was revealed in each of the separate readings confused her the most, and troubled her more than all the others. It hinted at something she had been wondering about for years. Dreaming about. And *fearing* to the very depths of her soul.

The card showed an unknown woman, linked with death.

And though the cards played themselves close to the chest, she *knew* somehow that the woman was the same one that was such a force in Audrey Bock's reading. But how could that be? She'd never met Audrey before that day and, as far as she knew, they had no mutual acquaintances.

Her hand kept straying to *The Hanged Man,* with its incongruous image of the woman peering down into the murky pool. Something in the woman's face was disconcerting for her. Was the woman seeing things in the future or in the past? Was she searching for salvation or casting a spell of death? Babs sensed that the woman was a focal point, drawing in a twisted web of lines that attached to people and events she couldn't begin to understand, but people and events that were destined to come together in a terrifying conclusion.

But was that before or after *she* was dead?

Cooder hadn't made it more than a hundred yards in the hours since the man and woman had passed him. In that time, several other cars and trucks had come along. A couple honked and waved and Cooder studied them as they passed, uncertain as always if he knew the people, if they were strangers being friendly or someone making fun of him. Not that it mattered. He always got around to waving long *after* a car was out of sight anyway.

He stood now in the gathering gloom, watching the moon rise over the rear of the old farmhouse. Backlit, the meandering building looked even more menacing, with only two downstairs windows emitting the vaguest of light, like the eyes of a weasel in a dark woods.

The house seemed to be tugging at him and it stroked his natural curiosity. He studied the ramshackle structure, wondering what it was about the place that touched him so. He'd passed a million old farmhouses in his day. Full of dusty corners they were. Empty rooms a lot of them. Funny, withered-looking sunlight beating its way in through dirty glass, turning into dusty beams in gray spaces filled with falling wallpaper and the smell of wood so dry it clogged the nose. He'd explored them before.

With one foot on the gravel shoulder, the other balanced in the grass that dropped off to the old galvanized drainage culvert, he angled his head, squinting his eyes. Cool wind soughed through the branches of a thick stand of spruce behind him. Other than the breeze, the early evening was unusually quiet, and in that silence, Cooder felt himself slipping even further away.

It wasn't a frightful sensation. He'd experienced it countless times before. He gave himself up to it, knowing immediately what was happening. He'd found his guide inside the house. He was seeing through other eyes. Using the senses of another, smaller creature. He felt curiosity, and hunger. And he felt a terrible, tiny heart thumping fearfully in his chest.

He was bathed in darkness thicker than night. He reached out with both hands, but his fingers felt weird, feeble and thin. A door, so huge it seemed to disappear overhead, slowly opened.

A man stood silhouetted in the golden light from the doorway and—as always—it took Cooder a moment to realize that the man wasn't a giant. *He* was little. The man passed him and spoke in a soft and tender tone.

"Come on, Zach. Time to get out for a little."

Zach! That was the name! In the corner, a child rose to his feet, shielding his eyes. The giant glanced toward Cooder and froze.

"Goddamned rat!"

Cooder saw a boot sole the size of a refrigerator dropping toward him and he scurried around the wall, underneath the child's bunk and back inside a crevice in the foundation. The man kicked at the wall and the sound was like thunder, the giant boot sole blocking out the light as it struck the wall. Cooder shivered against the stone, the rat's thick whiskers picking up every vibration like an insect's antennae. The boot hammered down at his cave opening like a guided missile, over and over, until finally he heard heavy breathing and the kicking had stopped.

"I'll get him later, Zach. Don't worry."

Cooder peered shakily out of the hole as the giant turned and walked out, followed by the boy. Cooder focused, forcing the rat to follow, skittering along the baseboard, its whiskers flicking like swords, testing the air, every muscle tensed lest the boy or the man glance over their shoulder. But Cooder knew that the last thing the man would think of was the rat getting up the guts to tag along.

The giant strode down a long, dimly lit corridor, with thin carpet and concrete block walls. Through a heavy metal door they came to a wooden stair, and the boy took the man's hand and followed him upward. Cooder felt every quivering clawnail as the rat shimmied up the open treads behind the booted feet. The rat struggled to regain control of its body, terrified by the light, the open air, and the giant man hulking over it, but Cooder wouldn't let go.

At the top, rather than a landing, a trapdoor apparatus blocked their path. The man reached up and lifted it easily, still guiding the boy with his hand. He raised the youngster above his head and followed him out, with the rat scurrying after. The shaking animal dropped onto the concrete floor of the large dark room, just as the man flipped a switch turning on a couple of bare bulbs high overhead. But even then, the area was so large that the dusty fixtures gave off only the barest of light. The ceiling disappeared in deep black shadows and, when the rat glanced in his direction, the man had vanished as well. But the boy didn't move.

The rat slunk back into the shadows and watched. There was a rustling sound and in a moment the man returned carrying a child's bike.

"Here," he said.

The boy climbed on and pedaled around the shadowed perimeter of the room. Over and over. In tighter and tighter circles. Faster and faster. Until he was out of breath and the man lifted him off the bike and left with the bike once again. The boy stood in the center of the giant room then, glancing toward the far end of the building, but the rat could not see that far, its eyes were made for small dark spaces.

"Sorry," said the man, returning and shepherding the boy back toward the hidden entrance. "We can't stay up long tonight. Trouble's coming."

Cooder knew the man was right. He could sense the trouble, in the basement and in the forest around his *real* self. It was coming right now. Right here. He took two steps backward and dropped over the lip of the road, landing on his hands and knees on the steep slope and sliding roughly to the bottom. He buried his face in the tall grass and listened as tires hummed across asphalt and then the exhaust thrummed away around the far curve. And all that time— as the car neared and then drew away—he sensed the danger the way a rabbit senses a coyote lying just outside its burrow. Danger so terrible that the boy and the giant and the rat were completely forgotten in the rumbling of his own heart and the chill sweat that trickled down his brow.

She's back.

The words flashed across his mind a full minute before he understood them. He had the feeling a small child gets, hiding beneath the covers, listening to footsteps in his bedroom in the middle of the night. His mouth went dry and he shivered, sharp pebbles cutting into his palms and his cheeks as he clutched at the slope.

"Try a little harder!"

The words echoed down the halls of his memory and he felt the electrical jolt that blasted through his brain and exited out every tortured pore in his body. And he had tried harder, but not the way she meant. There was nothing he could do to stop the pain. He could not please the voice in the darkness. In fact, he knew if he *did* please it, then he would surely die.

And now she was back. The witch that had been hiding in the back of his mind, in the deep black hole of his memory all this time, had returned. Just like he always knew she would. When a car shot past in a whirr of tires and rumbling exhaust, headlights disappearing around the far bend, it was like being shot at and missed. But she was gone now and the woods were silent as death once again. Cooder's heart took a long moment in slowing, his chest still pounding for air, but the air itself seemed fouled by the auto's passage.

"She's back," he whispered, spitting grit out onto the grass.

38

VIRGIL LEANED AGAINST THE HEADBOARD and stared blankly at the TV. He had no idea what the program was. The volume was turned off, but the flickering screen seemed to soothe Doris whenever she awakened, as she did often now. Every few minutes she would start, her eyes would pop open, and she would be as disoriented as a newly hatched duckling.

Virgil knew the end was near. She'd be lucky to make it through the week. He couldn't believe how fast she'd sunk in only a couple of days. She felt as light as a feather against him. Grasping her tiny wrist in his palm, bone was all he could feel.

"Virg?" Her voice sounded like a whisper, but he didn't think that she meant it to.

"Yes?"

She slipped her hand out of his and patted his thigh. "Are you all right?"

He was glad that she was leaning back against his chest and couldn't see his eyes. "Am *I* all right?"

She nodded weakly. "You don't look good."

"Yeah, sure, honey. I'm okay."

"I don't have the strength to argue."

"I don't want to argue."

"Then answer me true."

"All right."

"What are you going to do when I'm gone?"

How could he answer that? Tell her he was going to slip his service pistol out of his holster, lie down beside her, slide the barrel between his teeth until he could feel it biting into the roof of his mouth, pull the trigger, and blow his brains all over the inlaid headboard? "Try to go on."

"You promised."

"I don't know if I can live without you."

"We'll be together again soon."

"I want to be together now."

He couldn't tell if she was sighing or just trying to catch her breath.

"Promise me you won't do anything to yourself. You have unfinished business here."

"What business?"

"You didn't promise."

"What business?"

"Those boys, for one thing."

"Someone else can work on the case." That was the closest he'd ever come to admitting to Doris what he intended to do.

"Why did you go out to the Bocks' on Saturday?" she rasped.

"Who told you about that?"

She turned her head to him and smiled. He struggled to imagine her old face over this new one. "I still have my informants," she said, coughing into her hand.

He sighed. "Audrey thought she saw a Peeping Tom."

"Oh, my Lord. Did you find out who it was?"

He shook his head. "I don't know if there really was one."

But he didn't believe that anymore. He believed Audrey. She was too sure. And Richard backed her story. But it was the trail that had shaken Virgil, because although he had been denying it to himself, he could tell from experience it was man-made. Critters didn't make trails like that. They went from point a to point b in a beeline, or at least the straightest path they could manage.

"I'm worried about Babs," said Doris.

"Why in the world are you worried about her?"

"She thinks she's going to die today, you know."

"What? Why on earth would she think that?"

"Babs knows things."

He sighed loud enough for her to hear and she dropped it and skipped to another fretful thought.

"I'm worried about the Bock girl too."

"I'll have one of the boys drive out that way every night," he said, kissing her on the forehead.

She tried to twist in his arms but didn't have the strength. He had no idea what this conversation was costing her, but her breathing was as labored as though she were running a marathon. "So you *are* planning something."

"I don't want to talk about it."

"We won't be together if you do."

The finality in her frail voice sent razors up his spine. She sounded so certain.

"Virgil, if you hurt yourself, you won't get to the other side. At least not to where I'm waiting. Do you want to leave me there by myself forever?"

"No."

"Then promise."

"I promise."

"You've never broken a promise to me in your life."

"I promise."

"Good."

She dropped off to sleep again, and Virgil took that respite to wipe his cheeks and nose with the back of his sleeve. He'd never broken a promise to her.

Only he didn't think he could keep this one.

39

BABS SIPPED HER TEA and stared at the tarot deck on the table in front of her.

She'd spent the day organizing the house. Every dish was washed, dried, and put away. Every linen was ironed and folded and stashed in the cedar chest. Every item of her clothing was clean as it had been the day she bought it, and hanging in the closet or folded in the dresser drawers. The carpet in every room was vacuumed, the last bag taken out of the machine, placed in the garbage, the garbage emptied into the can on the front porch awaiting pickup day. After that she'd balanced her checkbook, paid all her bills, and wrote a simple here's-what-I-want will. It sat in a plain white envelope on the table beside her tarot cards.

She prayed heavily, confessing her sins to every deity she could think of, and asking forgiveness. She knew that she should probably be choosing a winner, but she just couldn't bring herself to do it. Regardless of what the preacher or Doris thought, the deities were just going to have to decide who got her when she got there. But at least if she was going to meet her Maker, Babs St. Clair was going to glory with a clean slate in every other way.

One thing that bothered her was the suddenness that the tarot foretold. That was the only way she could read the cards. If she had laid them out for anyone else she would have excused herself calmly and called all her friends over to restrain the person before explaining the significance of her interpretation. Her best reading of the cards was that she was going to rise up to heaven like one of the saints.

The reading made no sense and, if it had been only the one time, she might have been able to dismiss it as a joke of the fates or a misshuffle on her own part.

But not four times.

So now she sat on the sofa, composing herself, practicing meditation, and awaiting whatever ending destiny decreed for her. She was perfectly at peace now. She knew that no matter what came, she could face it, knowing that it was only a brief instant in the scheme of things, and in the blink of an eye she would achieve eternal peace.

She was just emerging from the depths of her meditation when the doorbell rang.

Audrey sat in the old vinyl lawn chair, staring across the dark backyard at her garden. The drone of the television in the living room barely filtered through the screen door. Crickets *chirred* in the woods and somewhere in the distance an owl hooted. The occasional bat swooped across the moon, gorging on the night.

Ever since she'd freed herself of the dulling effects of the Halcion, she had been trying to reach out and contact Zach, testing her so-called *talent*. Once or twice over the past two days she had thought she had something, but then the feeling drifted away like smoke. The images she and Cates had dredged up were haunting her as well. She sensed deeper truths buried beneath the images, just out of reach, and she wanted desperately to move on, to work her way through them, to get better. And if Cates *was* right about her talent, then—regardless of what he said—she was certain she *had* been in touch with Zach. He was alive *somewhere* and he needed her.

The key to both problems lay in her mind, and the only way she knew to get to the answer was hypnosis. She leaned back on the chaise longue and closed her eyes, starting the sequence of counts that took her into a self-hypnotic state. She relaxed first her toes, then her ankles, her calves, her thighs, right up to her neck and head. She floated in a universe of nonbeing, her senses dulled by lack of input, until she was only a thought. She felt herself being pulled away and she realized that the tug was wrenching her, not deeper into her mind, but out of it. To some other place.

The gloom around her formed itself slowly into a windowless room and light was coming from beneath a door. A hand reached out in front of her eyes—as though they were her own eyes, only smaller—and opened the door. At that moment she knew with every fiber of her being that she was not dreaming, not hallucinating. She was inside Zach's head. She sensed him the way she had sensed him every time he was with her. The way she had discerned his restlessness in the night. The way she had experienced his pain the time he cut himself on a kitchen knife. She was telepathically feeling what Zach felt, seeing what he saw. He *was* alive! He was alive and he needed her. Her breathing quickened and she sat up stiff-backed in the chair.

He was wandering down a long, sloping hallway. The walls were stone or concrete block and the floor was undulating carpet, as though the base were bare bedrock. The lighting was poor, old bare incandescent fixtures, and there seemed to be fog, though Audrey was not certain whether Zach was actually seeing that or whether it existed only in her mind, clouding her vision. The scene reminded her of movies like *Alien,* where everything was dimly lit by flashing emergency lights and veiled in hostile shadows and mist.

She could feel Zach grasping at some newfound power of his own, the way a four-year-old will frown and bear down on a crayon. She couldn't quite understand what he was trying to accomplish, but she experienced his concentration like a heavy presence weighing on her own mind.

"Where are you?" she whispered.

Her words carried on a wisp of breeze like butterfly wings. He gave no sign that he had heard, simply continued down the long, bleak corridor, exploring his dungeon. Ahead, through the fog and to the right, she saw another door. Zach approached it hesitantly. The handle, with its large, keyed escutcheon, was just below his line of vision. The door itself appeared ordinary enough. It was painted with white primer and Audrey could see scratches revealing the gleaming aluminum beneath.

Doors and corridors. It seemed as though her entire world was somehow wrapped up in doors and corridors. The bleak dungeon in her barely revealed past. The long hallway of locked doors she and Tara had created in her mind. And now this. Even as strongly as she felt Zach's presence right now—as though he were almost within her grasp, as though she could hear his soft susurrant breathing—the coincidence worried her, touched her with ice-rimmed fingers of doubt. Was she imagining this after all?

It seemed like minutes before Zach's small hand reached out for the handle. His fingers hung a millimeter above the brass, quivering, as though the handle were electrified. Audrey thought that it might be. If not electrified, then somehow *horrified*. She willed him not to touch it. To back away and run. Somehow she knew that this was not the exit. Was Zach telling her that? Or was it the tiny voice in the back of her head that kept telling her that it wasn't a real door at all, that it was like one of the doors in her mind and that if the Zach in her mind opened it now, all hell was going to erupt out of it.

Still, she had no control over him, he clasped the handle and pulled down.

Audrey felt the cold metal as though it were *her* hand grasping the handle. She felt herself drawn deeper and deeper into Zach's consciousness until she couldn't separate his thoughts from her own. She stared at the lock through the eyes and understanding of a small, very talented young boy. A boy who could do things she'd never imagined him doing.

The lock seemed frozen at first, but then there was a slight, grudging give to it, as though it were rust and not lock holding the door in place. Zach pulled it down a tad more. The scraping sound from inside the lock rattled down the dark corridor, but still the latch would not give.

He shook his head and pushed the handle again and Audrey could feel him, twisting the workings of the lock inside his mind, pushing a tumbler here—though he thought of them as *pins*—then another. He knew where he was inside the mechanism, understood the workings of the lock, because *it made sense.* That was the only way he could think of it. It just made sense to him.

But none of it made sense to Audrey.

40

ZACH PUSHED and the door swung inward. He was pulled a step into the darkened room with it, sucking in his breath. His heart pounded in his ears and one foot tapped rapidly on the floor. The sound frightened him, until he pressed all his weight on the ball of that foot to stop it.

The barest razor of light cut the concrete floor, all else was clad in gloom. But he sensed no one else in the room. Some people he could detect even at a distance. Others had to be very near. But here there was no one. He bit his lip, reaching up along the paneling to his right to find the light switch. A lightbulb buzzed on overhead.

The room looked more like his mother's closet than anything else. Men's and women's clothes hung from pipes along the concrete walls. Shoes, some still in boxes, lined the floor. Paperback books were stacked in one corner, collecting dust, and a double-wide dresser rested against the rear wall. He recognized a large, dusty photo album on the dresser. Dropping it onto the floor, he squatted down and opened it, glancing at the pictures in the shadowy light that seeped through the coats and plastic-covered dresses.

The photos were faded and warped. Some were black-and-white, which seemed positively ancient to him. Others he recognized as thick Polaroid prints, mostly out of focus. Almost all of them were of children. There were numerous group and single photos of one little boy and twin girls at different ages. He flipped one last page and stared at the woman looking back at him out of an unknown past. She was twenty pounds heavier. Her face was broader, and her hair was thick and black, but she looked like his mother. He pressed his back against the dresser, cocking his head, checking the photo from every angle.

There were pictures of the children with the woman and pictures of her with some man he had never seen before. On the last page was a photograph of the man and woman and a third person, standing directly on the other side of the man.

The picture was ripped, the edges jagged, and someone had tried to peel the photo off the sticky backing but it had beaten their efforts. The third person's head was missing and a shiver raced up Zach's spine. When he ran his fingers across the photo, dark, violent images flooded his mind. It was almost as though he could get *inside* the picture the way he could slip inside a lock. But he didn't understand the workings of the photo the way he understood mechanical things. He didn't want to. He shoved the book away in disgust, leaving it open, still staring at the photo. Locked onto it like a video camera.

He's showing me the book, thought Audrey. My God, they're pictures of me and my sister and brother, and that must be Mother!

She could feel Zach intensely now, stronger than she had ever sensed him before, and she knew he sensed her as well. She wanted to wrap her arms around him, to hold him tight, and she knew he wanted to *be* in her arms just as bad. She felt his relief at finally making contact as much as she felt her own. But *her* relief was short-lived.

She watched as Zach's finger pointed directly at the woman on the porch, and she felt a terrible blast of realization exploding from Zach's mind into her own. A deep-welled fear that seemed ever so familiar now slipped over her heart.

Her mother was back. It *was* she who had taken Zach. Just as she had taken Craig. As she had taken Paula. And neither of them had ever returned once they were *gone.*

Mother has him.

41

AUDREY OPENED HER EYES slowly. When she realized she wasn't breathing, she gasped until she choked and had to cough to catch her breath again. She was bathed in sweat and shaking badly. She knew where Zach was, regardless of what Richard or the sheriff or anyone else thought. And she was going to save him. Her mother was not going to destroy another life. Certainly not the life most precious to her above all others. But as much as she wanted to leap from the chair and race to Zach's side, Audrey was still half-caught in her inner vision.

Without warning, her sense of closeness to Zach had been shorted out somehow. She had lost immediate contact with him, but she could still sense his presence nearby, like a radiant heat. She *knew* now, beyond question, that her terrible premonitions on passing by the old house next door had been real. That was where her mother had Zach. The bitch had stolen him right from under her nose and held him so close that Audrey could have *touched* him all that time! The rage in Audrey's chest constricted the muscles of her heart.

She gazed at the saddle in the trees where a few stars were barely peeking through, and unseen hands lifted her to her feet. She moved like a sleepwalker, down off the porch and across the lawn. When she reached her garden, she paused, as though suddenly awakened, and glanced around.

Was the night quieter than before?

She peered upward at the saddle again. The moon formed bony shadows in the trees, creating an army of jagged skeletons. She stepped quickly through her garden, throwing herself into the alders on the slope. The rough brush scratched at her cotton blouse and nipped her bare arms. Cuts stung both hands, but the pain seemed distant, as though she were viewing the outer world through one of the long, dark tunnels in her head. She was forced to maintain her balance by grabbing the spiny branches, creating fresh wounds.

Halfway up the hill she stumbled upon the trail Richard had mentioned. She glanced both ways, but it seemed to run along the slope, not upward, so she crashed once more through the alders. When she emerged onto the trail yet again, she realized that it wove back and forth up the hill and she began to follow it.

She was winded by the time she reached the top. A stitch stung her side and she gripped her waist with both hands, ignoring the blood soaking into her blouse, but even that pain didn't stop her. She stumbled along the narrow path between the giant spruce until the slope dropped away in front of her and the moon illuminated the valley beyond. One cold gray beam shone directly down on the Coonts farm. She couldn't believe how close it was. If the hill had not been in the way, they would have been next-door neighbors.

She strode down the rough slope and out into the moon-lit field with clinched fists, tightened jaw, and raspy breath. If she'd carried a sword, she would have looked like an avenging angel.

42

THE PHONE RINGING was like a slap in the face. Virgil had dozed off and it took him a moment to remember where he was.

The TV was still on with no volume and Doris was lying on his arm, which was now sound asleep and throbbing. He tried to slide out from under her as gently as possible, placing her head on the pillow and waiting a second to assure that she was just asleep. He snatched the cordless phone out of its holder and stumbled into the hallway, closing the bedroom door behind him.

"Yeah?"

"Virgil? This is Ken over to Crane's Hardware."

Virgil glanced at his watch. It was almost eight.

"What's up, Ken?" He tried to keep the irritation out of his voice but he wasn't very good at it.

"Your deputy said to call you at home."

"He did?" He'd have to have a talk with his deputy, whichever one it was. "What's up, Ken?"

"Well, Birch thought it was nothing. Wouldn't even come check. That's why he finally suggested I call you."

"And you figured that I wouldn't think it was nothing?"

"I don't know. Just strange, that's all."

"What's strange, Ken?"

"Well, you know we're staying open later this year. Trying something new for the summer."

"Uh-huh." Virgil figured he'd give Ken about two more sentences to come to the point.

"About thirty minutes ago your friend Mac comes in and buys four five-gallon gas cans."

"Mac?"

What the devil was Mac doing in town tonight? And gas cans? It was a riddle all right. But it didn't sound like an emergency to Virgil.

"I thought that was kind of funny," said Ken.

"Did he say what he wanted with the cans?"

"No."

"Is it illegal to buy gas cans?"

"No."

"Is that all?"

"He looked strange, Virgil. Irv noticed it too, didn't you, Irv?"

Virgil could hear muffled conversation in the background.

"Strange how, Ken?"

"Like he was on drugs or something. He never looked me in the eyes. Just stood at the counter, told me what he wanted, and signed the credit card slip. That was funny too. He almost left his credit card on the counter. I had to put it in his jacket pocket for him."

"Did he look like he'd been drinking?" Mac had never had a drinking problem that Virgil knew of. He was just fumbling for answers.

"No," said Ken. "He wasn't wobbling or slurring his words or anything. He just seemed dazed, if you know what I mean."

Ken and Irv chattered in his ear, but Virgil could only make out bits and pieces of the conversation.

"He's back," said Ken at last.

"At the store?" said Virgil.

"No. Irv says he's parked out front of Babs St. Clair's house and he's getting out with the cans."

Alarm bells went off in Virgil's head.

"I'll be right there!" he said, tossing the phone onto the side table in the hall.

43

ADLER GRINNED IN THE PASSENGER SEAT. He loved riding in the hills where the car dipped and rolled, and he leaned his agile body with it, feeling the power surging beneath his feet. Occasionally the headlights would illumine subtle movement in the trees that his master didn't notice. Adler would raise his chin and peer into the darkness as the car whirred past in the night, and imagine himself racing through the damp stillness after the swift beast, trying to catch it before it could drop into hiding.

Tara shifted beside him and Adler glanced in his master's direction. The dog immediately acquired some of his master's agitation, swaying anxiously on *his* seat. Driving back and forth up the same stretch of road had the dog nervous, especially since Tara made whirling U-turns so frequently. When Tara sighed, it seemed to depressurize the car and the dog eased a little.

"You have to do what you have to do, Adler," said Tara, fingering a small automatic pistol in her lap. "I keep putting off the inevitable. That isn't like me."

She glanced over and smiled and Adler relaxed even more. Dropping his head, he accepted a friendly pat.

"You okay, old sport?" said Tara.

Adler, of course, didn't understand what Tara said, but he recognized the caring in her voice and responded to it by nudging Tara's arm with his nose, begging for another pat.

Tara laughed and rewarded the dog with a good grinding behind the ears. But as she drew her hand away and returned her attention to the road ahead, her face hardened. "I'm doing what I have to do, Adler. I don't have a choice. I can't keep putting it off any longer, I guess."

Adler rolled with another sharp curve and caught himself on the seat with sharp nails.

"I thought the doors would hold forever. I was wrong. It was Zach. When Zach disappeared, the stress must have been too much for Audrey. I should have seen it coming. But if Cates hadn't started digging . . . then the St. Clair bitch had to start exhibiting real talent. It was just a comedy of errors. Who would have thought Audrey would talk to a psychic, for God's sake? Audrey probably had as much to do with Babs's starting to break through as Babs had to do with Audrey. What an unbelievable mess!"

Adler sensed anxiety growing in his master's voice again and the animal grew restive, lifting first one leg, then the other, balancing on his skinny butt in the leather seat.

"I wish there was time to come up with an alternate solution. I'd like nothing better than to investigate the limits of Babs's talents. But I can't chance having either of them remember."

Tara was nodding, speaking more to herself now than to Adler, although the dog could hear her slightest whisper. "Why couldn't you leave it alone, Audrey? There was no danger for you. I would never have hurt you. Why couldn't you just forget like you were trained to do?"

Adler whimpered gently, panting and offering his master his down-turned nose in obeisance. Tara stroked the dog's neck again, the final decision gleaming in her eyes as her fingers returned to the pistol. She'd driven much farther up the road than before and, when she finally spotted a place to reverse direction, she put the car into a gut-wrenching turn, heading back for Richard and Audrey's house.

"We do what we gotta do, Adler. Eh?"

The dog *woofed* and Tara smiled.

44

RICHARD HAD JUST STEPPED OUT onto the porch in search of Audrey when the moon caught her back as she crept out of the underbrush and into the saddle high above. His first thought was that he was seeing the mysterious visitor who had left her tracks on the lawn, but then he recognized Audrey's bright red blouse and shock of golden hair.

"Audrey!" he shouted, leaping out onto the lawn, standing on tiptoe to see over the brush. "Audrey! Come back!"

She ignored him, disappearing into the trees like a frightened deer.

Richard shook his head. Of course she was headed for the Coonts place. Where else would she be going? And what was she going to do when she got there? Virgil had told them to leave Merle Coonts alone, to let *him* run the investigation. He'd take care of it if Merle was guilty of trespassing or worse. Richard had told Virgil he was sure it wasn't Merle Coonts. The tracks were too small. He didn't know whose tracks they'd been. But they didn't belong to a man as big as Virgil assured him Merle Coonts was.

"Jesus, Audrey," he muttered, racing to their car. He wasn't going to catch her by scrambling up that slope, but he could cut her off before she got to the house.

He slammed the car door and then fumbled for his keys, shaking so badly he had to use both hands to insert them in the ignition. He gripped the wheel for a moment, listening to the powerful *thrum* of the engine, catching his breath, trying to slow his pounding heart. He backed down the drive so fast he almost lost control as he whipped out onto the road, burning rubber when the tires hit the pavement. The car nearly went airborne cresting the hill and as soon as he spotted the farm ahead he glanced at the fields, searching for Audrey. He had to slow to a crawl then, staring out over the rusted barbed-wire fence into the tall grass, trying to make out the distant shadows along the tree line.

There she was, looking like a ghost floating through the moonlight. The sight of her, alone in the wide-open darkness, touched the deepest pain in Richard's soul. She'd been alone like that for over a year, in darkness. Searching for their son. And he hadn't been there for her. He'd held it all in. He'd hidden in the goddamned basement and let her hurt.

He glanced up and down the road, but there was hardly any shoulder here, only deep drainage ditches on both sides of the road. He had no choice but to pull into Merle Coonts's driveway and park behind the semi, the tail of the Camry just barely off the road. Every light was out in the house now and he hoped that no one inside had heard his arrival. With any luck he could grab Audrey, help her to the car, and go home with no one the wiser.

He ran around the front of the dark house to where he could see the field again, but he couldn't make her out where he thought she would be. He tried to move silently through the tall grass alongside the house, heading toward the barn, but he kept stumbling on the uneven ground.

A movement against the trees might have been Audrey, but he couldn't be sure. The moon had slipped behind a cloud and the night was even darker than before. He wanted desperately to call out to her, to let her know he was here, but she might not even hear him if she was having another one of her night terrors, and he didn't want to alarm anyone in the house. He took two more steps out in the direction of the open field, still glancing toward the corner of the barn.

45

BY THE TIME VIRGIL got to Babs's house, Ken and Irv were out front of the hardware store, and two or three other people were chattering noisily at them. Flickering lights shone through the curtains and Virgil couldn't help but think of the gas cans and the forest of candles in Babs's living room.

"Tell me what happened, Ken," said Virgil, pulling the bigger man away from the group.

"He carried three of those gas cans into Babs's house," said Ken, nodding as though that was exactly what he knew Mac had intended all along.

"Carried them from where?" said Virgil, searching for Mac's car.

"Out of his car," said Ken, pointing around the corner to where a blue Ford sedan sat parked beside the stop sign.

Virgil stared at the car in disbelief. He had no proof, but at that moment he was absolutely certain that it was the same car that had followed him, the same sedan that had damn near killed him. The thought that Mac might have been driving made no sense whatsoever. But the thought that Mac had just carried three gas cans into Babs's house didn't make much sense either.

"How long ago?" he asked.

"Maybe ten minutes."

"Stay here," said Virgil loudly, glancing around to make certain none of the gathering crowd got any other ideas.

Whatever was going on here, it wasn't good. And Virgil *really* didn't like the fact that Babs had warned him about bad things, just like Cooder. That wasn't quite the way she'd put it, but he couldn't get Cooder's words out of his skull. They kept beating around in there like the words to a song.

Virgil had called Birch on the radio before leaving home. He could already hear the siren of the approaching cruiser behind him. As Virgil climbed Babs's stoop, he unsnapped the strap on his pistol. Gas fumes stung his nostrils and his mouth went dry. He pictured himself pulling the trigger of the pistol, flames shooting from the barrel, catching the fumes. He could imagine the roar of exploding gasoline.

Sweet Jesus.

He rapped on the door but there was no answer.

"Babs?"

Still nothing. But the smell of gasoline was stronger right in front of the door. He wondered how thick the fumes would have to be before the candles in Babs's living room blew the place to kingdom come. Adrenaline raced through his veins like steam through a heat pipe. His hand shook as he gripped the doorknob.

"Babs?" he said again, opening the unlocked door.

The fumes hit him directly in the face and he grimaced. The scene that confronted him reminded him of something he'd seen before. A movie. Or a film clip, maybe.

In what seemed slow motion, he drew his pistol and aimed it at Mac's back. Mac had his own pistol pointed directly at Babs, who was calmly dousing herself with gasoline. Her hair clung to her head and she squinted, coughing and gagging, but still she poured the remains of the can over herself. As Virgil's eyes flashed from her to Mac, he noticed that Mac's suit was soaked as well.

"Oh, my God," said Virgil as Mac turned full toward him.

"Hi, Virg," said Mac. His voice was so calm, his demeanor so collected, that for a moment Virgil was sure he was dreaming.

"What are you doing, Mac?" said Virgil, keeping his voice controlled, his face calm and reassuring. He noticed puddles of gasoline on the tabletop, so near the spluttering candles he couldn't believe they hadn't caught. Maybe it was all a joke. Maybe it was water in the cans. But the overwhelming odor of the fumes put the lie to that idea. He was grasping at straws and if he didn't do something, those straws were going to go up like a Roman candle.

Mac shrugged. "Babs and I are going to join the others. It's our time now."

His calm words conveyed a horror to Virgil that Mac's eyes didn't reflect.

"Mac," said Virgil, easing a step forward, still aiming the pistol at his friend, "you need to put the gun down and step out onto the front porch with me."

He glanced back at the open door, hoping the fresh air would waft away some of the fumes. He couldn't believe that the vapors hadn't reached the candles yet, or built up enough to explode the three of them out to hell and gone, but he knew that it was only a matter of seconds before they did.

Mac shook his head. "We *want* to go," he said, glancing at Babs for confirmation.

Babs looked at Virgil, shaking her head. "There's nothing you can do now, Virg," she said. "You need to get yourself back outside before you get hurt."

"Babs," said Virgil. "I want you to stand up slowly and move toward the door."

"He won't let me," she said, nodding toward Mac, who still wore the same nonexpression. "He'll shoot me if I move."

"Stand up," said Virg.

Babs shrugged, easing the gas can onto the soaking sofa. She started to stand and Mac's attention instantly riveted on her again. He pointed his pistol directly into her face.

"Mac!" said Virgil, aiming his own pistol at the center of Mac's back. "Put the gun down. You have no reason to do this. Snap out of it. You don't even know this woman!"

But Babs was shaking her head. "Yes, he does," she said quietly. "Mac and I spent time in hell together."

"What?" said Virgil, his attention wavering.

Babs was staring directly into Mac's eyes now. "Remember, Mac? Remember Perkins?"

Virgil was stunned. "You were in Perkins, Mac?"

But Mac didn't hear. His attention was still riveted on

Babs. "We're all going to be together now, Babs," he whispered. "And everything is going to be all right again. Don't you feel it?"

Surprising Virgil, Babs nodded and reached out to place a consoling hand on Mac's shoulders, his pistol almost resting against her nose. "Yes, Mac," she said gently. "Yes. It's going to be all right now. All the bad dreams are going to end. You've been having the dreams too. Haven't you?"

Mac nodded, a touch of sadness creeping across the otherworldly calmness of his face. "I don't want to see them anymore," he said.

"Mac," said Virgil. "It was you in the car. You following me. Wasn't it?"

Mac turned to face him and for the first time Virgil saw emotion in his friend's eyes, sadness. He nodded slowly.

"Why, Mac? You almost killed me."

"I'm sorry, Virg," said Mac, blinking. "I'm awful sorry."

Virgil sensed that he was almost breaking through. That he was close to reaching Mac, to taking control of the situation. But the candlelight was still reflected in puddles of gas.

Babs glanced around Mac toward Virgil. "You need to get outside now."

Virgil shook his head. "I'm not going without both of you."

But it all happened too fast. The fumes didn't explode as Virgil had expected. Instead, all in the space of one gasp, flames licked outward from the candles, following an invisible path of gas through the air, leaping onto Mac's suit. Then, as he stumbled forward, the flames blasted out and engulfed Babs. From there they raced along the floor to the sofa, leapt up the walls, and arched across the ceiling. Virgil's body was assaulted by a fierce wave of searing heat and his mind, unable to accept the entirety of what he was witnessing, locked onto details.

Babs's face melted like plastic as she fell backward onto the flaming sofa, her eyes bulging from sockets where the lids had been seared away. Her hair turned into the tip of a giant candle flame as her head writhed in eerie silence from side to side.

Mac, now a human torch, slapping at his chest and face

ineffectually—as though he had changed his mind at the last instant—then falling to the floor and disappearing in the engulfing flames and smoke.

And the candles.

Melting as one, as though a giant magnifying glass had focused the sun upon them. Puddling onto the round table that was already immersed in flame.

Hands on his shoulders.

Dragging him backward out the door and down the porch steps as the fire reached out the doorway, grasping at him.

Sirens in his ears.

Women screaming.

People running.

Someone shouting at him.

"What?" he said, unable to take his eyes off the front of the house where the flames were already lapping at the eaves. The heat was more intense than he could have imagined. Of course, if you dumped a few cans of high-test in a living room, that was likely to happen. If he hadn't opened the door when he had, it probably would have blown the damned house to kingdom come.

It was Birch who'd slipped inside the inferno to save him, and he tried to focus on Birch's face. Birch stared at him wide-eyed, tossing glances over Virgil's shoulder at the spreading blaze.

"What the hell happened, Virg?"

"Ken was right," muttered Virgil. "Mac was crazy. He brought the gas back here, doused himself and Babs, and set it alight."

Well, that wasn't exactly the truth. Mac hadn't *lit* the fire. The candles had. But no way it was an accident.

"Wow," said Birch.

"Virgil!" shouted Marg, grabbing him by both biceps. She was winded as he'd ever seen her. Must have run the half-block from the hospital. "My lord, are you all right? I stuck my head out when I heard Birch's siren and the next thing I knew the house went up. What happened? Is Babs all right?"

"No."

"Oh, God."

Virgil nodded. "Come here, Marg," he said, dragging her aside and motioning for Birch to make sure they had some privacy. The first fire truck had just screeched to a stop next to his cruiser, men were dragging hoses out, and the chief was starting in Virgil's direction when Birch cut him off.

"What happened?" asked Marg, staring over Virgil's shoulder at the roof where shingles were beginning to smolder. The house was going up like a tinderbox, the gasoline turning the wood blaze into a raging firestorm. They had to back even farther away, out into the street.

"When I opened the front door, Mac had a gun on Babs and was forcing her to pour gasoline over herself. He'd already soaked himself."

"Holy shit."

"Yeah. The candles caught the fumes and the place went up like a bonfire."

"Babs never had a chance to get out?"

"Mac had a gun on her the whole time."

"That's just crazy. What the hell did he do that for?"

"It was weird. Mac goes to Crane's and buys four gas cans. He fills up the cans, comes back to Babs's house, and douses both of them in gasoline. He's calm as a cucumber when I open the door, and Babs is sitting there pouring gasoline on herself like she's taking a warm shower. Mac kept saying they were going to join the *others* and Babs said they'd both been in Perkins. Does that ring a bell?"

"Babs worked at Perkins for a while in the eighties. I thought you knew that. I didn't know Mac worked there."

"Evidently he wasn't an employee."

"Oh. I didn't know that. You think maybe he had a grudge against Babs?"

Virgil shook his head. "It didn't sound like that. It was more like they were old friends. Why would Babs sit there like that?" He stared at the grass, watching the fiery light play across it. "He acted so damned calm. Like it didn't bother him at all that he was about to murder Babs or that he was fixing to . . . burn himself up like that. Could he have been hypnotized?"

Marg shook her head. "That's pretty thin, Virgil. Hypnosis takes a lot of effort. Not everyone succumbs to it and, even if they do, the theory is that they won't do anything they wouldn't do awake. You might convince Babs to sit still for it if she didn't realize it was gasoline. I guess you could hypnotize her into believing it was holy water or something being poured over her head. But it's hard for me to believe you could get someone to kill someone else, if it wasn't really their idea. You think both of them were hypnotized?"

"Babs seemed clear-headed enough. She didn't want to move because she was afraid Mac would shoot her. How stupid is that? She knew he was about to torch both of them."

But Babs acted more like she was fulfilling a prophecy. She'd told Doris she was going to die and she had. Was seeing her prediction come to pass worth letting herself be burned to death?

"People have strange reactions under stress."

"What if *Mac* didn't know what he was doing?"

"What do you mean?"

"Couldn't a hypnotist convince *him* that it wasn't gasoline? Mac didn't *light* the fire. All he did was force Babs to pour gas over herself. What if he thought it was something else?"

"What?"

"I don't know! I'm just trying to come up with a theory here."

"Pretty wild theory, Virg. Sounds to me like Mac was a little looney all these years and he had fixated on Babs, whom he remembered from his days in the institution. He wouldn't be the first guy to crack like that."

"Maybe. Anyway, stay back and don't get hurt," he said, heading toward Birch and the fire chief, who was shouting instructions at volunteer firemen hanging safety tape around the front yard. The first hoses were just beginning to spray. But Babs's house was already a lost cause and everyone present knew it. Her candles were gone. Her cards were gone. Her weird curtains and her fake-fur sofa were gone. Everything that had made Babs St. Clair who she was, was disappearing with her, spiraling heavenward in the rushing black smoke. Virgil stared at the roiling ebony fumes, lit against the sky by the flames fingering their way out from under the eaves and bursting through the melted windows.

Go with God, Babs. I hope you make it over there where you want to be.

Virgil gave the chief all the information he could, instructed Birch to maintain crowd control and contact Mac's and Babs's next of kin, and then marched down the street to where he saw Ken and Irv watching the show, still out in front of the hardware store. Ken stepped out of the milling crowd to greet him.

"Virg! Holy shit! You were almost toast!"

"No, Ken. I'm all right."

"That was close! I saw Birch drag you off the porch. The flames looked like they were licking your face!"

"Really wasn't that close, Ken."

"Babs?"

Virgil shook his head.

"Shit," said Ken.

"Yeah, look, Ken. You said that when Mac came in he seemed out of it?"

"Yeah. It was like he was really preoccupied. Hell, I guess he would be if he was gonna go out and kill himself and somebody else. He's dead, isn't he?"

"Yeah. He's dead."

"What did you see in there, Virg? What happened?"

"I'd rather not say right now. Not while there's an ongoing investigation."

"Sure. I understand."

"Was there anyone else around that looked suspicious?"

"Well, I don't know what you mean, suspicious, Virg. There was that woman."

"What woman?"

Ken frowned. "She was driving a light SUV, a Ford I think. She parked beside Mac when he was putting the cans in his car and they talked for a minute or two, I guess. I couldn't see much of her because Mac's car was in the way."

"What did she look like?"

"Like I say, I couldn't see much. She had short gray hair. I remember that."

"How old?"

"Late forties maybe. Good-looking."

"That's all you remember?"

"Did you see her, Irv?" said Ken.

Irv shook his head. "I remember her car. There was a big Doberman inside."

"Yeah," said Ken. "That's right. I forgot the dog."

"How long ago did she leave?" asked Virgil.

"An hour, hour and a half, maybe," said Irv, glancing at Ken, who nodded. "That was about how long ago Mac left. I guess he was going to get the gas. It took him a long time now that I think about it. But he wasn't right. Right, Virg? Maybe he was building up his nerve."

"Do you think the woman had something to do with the fire?" asked Ken, glancing toward the holocaust Babs's house had become.

"See which way she went?" asked Virgil, ignoring Ken's question.

Both men shook their heads. "Didn't see her pull back out," said Ken. "One minute she was there. The next she and Mac were gone. We had customers."

"Thanks," said Virgil, heading back toward the fire.

Most of the crowd had now gathered on the sidewalk across the street from the house. Two more fire trucks had arrived and arcs of water gushed through the sky above the raging flames, but the building was already crumbling in on itself. It occurred to Virgil that Mac must have soaked the entire downstairs in gasoline before drenching himself and Babs.

Virgil couldn't figure out how anyone could possibly convince a man to do that to himself or to anyone else. He imagined himself, cloaked in flames, his skin crackling, nerves screaming, muscles refusing to obey him as the intense heat turned them from flesh to charred meat.

God, what a way to go.

Birch was leaning on the open door of his cruiser, radio mike in one hand. "You think Mac was a closet psycho?" asked Birch as Virgil stopped alongside him.

"Maybe he wasn't in control of himself."

"I'd say that was obvious."

He spotted Carl Robison, editor of the paper, trying to bust his way through the cordon. Virgil gave a hand signal to one of his deputies and Carl was politely shepherded away. Time enough to deal with Carl later.

"I meant, maybe someone *made* him do what he did," he said. "Why did he have to buy gas cans at the hardware store *here* if he was planning on driving up and killing Babs all along?"

"You can't figure out a nut's head. It was probably spur of the moment. You know something I don't, Virg?"

"All I know is there's more to this than meets the eye. Find out from Marg where they moved the old records for Perkins Mental Health Institute. Then find out what I need to do to get to see them. If I need a court order, start working on it."

Birch frowned. "Perkins?"

"Evidently Mac was a patient a few years ago."

"So he did have mental problems."

"I think maybe he had more after he got out than when he went in," said Virgil. "Just see what it takes to get into the records."

"You're not telling me something, Virg."

"I don't know anything to tell you yet."

"All right. Where you gonna be?"

"Home. Doris isn't good."

"Want me to call you in the morning, then?"

"No," said Virgil at last. "Call me as soon as you find out about the records. I don't care what time it is."

He glanced at the blue sedan and Birch followed his eyes.

"It's rented," said Birch, and Virgil nodded.

46

COODER HAD NO IDEA how long he had lain splayed against the slope, his cheek pressed into the ground, grass clutched in either fist, the tinkling sound of water dribbling through the corrugated pipe beside him. He was breathing in jerky gasps, tears welled in his eyes, and salty snot dripped down his lip.

She was back.

So close he could feel her. He felt like the rat, cornered in a dark hidey-hole, quivering, waiting for a giant hand to drag him out into the light.

The headlights had raced around the curve in the distance like the flickering flame on a dynamite fuse, and he'd barely dropped down the slope again in time, to avoid being caught in their glare. As the car approached, his mind had exploded with images of light and darkness. Visions of half-seen faces. Men and women in hospital gowns. And a pain that was as terrible as anything he could remember, that began somewhere deep within him and spun outward in burning spiderwebs. The car had passed numerous times, slowing, then speeding up, like a shark, trolling for prey.

"Try!"

The remembered command echoed down the dusty tunnels of his mind in a shrill woman's voice. Vaguely he could feel his body convulsing, held in place by strong straps, his neck stretching to the breaking point as his back arched violently upward.

"Try!"

The pain again, searing through his skin. He could smell smoke. But was he imagining it or was his brain really burning? What did she want?

He wanted to forget the woman's voice. To forget everything and blank out completely. But the pain forced him to remain. He burrowed away from it in his mind, trying to find sanctuary, but all that accomplished was to bring him closer to his memories of the woman.

The Severely Disturbed Ward.

Cooder wasn't certain how he had ended up in that section. He hadn't been assigned there in the beginning. But the hallway was indelibly registered in his brain.

That door there was where Crazy Feeble lived.

Crazy Feeble was what the attendants called the old man with the leering grin and one bad eye who was allowed into the television room only once a week and by himself. Crazy Feeble had been in Perkins since the day it opened. He'd killed his wife and six kids with a butcher knife, and then cut them up into bite-sized pieces, and burned them in the fireplace. That was before Cooder was born. But everyone was still plenty afraid of Crazy Feeble. There were lots of people to be afraid of at Perkins, like the guys in the *special* activities room where some of them were allowed to socialize, but only under heavy supervision. Cooder always thought of that group as the Mixed Nuts.

The memory of the woman's voice echoed in his head.

"What did you feel?"

He shook his head. He could see her now, standing in front of him. Was she really there? He shook against the slope, grasping at the grass. At anything that was real. She wasn't there. He knew it. But she was so close inside his mind. The memory so strong he couldn't shove her away. "Scared."

"You felt more than that. What happened?"

"Nothing."

"Come with me."

"No."

The memory woman moved her lips but he didn't hear her words.

Instead he remembered his body responding to commands he hadn't given. She was moving him just like he'd moved the crow... and the rat.

She walked away down the corridor and he followed complacently along like a faithful hound. She stopped in front of another of the white doors. Cooder knew that when this memory had actually happened, he had walked on through, but now he stopped. He couldn't make himself take the next fateful step. He knew that on the other side of that metal threshold was horror and even worse, pain. He knew then that once he had been different. Like other people. Something on the other side of that door had changed him forever. Something buried within the terrible flashes and visions that had haunted him ever since Perkins, had made him what he was now. It wasn't the loss that horrified him. Cooder was perfectly happy with who he was.

It was the fear that the woman was here to finish what she had started.

Try!

The command rattled in his brain, insistent.

He was wracked with terror at the thought of passing through the door, but finally the memory took over and his slippered foot stepped forward, entering a place as clean and bright as morning sunlight. A place that smelled like death.

Faces passed before his unmoving eyes. In the corner he saw cages filled with rats, their tiny eyes peering at him through the wire mesh. But one face became more and more prevalent until it swelled to the width of his vision.

Doctor Beals. So close he could smell the tangy sweetness of her toothpaste.

Try!

"Try what?" he screamed. His voice rang against the tinny sides of this place.

"Try to see inside their heads! The same way you do with the birds! I know you can do it! Do you want me to use the machine again?"

"No! Please!"

He couldn't fight her. Couldn't move. She strapped the blinding mask over his head. Connected wires to his body. The wires and the mask were where the spiderwebs came from.

Blind panic surged through him. His breath was ragged, his heart raced, never knowing when the agony would strike. And then it did. Gut-wrenching. Breath-stealing. Mind-shattering pain.

"Try!"

He knew that he could do what she wanted. He had done it before often enough when he thought he wasn't being watched. All he had to do was relax and let it happen. But he also knew that if he did he would die, because then she would use the mask more and more, turn the machine up higher and higher until the pain killed him.

So he hid it away. Screamed that it was impossible. Cried over and over that he didn't know why the animals liked him. And eventually she would take the mask off and talk to him, and sometime during that talk he would begin to forget again. And each time there was less and less for him to forget.

That was what this was about. The machine. The little boy. The woman in the car. Doctor Beals. He opened his eyes and listened to the night. In the distance, an owl hooted. The water still trickled beside him. He rolled over onto his back and stared at the cloud-dusted stars overhead.

Why didn't she kill me? She killed the others.

Like so many things in his life, the other deaths were something that Cooder just *knew*. The way he had known that she was coming back. The way he knew that the bad things he had seen were returning and people were going to start dying again.

Another car drove slowly by and Cooder recoiled in fear until he realized that it wasn't Tara. It was the other woman's husband. He listened as the car parked somewhere across the road and then a door slammed. Now all was quiet. He allowed himself to relax again, just a little.

But now, in the distance, he sensed Doctor Beals returning.

47

AUDREY HAD NEVER EXPERIENCED such a powerful sense of awareness before. The night seemed electrically alive, her mind filled to bursting with sights and sounds and smells. It was as though she had been statically charged with some otherworldly energy and all her senses were magnified, acute.

The closer she got to the farmhouse, the stronger her sense of Zach's presence became. It wasn't a dream. It wasn't a night terror. And it wasn't a hallucination. She could feel him and she knew that he could feel her as well. She could hear him inside her head, jabbering at her, excited the way any child would be to be with his mother after more than a year apart. It was almost as though she were already holding him in her arms, hugging him tight against her breast.

I'm coming, honey! I'm coming!

She knew that he heard her as clearly as though she had spoken aloud because he answered her. She stumbled on a root and scolded herself. If you're going to walk in two worlds you'd better pay attention to both.

When she spotted the two figures alongside the house, she froze. Richard she recognized immediately as he rounded the corner. The other man had to be Merle Coonts. He was hiding in the shadows alongside the house, watching Richard. He hadn't spotted Audrey, though, and she eased stealthily back along the tree line to fade into the shadows, continuing her advance toward the barn. Now she was almost parallel with the rear of the old building and Merle was slipping along the house, away from her, toward the unsuspecting Richard.

Should she shout a warning? But that would give her away and she knew that Richard wasn't here to help her. He was here to take her home. But what were Merle Coonts's intentions? He wasn't making his presence known. What if he hurt Richard? What if he killed him?

She hugged the deep shadows along the tree line, studying the two men. Richard wasn't trying to conceal himself. Merle, on the other hand, moved like a fat old weasel, taking cover in every patch of darkness along his path. She couldn't tell if he was armed, but he was a lot bigger than Richard.

Just when she had decided to call out, Zach's voice pleaded with her again to come and rescue him. And it dawned on her that if Merle Coonts was here, then Zach was alone with her mother! She had to find him, and Richard wouldn't help her. He'd *stop* her!

She stared across the fifty yards of open field toward the back of the old barn. A large sliding door was open just a crack. That must have been where Merle had snuck out. She eased along the trees a little farther until the corner of the barn obscured her from Richard and Merle, then she ran, not stopping until she hit the back of the barn, gasping for breath. But she couldn't stop now. She eyed the barn door, listening to Zach in her head.

Just a minute, honey. Just one minute!

She edged up the sloping ground to the corner of the barn and peered around into the gloom. There was Merle, crouched like a cat.

"Richard!" she screamed at the top of her lungs. "Look out! Merle is hiding beside the bulkhead!"

Then she ran. Stumbling back down the slope, grabbing the old door, whipping herself inside. She was winded and her heart pummeled her ribs. The barn basement was dark as pitch. It smelled of damp concrete and ancient, dust-dry hay and mildewed wood. She wished she'd had the foresight to bring a flashlight.

I'm lost, Zach. In the dark.

Look for the big suitcase. In the back.

His voice, echoing in her mind, was as heady as strong whiskey and teasingly close. Almost like a real voice, getting louder as she drew near.

Suitcase?

It's how we get upstairs.

I don't understand, Zach.

Look in the back! Against the wall!

She couldn't make out anything in the darkness, so she'd have to follow the foundation blindly to the rear. She swallowed a dry lump in her throat and stepped gingerly along the side wall, into the deeper darkness hidden there, her hands bumping over the splintery barn boards, sliding her feet along the cement floor. Sooner or later she had to bump into the first corner, and then she could work her way to the back and find the suitcase.

When Audrey screamed, Richard spotted Merle immediately. The big man thought he was being cunning but his clumsiness was almost laughable. He was hunched over beside a large lilac bush as though he could hide his huge bulk there. Only it wasn't funny. Why was he being sneaky at all? Why didn't he just come right out and say "Hey, what are you people doing on my property in the middle of the night?"

Richard thought again of the footprints in the grass. They were too small to have been Merle Coonts's tracks, but *someone* had made them. He'd wanted to believe that the possibility they might really have a Peeping Tom didn't have anything to do with Audrey's dreams, with her night terrors. He wanted to believe that *that* was just imagination. Only maybe Audrey wasn't imagining things. Someone with small feet had been outside their bedroom window, someone who had passed over the same cut in the hills that Audrey had just climbed through, and this was the only house in the area. What if Audrey wasn't just having bad dreams or hallucinations? What if Zach really was here? Was it possible? Could he really be alive?

Richard didn't want to go back to wondering every

minute if some miracle would happen, if the phone would ring or a knock would come at the door, wondering if he would wake up and discover that it had all been just a terrible dream. He didn't want to let his heart start beating faster in his chest at the thought of his son. He'd been there so many times and every time he had awakened, only to discover that the dream was a nightmare.

But Merle Coonts was hiding *something*.

And where the hell was Audrey?

He'd lost her in the shadows again, and now the moon had slipped behind a cloud. The field was barely lit by the faint starlight, and Richard wondered again why not one light was on in the house. Why were all the lights out if Merle was wide-awake and dressed?

Merle seemed to think the shadows made him invisible. He kept edging closer, sliding clumsily along the wall of the barn. Richard sized him up, wondering what was going to happen. He hadn't been in a fight since grade school, and he knew he was dangerously out of shape. But maybe Merle was too. He didn't see a gun and he figured if Merle had one on him he probably wouldn't be hiding like that. No, Merle was planning on jumping him when he got close.

He's going to attack me without warning. Why?

Suddenly Richard was absolutely certain that Audrey had been right all along. He didn't understand how she knew or how Merle had pulled it off. But somehow this bastard had taken their son. He could only pray that *all* of Audrey's premonitions were correct, that Zach was still alive. Wild rage welled up inside him.

I can take you, you son of a bitch. If you've hurt my son, I'll do more than take you.

He strode along the side of the house as though he had no idea that Merle was lurking in the shadows. When the bigger man leapt out in front of him, Richard surprised himself as much as Merle by rushing forward, gripping Merle by both shoulders, and powering him to the ground. Suddenly, with his hands grasping the man's flesh, he *knew* that Merle Coonts *had* taken Zach.

"What have you done with Zach, you bastard?" he screamed, slamming his fist into Merle's jowly face. "Where's my son?"

48

VIRGIL DROVE HOME in a daze, letting the cruiser steer itself like an old plowhorse headed for the barn. But when he pulled into his drive, he knew instantly that something was wrong. The lights were on in the kitchen and he distinctly remembered turning them off. He thought of the look on Babs's face as she poured the gasoline all over herself and suddenly Virgil knew what it was that he had felt, standing outside on her porch, just before going inside.

Death.

He had never before believed that you could sense death in a *place*, reaching out for another innocent victim, but he had felt it then and he felt it again now. His whole body went limp. He dragged himself out of the car and raced across the lawn on shaky legs. Pounding up the porch steps, he crashed through the front door that had never been locked in all the years he and Doris had lived there.

Doris lay on the floor beside the refrigerator.

How she had made it down the stairs he couldn't imagine. Her nightgown was bunched up around her wrinkled thighs, and he was shocked by how white her skin seemed against the brown tiles. He dropped down beside her, feeling for a pulse on her bird-thin wrist.

"Thank heaven," he muttered, carrying her hurriedly up the stairs and slipping her back into bed. He called the hospital and Marg answered.

"What's the matter, Virg? Jesus, I just saw you two minutes ago. Have you got into trouble again?"

"It's Doris."

"Oh, shit. Should I send the paramedics?"

"I found her downstairs passed out beside the fridge. I brought her back up to bed, but she hasn't woken up. I'm scared, Marg."

"Is she breathing all right?"

"She seems to be."

"Check her eyes. See if they dilate."

They did.

"Is she cold?"

"She feels clammy. But she always feels that way."

"You want Doctor Burton?"

"Hold on, Marg. I think she's coming around."

Doris groaned and rolled against his side. He slipped another pillow under her head.

"You scared the bejesus out of me," said Virgil when she opened her eyes. "What did you think you were doing? Are you all right? Did you break anything?"

"Sirens."

Virgil sighed loudly. "It was Babs. Her house burned down."

Doris's head barely bobbed. "She's dead. She told me she'd die today."

"I'm going to call an ambulance for you."

"No," she said weakly, grabbing his hand. "They'll take me to the hospital."

"Not if I tell them not to."

"Please," she whispered. She swallowed dryly and he lifted a glass off the bedside table, holding it to her parched lips.

"What were you thinking, going downstairs?"

She shook her head. "I was worried. I knew Babs was going to go today. What happened?"

"Nothing you need to be getting upset about right now."

"Virgil."

He sighed loudly. "She was murdered. Mac Douglass carried gas into her living room and set both of them on fire."

She closed her eyes as though fighting down one of her

pain attacks. When she opened them again, she stared directly at him. "The tarot cards foretold it."

He kissed her gently on her parchment brow and held her close.

"Coincidence," he said.

"You don't believe in coincidence and you know it."

"I don't believe in a lot of things."

"Just what you see."

"Yes."

But was it just coincidence running into Cooder when he did? Was it just coincidence that Babs blathered something about the Merrill boy's bike and he found it right where she said? Was it coincidence that two people who were at Perkins at the same time as Tara Beals suddenly ended up dead? And what kind of coincidence was it when a woman said she was going to die on a specific day and she did? How could she possibly have known something like this was going to happen?

"Do you still believe that, Virgil? After everything?"

He shook his head. "I don't know what to believe anymore. I believe Tara Beals is behind it though."

"Talk to Audrey again," whispered Doris. "She's not crazy and you know it. And you shouldn't leave her thinking you believe she is."

He stared at her and, for just an instant, he saw the old Doris. The Doris with gleaming eyes and sun-bleached hair and glowing skin. The Doris with a ready smile or a quip. He kissed her again.

"I'll do that. But I won't leave you right now."

A buzzing noise caught his attention and he realized that he had laid the phone facedown on the bedspread. "Sorry," he said, putting it to his ear. He was surprised when Doris reached up and took it away from him.

"Marg," she said in what was left of her husky soprano. "Doris. Could you come over and baby-sit me while Virgil goes out on official business? Yes. That would be nice, thanks."

He stared at her dumbfounded. "I told you I'm not going anywhere just yet. That was a heck of a spill you took."

She shrugged. "I'll be fine. You go tell that young woman you believe her."

"I can't tell her what I don't know."

"You know she's not crazy."

"I don't. She thinks Merle Coonts kidnapped her son and I know there's no way he did."

"Sometimes things aren't what they seem. You go talk to her and at least tell her you don't think she's crazy. I won't sleep worrying about her." She stared at him with that do-it-or-you'll-be-sorry look that was always the end to a conversation like this.

"All right," sighed Virgil, climbing wearily to his feet.

Doris snatched his hand. "I need you here with me. But you have to stay a good man through this. The man I married. You know?"

"I know."

Her voice was raspier than before and each word seemed dragged from her throat, but she was determined to have her say. "I don't know if you do. I'm ready and all that. I know everything will be okay. But I don't want to be alone when I go. I'm glad I'm going first. That's not fair to you, because then *you'll* be alone. But you're stronger than I am. You promise me you'll take care of yourself."

"I promise," he said, knowing that *she* was the strongest.

"I love you."

"Love you too."

"Eat something now and fix something for Marg."

He did as he was told, taking his time making sandwiches, soaking up the sounds of life: cars on the street outside, the hum of the fridge, water rushing in the sink, even the sound of another fire siren down on Main Street. He'd been certain that Doris was dead when he pulled into the driveway. Now everything seemed as normal as normal had been for the two of them in the past few months. But he couldn't get over the sense that he'd missed something.

49

COODER HEARD THE MEN'S CRIES coming from around
the side of the house and—like Audrey—the sights and
sounds of the night touched him on more than one level. He
knew that someone was fighting for his life *now*. But a part
of his mind related it to a fight *then*. And he had difficulty
separating the two. Cooder wasn't telepathic—at least not
where human beings were concerned—but he could read
strong feelings, even at a distance.

Now his mind was like a television badly tuned, picking
up more than one channel at a time, filled with static and
snow and weird images that came and went like ghosts. He
could sense the powerful emotions around him. Most of all,
he felt the little boy. But suddenly a pall seemed to drop
over the night. A chill hovered in the air.

Doctor Beals was almost here.

He sensed her well before he heard the hum of the tires
on asphalt, approaching from the direction of town. What
had she been up to? She'd kept passing by, back and forth
like a lion in a cage. Now he heard the car slowing, just
over his head. Stopping.

Had she found him? Had she finally found him again?
The thought turned his blood to ice. His fingers dug into
the loose gravel up to his knuckles, trying to crush the cool
stone and sand. But no footsteps approached. No terrible
presence lurked above.

With dreadful slowness, he found the courage to climb to the edge of the road and peek over the lip of pavement. She was parked in the road behind the other car. Her door slammed and Cooder caught just a glimpse of her slipping silently across the front of the house and disappearing around the corner. There was a dog with her. A powerful, excitable, loyal, brave dog.

Cooder steeled himself. He knew in that instant that she was after the boy, not him. She wanted to do to Zach Bock what she'd done to him, to so many others. He couldn't help but picture it, and the thought of a child in that terrible place was more than he could bear. He didn't know what he could do. If there was anything he *could* do. But the picture of it was more terrible to him than any pain he had ever imagined. He closed his eyes and stiffened, concentrating harder than he had in years. Thinking until his head hurt. When he opened his eyes again, he had the awful sense of being within touching distance of Doctor Beals.

He could feel the cool earth beneath his paws.

50

AUDREY LISTENED TO THE SOUND of her own breathing and her pulse pounding in her ears. She was still in contact with Zach, and from that strange, soundless dialogue she was forming a skewed, filmy picture of what she was supposed to be looking for. It wasn't a *suitcase*. It was a trunk.

She had reached the end of the wall beside the door where she'd entered, and turned the corner, heading toward the main house, creeping slowly along the rough stone foundation, only to discover that she was in a stall. She could feel the top of the hewn pine barrier and she sidled quickly around it. Then she followed it back into the next stall.

Again and again.

She had just an inkling of vision. The occasional moonbeam that peeked through the slit of open door did nothing this far into the barn. But here and there the faintest tendril of starlight struggled through a crack in the floor above, lending the huge open area a cavelike appearance. And if the vague visions that were passing between her and Zach were accurate, then she was approaching the last stall. She rounded it and discovered, as she slid her hands along the wall, that there were indeed no more barriers. She quickened her steps until her fingers struck something hard and she moaned. She'd found the back corner. Without stopping, she followed the wall to her left until her shins struck something solid.

She knelt and ran her fingers over the old trunk, her hands caressing the front, feeling for the hasp. When they reached it she gasped. Locked. She spun the cylinder ineffectually, cursing under her breath. She ran her fingers over the top, along the rusted iron straps to the thick hinges that were solid and unyielding. She felt as though she had been struck in the gut. She knew this was the hidden entrance to the cellar where Zach was held. It was just as he had shown it to her. But what good did knowing do?

She jerked hard at the lock, but the hasp was as solid as the hinges.

Zach! What's the combination?

But even as she thought that, she realized she wouldn't be able to see the numbers on the dial anyway. There had to be another answer.

I don't know.

Is there another way in?

I don't think so.

I have to find some way to open the lock.

"You son of a bitch!"

Richard's scream cut through the old barn boards and Audrey was torn. Help Richard? Or save her son?

The sounds of the two men struggling seeped into the darkness. Boots and bodies striking wood. Panting. Cursing. She started to rise.

I can open it.

What?

Watch.

She sensed a young boy's pride in the thought. Here was something he could do to help himself. To help her. Barely audible beneath the sound of the fight outside, a tiny clicking reached her ears.

What are you doing?

But she knew. He was inside the lock.

Wait.

Silence outside.

Audrey's hands quivered against the trunk.

"Richard?" she called weakly. Could he hear her through the barn wall? Was that another tiny tinkling noise inside the lock or was she just imagining it?

"Richard?" A little louder this time.

Nothing.

Had she made a mistake? Was she going to save Zach only to lose Richard? She rose to her feet and turned toward the big barn door.

She's coming.

Zach's voice echoed in her head just as a loud *clack* sounded inside the lock and it fell open. She jerked at it, fumbling it out of the hasp. She ripped at the clothing inside the trunk, scattering it wildly until there was nothing but wood bottom.

Lift it up.

She ran her fingers along the old paper-covered panel, discovering a small hidden finger grip at one end. She lifted it out of her way and stared in surprise at a steep, well-lit stairwell. She drew in a short breath that tasted of barn dust and dark, half-remembered yesterdays.

Another cellar.

Her throat was dry as sand and her chest was so tight she could barely catch another gasping breath. But Zach was down there, waiting for her to come and save him. Shaking like an old woman, she descended step by shaky step to the floor below. The ceiling was barely a foot above her head and the smells here were of dampness and mildew, reverberating even stronger with the surfacing memories in her mind. It was impossible, but Audrey knew it was true.

Somehow, after all these years, her mother had come back to haunt her.

51

RICHARD COULDN'T SEE out of his right eye. It stung like blazes and his throat felt as though someone had fired a bottle rocket down it. He'd twisted his knee and a couple of ribs were beginning to ache every time he drew a breath. But Merle was in worse shape.

The battle had been brief and Richard's emotions had careened from mind-numbing terror to murderous rage. At times he'd been certain that Merle was about to kill him. He'd struggled wildly, gouging Merle's eyes with his fingernails, grasping the man's throat between broken fingers, kneeing, punching, head-butting. At other moments he was afraid that he was going to murder Merle and there seemed to be no stopping himself.

Merle had a torn cheek where Richard had bitten his lip, and part of Merle's ear hung away from his skull. But there was little strength left in the man, and now he had Richard's knee on his abdomen and both of Richard's hands around his throat. It was only when Richard saw the light fading from Merle's eyes that the fire went out of him and he eased his grip on the man's soft larynx, removing both thumbs from Merle's bobbing Adam's apple. Slowly Merle began to cough and shake and some color returned to his cheeks.

A noise to Richard's right caused him to jerk and he spun, trying to make out the shadowy figure silhouetted against the stars. At first he thought it was Audrey, but then his eyes adjusted and he stared in shocked disbelief, barely able to speak. "Tara, what are you doing here?"

"I saw your car out front."

Merle shook beneath him. "You!" shouted Merle, pointing a shaky finger at Tara.

Richard saw the light of recognition in Tara's eyes. "You know each other?" he said, struggling weakly to his feet.

"Yes," she said, stepping away from Richard and removing a small automatic pistol from the back of her pants.

"Tara, what..." sputtered Richard.

She shot Merle once in the forehead and once in the chest before Richard could blink.

"My...my God," he gasped.

"Yes. Pity you had to murder poor Merle."

"What?"

"Where did Audrey go?"

"Tara, you just shot that man!"

Tara aimed the pistol directly at Richard's face. "Take me to Audrey."

"What are you doing? Why are you doing this?"

She fired a shot over Richard's shoulder and he jerked. "I don't have time to waste, Richard. Take me to Audrey. Now!"

52

VIRGIL FILLED THE COFFEEMAKER, not paying attention to what he was doing, spilling water over the counter. He glanced at the spot where Doris had fallen and he almost broke the glass pot, shoving it back into the machine. He locked his hands on the countertop and took a deep breath. Doris had almost died right there. If he hadn't come home when he did, she *might* have died. Right there. On the goddamned kitchen floor! And she looked like hell. Like there was nothing left inside her. He rested his head in his hands and tried to calm himself.

It wasn't the first time she'd gotten out of bed and fallen when he was gone. During the first few weeks being houseridden it had irked her, coming to terms with the new realities of life. She hated being an invalid. But lately she hadn't had much strength, so he at least hadn't worried about her going down the stairs. The thought that she might have taken a worse spill, that she might have tumbled down that long flight while he was away, made him physically ill.

He dropped into a chair at the table, waiting for the coffee. A car honked somewhere downtown and he thought once again of the fire. He couldn't get the look he had witnessed in Mac's eyes out of his head. Why would a man like Mac commit murder or suicide? Even with a gun on her, why would Babs pour gasoline over herself like it was baby lotion? Surely she had to know it would have been better to get shot than to burn to death. When the fire blasted them, they knew. Wherever Mac was before that instant, when the heat scorched his skin, he was awake then.

The phone rang and when he answered it, Charlie was on the line.

"I did what I could," he said. "But whatever Tara Beals was into at Perkins, most of it is buried real deep. I have an old friend on the inside and he got me what little info I could dig up."

"The inside?"

"Well, some people way back used to call it the *Company.* It's in better favor now than it was then, okay?"

"Okay. So tell me."

"Tara Beals was the last researcher involved in something called Project LongLook."

"Long-distance viewing?"

"Yeah, right. I told you"—Charlie sounded like he was sipping coffee, or maybe something stronger—"Project LongLook was one of those sixties leftovers that somebody in the government kept funding forever, even though cooler heads had long since declared it a waste of time. During the sixties or seventies, word got around that the Russians were experimenting on mind control and ESP, and this long-distance viewing baloney. He claimed Tara's group actually had results where people could locate buildings and rivers and stuff they had never seen before, just by being told to focus on a certain area."

"It worked?"

"Evidently."

"But they stopped it?"

"Well, it was never any more accurate than the information they could get from spy planes and satellites and spies. I guess the technology outstripped the spooks. And he said it was never all that reliable. If you're going to start a nuclear war, you don't want somebody coming in thirty minutes later and telling the president it might have been church steeples he was seeing and not ballistic missiles. Beals was the last one to lose her funding. My friend didn't know why, except that she must have had friends in high places."

"Anything else?"

"Yeah. Beals was working on mind control. Drugs. Hypnosis. That was a different project and I couldn't get much out of my buddy about that one. Just talking about it made him real nervous. The way he talked, Tara's research made even his people nervous."

"Why?"

"I think maybe her methods weren't all that nice."

"What kind of mind control?"

"How many kinds are there? Hypnosis, I suppose. That's her specialty."

"Everybody I talk to tells me you can't control someone with hypnosis. At least you can't make them do anything they wouldn't do when they were awake."

"Yeah, well I think Beals got around that by using drugs. Apparently there was something fishy about her *treatment* of some of the patients at Perkins. It was hushed up, but she lost her license. Whatever she was working on, my buddy got *real* nervous talking about it. I kind of got the idea her system might have worked *too* good."

"How could it do that?"

"Maybe they were afraid she'd get so good at it she'd start using it on them."

"Mmm. So what we have here is a doctor who knows how to control people using drugs and hypnosis."

"Yeah. And she likes to play around with ESP."

"Why would she do that at a hospital for mentally disturbed patients?"

"Got me. Maybe crazy people are easier to work with. And mind control there might be a *good* thing. Who's going to talk? And if they do, who's going to believe them?"

Virgil thought of Cooder and shuddered.

"Anything new on your end?" asked Charlie.

"Mac Douglass killed a woman in town a little while ago. Killed himself at the same time."

"Shit. Mac?"

"Yeah."

There was a short pause and another sip. "You thinking Beals had something to do with it?"

"Maybe. I'd like to see the autopsy after they're checked for drugs."

If they got enough out of the blaze to autopsy.

"Might not be any evidence. I got enough out of my buddy to get the idea that the drugs were only required in the beginning to break down the patient's will. After that, it was all just hypnosis."

"Great."

"I'll keep digging, but I think I might have hit rock bottom on the info well."

"Thanks, Charlie. I appreciate it."

"Say hello to Doris."

"Yeah."

Virgil hung up and called the station. The dispatcher answered on the third ring. "Are you all right, Sheriff? Birch said you looked a little shaken."

"I'm fine. Who's on call?"

"Birch is still at the fire. Bob's investigating a possible firearm discharge in South Eden. That's probably just a night hunter. I could call Mike at home. What's up?"

"Call out *all* the deputies and make the search for Doctor Tara Beals top priority."

"Are we charging her?"

"Just bring her in. I'll make it up as I go along if I have to."

"Okay, Sheriff."

Tara Beals hypnotized Audrey to make her forget. What else did she do to her while she was under? Did she use drugs on her and Mac and Babs, something to strengthen the hypnotic suggestions? And what was so terrible in Audrey's past that it *had* to be forgotten?

The sound of the coffee hissing into the pot reminded him of Mac and Babs's skin, singing under the flames. Instead of the aroma of French roast, his nose was assaulted by the stench of burning flesh and he flinched. What did this all have to do with Zach Bock? Tara had been working on a lot of weird shit at Perkins. Messing with people's minds. But Perkins closed before Zach Bock was born.

And what about Audrey's mother? Where was she? The state had granted Tara custody of Audrey, after all. Maybe he was making this too complicated.

He poured himself a cup of coffee, holding it under his nose and sniffing deeply to rid himself of the hateful odor in his mind. He sipped it black, relishing the sting on his tongue and the bitter flavor.

"I don't believe in coincidences," he muttered.

"Neither do I," said Marg through the screen door.

He glanced over his shoulder. "Come on in."

She waddled through and plunked herself across a kitchen chair, accepting the coffee he handed her.

"Doris all right now?" asked Marg.

"She's conscious, if that's what you mean."

"She didn't break anything?"

"Doesn't seem hurt. Just more run-down than I've ever seen her."

Marg made certain she had eye contact before she spoke. "It won't be long now, Virg. You know that, right?"

"Yeah," he said, turning away.

She slipped her wide hand over his. "You did everything for Doris a man could do. She could never have wished for a better husband."

He nodded, but his brain was seething. Doris was dying. She could go at any minute. He had sensed it in the way she spoke, the weariness in her eyes, the low rasping of her breath. He should be with her right now, not sitting in the kitchen calmly drinking coffee with Marg. But there was something else torturing him as well, something he'd missed about Tara Beals, something simple that he should have grasped immediately. Doris's health had ruined him as a cop, but his old police instincts wouldn't be denied.

"Virgil, you need to get some rest," said Marg, squeezing his hand. She set her coffee cup down on the table.

He shook his head. "I'm trying to put it together in my head. It doesn't make sense, but there's too many threads that all end up in the same weave for it to be just coincidental. Mac wasn't a murderer and when I saw him *something* was wrong with him. And for him and Babs to be at Perkins at the same time, well . . ."

"*Something* doesn't have to be hypnosis, Virgil. That's a real longshot. I know Mac was your friend. But people do insane things that they don't really mean to do. It happens all the time."

"There's a lot that you don't know."

"So tell me. Why would Mac kill Babs and himself?"

"I don't know. Unless it has something to do with Tara Beals' experiments at Perkins."

"What kind of experiments?" said Marg, frowning.

"Tara was working for the government on classified stuff. Mind-control experiments. Babs worked there and Mac was treated there."

"And Tara wanted to cover them up? The experiments?"

"Yeah. I think so."

"Perkins has been closed for years."

"Maybe Mac and Babs just remembered."

"After all this time?"

"What if Tara made them forget and something just reawakened the memories?"

"Like what?"

Virgil poured himself another cup of coffee from the pot on the table and stared into the swirling blackness.

"Audrey Bock," said Virgil. "She's Tara's niece. Tara Beals took her away from her mother when she was young and then hypnotized her to help her forget her traumatic childhood. Audrey went to Babs for a reading. Maybe she mentioned Tara Beals. Who knows what she mentioned? Maybe something in those dreams she's been having triggered something in Babs's head. But I think it got back to Tara and Tara didn't like it."

"But what about Mac? Mac didn't know anything about Audrey."

Virgil frowned. "Not until I asked him to start investigating Audrey's past."

"You asked him to investigate Audrey?"

Virgil nodded. "And he led me along, aiming me at Audrey's mother when it was Tara Beals I should have been investigating. I think she was controlling Mac all along."

"You make Tara Beals sound like some kind of voodoo witch doctor."

"Maybe she is. I think she did something at Perkins that she doesn't want to be discovered."

"But Audrey was never at Perkins. Was she?"

"I don't think so."

He sipped the bitter coffee; thoughts twisted and merged like dark swirling clouds in the back of his head. Doris. Babs. Mac. Doris. Audrey. Tara. What the hell was it he'd missed? Something Ken had said. Mac had come in looking all drugged up and bought four gas cans. Ken said a woman who fit Tara Beals' description had spoken to Mac. But it wasn't that. It was something else. Ken said when Mac came back he carried three gas cans into Babs's house.

Three.

Not four.

"Shit!" he said, flinging the coffee cup into the sink, shattering it.

"What?"

"Watch Doris!" said Virgil, heading for the door. "I'm such an idiot!"

"Where are you going?"

"The Bocks! She'll go after Audrey next!"

53

AS AUDREY INCHED toward the door, her entire body stiff as a board and sheened in cold sweat, she noticed that the ceiling and walls of the small anteroom were all covered in dull gray sheets, nailed in place.

Lead.

This room was not the one in Audrey's memory. For one thing, a heavy metal desk stood to one side of the door and an old wooden chair on castors sat beside it. The room in her memory was empty. But the secret entrance and the sense of being buried were so suggestive of that traumatic night long ago, that she could barely separate her past from her present. There was no little girl crying in the darkness ahead, but she could still hear Zach inside her mind, pleading with her to hurry. She twisted the knob, hating the feel of the icy metal against her palm, opening the heavy door ever so slowly, ready to leap out at whoever might be on the other side, but there was no one there. Instead a long, sloping corridor confronted her and she gasped.

Like the corridor in my mind. Like the white doors.

But the more she stared at the corridor, the less the two seemed alike. This hallway was strangely constructed, with an undulating floor and heavy, painted block walls in place of the redbrick in her memory. And these doors were all on one side of the hallway. All except for the one door to her right.

She didn't see any lead shielding in the hall, but the paneling on the ceiling overhead was damp with condensation. A single metal conduit ran the length of the hallway and every few yards an exposed bulb lighted the way.

She sensed Zach so close she could almost smell him. She stared at the first door to her left and she *knew* he was in that room. She'd found him at last. She began to shake and she had to stop for a moment to catch her breath. The walls closed in around her and her vision seemed off, fuzzy. The terror that gripped her was so strong she wanted to turn and run from the place, just as she had in her youth. She listened intently for the hideous sound of laughter like darkness.

She reached the door and stood there for a moment, trying to erase the corridor in her memory which kept superimposing itself over the real corridor she was in. She grasped the handle of the door in front of her—praying it was real—and jerked it wide.

The woman clutching Zach had Tara's face, but her hair was completely white and her features were worn and weathered like old stone. Her eyes shone with the light of madness as she crouched in the far corner like a wounded animal, her gnarled hands wrapped tightly around Zach's chest, holding the boy so close against her withered breast that he could not escape to run to Audrey.

Mother.

Audrey froze in the doorway, staring at her mother's Nikes peeking out beneath a worn cotton dress, the wild look on her face resonating in her animal stance, her flitting eyes. But there was no hatred in them, none of the rage that Audrey had remembered, and the hands caressed Zach lovingly, not like the hands of some deadly madwoman. She looked more the way Audrey pictured herself, a woman who had lost everything, clinging to one last ray of hope before going completely over to the other side, into the bottomless pit of insanity.

Suddenly Audrey could feel her memories falling into place like tumblers in a lock, as door after door flew open in her mind. She collapsed against the wall for support as the foundations of her shattered memory fell apart. It wasn't Mother that had tortured Paula. It was Tara.

It was Tara's basement Audrey had been in. Not the basement of her mother's house. It was Tara on the floor, wrestling with Paula. Over a period of time, Tara had taken both her brother and sister from Audrey's mother. It was Tara who tortured and killed them. And it was Tara who superimposed Audrey's mother's face over her own in Audrey's memory. Tara hadn't only *buried* memories. She had distorted them! Created new ones!

"I'm here, baby!" gasped Audrey, stumbling across the floor toward the two of them, never taking her eyes off her mother's hands, lest she was wrong and they shoot up toward Zach's throat.

"All my babies," said her mother, staring past Audrey, out into the corridor. "She took all my babies."

Audrey staggered as more memories hit her.

It had always been Tara. It was Tara who strapped Paula to the machine in her lab and then she turned the dials on the machine. And Paula's cries became animal wails of terror and pain so loud Audrey had careened wildly backward, away down the corridor. It was Tara she'd heard laughing, following the sound of Audrey's telltale running footsteps down that long dark tunnel.

It was Tara all along.

Audrey dropped onto her knees beside Zach and wrapped her arms around him, still staring into her mother's eyes, trying to make contact. Zach pulled free of her mother's embrace and buried himself in Audrey's arms, quivering.

"You're safe now, sweetheart," she said, hugging him tightly.

He shook against her. They both sobbed together, clinging tightly, tears running down their cheeks.

"Mommy!" he managed, tucking his head against her breast.

She reveled in the feel of him, the clean soapy smell of his hair, his skin, his solid healthy weight against her. She was never going to let him go again. Never.

Martha brushed against her and Audrey smelled her as well. She smelled like the past. But it was a sweet past. Jasmine and dust.

"You can't stay here," said Martha, as Audrey glanced up into the dry old eyes that were as sad as death.

Zach nodded. "She's coming," he whispered in Audrey's ear.

The words chilled Audrey to the bone, because at that instant, for the first time, she sensed it too. It felt like a million venomous insects crawling up her legs, her back, inside her clothes where she couldn't reach them. Her entire body was sending out a warning.

Tara *was* coming.

"All my babies. All my babies," muttered Audrey's mother.

"She didn't get me, Mother," Audrey whispered. "She didn't get Zach."

"Not yet," said her mother, still staring toward the door.

But it was Richard, not Tara, who stepped into the room.

"Honey!" said Audrey. "Zach's alive! He's—"

Tara strode into the room behind Richard. Audrey's eyes were drawn instantly to the pistol in her hand.

"Tara," said Audrey, swallowing a large lump in her throat. "What are you doing here?" But of course she knew. Tara had come for Zach. Just as she had come for Craig. And Paula. And finally for her. But she wasn't getting Zach. Not even over her dead body. Audrey clutched him so close against her he shoved her, trying to breathe.

"So he is alive," said Tara, staring at Zach.

She reached into her pocket and removed something small. There was a metallic clicking noise and her lips moved but Audrey didn't hear her. Instead she felt a sudden dullness within, as though she had taken an entire bottle of Halcion. It was a strange, familiar sensation and a tiny voice within her rebelled. She knew this place. It was where she went when she was under the force of hypnotic suggestion. She had brought herself here often enough, and because of that she realized that she had it within her power to leave. She imagined herself trudging out of some narrow opening inside her mind and back into the light. When her eyes focused once more, she found herself staring directly into Tara's bewildered face.

"Exit!" said Tara, snapping the clicker again.

This time the sensation was far briefer for Audrey, just a momentary sluggishness, and she realized immediately what had happened. Tara had implanted a word and a sound into her subconscious that would put her under, but her recent work with Doctor Cates, and her own practice with self-hypnosis and opening the doors in her mind had freed her of the word's power.

"No," she said, shaking it off. "I know what you did. But you're not going to hypnotize me again. Why? Why did you murder Paula and Craig?"

"I didn't murder anyone," said Tara. "Paula and Craig were telepathic. I wanted to help them discover the limits of their abilities. To stretch those limits. I wanted to make them gods."

"You killed them."

"They died as a result of the experiments."

"How many people died as results of your experiments?"

Tara didn't answer.

"Did any survive?"

"A few."

"All my babies," cried her mother, dragging herself out from behind Zach.

Tara's eyes widened and when she laughed the sound chilled Audrey. Why had she never realized the laughter in her head was Tara's? Had Tara made her forget that too? Audrey noticed that Richard was watching Tara over his shoulder, tensing. But the pistol was aimed right at his back.

"I spotted Richard's Camry in the drive and I knew I'd find Martha here when I saw Coonts outside," said Tara, glaring at Audrey's mother. "What he saw in you I'll never know. He's dead, by the way."

A low moan escaped Martha's lips. "All of them," she muttered darkly. "I'd wake up and another of my babies would be gone and I wouldn't even remember it for days, months. She killed your father, Audrey."

Audrey gasped.

"I tried to make you forget altogether, Martha," said Tara. "I'm better at it now, but still the mother–child bond is incredibly strong. I believe that must be what finally broke through the barriers I installed for you too, Audrey."

"You took all of them," muttered Martha. "But you won't murder Zach. You won't murder Audrey."

Martha stumbled forward. She looked stunned, her eyes

barely focused on Tara. Tara shot her at point-blank range. Audrey screamed as the old woman crumpled to the floor, and Tara swung the pistol around quickly to point at Richard before he could move. But he turned slowly to face her anyway, daring her to fire. "Get over beside Audrey," she said.

"No," said Richard. "Why don't you just shoot me now?"

"Adler!" said Tara, nodding toward Richard.

The dog growled, bared his teeth, and took a menacing step forward. Between the pistol and the dog, Audrey could see that Richard didn't stand a chance.

"Don't!" said Audrey, knowing that Richard was about to attack Tara anyway. He turned toward Audrey and when she shook her head he reluctantly did as he was told, but after that his eyes never left the gun.

Tara glanced around the room and then at Audrey, shaking her head. "She probably came and got Zach the instant she and her boyfriend had constructed this place." She laughed and Audrey recoiled again at the dark, too-well-remembered sound of it. "She lined the walls with lead. As though that would stop psi. My sister had this mad idea that if she could hide the children behind lead-lined walls I wouldn't find them. But I didn't find them because they *had* talent. I came to get them because I *assumed* they did. I told her that often enough. But her memory was shot. You're lucky you didn't all die of lead poisoning. Luckily she had the sense to panel over most of it."

"Why did you assume the kids had psi talent?" asked Audrey.

Tara studied her face. "Of course, you wouldn't remember. I'd ask Martha to show you, but now she can't."

"Show me what?"

"Your mother was a gifted clairvoyant. That's how she made a living. Reading people's fortunes." She said it scornfully, as though not only Martha's profession but *she* herself were beneath contempt.

"And she knew you were going to come for them," whispered Audrey, nodding to herself, slipping closer to Richard, drawing Zach along. "So as each child grew older, she locked them in the basement."

"Not much of a basement back then, nothing quite as elaborate as this." She waved her free hand around the room. "One little cell with lead shielding. And she'd have spells all the time, thinking I was coming. I think she made you kids sleep down there whenever she was having one of them."

"It was your basement where they died," whispered Audrey.

Tara's frown became more menacing.

"You murdered Paula and Craig with your machine!" screamed Audrey, the memories flooding her mind. The mask—the hideous metal monstrosity—wasn't in her mother's basement. It was in Tara's. It had always lurked in Tara's.

"Stop saying that! It was an experiment that was necessary for the good of mankind. It wasn't just them. I worked on as many subjects as I could find."

Audrey shook her head. "But that doesn't make sense. Why didn't you do it to me? Why didn't you kill me?"

"It was science!" screamed Tara. "I didn't try to enhance your talents because you never exhibited any. I'm sorry, Audrey. I never meant for you to stumble onto the experiments the way you did. I did everything in my power to protect you, to erase the memories, but I suppose sooner or later you were going to remember, and I can't have you babbling. My work is more important than any one person, no matter how much I love you."

"Love me?"

"I raised you."

"You wrecked my mind. You murdered my sister and brother and my mother. You came here to kill me."

"No. That's not true. I'm sorry this had to happen. But I can't leave any loose ends. Everyone who knows about my experiments has to be eliminated." She pointed the pistol at Richard and pulled the trigger just as he made a move toward her. The shot drove him back against the wall and he slumped to the floor, staring in disbelief at the hole in the left side of his chest. His feet splayed and his hands fluttered toward the bloody wound, shaking against his shirt like a fish flopping on a beach. Audrey screamed, releasing Zach and dropping to Richard's side, just as Tara aimed the pistol at her.

"Come with me, Audrey," she said. "It's time for *you* to meet the machine."

Audrey shook her head. "I'm not going. None of us are going."

"I can only take the one," said Tara. "More's the pity. But I have no lab help nowadays. And since you've worked yourself out from under my conditioning and Zach has never been programmed, I can't chance either of you getting away." She studied Zach as though he were not her own nephew but a poor lamb that unfortunately needed to be slaughtered. "You seem to have some small talent that I missed, Audrey. You managed to find your offspring even when the whole world told you he was dead. That's a bit of work I'd like to examine."

It took Audrey a second to grasp her meaning and when she did the horror of it stilled her heart. She glanced at the pistol swinging slowly toward Zach. Tara wasn't leaving any witnesses. Neither Zach nor Richard nor mother would be left to incriminate her.

"No!" Audrey screamed, reaching out ineffectually.

There was a metallic click inside the gun, but when Tara pulled the trigger nothing happened. She drew back the slide to check the chamber, shaking her head. She pulled the trigger again. Another dry fire and then another unexpected clicking sound.

Tara backed away a step, glancing at Zach who was focused like a laser on the pistol. She dropped the gun onto the floor as though it were on fire.

"You did that!" she said, as Zach's attention slowly rose from the floor to her face. Tara moved before Zach could react, gripping his arm like a vise, shoving Audrey back onto the floor beside Richard. "Adler!" shouted Tara, waving at Audrey who was already starting to rise. The dog leapt in front of Audrey, its teeth glistening, the death threat in its throaty growl unmistakable.

"How did you do that?" said Tara, lifting Zach's chin.

Zach shrugged, glancing at his mother who was shaking her head.

"I didn't do anything."

"Yes, you did. I felt it. What did you do to my pistol?"

"Nothing."

"Adler! Ready!" The dog bared even more of his teeth and stiffened. Audrey crunched back against the wall beside Richard, her hands in front of her. "If I give the command, the dog will rip your mother to little pieces," said Tara. "Now one more time, what did you do to my pistol?"

"I fixed it so it wouldn't shoot."

Tara's eyes gleamed. "How did you do that?"

Zach shrugged again, still glancing at Audrey, who's face was a mask of fear. "I just got inside it and fixed it, that's all."

Tara nodded. "Amazing! You could be the one I've been looking for all these years, Zachary."

"No, Tara," said Audrey. "Please. Take me."

Tara didn't even look back. "We have to go, Zach. Adler! Stay! Guard!"

The dog twisted his head back and forth, as though there were something in his ears. But he shook it off and held his position directly in front of Audrey.

"Zach. Come along," said Tara, jerking his hand.

"No." He planted his feet, leaning back hard against Tara's tug.

"Tara, please! For the love of God!" whispered Audrey.

"Adler!" Tara pointed at Audrey and the dog growled ferociously, scratching the carpet with his paws and leaning menacingly closer to Audrey. "One more command, Zach, and Adler will kill your mother."

Audrey shook her head. "All these years I never knew what kind of animal you were. You gave me memories of the wonderful aunt who had saved me from a horrible mother." She glanced down at the pool of blood surrounding her mother on the floor, then back at Richard, who was barely conscious beside her. "It was you. All along. It was you."

Tara dragged Zach out of the room and as she disappeared she screamed, "Adler! Now!"

The dog lunged at Audrey's face, planting its paws on her chest. She slid sideways along the wall, over her mother, forgetting the pain, slapping frantically at the dog, praying it couldn't plant its flashing fangs in her. Before she could stop it, the dog's breath was hot on her throat, the scalpel-like teeth just touching her skin like a promise, the growl filling her ears, but for some reason the dog never clamped down. The two of them hung there in suspended animation, Audrey feeling the dog's warm saliva dripping down onto her shoulder for what seemed hours.

"Adler!" shouted Tara from somewhere down the hall and the dog slid its cruel nails down across Audrey's breast and raced out of the room.

Audrey climbed wearily to her feet and rushed out into the corridor just in time to hear the heavy metal door clang shut and the lock click into place.

Cooder drew back into himself when he realized that the dog, the boy, and Doctor Beals were approaching Doctor Beals' car. He slipped back down the slope above the drainage ditch and tried to disappear like a worm into the dirt. Car doors slammed and he waited for Doctor Beals to drive away, but nothing happened. Finally curiosity got the better of him but, rather than climbing back up to the road again, he took a deep breath, pushed real hard, and peered through the dog's eyes again.

The boy was sitting crossways in the backseat, staring straight ahead with a dazed look on his face, and Cooder realized that he—the dog—was growling at the kid. He concentrated hard and forced the dog to nuzzle the kid's side instead, but the boy shoved him away.

So where was Doctor Beals?

Cooder forced the dog's eyes to glance in every direction. Then he saw her, hurrying back around the corner of the house. She leapt into the car, slammed the door, and started the engine. The SUV rocketed away in a spray of gravel and a shriek of asphalt. Even before it rounded the bend, Cooder felt himself losing contact with the dog. He rested his head on the dirt and closed his eyes. She was gone. He was safe.

But she had the boy.

That thought rocked him like a blast of Arctic wind. No matter where the kid had been before, no matter what had happened to him, it was nothing to what would happen to him now. Doctor Beals had killed the man outside the house, and the old woman in the basement, and the boy's father. She had tried to kill the boy's mother, but somehow the boy had stopped her from doing that.

For just an instant Cooder had felt as though he were making contact with the boy. But it was so hard just staying inside the dog's head that he couldn't let go. The boy had done something to the gun so that it wouldn't fire.

How would a kid know how to do that? Like getting into a bird's head, maybe? Cooder didn't see how the inside of a bird could be anything like the inside of a gun, but he sensed that he and the kid shared something now. Something Doctor Beals wanted.

He shook his head, trying to clear it, bouncing his forehead off the gravel ditch side. Doctor Beals talked and the woman went stiff. The woman was trained like the dog. Hypnotized.

He shivered, knowing right then that somewhere inside his twisted skull, there was a word waiting for *him,* that when he heard it he would do anything Doctor Beals said. And he was afraid that the way things were going, she would tell him to kill himself. Because she was coming back for him. He knew it. Maybe not right now. Maybe not right away. But she was coming back. He'd seen enough to figure that out. As he climbed fearfully to the edge of the road, he began to notice a slight lightening in the night, a flickering against the tops of the trees behind the barn. Then, as he stood up on the road again, he saw the flames licking at the sides of the old barn, catching in the dry wood, racing like rabid squirrels up the walls.

He was caught up in the magic of wild fire, like a rat staring at a snake. He couldn't take his eyes away. He was standing that way, one foot on the grass, the other on the road, when Virgil's cruiser shrieked to a stop almost directly on top of him.

"Cooder!" Virgil screamed, jumping out of the car and racing to face Cooder.

"Hi, Virg," said Cooder, glancing at Virgil, then back to the flames that were already tickling their way up toward the barn eaves, two stories above the ground.

"What are you doing here, Cooder?" said Virgil, shaking him by the shoulders and glancing across the road at the Bocks' car. "Have you seen Audrey Bock or her husband?"

A space of time.

"I think so."

"You *think* so?"

Cooder nodded. "Yeah. I saw them."

"Where are they?" asked Virgil, praying for any answer other than the one he was afraid Cooder was going to give him.

"In there," said Cooder, nodding toward the fire.

"Shit," said Virgil, as the flames began to climb the steep cedar shingles. Down below they were fanning out, creeping along the base of the wall, working their way from the barn toward the house. But they didn't seem to have reached any of the residences yet. Virgil grabbed a flashlight off the front seat and started across the road.

"You won't find them," said Cooder in that perpetually calm voice that drove Virgil right out of his gourd.

"Where are they, exactly, Cooder? I don't have much time."

Cooder shrugged. "I'll show you."

"Then show me."

A space of time caused Virgil to shake Cooder by the shoulders again.

"The barn," said Cooder, as though he'd just remembered.

Virgil stared at the wall of flame beginning to turn the barn to a pyre.

"If they're in the barn, surely they'll make their way back into the house to get out," he said.

"Can't," said Cooder, shaking his head. "They're in the basement."

"The basement attaches to the house."

Cooder just kept shaking his head. "Bad things, Virg."

"Shit," said Virgil at last. He waved for Cooder to hurry up and follow him. "Show me."

Audrey kicked at the heavy door, jerking the handle so hard her wrists ached, but there was no opening it, no give whatsoever, and she could sense Zach slipping farther and farther away. It was infuriating having come so close, having held him in her arms, to surrender him now to the woman who had been at the center of the insanity all along. It wasn't going to happen!

Audrey tugged at the door, throwing her shoulder into it, ignoring the pain. But after several such attacks, she was out of breath, leaning against the cold metal, ransacking her brain for another way. She turned and raced back down the corridor, slamming open doors, exploring the subcellar room by room, stopping only long enough at the first door to ascertain that Richard was still breathing.

The layout seemed to follow the house above, for the most part. To her right lay the foundation. All of the rooms but one were to her left. What she could see of the old granite foundation had been undermined and shored up with solid concrete walls, although here and there—where the wall met the ceiling—a section of stone might show through. When she discovered Zach's cell at the far end of the subbasement, she had to take a moment to catch her breath, shaken by the size of it, barely bigger than their bathroom at home, and the bleakness, with only a metal cot to break the barren walls.

He lived here for a year. In this hole. Mother did it. But it was because of Tara. Mother brought him here to protect him even though she hadn't been able to protect any of her own children. Still, Audrey couldn't forgive her, even in her madness, for the barren cell. She *could* have given him some semblance of a life. What was she thinking locking him away like a murderer in solitary confinement? Had her mind slipped so far over the edge that she didn't even realize what that would be like for a small boy? And what about Coonts? Who the hell was he and why would *he* be a part of this?

She hurried out into the corridor again and backtracked to the small workroom next to the room in which Richard and her mother lay, intending to find something, *anything,* she could use to cut or batter their way out of the cellar. But just then, Richard stuck his head out into the hall. He was pale as death, kneeling, clutching the door frame for support, but he was conscious. Still alive. And she had left him in her panic to get to Zach. She raced to him, dropping beside him, easing him back against the wall.

"I blacked out," he whispered.

She nodded. "Try not to talk. I'm going to get us out of here."

He glanced past her toward the metal door.

"Locked," said Audrey. "I have to find some way to bust out."

Richard shook his head, glancing back into the room toward Martha's body. "She must have a key."

"Maybe Merle has it," said Audrey. "And he's outside."

Richard shook his head again, but it was clear the effort cost him dearly. "She wouldn't stay in a hole in the ground without being able to get out if something happened to Merle." His voice was raspy and harsh but his reasoning was sound. Would her mother be crazy enough to chance being buried alive? Maybe. In her overpowering terror of Tara, *anything* might have been preferable to discovery. Still, it was the best chance they had.

Audrey tore his shirt aside and inspected the wound, grimacing at the blood, but the hole was small and oozing, not pumping. She thought that was a good sign. She reached behind him, feeling for an exit. The skin was unbroken.

"Need to stop the bleeding," said Richard, glancing groggily at the wound.

Audrey ripped his shirt completely off, and biting her lip, stuffed part of it into the hole with her finger. Richard moaned and blacked out again. But he came around quickly, taking deep breaths through his teeth.

"I'm sorry," she whispered.

"Had to stop it."

"For everything."

"It wasn't your fault, Audrey. None of this was your fault." He glanced back at her mother, but Audrey shook her head. "Have to check, Audrey. She might be just out of it."

Audrey climbed to her feet and strode to her mother's side. The old woman's face looked peaceful, reminding Audrey of the photograph. She wondered how many times in her mother's life she had looked like that. But she knew before she knelt to touch Martha's throat, that she would find no pulse. Tara's aim had been better the first time and Audrey wondered if Zach had had anything to do with her missing Richard's heart.

"She's dead," she said.

"Check for a key."

Audrey felt through her mother's skirt and blouse. But there were no pockets, no key secreted on her still-warm form. "Nothing!"

Richard nodded. "It's here somewhere, Aud. You have to find it." He leaned his head back against the wall and closed his eyes. When she knelt beside him again, he opened them. "I'm okay. Find the key."

She glanced around the room. Besides three arm chairs and an empty side table, there was a floor lamp and a chest of drawers with a TV and some medicine bottles on top. She dumped each of the drawers on the floor, kicking through the photographs and papers. A stack of brown notecards bound with a rubber band caught her eye and she flipped it over. Twenty-year-old report cards—hers. But no key. She glanced at Richard and shook her head.

"Check the other rooms," he whispered.

This time through the maze she moved slower, more deliberately. Zach's room didn't bear searching of course. There was nowhere in there to hide a key and that would have been the last place either Martha or Merle would stash one. The closest room to the one Richard was in was a bedroom, and it was only slightly less Spartan than Zach's. So maybe Mother hadn't been punishing him. Maybe she had simply lost any concept of the needs of a small child beyond the requirement that he be protected from Tara. Or else this was Merle's room. But going back over the layout in her head, Audrey realized that there were only the two beds downstairs. So Merle had lived in the house above. Of course he would have. He had to keep up the front that *someone* lived there.

Martha's bed stood beside a dresser that matched the one in the sitting room. Again Audrey dumped the drawers onto the floor and this time she carefully sifted through the contents by hand, shoving aside white nylon panties and knee-high stockings, praying to find the key somewhere in the jumble.

She could no longer feel Zach at all and panic started to well up inside again. Audrey didn't know how much longer Richard could last and she knew that she was missing something. Something important.

But there was no key in the pile of clothes. In desperation she shook out each item separately, willing the key to clatter to the floor. Finally she threw the last cotton blouse onto the bed in disgust.

Where was it? Richard was right. There had to be another key down here somewhere, but where? In the tool room? Hidden in the bathroom? Why would mother do that? Surely the idea was to keep the key away from Zach, and naturally both Martha and Coonts had to know that Zach would have found opportunities to explore the bath. She couldn't picture her mother using the tool room. That would have been Merle's domain. It had to be in here or in the storage closet where Zach had discovered the photo album. She'd search it next, but first she was going to make absolutely sure of the bedroom.

She tore the linens off the bed, shaking them out carefully before discarding them in the corner. There was nothing under the pillow or stashed in its case. She flipped the mattress off. Nothing between it and the springs. Finally she leaned them against the wall and stared at the frame. The room was a disaster area, but no key had appeared. She slammed the springs back down into place, frantic. She started toward the door, ready to search every nook and cranny of the storage room, when a photograph on the wall caught her eye.

When she looked closer, she realized that it wasn't really a photo at all. It was a *photocopy* of the image Zach had shown her. The one with Tara's face torn away. Only the copy was made *before* the image had been torn and Audrey was stunned at the likeness of Martha and Tara. They were twins. Just like she and Paula. Maybe that was why it was so easy for Tara to mix up Audrey's memories about the two of them.

The photo hung beside the bed where Martha could stare at it before going to sleep. Stare into the eyes of the woman who had destroyed her life and turned her into a hunted animal living in a burrow in the ground. Audrey could only imagine what it must have been like to lose not one but three children, and a husband, and to know all along—at least on some level—who the monster was that was stealing them away or killing them. No wonder her mother had gone mad.

As Audrey lifted the picture off the nail on the wall and studied the faces, her finger touched something cold and metallic on the back side of the frame. She flipped the picture over in her hand and there was the key, the tape that held it to the dustcover yellowing with age. She ripped it off and raced down the corridor, the *something* in the back of her head still screaming to get out. But she was too focused on escape—on finding Zach again—to listen to it.

"I've got it!" she shouted at Richard in passing.

It was all he could do to nod and smile.

She slipped the key into the lock with shaking fingers, careful not to break it in her haste to open the door. The metallic clicking of the lock reminded her again of Zach, the way he had opened the lock in the barn, the way he had fixed the pistol. But it reminded her of Tara too, of the metal clicker she used to put Audrey under, reminded her of what Tara would do to Zach when she got him into *her* basement, and she jerked the door open and raced to the stairs. To her dismay, she could not shove the trapdoor open. Tara must have placed the clothes back inside and locked the hasp shut again! Audrey slammed upward again and again, but the pile of clothing deadened her blows and finally she collapsed on the stairs, her mind racing, trying to think what tool she'd need now to bust her way to freedom. She heard Richard gasping down the hall and she caught her breath, sliding down the stairs on her butt before heading back down the corridor.

She smelled the fire before she saw any evidence of it. Glancing up she noticed a thin layer of gray smoke winding across the ceiling like a flat snake. Richard was hacking and each cough seemed to send a wracking pain through him. His hands were flat on the floor as he tried unsuccessfully to brace his body against the agonizing vibrations of his own exhalations.

Fire. *That* was the something she'd missed. Of course Tara wasn't going to just leave her here alive. She wouldn't take a chance that the dog might not have done her in, although Audrey still didn't understand why it hadn't. She and Mother and Richard were supposed to end up a pile of ashes in Merle Coonts's cellar. When and if they were ever found, Audrey had no doubt that Tara would have things set up to look as though *Audrey* was somehow to blame. Audrey *was* crazy after all. Everyone knew it.

"She set the house on fire!" whispered Richard, nodding up toward the ceiling. "You have to find the ventilator and turn it off before we suffocate."

"How do I do that?"

Richard could barely shake his head. "Trip the breaker. There must be a panel somewhere. And find the main vent and plug it."

She started down the hallway again, figuring the panel would probably be in the tool room, when Richard called to her. "You have to brace that door shut!" he said, nodding back at the metal door she had wanted so badly to open. "The whole barn might collapse down into the hole and if it breaks through into this basement the cellar will burn too."

Audrey stood for just a second, unsure of what to do first, but the smoke caught in her lungs and she raced for the tool room. That was the logical place to find the breakers.

54

AS VIRGIL AND COODER rounded the front of the house, Virgil was surprised to find the entire barn already engulfed in flames. The blaze was rapidly flowing along the walls of the outbuilding that attached the structure to the house.

It was the gas, of course. Stan said Mac carried in three cans. But he bought four. The first thing Virgil had done when he got back to his cruiser was call Birch. Just as Virgil feared, Birch hadn't found the fourth can in the rented sedan. And Tara had had plenty of time to make off with one.

"You're sure they're in there?" said Virgil. He was standing in front of Merle's door, glancing over his shoulder at Cooder.

Cooder nodded and Virgil kicked the door in. A faint whiff of smoke caught in his lungs as he stumbled into the house.

"Where are they?" he shouted back at Cooder.

No answer. Jesus. This was no time to be having a Cooder conversation.

"Where are they, Cooder? We don't have much time!"

"The barn."

The picture of the barn, blazing like a football bonfire, lit the front of Virgil's brain.

"If they're in there, they're dead!" he shouted.

Cooder frowned and shook his head. "Basement."

"Even the barn basement ceiling's got to be on fire!"

Cooder seemed to be studying something hidden behind his eyeballs. "Underneath."

"What?"

"Underneath."

"Shit," muttered Virgil, stepping full into the doorway and motioning Cooder to follow. "Come on. You've got to show me, and for the love of God, hurry up!"

As they stumbled down the stairs into the box-lined cellar, Virgil thought of the old steamer trunk. His claustrophobia started to tickle at the back of his brain and he shook it off. That was the least of his worries right now.

"Dear God," he muttered, stopping. "Are they alive?"

"She is," said Cooder, pushing him ahead.

"In that trunk?"

A pause to study again. "Yeah."

"Cooder, if you get me killed down here," said Virgil, kicking and tossing the boxes aside rather than searching for a path, "I'm going to hurt you bad. Okay?"

"Okay, Virg."

But long before Virgil or Cooder reached the basement of the barn, they could see the flames ahead. The heavy beamed floor had collapsed at the back of the building blocking the rear doors and the upper walls were coming down with it, creating a mountain of blazing embers and sucking air through the house above and behind them like an interior tornado. To Virgil's surprise, Cooder edged past him and disappeared through the door into the barn basement.

"We can't go in there, Cooder!" shouted Virgil, getting a lungful of smoke and hacking ferociously. He leaned against the stone wall, dragging his T-shirt up across his mouth to catch his breath.

"We can't go back!" shouted Cooder, leaning back through the door and pointing over Virgil's shoulder.

"Mother!" rasped Virgil, glancing behind him. Burning embers of dust were falling like a hellish snow from the low ceiling joists into the tinder-dry boxes, which lit up one by one. The house must have gone up like a pile of straw as soon as they'd entered the cellar. A wide claw of fire scratched its way down the cellar stairs and the roar of the blaze was now coming from the house as well as the barn.

"Over here!" shouted Cooder, dragging Virgil through the door toward a pile of burning beams that had collapsed from the floor above. Right over the spot where Virgil remembered the old trunk sitting. Cooder started kicking at the beams and boards. Virgil heard the sound of all the boxes igniting in a loud *whoomp*. The fire was tracking them through the cellar, a golden-eyed serpent with glimmering teeth. Virgil ripped his shirt off and wrapped it around his hands. He grabbed one of the beams and heaved while Cooder kicked.

"Are you sure she's in there?" he shouted at Cooder. If Audrey was locked up in the trunk, they couldn't leave her. But if Cooder was wrong and they ended up wasting their last seconds of possible escape time busting into a trunk full of old clothes, Virgil figured he just might hurt Cooder.

Cooder ignored him, kicking at the now smaller pile of burning wood until his pants caught fire. He ignored the flames licking at his legs, lashing out with his heavy boots until the old trunk stood revealed, black and inflamed. Virgil dragged him back, slapping at Cooder's legs with his shirt until the last of the flames were out. Cooder reached down and ripped open the trunk lid.

Virgil peered inside. The clothes were stacked just as Virgil remembered them. "It's just a goddamned trunk, Cooder! We've got to get out of here."

Cooder shook his head, tossing clothes over his shoulder like a threshing machine firing wheat into a truck. "It's how we get in," he said at last.

"What?" said Virgil. He kicked the old trunk, surprised at how solid it felt, as though it were bolted in place. When the last of the clothes were gone, he shoved Cooder aside and leaned down into it, slapping the sides, testing the bottom that *did* give off a hollow ring he hadn't noticed before. With nimble fingers, he felt for the joint where the bottom met the sides. There was a space as wide as a fingernail all the way around that shouldn't have been there. He jerked his pocket knife out, slipped it into the gap, and folded back the false bottom.

To Virgil's surprise, Cooder shoved *him* aside, leapt into the trunk and disappeared, like Alice vanishing down a rabbit hole. Cooder's head—reappearing seconds later, like a prairie dog on the lookout for hawks—would have looked humorous if it hadn't been accompanied by the sound of rending wood directly overhead. Virgil hiked his legs over the side of the trunk and dropped into the stairwell almost on top of Cooder. They slid to the bottom on their butts, just in time to be showered by sparks as another load of burning timbers crashed atop the trunk. The heat on Virgil's back was intense. The only light in the tiny room was the red glow of the blazing lumber directly overhead, but he spotted the door into the subcellar instantly.

"Go on!" he shouted at Cooder. "Get out!"

He pushed himself up off the stairs and ended up standing beside Cooder, uselessly twisting the knob that would not give. He kicked the door with his boot, panic starting to win out. The tight little room and the sense that the entire building was collapsing around them like a house of cards had Virgil's fear reaching its breaking point. And they were about to suffocate to boot. It wasn't so much that the smoke was getting thicker in the room, it was the sense that the air was disappearing. Virgil knew what was happening. The fire was eating up all the oxygen in the basement, leaving them nothing but carbon monoxide to breathe. And a man couldn't breathe carbon monoxide.

"We have to get out!" he shouted, edging around Cooder to face the door squarely. He kicked it hard just below the knob, but it was a heavy metal unit with a steel frame set into a block wall. He kicked it again with no more effect, already beginning to feel weak from exertion and lack of oxygen.

"Kick it, Cooder," he gasped.

Cooder shrugged, but did as he was told.

Twice.

"It won't open, Virg."

"It has to open, Cooder. I didn't come here to die in a hole in the ground."

"They must have locked it from inside."

Why hadn't *he* thought of that? Cooder swore Audrey was down here. Their family car was parked in the drive. That meant there was somebody to unlock the damned door!

If Cooder was right and she was alive.

"Audrey! Anybody! Can you hear me? Open up!" He pounded on the door with both fists and kicked it again with the toe of his boot. A large section of beam, sparking like fireworks, clattered down the stairs and landed near their feet.

55

AUDREY WAS CERTAIN she'd heard something. She was wedged in close to Richard in Zach's cell, in the farthest corner of the underground complex. She'd found the breaker for the ventilation system, shut it down, and stuffed blankets and sheets in the vents. Then she'd half-dragged, half-carried Richard down the hall and shoved loose clothing beneath the door. She hoped they were deep enough to survive the firestorm above them if they waited it out.

"It's just the noise of the fire," she said, trying to keep Richard alert, but he kept nodding in and out of consciousness. "Hang on. We're going to be all right." She'd snagged a flashlight off Merle's workbench just before the lights went out for the last time. Now she rested it on the floor and tried to make Richard more comfortable on his blanket.

"She kidnapped Zach," she said, not knowing if he was hearing her. "All these years, I thought it was my mother that did those things. I even thought that maybe I was somehow responsible for some of it. But now..." She shook her head. "Mother took Zach to keep Tara from getting him. In her own way, she was trying to protect him." She cocked her head. "Did you hear something?"

Richard half-opened his eyes and looked at her groggily. "What did it sound like?"

"I thought I heard someone shouting. Maybe it's help. Listen."

A sound that might have been a voice teased at her ears. "There. Did you hear that?"

Richard shook his head. "Just the fire."

She tucked the blanket tighter around his shoulders and he tried to smile with his eyes closed. She held his hand and noticed how cool it felt. When he opened his eyes again, she told him to hold on. She wasn't going to lose *him,* not after losing Zach *again.*

"You found him, Aud," whispered Richard. "You really found him."

"He's gone," she said. Her chest tightened but she refused to break down now, when Richard needed her.

Richard's eyes clouded, but he fought to stay with her. "You found him once," he said. "You can find him again."

She wanted to believe that. But could she? Would she survive to find him? She felt no sense of Zach at all now. The wonderful feeling of being able to reach out with her mind and touch him, had disappeared. She tried to put herself back into a self-induced trance, slowing her breathing, relaxing her body. But something kept intruding. A tapping noise. Like coins falling in a cup. And then, far off, whispered voices...

"Listen," she said, easing out from under Richard and placing her ear against the door. "It sounds like someone's calling for help. What if it's Zach? What if she left him?" But she knew that was too good to be true. Tara thought everyone in the basement was dead by now. There was no reason to leave Zach. Not when she wanted to experiment on him.

Richard closed his eyes and Audrey couldn't tell if he was nodding off or concentrating.

Two pops sounded. Like firecrackers. Then she heard the faint cries again.

"Someone's down here," said Audrey, ripping out the rags that she had laboriously stuffed under the door.

Virgil's skull felt like someone had crawled inside it with a sledgehammer and now they were trying to pound their way out through his forehead. He had dented the heavy door with his boots and he was pretty sure a couple of his toes were broken. Finally, he'd shot through the lock, but someone had packed something heavy up against the inside of the door, and the best he and Cooder could manage was to wedge it open an inch, just enough to get a breath of air, but not nearly enough to save them from the heat that was turning the tiny room into an oven. Already Virgil could feel the skin on the back of his neck starting to blister and his lungs felt as though they had been belt-sanded. He kept slapping at his hair to make sure it wasn't alight.

"Let's try one more run at it," he said, urging Cooder on. Cooder gave him a long, suffering look but backed away the eight feet to the far wall, preparing for their charge. Shoulder to shoulder they struck the door at full tilt, but all they got for their trouble were aching shoulders.

"We're finished," said Virgil, leaning heavily against the door frame, staring up at the hole over their heads that now looked like the bottom of a giant campfire.

Cooder shook his head.

"You got an idea?" said Virgil.

"She's coming."

"Who?"

"The woman."

The sound of metal dragging across carpet alerted Virgil, and he shoved hard on the door, gratified to feel it give a little.

"Wait a minute!" a woman screamed.

"Audrey?!" he shouted. "Is that you? We've got to get out of here!"

"I'm trying to move the desk! I barely got it into place by myself. Hold on!"

As Audrey struggled to drag the heavy desk back, Cooder and Virgil put their weight into it again. The door finally screeched open and the charbroiled pair fell through into the corridor, gasping for breath.

"Is anyone else out there?" asked Audrey, peering past them at the flames that were starting to catch on the upper stair treads.

Virgil shook his head.

"Zach was here," she said. "Just like I told you." The pain in her eyes slashed him like a knife.

Virgil figured now was not a good time to stop to say he was sorry. "Where's he now?"

"Tara's got him."

Virgil glanced back through the door as the flames danced down another two treads. He kicked the door shut.

"I barricaded us in to keep the smoke from getting down here and to conserve oxygen," said Audrey. "I was afraid a beam or some of the masonry might collapse down into that little room and bust the door open."

"Good idea," said Virgil, helping Cooder shove the desk back into place after Audrey stuffed rags under the door again. With the door closed, the hallway was once more bathed in darkness broken only by the flashlight's glow. Audrey pointed it at the floor.

"Richard's been shot in the chest," she said, scurrying back down the hall.

Virgil and Cooder followed close on her tail. Virgil glanced at Martha's body lying on the floor of the sitting room as they passed it.

"Tara shot her too," said Audrey, stopping. "She's dead."

"You sure?"

Audrey nodded. But Virgil dropped down beside Martha anyway, sliding his fingers onto her throat. He glanced at Audrey and shook his head. She shrugged.

She led them up the hall to the room where Richard now lay unconscious on his blanket. Virgil knelt beside Richard and pulled aside the bloody shirt Audrey had used for a bandage. He shook Richard gently and Richard came around again, enough to recognize him.

"You're going to be all right," said Virgil. "Don't worry, we'll get you out of here."

Virgil glanced at Audrey and she gave him a brief, tentative smile as he gently tightened the shirt back around Richard's chest.

"The bleeding has about stopped," said Virgil. "You did the right thing, plugging the hole like that."

"He's not going into shock, is he?"

Virgil glanced at Richard. He *might* be. But they'd done everything for him they could right now, and there was nothing to be gained by worrying Audrey. "Not yet. But we need to get out of here and soon. You looked for another way out?"

Audrey shook her head. "There isn't one. Just the stairs you came down. But the firemen will find us, right?"

Virgil's expression said as much as his words. "Not for a while. The fire trucks will be hosing this one down all night. Then it could be a few days before the fire marshal really gets to investigating, and even then he might not find us down here for a week. The remains of the barn will collapse over the hole up there. Audrey, I'm afraid we're buried." He grabbed her by the shoulders when she started to sag. But there was steel in her eyes.

"Our car's out front," she said. "Your car must be out there. Won't they be looking for us?"

"Oh, they'll be looking all right. But even so, it could take days. They'll be careful, sifting through the ashes. They'll most likely assume we're dead, so they'll be looking for evidence, not survivors." He glanced around the room. "I don't feel the heat so much here just yet. I think we're safe for the moment." He had no idea of just how hot it might get in the basement. Maybe the surrounding soil would keep it at least liveable. Maybe not. But he didn't think it would do any good for Audrey to think about that either. One problem at a time. "The trouble is oxygen. The fire is sucking it out and now all of us are using it too. I don't know how long we can stay down here. You absolutely certain there's no other way out?"

"Pretty sure," said Audrey. "I found this cell where they kept Zach, another bedroom, a bathroom, a storage room, a workroom, and the room you saw. But no other exit."

"Show me the workroom," said Virgil, following Audrey two doors down. The one door on the other side of the corridor was closed. "What's in there?" asked Virgil, pointing.

"The bathroom."

Virgil passed by her into the workroom. Audrey stood in the doorway.

"Tara has Zach," Audrey reminded him. "She's going to kill him."

"Why would she want to do that?" asked Virgil, wondering if she was going to confirm his theory about Tara's research.

"She wants to experiment on him."

Virgil closed his eyes, nodding.

"She thinks Zach has some kind of supernatural powers," said Audrey. "And she believes she can enhance them. She'll kill him. Just like she killed my sister and brother."

"I thought your mother did something to your sister and brother."

Audrey shook her head. "I did too. But it was Tara. I never *remembered* it before."

Virgil rubbed sweat off his brow with the back of his sleeve.

"All right. Well, we have to find a way out."

"How?" said Audrey.

"The obvious way would be to dig."

"The walls and ceiling are concrete and they're lined with lead," said Audrey.

"What?" said Virgil, glancing around. He hadn't paid any attention to the walls before. But the walls and ceiling in the little workroom seemed normal enough, painted a uniform shade of beige. He recalled Charlie telling him that Martha Remont's cellar had been lead-lined. "Why lead?"

"I think my mother thought it would keep Tara away."

"But it didn't work."

"Obviously not."

"Not much here," said Virgil, glancing at the worktable and shelves. He eyed the woodworking tools and small table with a vise attached to the side. "And mostly power tools. That's not going to help us much."

"Shine the light over here," said Audrey, shoving aside a wooden crate. Virgil's flashlight illuminated a row of metal ducts radiating off a single flue that dropped down through the ceiling. A large fan system was wired directly into the breaker panel.

"Did you do that?" said Virgil, pointing toward the blankets plugging the vents.

Audrey nodded. "Richard had me shut off the breaker to the fan. The ventilation system was sucking smoke down here."

Virgil glanced at the dead lightbulb overhead, feeling a faint ray of hope. If they could use the power drill and circular saw, *that* might help. "Did you trip them all?"

"No," said Audrey. "The power went out right after that."

The hope faded.

Cooder hefted a small sledgehammer with a short handle and pulled a wide-bladed chisel off the wall.

"Whatcha gonna do with that?" said Virgil.

"Dig," said Cooder, nodding up toward the ceiling.

"Case you didn't hear anyone mention it," said Virgil, "there's a burning building right on top of us."

Virgil watched that roll around inside Cooder's skull. Audrey looked at Cooder, then Virgil. Virgil shook his head and rolled his eyes.

"Not in the bathroom," said Cooder.

"Huh?" said Virgil, blinking.

"Feel the ceiling," said Cooder.

Virgil reached up and placed his hand against the lead. It was warm, a lot warmer than a cellar wall or ceiling had any right to be. There was a fire directly over their heads.

"Not in the other room," said Cooder again.

"How do you know that?" asked Virgil.

Cooder shrugged "The door's cooler there."

Virgil glanced at Audrey.

"Maybe," said Audrey. "You get kind of lost down here. But I think the cellar follows the outline of the house above. Maybe the bathroom was added on later?"

"Maybe," muttered Virgil, trying to orient himself. If the house *was* right over their heads here, then the bath across the hall might be out from under the fire, somewhere in the vicinity of the driveway. He found a household hammer and a short steel crowbar, and Cooder led the way back across the hall. Sure enough, the door did feel cooler. Virgil shoved it in, surprised to find a set of stairs leading up half a floor to the bathroom.

"Merle probably raised the bathroom so he didn't have to put in a sewage pump to get the waste to flow to the septic system," he said.

Audrey shook her head, not understanding.

"Sewage flows downhill," said Virgil. "Plumbers'll tell you it's a pain to install a pump. Someone like Merle probably wouldn't know how. With any luck, the bathroom isn't much deeper underground than the regular house basement. Come on."

The three of them marched single file up the tiny stairs,

wedging into the bathroom. A small vanity and sink took up one wall. The toilet was on the other and a built-in fiberglass tub at the far end butted against a small closet. The walls were decorated in a floral wallpaper and most of the floor was concrete painted pink. The section under the tub and toilet was raised, however, sheathed in bare plywood. Clean towels hung from wooden rods and two toothbrushes rested neatly in a clean glass on the vanity. The room was definitely cooler.

"You have your moments, Cooder," said Virgil. "I'll give you that."

Cooder grinned like a stroked puppy.

Virgil stared at the sink. "Looks like your mother lived down here with Zach."

Audrey nodded. "She was so pale. I don't think she's seen daylight in ages."

Virgil dropped the hammer and crowbar and took the tools Cooder was carrying, instead. He began to chisel a square opening overhead. He had only been working for a couple of minutes—he hadn't even been able to tear the thin paneling away from the lead yet—when his arms dropped to his sides, and his heart throbbed in his chest. Cooder took the tools out of Virgil's hands and *his* blows reverberated in the cellar. He managed to peel away the plywood and went to work on the metal. When Cooder began to tire, Virgil took over again. They worked that way for half an hour before they were finally able to pull down a man-size square of the quarter-inch sheet of soft lead.

Virgil immediately began chiseling at the concrete.

When his hands sagged again, the ceiling was chipped and grooved, but nowhere had he gouged deeper than the width of his little finger into the hardened cement. Cooder took over again, but still only cornflake-sized chips flew from the ceiling. When he finally tired, Audrey slipped beside him and began hacking wildly over her head with the sharp end of the crowbar, but all that accomplished was to send a low-pitched ringing echoing around the room.

"How thick do you think it is?" she said at last, leaning on the crowbar, catching her breath.

"No way of telling," said Virgil. "Unsupported ceiling

like that, might be six, eight inches or more and it's probably steel reinforced."

"Shit," said Audrey, staring at the tiny bit of damage they had managed to cause.

Virgil sat down on the floor. The fire was barely audible down the hall, and he wondered again just how long they would be buried. Richard wasn't going to survive long without medical attention, and even if the fire didn't drain the air, he knew they couldn't breathe in here much longer. To top it off, the temperature was steadily rising. It had to be near ninety even in the cooler bathroom. Virgil felt the walls of the cellar closing in on him.

"I have to get out of here," said Audrey, mirroring Virgil's thoughts. She didn't raise her voice, but there was panic in it just below the surface.

"We will," said Virgil. "We're going to get out. Just give me a minute."

"How?" she said.

"I don't know yet."

"A rat could get out," said Cooder.

Virgil gave him a look he was certain Cooder had seen often enough before. "We're not rats, Cooder."

Cooder shrugged. "A rat could get out."

"How would it get out?" asked Audrey.

"Audrey," said Virgil. "Cooder . . . Cooder has some issues."

"Through cracks in the walls . . . or the plumbing," said Cooder.

"We can't go through the plumbing," said Audrey. "And the walls are stone or concrete. Just like the ceiling."

"No," said Virgil. "We can't." But he was rubbing his chin, musing. "The plumbing has to go through the wall or floor though. The concrete might be weaker there. At least there'd be a hole we could start with." He stared at the plywood platform beneath the toilet and tub. "Pry that up," he said, motioning Cooder to go to work with the crowbar.

They knocked the toilet off its stand and snapped the copper feed pipe. It pumped out about a gallon of water and then bled dry.

"No electricity. Pump's off," said Virgil.

The smell of raw sewage filled the room. Audrey backed into the doorway as Virgil and Cooder struggled with the flooring. The sound of groaning nails and rending lumber shrieked through the cellar. Virgil moved in beside Cooder and the two of them hacked and cranked at the ornery flooring. When Cooder shifted out of Virgil's way to give him room, Audrey found herself staring directly into Cooder's mesmerizing eyes.

"I'm Audrey Bock," she said, realizing they'd never been introduced, offering her hand.

It disappeared in Cooder's huge mitt. "Cooder."

"You help the sheriff?" she said, still unable to take her eyes away. Cooder's hands seemed impossibly warm and soft and she experienced a strange sensation of overpowering calm. Cooder appeared to realize the reaction he was causing. He smiled gently, but there seemed more to it than just a smile, as though he were discoursing with her on some level far below normal human communication. She knew that whatever was happening, it wasn't about her telepathy. Cooder was touching her with something so basic it could only be understood as love. She felt wrapped inside a strong, safe place, the likes of which she had never experienced before. And without understanding how, she realized she knew things about Cooder he'd never told anyone.

Cooder frowned, ending the moment. "I seen bad things," he whispered.

Audrey stood silent, trying to speak. Finally she nodded slowly. "I've seen bad things too, Cooder."

"Sometimes I can feel things."

"Things about other people?"

Audrey waited as Cooder struggled to form a response.

"Yeah. Sometimes."

"What do you feel now?" she asked, glancing down at her hand still wrapped protectively in his.

Cooder's frown turned hard and his eyes grew distant. "Scared."

She felt it too, now, radiating through her. "Because of the fire?"

"No."

"Because of my son."

"Yes, ma'am."

"I feel that too, Cooder. But I don't know what to do. What am I going to do?"

Cooder couldn't possibly have the answer to Audrey's question, and yet she found herself listening with bated breath.

"Don't ever let her know."

"Tara?"

A nod. "Doctor Beals."

"Don't ever let her know what?"

"That you feel people."

"What did she do to you?"

Tears welled in Cooder's eyes and Audrey felt as though she were melting. For just an instant her fear for Zach faded and she experienced some of the horror she had been tormented with in her garden. The blindness. The pain radiating outward in all directions. But she knew that she was feeling not only her own pain, but some of Cooder's as well.

"Don't let her know," he whispered.

"She hurt you like that and you still lied to her?"

A nod.

She stroked the whiskers on his cheek and he smiled.

"He's okay," he said.

"I want to believe that, but I can't feel him anymore."

Cooder placed a brawny hand over her tiny shoulder. "He's okay."

"Shit!" said Virgil.

He dragged part of the dismembered box that had been the platform past Audrey and Cooder, and tossed the pieces down the stairs, shaking his head.

"What is it?" asked Audrey.

"There's a hole all right," said Virgil. "But it's barely big enough to get a rat through." He gave Cooder a discouraged look and disappeared back into the bathroom just as the sound of the sledgehammer pounding on concrete rumbled through the room again.

"This isn't going to work either!" shouted Virgil, throwing the hammer into the tub.

"There has to be a way out!" said Audrey, crowding back into the room. "There has to!"

Virgil was on his knees staring into a square hole in the

cement floor with the open toilet drain reeking in his face.
He had busted the PVC pipe and dug out the loose soil
around it, but the hole itself was barely wider than the
plumbing and, with the dirt removed, the thickness of the
concrete was revealed. It would take them days to break
through with the tools they had on hand.

"There's got to be a way out," she repeated.

Virgil gave her a sheepish look, shrugging his shoulders.

"There's got to be!" she shouted, slapping the closet
door. She jerked it open so hard it ripped off its thin brass
hinges, and she tossed the door into the tub atop the
hammer.

The flashlight was still lying beside Virgil and the inside
of the closet was a weakly lit maze of shadow. The rows of
shelves were filled with towels and toiletries, but it was the
plumbing behind them that caught Audrey's eye.

The tub drain ran through a small hole in the floor just
like the toilet, but the copper water line and a large plastic
vent pipe passed through the rear wall at knee level. And
rather than a small hole, whoever had poured the concrete
had left a large square opening for the plumbing to enter, as
though they weren't exactly certain where it should be located inside the basement. The hole had been filled with
urethane foam which looked like hardened lava. But
Audrey knew it was much softer than that. She'd used foam
just like it to plug holes in her storage shed.

"Let me see the light," said Audrey.

"What have you got?" said Virgil, struggling to his feet.

"Shine it in here," she said.

"I'll be damned," said Virgil, easing her out of his way
and tossing towels and shelves aside. "Cooder! Hand me
that crowbar!"

56

THE NIGHT WHIZZED BY in a blur of stars, trees, and on-coming headlights.

Zach stared straight ahead from the backseat, but he kept a close watch on his aunt from the corner of his eye. Everything his grandmother had said was true. Tara really *was* a bad person, and she really had come to take him away. He could hear the dog panting lightly right beside his head. He had no doubt that the dog would rip his throat out if Tara ordered him to.

For over a year now, the woman who claimed to be his grandmother had told him that her evil sister was coming for him and his only salvation was for him to hide with her in the tiny cellar, coming out only in darkness to ride his bike. For over a year he had cried and pleaded for his freedom, for his mother and father, and the worst part of his captivity had been the understanding in the woman's eyes. It would have been better if she'd been a terrible monster who laughed and beat him, or an evil witch, but she would just nod her head and say "I know. I know. It's hard for you, my baby. I'm so sorry. But I can't let you go. You have to try to understand."

He had finally realized that the only way he was ever going to get out was on his own. That was when he began exploring with his mind. When he discovered that he could *see* inside of locks and machines. When he began to learn how to reach out and touch his mother.

He still wasn't certain how he'd done those things. The lock on his room had come first. He had lain down on his bed and closed his eyes in exhaustion, prepared to sleep, when suddenly he felt as though he had gotten up and walked across the room.

Only he hadn't.

When he opened his eyes he had the weirdest sensation of being in two places at once. He closed his eyes again and let his mind drift where it wanted to go. Inside the lock.

He instinctively understood the workings of the mechanism even though he couldn't understand how he was inside it. Mental fingers reached out and pressed tiny pins here—*tumblers,* he reminded himself, his mother had called them *tumblers*—then there, then twisted the knob until he heard the distinctive click of the door opening.

But there were several doors between himself and freedom, and, once Merle discovered Zach's new talent, Merle and the old woman were even more watchful. Zach had tried over and over again to get away. Merle removed the lock from Zach's door and installed a latch. Then Zach learned to work the latch without touching it. So Merle screwed his door shut. That was harder. It took a lot more concentration to back the screws out of their tight holes in the wood and by the time Zach had completed the job the first time he was too exhausted to move and Merle had learned his lesson. After that *all* the doors between Zach and freedom were locked and either the woman or Merle stayed home, between Zach and the trunk. Zach could slip slyly around the underground complex all he wanted. But he could never get past them.

Then he had made contact with his mother or she had made contact with him, he wasn't sure which, and he had known then that he was saved. No matter how long it took, he knew that his mother and father would come to get him. And they had.

But now that hope was dashed and he was alone in the speeding car with his aunt and the dog, and the night was big around him.

57

VIRGIL FELT LIKE A CIGAR in a tube. He'd stripped off his gunbelt and his undershirt and he could feel dirt sliding down around his pants into his boxer shorts. He fought to stay calm. There was no turning back now. Audrey and Cooder couldn't do the job by themselves. She wasn't strong enough and Cooder was too big and too damned slow. Besides, he was the sheriff, the man in charge. He had to do it. Cooder had dug as far as he could. Now it was Virgil's turn again. Still, the warning voice in his head screamed at him to get out of the tiny little hole.

Virgil and Cooder and Audrey had busted up the plywood toilet platform and torn the thin plywood into small but workable spades. Taking turns, they'd weaseled into the tiny closet and dug out the foam insulation, ripped the copper pipes out of their way, and begun to dig. Each in turn would shovel at the rough, tightly packed brown clay until a pile formed beneath their bellies. Then they would climb out of the closet and while they sat exhausted in the corner by the tub, fighting for a breath of fresh air, their replacement would shovel the pile out into the bathroom and slip inside the closet to take their place.

Once the hole was deep enough to slide the digger's torso into it, things became even more interesting. Now they had to dig *up*. What that amounted to was lying on their backs, closing their eyes and scratching at the soil right in front of their faces as chunks of packed dirt and grains of loose sand fell into their mouths, their noses, and sometimes covered their faces altogether. They twisted and snorted and coughed, but the hole was getting bigger. The trouble was that twice already Virgil or Cooder had been buried under large falls. Their digging partner had jerked them out by their feet, Audrey wiping their faces with a towel, while they sputtered and hacked and cursed. Now it was Virgil's turn again and the hole was just large enough for him to stand in.

What if it collapses and buries me standing up? It'll take time for them to dig in to my feet and even when they find them, no way they'll bend me back through that hole if I'm locked into a cave-in. This is fucking crazy.

Weak light reflected into the hole from the flashlight. Inches above his head the clay became ever more gravelly. Good cave-in material.

He tried to guess just how far it might be to the surface, but he had no way of knowing how deep the low-ceilinged room might be buried. He could be a couple feet beneath the driveway or he might be eight feet down. Still, the gravel gave him some hope. How deep would they make gravel for a drive? Not too deep probably. Unless it wasn't just the driveway. What if this was the natural soil? In that case, it could be yards.

"Give me the crowbar!" he shouted.

Was that voices overhead? He worried the sharp end of the bar up through the hard-packed gravel, dodging clods flying at his face, expecting at any second to be buried.

"See anything yet?" called Audrey. Her voice sounded hollow in the tiny opening.

Virgil's sinuses were filled with the damp smell of earth and the leftover aroma of the septic tank still bleeding out of the toilet hole. The light flickered and yellowed.

"I think the flashlight's dying," said Audrey.

"Great," muttered Virgil, giving the bar another hard shove.

It gave a little easier this time. He twisted the curved end, spinning the shaft.

"I think the bar's broke the surface!" he called.

Cooder and Audrey hooted.

Now what do I do? It feels like two feet of gravel up

there. If the hole caves in diagonally that's more than enough to bury me.

But there was nothing else to do. He ever so gently withdrew the bar to see if light from the fire might travel down the tiny shaft, but the soil filled in the hole as fast as he removed the crowbar. He took a deep breath and plunged the bar into the dirt once more, twisting and punching at the gravel with the chisel end. More and more soil broke away and then he hit the keystone. The rough gravel cascaded around him in a furious pounding roar. He clapped his hands over his face and held his breath. The entire cave-in was over in less than a second.

When he pulled his hands away, he was staring at starlit sky and low, fast-moving clouds tinted crimson by the fire. He could hear the blaze roaring behind and above him, but his back was pressed against the cold concrete wall and he was pinned up to his shoulders in a four-foot-wide pit that had opened somewhere in Merle Coonts's driveway. The crowbar was gone.

He felt hands scrabbling around his feet; he was afraid they'd break his legs trying to drag him back down into the hole. He shouted down to them. "Audrey! Cooder! I'm out! Can you hear me?" Above the roar of the fire, it was impossible to tell if the muffled noises he heard were replies. Birch's face appeared over the lip of the tiny crater.

"Sheriff? Jesus Christ! How the hell did you get down there?"

Birch leapt into the hole, shouting over his shoulder for help. He brushed off Virgil's face and started digging with his bare hands around Virgil's chest. "What the hell are you doing down here, Virg?"

Suddenly more faces appeared. Volunteer firemen in full gear with shovels. As each caught sight of Virgil, they froze for an instant.

"Dig!" shouted Birch, breaking the spell. But even so, all of his rescuers chattered as they dug.

"Sheriff, howdja get down here?"

"What the heck happened?"

"Just get me out!" shouted Virgil. "There's more people down this hole. Bob! Get the paramedics over here! There's a man with a bullet wound down there."

"They're coming," said Birch, jerking at Virgil's shoulders, trying to lift him out of the hole. But the soil had Virgil locked in place. Birch moved aside to let a couple of firemen work with their shovels. "When we couldn't find you or the Bocks, we were afraid all of you were in the house when it went up. One of the firemen found a man shot to death at the back of the house. Damn, Virg. You gave us a hell of a scare."

"The body must be Merle Coonts," said Virgil. He'd made a mistake about Coonts. Merle wasn't a bad guy after all. Or not the bad guy Virgil had thought he was. He'd kidnapped Zach Bock. But still, Virgil didn't think under the circumstances he deserved to die for it.

When enough gravel was removed, Virgil clawed his way past the rescuers and out of the hole. He was instantly surrounded by more firemen and paramedics, all talking at once.

"You'll all get the story! Right now I don't have time. Get the rest of them out."

Glancing around, he saw that someone had moved Merle's truck and the Bocks' Camry. Two fire trucks had taken their place and lines led from a pump truck out on the road. They'd be refilling it from the nearest pond when it ran out of water. Maybe it had already been refilled a couple of times. The barn was gone, just smoldering timbers. There was still a good deal of bright red fire evident in the house, even beneath the streams of water, but the flames had died enough that it wasn't *too* uncomfortable standing as close as he was. The gray mist rising thickly into the night air was more steam than smoke. Virgil glanced at the trucks again and noticed they were all from outlying towns. Ouachita County had been hit pretty hard with fires in the past couple of hours. The Arcos trucks were probably still at Babs's place.

He turned to Birch, who waited patiently beside him. "Put out an all-points bulletin. Tara Beals is now wanted for kidnapping and murder."

"The boy?"

"The boy's alive and she has him. Let the troopers know Tara is armed and extremely dangerous."

"Okay, Sheriff," said Birch, turning to go.

"Birch!" said Virgil, grabbing his arm. "Give me your shirt and your gunbelt."

Birch stopped to do as he was told.

"My gunbelt's in the cellar," said Virgil. "And my shirt. Get 'em for me when you can."

"Okay," said Birch. He disappeared around the back of Merle's truck and Virgil peered down into the crater as he slipped on the uniform shirt that was two sizes too big for him and tightened the belt to its last notch. Two firemen were pulling Audrey out. Virgil leaned down and took her hand, helping her to the top.

"Richard," she said, glancing back into the hole.

"They'll get him," said Virgil, moving her away from the heat.

"State troopers will be on the way to Tara's house in a few minutes," Virgil told Audrey.

Audrey shook her head. "The police won't find her."

"Tara thinks you're dead. She did all this"—he waved his hand at the fire—"as a cover-up. She's crazy, Audrey. I'm sure she thinks no one's even looking for her. More than likely she'll go straight home."

"Even so. They won't find her."

"Why are you so sure?"

"My mother kept Zach here for a year," she said, nodding toward the hole. "Did you find him? And Tara is more expert at deception than anyone else in my family. She may be crazy, but she's a hell of a lot smarter than you think."

One of the paramedics disappeared into the hole. Another passed a medical case and flashlight down to him. Then Cooder stuck his head out and smiled. Virgil couldn't help but smile back.

"Come on out, Cooder!" he shouted, motioning for one of the firemen to help Cooder up out of the hole. Cooder scrabbled to the top. Another paramedic disappeared and then they were passing Richard out. Firemen lifted him out of the hole and Audrey hurried to his side as they eased him onto a stretcher. A big paramedic checked his blood pressure and inspected the wound with a flashlight. Richard was conscious again, but that was a mixed blessing since he seemed to be feeling the pain more now, slitting his eyes, gritting his teeth.

"You're going to be all right," she said, glancing at the paramedic who gave her a thumbs-up.

Richard tried a nod but the effort hurt and he grimaced. "Where's Zach?" He seemed to think that Zach should be there with them. His head bobbed.

Audrey frowned. "Tara's got him."

Richard let out what might have been a sigh but sounded more like a gasp, closing his eyes tightly. When Audrey took his hand he squeezed back and she could feel some of his pain. She hoped by doing so she might be taking some of it away, but she had no idea if her talent worked that way. Richard opened his eyes again slowly and Audrey saw both desperation and determination in them.

"Go get him," he whispered. "Go get Zach!"

Virgil looked at her and shook his head. "I'm leaving in a minute to go join the troopers. Let us handle it, Audrey."

"No!" rasped Richard, slapping the side of the stretcher. "The keys are in the car, Aud."

Audrey nodded but Virgil grabbed her arm.

"I'm going," she said, staring at his hand. He took a moment before releasing her.

"All right," he said, frowning. "I'll drive you."

To their surprise, Cooder was already seated in the rear of Virgil's cruiser, staring calmly out the window into the dark woods across the road.

"Cooder," said Virgil as he slid into his seat and reached across to open the passenger door for Audrey, "you'll have to get out. We're leaving."

Silence.

"Cooder?"

"Going with you, Virg."

"Sure," Virgil sighed, starting the car. "Why not?"

58

AS THEY RACED THROUGH THE NIGHT on the eighty-mile run to Augusta, Virgil filled Audrey in on what had happened in town and what he knew for sure about Tara. The radio buzzed with traffic about the two fires and Virgil spoke to the troopers, who were already searching Tara's house and grounds. Tara's car was gone and so far they'd found nothing suspicious. Audrey told them to keep looking in the basement.

"We've been over it twice," said the trooper's scratchy voice.

"Go over it again!" she screamed.

Virgil rested his hand on her shoulder and squeezed, hard. She took long deep breaths and stared out through the headlights into the darkness ahead. Now she sat silently, staring into the dregs of the night. It was almost four o'clock. How could so much time have passed?

They had been trapped in the basement for hours. And all that time Tara had had Zach. Audrey closed her eyes and tried to sense him. Tried to find the place where he had contacted her before. But he wasn't there. She wondered if sometime, in all the years that Tara had known Zach, whether she had secretly hypnotized him, implanted a command in him the way she had in Audrey. But surely Tara would have used the command in the basement to subdue him, and Audrey couldn't imagine when Tara might have had an opportunity to work with Zach. Audrey had always been instinctively protective around Zach when Tara was around, never leaving the two alone together. Her maternal instincts and her subconscious must have been conspiring to protect her son even then.

"North of town," said Audrey, pointing to the turnoff. "Tara lives about ten miles outside the city."

"I know how to get there," said Virgil, nodding.

"I seen bad things, Virg," said Cooder, from the backseat.

Audrey glanced back at Cooder and her breath caught in her throat. She peered into his soft brown eyes and suddenly she *knew* where Zach was. She turned to stare out her window and realized immediately where they were. When she and Richard were dating they must have passed this way a thousand times, hardly giving the old run-down complex a passing glance. But now the place drew her like a magnet, pulling with a dark loathsome force so unsettling that she *knew* she was right.

"She's in there," she whispered, pointing through the window.

"Where?" said Virgil, slowing the car.

"There!" she said, slapping at the windshield as a pair of cracked brick pillars supporting a heavy wrought-iron arch appeared just ahead. A black iron gate was secured with chain and a padlock. Long-dead ivy embraced the square columns, reaching upward toward the sign with bony brown fingers.

PERKINS MENTAL HEALTH INSTITUTE

"He's in there," she whispered, pointing through the gate.

"Are you sure?" asked Virgil, staring at the heavy chain.

"Yes," whispered Audrey, unable to take her eyes off the sign.

"Have you ever been here before?" asked Virgil, turning to study her face.

Audrey's brow furrowed. "I think so."

Cooder nodded vigorously to himself. "Bad things," he muttered, slapping his thigh over and over. "Bad things."

Just then the trooper came back on the radio. "You're

ight! There is something here. One of my men just found a
idden door down into another basement!"

Virgil stared at Audrey, waiting. She shook her head.

"Zach's in there," she said. But she wasn't *quite* as cer-
ain as before. It felt right, but what if she was wrong?
What if she was searching an empty building while Zach
eeded her somewhere else? She closed her eyes and
eached out for him. A faint tingling at the base of her skull
aused her to jerk and then she *did* sense him. Just the tini-
st tug. But he was close. Real close.

She nodded at Virgil.

Virgil glanced in the mirror at Cooder and sighed.
'Good enough for me," he said, picking up the mike. "Pete,
his is Virgil. I'm investigating over at Perkins."

"Perkins Mental Health?"

"Yeah."

"Why?"

"I got a hunch she might be here."

"Just a hunch?"

"Yep."

"You got any backup?"

Virgil glanced at Audrey and Cooder. "No."

"All right. I'll send a car over as soon as I can break some-
ody loose here. But it's going to be a little while, so hang
ight."

"Right," said Virgil, knowing that he'd never keep Audrey
n the car that long.

"I seen bad things, Virg." Cooder's voice was shaky and
e kept slapping his legs as though still trying to put out a
ire there.

"It's all right, Cooder," said Virgil. "Stop saying that,
ow. Okay?"

Cooder nodded, clamping his jaw.

Audrey glanced over her shoulder. Cooder's face was
wisted and his eyes had a hunted look as he stared through
he gate and up the pitted drive. The building itself was ob-
cured in shadow and gloom, but the dark windows re-
lected the moon and stars, peering out into the night like
he glittering multiple eyes of some alien creature of prey.

"I have to find my son, Cooder," said Audrey. "I have to
;o in there. But there's no reason for you to go."

"I'll go," he said at last.

Virgil eased the cruiser up against the gates and gave it just enough gas to slowly rend the old iron from its hinges. As it clattered noisily to the pavement, he rolled right over it. The drive wound through widely spaced oaks surrounded by grass that had once been manicured but now grew in tufts like a radiation victim's hair. The asphalt was covered with dry leaves and scarred with potholes.

Apparently no one had considered that maybe a building that looked like a prison might be bad for patients. The windows were tall and heavily barred. The walls were built of massive limestone blocks, and the front doors were faded green metal with thick, wire-webbed glass. Up close, the hulking monstrosity glared down at them like a giant square-sided troll.

Audrey jumped out of the car and ran toward the entrance. Virgil shouted at her, but he had to open the rear door for Cooder, and he took the time to open the trunk and grab his shotgun. On second thought, he reached back into the car and snatched his phone out of its holder. By the time he caught up with Audrey and Cooder, Audrey was shaking the heavy doors furiously.

"I can't get in!" she shrieked.

Virgil pulled her aside. But he and Cooder had no more luck against the heavy deadbolts.

"How did Tara get in?" asked Virgil. "Assuming she's here."

"She'd have a key," said Audrey.

Virgil nodded thoughtfully. "But where's her car?"

He took off around the front of the building and Cooder and Audrey fell in behind him, moving at a slow trot. As they passed each pitch-black window, Audrey felt her stomach tighten. Although she knew it was only their own starlit reflections passing in the dusty glass, she seemed to be glimpsing faded specters from another horrific time. The faces were hard, brows furrowed, mouths down-turned, eyes deep-set and empty. The building seemed to inhale the present and exhale the past.

Dry grass crackled beneath their feet, and in the distance a siren wailed. It wasn't that far to Tara's and Audrey wondered if that was one of the cops, the backup Virgil had requested. Virgil twisted his head in that direction, then shook it as the wail drew farther and farther away. At the corner of the building Virgil stopped and peeked around, waving back to them to halt, but then he disappeared and they hurried after.

Tara's car wasn't in the side parking area either.

Over the distant trees the lights of Augusta were clearly visible, and Perkins' three stories of stone and glass and iron were lit in their feeble glow. Audrey pressed close against the cold limestone, the sheer sides of the building reaching toward the veil of night overhead. She had the sudden fear that Tara was on the parapet high above, about to drop boulders or boiling oil.

She glanced over her shoulder at Cooder. He looked for all the world like a small boy about to cry. As Virgil continued on to the far corner, she stopped and turned to face Cooder.

"Don't do this," she said. "I don't want you to go in there."

"Got to," said Cooder.

"Why?"

Hardly any hesitation this time. "To get your boy."

"We can do it," she said, nodding toward Virgil.

Cooder shook his head ever so slowly and, when he spoke, the certainty in his voice terrified Audrey. "You'd get in. But you wouldn't get out."

"What do you mean?"

"I been remembering things."

"Like what?"

He leaned down close to her face and she ignored his heavy odor. "They used to let me play with birds."

She frowned. "I don't understand, Cooder."

"But it wasn't just birds. I used to play with mice too. And dogs." He closed his eyes for a second. "Dogs know a lot, but they're harder than birds." He kept nodding as though reassuring himself that he *knew* what he thought he knew. "Dogs are hard. But when you can do them, you learn a lot that way." When he focused on her again, there was more confidence in his face.

"Come on, then," she said, still not understanding. She couldn't leave him here in the dark alone, and she didn't have time to walk him back to the car.

Just ahead she spotted another paved drive—the service entrance—as the rear of the building came into view. An attached two-story brick unit had two raised garage doors—evidently for unloading delivery trucks—and a set of concrete stairs led to a cement walkway with a painted iron rail. Virgil was already climbing the stairs as Cooder and Audrey raced to catch up. They all stopped in front of another wide metal door with wire mesh reinforcing its one window. When the door wouldn't open, Virgil kicked it. The sound echoed inside the large structure like a penny on a snare drum.

"Damn!" he said, slapping the glass. "I guess I'll have to shoot through the glass and open the lock."

"Do it!" said Audrey.

"I didn't want her to know we were here," said Virgil. "But I guess my hysterics already took care of that."

"Trust me, she knows," said Audrey, and Cooder nodded.

Virgil racked the shotgun and aimed it at the lower corner of the window. When he pulled the trigger the roar of the big gun slapped against the cold bricks like a giant hand. A hole the size of a fist appeared in the corner of the pane and spiderweb cracks radiated outward. Virgil smashed at the glass with the butt of the shotgun and the pane bowed inward but held. Another hard elbow strike and he was able to push his hand through and unbolt the lock.

"Well," he said, muscling the door aside and aiming his flashlight down the long corridor. "Everyone and his brother knows we're here now."

 **59**

ZACH FOLLOWED ALONG down the endless corridors, meekly holding Tara's hand, as though accepting his fate. But *inside,* his ten-year-old mind raced.

This is just another basement. I almost got out of the other one. I can get out of this one too. If I have enough time.

The thought of time sent a sinking feeling through his tummy down into his crotch. He had only begun to become accustomed to being separated from his mom and dad the first time when it looked as though he was going to be rescued, and now he was lost again. It had taken so long before anyone found him and he was absolutely sure he didn't have that kind of time now.

I will get away. I will!

Every now and then a picture of Tara aiming the gun at his dad and pulling the trigger would flash in front of Zach's mind and the sinking feeling would be worse than ever. He'd done everything he could, but it had happened so fast! He wasn't sure if his dad was dead or alive. He *thought* he was alive. It *felt* like he was alive. But he just wasn't sure, and the not knowing ate at him. But he couldn't think about that right now. He had to think about getting away somehow.

But Tara stopped in front of an open door into a darkened room and as the lights flicked on and he followed her into her lab, the last of his self-confidence melted. This wasn't a cellar that was made to look like anyone's house. There was no bedroom for him here with its hard iron bunk. No wide-open old barn in which to ride a bicycle. This looked more like a doctor's office, and like most ten-year-old boys, Zach had a healthy fear of such places. Doctors' offices were filled with antiseptic and bright lights and shiny steel instruments designed for unknown and frightful purposes. But at least his mother had always accompanied him to the doctor, and he'd had a sense that, no matter how terrible the place might *appear,* the doctor had his best interest at heart.

Here there was no such reassurance and the shiny instruments and odd devices in glass jars filled him with apprehension. He tried to stare blankly ahead but his eyes betrayed him, searching the cabinets, exploring the strange machines with their dark displays and endless switches and buttons. The far end of the room was unlighted, hidden in gloom, and he instinctively shied away from it, knowing without being told that that was where they were headed.

Tara gave Zach and the dog a meaningful glance, warning the boy not to move. Waiting until Zach nodded, she strode purposefully about, plugging in equipment, rolling out an oddly constructed wheelchair, chattering to herself. She looked like an elf, gaily preparing the workshop for Santa's arrival. Her eyes were alight with anticipation and that, more than anything, gave Zach an even worse case of the creeps.

He had no idea what all the equipment did, but he knew that it was all there for him. And he knew Tara wasn't going to give him the time he needed to figure out how to escape. In desperation he closed his eyes and reached out again.

60

AUDREY STUMBLED DOWN THE CENTER of the corridor. She was disoriented, two places at once again, no longer only in the upper reaches of the old building. Without warning, a part of her was thrown into what appeared to be Tara's research lab. She tried to focus on the room in her head, blanking out the space around her, feeling her own feet catching on the tiles of the corridor floor.

Help me!

Zach's voice exploded in her mind.

I can't get out! She's going to hurt me!

Audrey tried to scream, to warn Zach, to threaten Tara, to tell her to leave her son alone or else, but she could barely breathe. Instead she heard Tara, speaking calmly, as though reciting from a laundry list.

"Alcohol swabs, Dexedrine, adrenaline too. Eppie, just in case, check the voltage settings."

What's she doing?

Was that her own thought or Zach's?

Agonizingly slowly, the small, bright room superimposed itself over the dark corridor she was in. Tara stepped from behind a large green instrument panel, and Audrey felt her own knees buckling. Tara seemed to be studying Audrey's face, but Audrey knew that she was really looking at Zach.

"Be still," said Tara. "This won't hurt."

Tara receded as Zach tried to back away, but Audrey felt the wall strike her in the back and then she was struggling weakly with a much larger Tara. She was there with Zach. She could feel Tara's bulk jerking her along, feel a tearing pain in Zach's elbow. She screamed again, but this time she heard it, and so did Tara.

And then she realized that Zach had screamed with *her* voice.

"How did you do that?" gasped Tara, releasing her grip and taking a step back.

Zach shook his head, confused.

Tara lost only a moment in reflection, boxing in Zach before he could take advantage of her momentary incredulity to run. Her strong arms lifted him off his feet, tossing him into the wheelchair. He fought like a cat, slapping and scratching, but soon enough she had him lashed down with thick leather straps.

"Audrey!" Virgil's voice barely reached her, but she struggled to hold onto it. She knew that she had to take control of her own body again. She couldn't save Zach by entering his mind. She had to find his body. But it was so hard to be so achingly close and to let go. "Audrey! Snap out of it!"

"She's hooking him up to the machine!" she gasped.

"What machine?" asked Virgil.

Audrey shook her head. "It's all wires and dials and... and pain."

"Yeah," said Cooder, his eyes gleaming in the flashlight's glow.

"You saw it too?" said Virgil, glancing at Cooder.

"I seen..."

"I know, Cooder," said Virgil. "I know. Just tell us how to get there."

"This way," said Cooder. "Got to go by the Mixed Nuts."

61

LITTLE ENOUGH WAS LEFT of Tara's once formidable lab complex after the cutbacks, after the fools ended her funding and forced her to make her research even more clandestine. But she had salvaged what she could. All of her lab equipment—that had been the most important thing. And some of the original security system had been simple enough to maintain. She was proud of having taught herself the workings of the electrical and some of the electronics systems in the undergound complex. She scrutinized Virgil, Cooder, and Audrey's progress now on closed circuit cameras overhead. It riled her that Audrey didn't *need* technology like that to find her son. How had she missed Audrey's talents? How could Audrey have hidden them all these years? No matter. Everything had worked out for the best after all. Now Audrey would feel the machine like the others.

Tara had known psi existed, even before the government imbeciles admitted that they did. She knew because her mother had it. Her mother had made a good living forecasting the future for wealthy men who were willing to pay handsomely for advice and discretion. But unlike her mother or her sister Martha, Tara never exhibited any strange talents whatsoever, and Tara grew up ashamed at failing a test she didn't really understand. By the time she'd reached the eighth grade, she had thrown herself into the study of the paranormal. If Tara didn't *have* it, then she meant to understand and *own* it.

She wasn't one of the world's most proficient hypnotists by accident. She had learned at an early age how to control people's minds without psi, simply by the persuasion of the spoken word. Little things at first. Like getting her way with her parents when her sister couldn't, or manipulating them into blaming and punishing her twin for something *she* had done.

Tara had used her sister as a child and then, when her sister had children who had interesting powers, Tara had controlled her sister's mind, forcing her to give up the children without a fight, without a word to anyone. Looking back on those years, she often wished she had done things differently, that she had found some way to study Martha as well. But by the time Martha's children were old enough to exhibit their abilities, Tara's manipulations of Martha's mind had left her a burned-out husk. Craig and Paula, on the other hand, had been powerful telepaths, perfect for Tara's needs.

But Audrey had hidden her powers completely. Tara had been convinced that it was a twin thing, that, like she and Martha, only one twin could be born with psi powers. How had she been fooled so easily?

Tara stared at Zach, trussed like a chicken. Then she glanced over her head at the monitors again, watching as Audrey rounded a corner.

How did Zach imitate his mother's scream? And why did Audrey stumble just at that moment? Was Audrey's telepathy so powerful that she was able to insinuate herself into her son's mind *and* body? Wouldn't it be informative to give Zach the added incentive of reaching out to his mother? Trying to save each other's lives might be just the push they needed to expand their capabilities. Was the mother–child bond the key she'd been searching for all these years? Was it even stronger than the sibling bond?

Tara's hand rested on the rheostat connected to a series of impulse stimulators within the machine. Her eyes followed the path of the red wires leading to the mask covering Zach's skull. Pain was an unfortunate yet essential aspect of her research and Tara knew more about administering pain than any person alive. She had never had two talents such as Audrey and Zach to work with at the same time—since Paula's talents developed well after Craig was dead—and certainly never two so intimately connected.

Interesting, indeed.

![chapter decoration] **62**

AUDREY SCURRIED DOWN THE CORRIDOR ahead of the others. Virgil's flashlight glow bounced around her, sending her shadow dancing ahead and lending the sterile old structure a ghoulish air. The dark hallway looked like someplace vampires might gather. She wondered if this was how the building had always appeared to its inhabitants, who had lived more in their minds than inside the white, tiled rooms.

"This way," whispered Cooder, just behind her, stopping her in her tracks.

He was staring into a doorway she had missed in her haste, assuming it was just another cell. Virgil caught up and shone the light inside.

"In there?" he said, frowning.

Cooder took a deep breath and entered, Audrey just behind. Virgil took up the rear.

"What the hell is this?" muttered Virgil, his words echoing in the cavernous room. The hills were lined in a cold gray light through the tall windows covering the far wall. Deep carpet covered the floor. Virgil studied the framed documents on the walls.

"This building's supposed to have been abandoned for years," he muttered.

Audrey ran her fingers across the massive oak desk, taking in the profusion of bookshelves, the Persian rug beneath the leather chair behind the desk. "She never left here. Not really. When it closed down, she stayed somehow."

Virgil shook his head. "How would she have gotten power? Funding?" He stared at the library surrounding them. "How could she have kept this a secret?"

Audrey glanced around, feeling for Zach's presence. He kept coming and going in her mind now like a throbbing pulse. "Tara's resourceful," she said, following the tug inside her head.

"Hey! Let me go ahead," shouted Virgil, as Audrey and Cooder disappeared through another door. But they didn't stop until they'd reached the bottom of the stairs inside. When Virgil caught up, he shone the flashlight down the length of another set of stairs into the corridor beyond. No doors were in sight. The tunnel wound away in front of them like a subway line.

"What the hell is this?" he said, glancing at Cooder.

"I seen—"

"Yeah, okay," said Virgil, heading down the stairs. Cooder and Audrey followed side by side.

Please help me! Zach screamed in Audrey's mind. She could barely breathe. She wanted to race ahead. To get to him. But her sense of disorientation was growing, even worse than before. She had to pace herself until she could reach him, until the place in her mind and the place she *was* became one and she could act. By the time they found the elevator doors, she was stumbling again, clutching her temples. Virgil caught her as Cooder punched the red button. The doors hissed open immediately and light flared out around them.

Audrey stepped into the elevator beside Cooder and Virgil, instinctively pushing the button marked *S* below the *B* for basement. The lift dropped quickly and then shuddered to a stop. When the doors opened, Virgil held Audrey and Cooder back while he shone the light up and down the dark corridor. Finally he motioned them out.

"Not here," said Cooder, remaining in the elevator.

Audrey stayed as well, her brow furrowed, her eyes closed. Cooder was right. She could feel Zach stronger now, so close she could reach out and touch him. But he wasn't here. This was a ruse.

Virgil peered back into the elevator. "Then where the hell are they?"

"Come back in," said Audrey, nodding at the corridor behind him. "There's no light here. Where she has Zach, the lights are on."

As the door buzzed shut again, Cooder turned and faced the back wall.

"You know how to get there," said Audrey, placing her hand on Cooder's shoulder. "Don't you?"

"Bad things . . ."

"Yeah. I know, Cooder. But you have to remember how to get there. You have to."

Cooder nodded slowly as he glanced around the tiny elevator, a curious expression lighting his face.

"What are you hunting for?" said Virgil.

"He was always looking up."

"Who?" said Audrey.

Cooder shook his head. "The dog," he said. "There's a switch . . ."

Virgil glanced at Audrey and shook his head. But Cooder ran his fingers underneath the safety rail until a metallic click sounded. Another mechanical *whooshing* sounded as the back wall of the elevator slid away.

Another corridor appeared before them, this one dank and damp, lit unevenly by oddly spaced fluorescent fixtures. As they entered the hallway, their footsteps echoed away like rats skittering down a hole. The place had an underlying odor that set Audrey's nerves on edge. Virgil must have noticed it too. He grabbed Cooder's sleeve to stop him, then motioned a finger across his lips for silence. Replacing the flashlight in his belt holder, he put both hands on the shotgun. But staring down the length of the long corridor, Audrey knew the gun would not be enough.

We aren't hunting her, she thought. She's playing with us. I can feel her. Watching.

For the first time she glanced up and noticed the half-hidden camera peeking through a glass bubble in the ceiling tile. She tapped Virgil on the shoulder and pointed to it.

Virgil frowned. "Nothing we can do about that now. If she's looking, she's looking."

Just then, a public address system crackled to life through

hidden wall speakers. Audrey spun back toward Cooder. "Plug your ears!" she screamed. There were several metallic clicking noises, then Tara's voice. "Egress. Exit."

Audrey felt the sudden dullness again, but it wasn't nearly so confusing, so overwhelming as before. It seemed more like a natural sluggishness, like waking up slowly from a deep sleep. And she'd heard the words this time. She could control herself, take possession of her body again. She fought her way through the sludge, struggling to break out of the darkness back into the light of the corridor. She couldn't let Tara do this to her. If she went under, they were all dead.

 **63**

"WHAT THE HELL?" said Virgil. The weird combination of words still echoed down the hall. He glanced from Audrey to Cooder. Their faces were blank. They looked more like statues than people and then he knew what had happened. They were hypnotized. Just like Mac.

The public address system rattled again. "Kill the intruder. Take the gun away from him and kill him."

"Shit," said Virgil.

A new gleam of unquestioning obedience came on in Cooder's eyes. Behind Audrey and Cooder, the door to the elevator was sliding shut. The loud *click* as it locked back into place sounded like a casket lid closing. Virgil backed away down the hall, pointing his shotgun at Cooder since he looked to be the only one who had heard the command. Cooder's movements were jerky and unsure and his hands were spread like a 1930s movie monster. It would have been comic if his face hadn't been stony, and if Virgil hadn't been absolutely certain that Cooder would choke him to death with those same hands. Audrey was shaking her head and stamping her feet, and Cooder's movements were slow and unwieldy, his face a mixture of concentration and confusion.

"Stop, Cooder!" Virgil shouted, waving the gun in Cooder's face.

Cooder slapped at the shotgun barrel, his movements clumsy and slow. But he kept coming.

"I'll shoot him!" shouted Virgil, hoping the address system was two-way.

No answer.

"I'll shoot both of them if I have to!"

He thought he could wound Cooder. Shoot him in the leg, maybe. But he knew he couldn't shoot Audrey. No way he could do that. And just how powerful *were* Tara's commands? Would Cooder just keep coming, dragging himself down the hall on stumps? Cooder'd never hurt a fly in his life.

Virgil backed farther and farther down the corridor until another corridor appeared. He peered down it at another long line of white doors. Tara was behind one of the doors around here and if he could get to her he could get her to bring Cooder and Audrey back around. Either that or he'd have to shoot Tara, too, and she wasn't gonna like that idea. But which corridor?

He backed across the intersection, picking up his pace, putting some distance between himself and Cooder. Audrey was twenty steps back. Virgil stopped beside the first door, and, twisting the handle, kicked it in. It was an empty, tile-lined room. But the smell of death that he had noticed upon first arriving in the cellar was doubly powerful here.

"I'm coming for you, Tara!" he shouted in frustration. "And when I find you, I'm going to shoot you. You got that?"

Cooder was almost across the intersection. Audrey hadn't reached it yet. Virgil kicked in another door. Another empty room.

"You turn these people off now! I know you can hear me!"

Nothing.

Cooder seemed to be walking faster now. Virgil aimed the shotgun at Cooder's left leg, just below the knee, and continued backing up. "I'm going to shoot him!" he shouted.

"One more step and I'm going to have to shoot you, boy," he whispered sadly, his finger tight on the trigger.

Now he had nowhere to run. Cooder was slow and he was unarmed, but sooner or later he was going to get in close and there was no way Virgil could allow him to get his hands on the gun or on his throat.

God help me, I may have to kill him.

64

AUDREY COULD STILL SEE the corridor around her. There was no sickening sense of dislocation like before. She could control this trance, just as she had learned to control her self-hypnosis. The real power was in her own mind, not Tara's, and she could hear Zach again like a siren, calling to her.

Help me, Mommy!

I'm coming, honey. I'm coming!

But first she had to help Cooder, or Virgil was going to kill him.

She fought down the last of the lethargy and stumbled down the corridor, catching Virgil's eye to assure him she meant him no harm. Then she placed herself between the shotgun and Cooder, facing Cooder, focusing on his eyes.

"Cooder!" she shouted. "Cooder, look at me! It's Audrey! Look me in the eye."

Nothing. He was a stumbling zombie. Her mind raced. She tried to remember the words she had heard Tara calling just seconds before. The commands that had driven her and Cooder into a hypnotic trance. She remembered them immediately, because suddenly she realized their significance. How could she have been so blind?

They were doors.

"Exit!" she said.

Nothing.

"Egress!"

Again nothing. Of course not. Tara wouldn't implant just a *word*. What if it came up in conversation? She couldn't have her subjects popping into and out of trances like a carnival sideshow. Audrey glanced quickly around, finally settling on the shotgun in Virgil's hands. When she reached for it, he drew back a step.

"Give it to me!" she shouted.

Virgil shook his head, studying her eyes.

"I'm not crazy!" she said. "I need to make a clicking noise."

Virgil frowned, then understanding hit him. He cocked the gun several times, shells rolling across the floor at his feet. The sound stopped Cooder in midstride.

"Exit!"

A dullness settled over Audrey and she realized her mistake, fighting slowly back to the surface.

"Egress!" she coughed, as Virgil clicked the empty shotgun yet again.

A light came on in Cooder's eyes and Audrey nodded, patting him on the shoulder.

"Do you see what she did to you?" she said.

Cooder nodded, slowly, still focused inward.

"Can you control it next time?" she asked.

Cooder pondered that while Virgil hurriedly gathered up the errant shells, reloading the gun.

"I think so," said Cooder.

Just then Audrey felt a flicker of pain starting in her abdomen, shooting out in all directions, and she knew that she was feeling what Zach was feeling. What Paula had felt. That was what the seizure in her garden had been about, the memories of Paula's pain, and the pain Audrey had felt *from* her. The pain Audrey had hidden from Tara in order to save herself. She felt a sudden stab of guilt as she realized what she had done. She had allowed Paula to die, pretending all along that she felt nothing.

The three of them had reached the final door at the end of the hall. Audrey twisted the doorknob and the door swung open soundlessly, wafting foul air into her face. The room was half in light and half in darkness, and the stench of decay was even heavier here. But the room looked as clean as the hallway. She stepped through the door and she sensed Cooder and Virgil following her inside.

Zach was strapped into a wheelchair, backed against the far wall, his head covered with what looked like a heavily padded cotton cloth, his body connected to the hateful-looking machine by a hundred brightly colored wires. It was the same machine Tara had used on Paula and Craig and God knew how many other *subjects*. Tara stood over Zach like a vulture, Adler sitting on the floor at her side. Tara adjusted dials and switches on a machine the size of a large-screen television. Audrey noticed an examining table at the other end of the room where a small body lay covered beneath a sheet, and she wondered if that was where the smell was coming from.

She eased silently forward, but Tara raised one gloved hand over her shoulder to let them know that she was aware of their presence. Audrey followed Tara's pointing finger to the bank of closed circuit cameras overhead. As though for emphasis, Adler bared his teeth and growled.

"You have to stop, Tara," said Audrey. "Give me my son back. You haven't hurt him yet."

"Hurt him?" said Tara, whirling. Her face radiated surprise. One hand remained on an ominous-looking dial. "It's *you* who've hurt him. This boy has potential. I should have known! I should have gotten to him earlier."

"Please don't," said Audrey, easing forward.

"If you take one more step, Adler will rip your throats out."

Audrey froze halfway across the room.

Virgil raised the shotgun, aiming it directly at Tara. "Put both hands in the air, Doctor Beals!"

Tara laughed, turning to stare ominously at Audrey, her hand on the machine.

Audrey felt Cooder easing up close behind her, smelled him, sensed him the way fish sense each other in a school. She knew how fast his pulse was pounding, felt the sweat breaking out on his brow just like hers. She glanced at him as his eyes fell slowly from her and dropped onto the dog. As Audrey watched, Adler's lips began to relax back over his teeth.

Zach screamed danger signals into Audrey's head. He

knew the machine could kill. And the memory fragments that flooded Audrey's brain said it could kill incredibly painfully. Still, she and Cooder slipped one step closer.

"Put your hands in the air!" repeated Virgil, stepping around Audrey and Cooder.

Tara faced them and chuckled.

"You didn't say *Mother May I*," she said.

"What's the machine?" Virgil whispered to Audrey.

Audrey was afraid shooting Tara might set the machine off. "It causes pain. Terrible pain."

"She'd do that to her own nephew?"

Audrey didn't bother to answer. "Let my son go, Tara."

"I can't do that. He's much too talented. As are you. You lied to me, Audrey. Now that I have the two of you, I can get back to my research."

"What research?"

"Sheriff," said Tara. "Put the shotgun down and lay your gunbelt on the floor."

"Afraid I can't do that."

"Very well."

Tara twisted the dial a notch and Zach and Audrey screamed at the same time, Audrey taking a stumbling step forward before Cooder caught her. Tara eased off the power.

"Set your shotgun on the floor, Sheriff, or Zach and Audrey will suffer more pain than you can imagine," said Tara. "And they will surely die."

"Can she do that?" said Virgil, glancing at Audrey. When she nodded, he reluctantly did as he was told.

Tara stared thoughtfully at Audrey. "Amazing.. You felt more of Zach's pain than any other subject ever has. This is going to be the crowning achievement of my career."

Tara reached atop the machine, withdrawing a pistol, aiming it at the three of them but glancing at Zach.

"In Martha's basement Zach managed to do something to my other pistol. He's kinesthetic. Did you know that, Audrey?"

Audrey nodded.

"The low level of pain the machine is administering should keep *that* talent under control for now," said Tara.

Audrey could feel the pain, like a knife digging just its

point into a thousand different locations on her body, so that was why she'd been having trouble contacting Zach. He was fighting the pain as well as his fear.

Audrey shook her head. "You're insane, Tara."

"No more than Galileo or Einstein."

"They didn't torture children."

"Look," said Tara, pointing toward a wide row of colored wires running down Zach's leg. Audrey squinted as Tara flicked a light switch and bathed Zach in a fluorescent glow. Then she jerked aside the sheet covering his torso. The wires were attached to every portion of his body, now clothed only in a pair of jockey shorts. One heavy cable led up under the cloth covering his head. Audrey knew what lay beneath the cotton. The cable led to the mask, the metal monstrosity that had been haunting her dreams. It was all coming back to her now. Sensing the other's pain each time a new victim was in the chair. Hiding her feelings because Paula had warned her—revealing them meant that *she* would be strapped into the mask. She remembered everything. Even the cloth was no longer an enigma. Tara draped the cotton over the mask and down across the victim's torso to stanch the flow of blood. Sometimes the veins in the victim's neck burst from the stress.

"You're insane," she whispered.

"All geniuses are considered mad," said Tara. "You won't think so when Zach becomes a phenomenon. You have no idea of what I intend to accomplish. If the fools in the government hadn't pulled their support, I'd have managed to prove my theories long before now. All I needed was someone with more *juice*. Someone like Zach. You can't conceive of the potential he may have."

Virgil tried to edge forward without taking a step.

"If you think I'm joking about the machine or about Adler, Sheriff, then by all means come closer," said Tara.

Audrey shook her head at Virgil, but mostly she was watching Cooder and the dog. She thought she understood now what he was saying before, about talking to animals. She tried to distract Tara. "You're not going to let any of us out of here alive."

Tara frowned. "I don't want to kill you."

"But you will."

Tara's eyes flicked about the room. "I have to keep up my research."

"Tara, your research has been killing people for years!"

"People die. It happens. Science progresses."

"Distract her," whispered Virgil out of the corner of his mouth.

Audrey could see him tensing, but he was too far from Tara. Even if Cooder could control the dog, by the time Virgil reached Tara it would be too late. Audrey put her hand on his chest and he glanced at her as though she'd betrayed him.

"Wait," she whispered.

"She's going to do it, Audrey."

Audrey tried to make contact with Zach, but the pain was blocking him. He couldn't concentrate and she couldn't get through. Tara *was* insane. Her machine didn't make telepathy easier. It made it impossible.

Cooder's breathing seemed to have slowed to nothing. He grunted and Adler did a funny prance with his front paws. Audrey saw the look of surprise in Tara's face.

"So you were blocking your ability too, 79B! How did you manage to best the machine? Are you really that strong? Well, we'll see. My *new* machine is much better than the old one. Adler! Sit!" The dog settled but kept moving his head from side to side as though searching for an invisible mosquito. "I always suspected you were hiding more ability than you were revealing, 79B. Pity they released you while I was out of the country. I came close to getting you back a couple of times, but you always seemed to slip away."

"I felt you coming."

Tara nodded. "What do you remember about our sessions?"

"I seen bad things."

"Indeed. Like this?"

Tara flicked a switch on the machine and the room was bathed in swirling lights. Audrey felt herself losing her footing again, floating. The lights stimulated other lights inside her mind, and she knew that somehow Tara had tripped another switch in her subconscious. She didn't remember the lights, but she dimly recalled the pain that followed on their heels. The agony she had experienced in her garden was nothing compared to what she experienced now.

"What are you doing?" she shrieked.

"Stimulating the optic nerve and increasing Zach's pain level just a notch. The lights disrupt your ability to focus on things around you, forcing you to focus inward," shouted Tara. "Remember when I used this technique on Paula?"

Audrey did. She also remembered that she had had to hide the fact that she felt Paula's pain. Because she knew that if Tara found out, then Audrey would be placed in the machine as well. She remembered her own fear of discovery after Paula warned her of Tara's evil. "Tara must never find out! Tara must never know that you can do what I do!" That warning had pounded through Audrey's skull, and somehow she had acted as though the lights and pain had no effect on her. She struggled to do that now, but it wasn't Paula in the chair, it was Zach. It was her son suffering the agony, and the thought of it tore her heart.

Shut it out!

Suddenly Zach's voice was in her mind.

You have to not feel it.

How do you do that, Zach?

The pain raged over her. She felt beaten down by it. She wanted to die. Only she couldn't. She had to save him.

But there was nothing she could do. It took all of her strength just to keep from blacking out. In the distance she could hear Virgil asking if she was all right, feel him holding her upright, hear Tara speaking calmly. "Make your way through the pain. There is a place in your mind that understands. Don't be afraid. Reach out. I know you can do it."

Blinded by agony, Audrey stumbled toward the sound of Tara's voice.

65

ZACH SHUDDERED as more pain shook him. He had never experienced anything like it in his short life. But as it worsened, he noticed that he seemed to be able to *slide* slightly to one side inside his own brain, and the further he slid, the less the pain touched him.

In the short time that Tara had been fiddling with her equipment, his mind had traveled every hallway in this new underground complex, examined every room. He had raced through the building like a ghost and he knew that if he could get out of the wheelchair and get a running start, he could get away from Tara. But now his mother and the sheriff and the man called Cooder were in the basement, too, and Zach knew that Tara was going to kill all of them. That was a lock that he could not pick. There had to be another way. He slipped further aside from the pain and looked out *through* the mask again.

Cooder was barely able to stand in the middle of the floor. The sheriff was holding him up. His mother had jerked away from them and was reaching blindly toward Tara. But Zach knew that she would never get there.

I have to do something! But what?

The brightly colored wires attracted his attention again, and he began to explore them, following them to the inside of the machine. It wasn't anything like a lock or a pistol, but he sensed its workings nonetheless and he began to understand the underlying *sense* of it immediately. In fact, he understood the mechanics of it far better than his aunt.

As Tara regarded Audrey, Zach reached out with everything he had, willing a tweak here, an adjustment there. This was more than moving tumblers in a lock, a lot more. Even so, it required a light breath rather than a push. And he felt stronger by the minute. He seemed to be drawing power from somewhere. He felt almost as though someone was lifting him up, and he realized that he was no longer just drawing comfort from being in contact with his mother, he was taking strength from her too.

You can do it, sweetheart.

When Zach reached a nexus point in the machine, he flipped a series of digital switches and Tara jerked.

"What are you doing?" she screamed, turning on Zach. "Stop that!"

As she turned toward him, swinging the pistol in his direction, Zach shorted another circuit and Tara jerked again. As she did so, the lights stopped flashing and the pain died along with them.

Zach?

I'm all right, Mom.

It sounded almost like a different boy. The fear was still there, but it was held at bay and there was a growing confidence behind it.

But Tara didn't have the look of someone who knew she was beaten. She just looked confused. "He's inside my machine," she gasped.

Audrey took another step toward Tara, her fists clinched.

"Adler!" shouted Tara.

The dog started to lunge but stopped, balancing on its toes, its eyes suddenly blank. Tara glanced immediately at Cooder.

"You!" she shouted.

"Good dog," said Cooder as Adler trotted over to sit quietly at his feet. He reached out a shaky hand and patted the Doberman on the head. The dog jerked as though it had been shocked, but then settled back.

Virgil was eyeing the shotgun on the floor.

"Now what?" said Audrey, glancing from Tara to Zach.

"Take one more step and find out."

"For your own good," said Audrey. "Please don't do that!"

"For *my* own good?" said Tara, glancing at Zach and sliding her hand down the panel onto another row of dials. "You may be inside my machine, nephew. But this is a *lot* of machine for a little boy." She looked at Audrey again. "I have different amperages here, Audrey. A million different combinations of pain. He can't possibly override them all. Do you think Zach will be so successful with the *real* pain? It killed your brother and sister, but that took three days because I never turned it up over thirty percent. If I spin this dial, Zach will get hit with pain you can't even imagine. And you'll get it too, Audrey. Want to test it?"

Audrey shook her head.

"Zach," said Tara loudly. "Nod if you hear me."

Zach nodded.

"Smart boy," said Tara. "Too smart to play games. Do you understand what's happening here? Do you understand the word *standoff?*"

Zach nodded slowly.

"Let me show you the cards *I'm* holding," said Tara, spinning a dial on the machine.

Zach felt just a touch of pain from a different direction than before, radiating from another part of the machine, a part he had not explored. It struck like lightning, somewhere near his middle. As though someone had poked him just above his belly with the pointed end of a pencil. Hard.

"No," said Audrey, holding her own stomach. "Please don't."

Zach knew he had to find a way out, now! But it wasn't the machine he needed to control. It was a person who wanted to kill him and his mother and everyone else. But why? In frustration he reached out for Tara to try to find the answer, sliding into her mind just as he had slid into the lock, into the pistol, into the machine.

"No!" Tara shrieked. "Get out of my head!" She clawed at her temples with both hands, as Zach slipped deeper into her brain.

There were terrible pictures inside Tara's mind, but not the feeling of horror that Zach expected to go with them.

Instead the images seemed to be regarded as necessary, even useful. And there were even worse things than the images, memories that his aunt had buried deep in her past. He trundled through her brain like a small child discovering the weird treasures inside a dusty but very dangerous attic.

"Get out of there!" shrieked Tara, stumbling back toward the wall.

You wanted to see what I could do.

"You have no right to be inside my mind!"

Audrey reached out as well.

You wanted to get inside my son's head. Now he's inside yours. Are you happy?

But Zach had not yet learned how to control Tara's body. She managed to twist one of the dials as far as it would go, and Zach felt himself being forced out of her head by his own pain. And through Zach, the agony attacked Audrey and Cooder. Roaring fire raged through them all, searing their flesh, melting their nerves like plastic in an oven. Even their blood pulsed with pain. It wasn't as though the agony radiated from an arm, a leg, or a wounded torso. There *was* no body to attach it to. It started in the center of their minds and flowed out like lava. And as it raced through them, an object began to form in what had become their collective consciousness. They all saw it clearly, at the same time. White. Rectangular. Familiar.

Another door.

What's in there? Is there more pain? Or less? There can't be anymore. But what if there is? We can't stand anymore.

Three nonexistent hands reached out for the imaginary knob and jerked the door open. And there was nothing inside.

What is this place?

And then, ever so slowly, Audrey and Cooder began to remember.

This is where we hid our real selves, said Cooder, echoing Audrey's thoughts.

Yes, she whispered, feeling the power swelling within. This was where she had hidden away her power so that Tara could never find it and use it against her. This was where she and Cooder had locked away their talents and had forced themselves to forget that this door had ever existed for them. Cooder must have done the same thing in order to save his own life, only some of his talents had seeped through his door. That was why he could talk to animals. And enough had eventually slipped through Audrey's to allow her to find Zach again. Thank God.

Tara had no idea, thought Audrey. *Zach is powerful because of me, not in spite of me. I was the strong sister. But I locked the door, even from her. Now it's open again all the way. I am more telepathic than Paula was. More telepathic than Tara could ever have imagined. And the machine did work. It's done something to all of us.*

Audrey sensed Cooder's mind, bumbling along to the same answer.

It made us all stronger.

She knew he was right. Tara *had* accomplished exactly what she had claimed to be trying to do. Only it was going to cost her dearly.

Audrey reached out with a tendril of herself and entered Tara's mind.

"No!" shrieked Tara again, pounding at her forehead as Audrey spoke telepathically to her.

I used to go inside Paula's mind. But she warned me never to do it to you, Tara.

"Get out!" Tara screamed, falling back against the machine.

Audrey opened her eyes and stared at Tara, and Tara slammed away from the machine, back against the wall. She hung there like a doll on a rack, her hands still covering her face.

You have a lot of doors in here, Tara.

"Get out!"

You should have left my son alone.

Tara took a step forward but crashed back against the wall again.

She'll kill us if we let her go, Mom.

I know that, Zach.

What should we do?

Audrey stared at Tara, deciding. Every last vestige of pity, of remorse, of feeling for the woman who had *saved* her was gone.

Close the open doors and open the closed ones. You know how to do it. It's just like a lock.

"No! Please!" screamed Tara. "You don't know what you're doing."

Neither did you.

To Audrey it was as though a rushing torrent flowed through her, through Cooder, through Zach, and into Tara. But she knew that Zach was controlling it somehow. Just as he'd manipulated the lock in the basement, just as he'd figured out the workings of the machine, he'd intuited how to open the doors in Tara's mind.

For a split second, as Audrey stared into Tara's terrified eyes, she saw the woman she thought she had known, and a tiny mote of pity touched Audrey. She could see down the long corridor in Tara's mind that echoed her own, with the familiar doors on either side. What horrors were concealed by Tara's rigid control over her mind? What could this monstrous woman possibly fear?

At first the images made no sense to Audrey: Tara as a tiny child, weeping with anger and frustration. A figure in a lab coat, sneering. A patient on a gurney, flatlining. And through it all, the most intense feelings of self-pity and disgust, shame and fear.

Failure. Tara was afraid of failure.

Then, one by one, the echoes began. The sound of the doors slamming shut seemed so real. When the last one closed, Tara's head slumped and she slid down the wall to the floor, where she crumpled, feet splayed.

Babbling.

66

PERKINS MENTAL HEALTH INSTITUTE hadn't seen so many cars since its grand opening. The front of the building exuded a holiday spirit as red and blue lights raced across its bleak facade. The four survivors sat in Virgil's cruiser as Virgil finished talking to the state trooper in charge.

"I'll make a full report tomorrow, I promise," said Virgil, watching as Tara was rolled to a waiting ambulance on a gurney.

"There's more bodies down there, you know," said the cop. "One of the rooms was kind of a crude morgue, and I mean *crude*. That's where the smell was coming from." He glanced into the backseat at Audrey and Zach, then whispered, "That and the kid on the examining table."

Virgil sighed. "Call my office. They may be able to help you identify at least one of the bodies."

The trooper nodded and waved as they pulled away.

Virgil drove in silence for a while, watching in the rearview as Audrey smothered Zach in hugs. Virgil felt good. The best he'd felt in months. He thought for the first time that maybe, just maybe, life might be worth living after Doris was gone. But he'd make that decision when the time came.

He glanced over his shoulder at Audrey. "You want to tell me exactly what happened to me in there?"

Audrey shrugged. "I'm not sure, but I think Tara finally

got her wish. She amplified Cooder's and Zach's and my abilities so much that a part of the pain we were experiencing was transmitted to you."

"A part?" said Virgil, shuddering. He'd felt like a freight train had hit him. The next thing he knew, he was coming to on the floor and Tara was up against the wall, gibbering madly even though no one was touching her.

Audrey nodded. "Cooder and I had some experience controlling the pain and Zach seems to do it naturally. You had no defense."

"And what happened to Tara?"

Audrey glanced at Cooder in the front passenger seat. He seemed distant again, lost somewhere inside. But his eyes were at peace now. "Tara got everything turned back on her. Everything the three of us had. You can't imagine."

"I don't think I want to," said Virgil. "You want to go right to the hospital?"

"Oh, my God!" said Audrey. "I didn't even think."

"Dad's asleep," said Zach.

They all stared at him and he shrugged. "He's all right. He's just sleeping."

Audrey glanced at Virgil and laughed. "You don't believe him?"

"I believe him. I believe him."

"Doris is real sick though," said Zach, and an icy knife sliced through Virgil's heart.

"What?"

"She says you shouldn't worry. She says you'll be together soon enough."

Virgil flipped on the siren and flashers, flooring the accelerator pedal and throwing them all back in their seats.

"I don't think you're going to make it," said Zach, leaning into Audrey.

"Hush, honey!" said Audrey, hugging him tighter. But glancing in the rearview, Virgil saw the boy staring into his mother's eyes and shaking his head.

By the time they hit the outskirts of Arcos, Virgil had bottomed out the cruiser three times, sending sparks flying and bouncing Cooder's head off the roof. Audrey and Zach were pressed into the corner in the backseat as they rounded the last turn on two wheels. Virgil whipped into his driveway and exited the car at a run. Audrey, Cooder, and Zach followed him silently into the house.

Marg met Virgil at the top of the stairs, shaking her head.

"No!" he screamed, shoving past her. "Doris! Doris!"

He stumbled into the bedroom and dropped onto his knees on the floor, stroking her cheek and holding her hand. She couldn't be gone. She was still so warm. But his fingers couldn't find a pulse. "Doris. Oh, Jesus. I should have been here. I should have stayed."

Marg leaned in the door. "She was peaceful, Virgil. She went easy. There wasn't any pain. I promise."

He stared at Marg, trying to make sense of her words. Reality dropped on his shoulders like a stone.

Doris's gone. I'm alone.

He leaned over and kissed her gently, and it dawned on him that this was the last time he would ever kiss her. He stroked her hair, so thin.

"I love you, sweetheart," he choked. "I'll always love you."

The room seemed shiny, even the bedspread glistening through his tears, and he sniffled loudly. Doris had always been his first thought upon awakening and his last before going to sleep. Now she was gone and he would never hear her laughter again, never feel her warm breath against the nape of his neck in the middle of the night, never see her eyes light up in mirth or anger.

"I can't live without her," he whispered, thinking instantly of his pistol.

Somewhere in the distance, he thought he heard a commotion, but his focus was on the glow still lighting Doris's face. There seemed to be a real gleam to it that was fading. He wanted to catch it as it went.

"No, Zach!"

The sound of small feet pattering up the stairs caught Virgil's attention and he waved at Marg to stop the boy, but Zach slid under her fat arms and slipped around to Virgil's side of the bed. Virgil wondered if it was a good thing to be having the boy seeing Doris like that. Dead. There, he'd thought it. But then it occurred to him that Zach Bock had seen far worse tonight.

Virgil wiped his face on the back of his sleeve and sniffled loudly. He felt a small hand on his shoulder and he almost laughed.

He's consoling me. After all he's been through, this kid wants to make me feel better.

"She says you shouldn't be sad," said Zach.

"Is that right?" said Virgil, stroking Doris's hair back into place.

"Did you have a cat?"

"What?"

"She said not to be sad. Kitty's with her."

Virgil's jaw dropped and he turned to face Zach. He took the boy by the shoulders, trying to look inside the kid's head through his eyeballs.

"Tell me what she said about Kitty."

Zach frowned. "She says Kitty thinks it's funny you can't see her. You never could find her. Was she a bad cat?"

Virgil smiled. "Kitty was my kid sister. She died when she was seven."

"That's a funny name."

"I gave it to her."

Audrey peeked in past Marg, who stared at Zach in disbelief.

Virgil pulled Zach up close, staring at him wonderingly. "Babs said that people could only talk to souls who hadn't crossed over to heaven yet. She said nobody could really talk to heaven."

Audrey smiled. "Babs didn't know my son."

"She misses you, but she says to wait," said Zach.

Virgil closed his eyes and leaned until his forehead touched Zach's. The boy stood motionless until Virgil pulled away.

"Tell her I will, then," he said.

Zach shrugged. "She heard you," he said.

The crowd had left and the cemetery was empty except for Virgil, Cooder, Audrey, and Zach. The grave diggers stood patiently beside the tent, tactfully staring off into the distant trees and acting as though they were ignoring the conversations around them altogether. A light rain had fallen earlier in the day and now the sun glimmered in the droplets on the grass. Zach fidgeted in his new suit and tight-fitting shoes. Audrey stroked his hair and beamed at him as though he were a newborn.

Cooder looked resplendent in a new suit of his own that Virgil had insisted on purchasing for him. He had also insisted that Cooder avail himself of his shower and then he drove him to the local barbershop for a shave and a haircut. Ralph, the barber, had given Virgil a look, but kept his mouth shut through the entire procedure—which was completely out of character for Ralph.

"I want to thank you all for coming," said Virgil as they walked toward their cars.

"We wanted to," said Audrey.

Cooder and Zach nodded.

"Richard would have been here if he could," said Audrey.

Virgil nodded. "Doc Burton says he'll be fine in a few weeks."

"We all will," said Audrey, hugging Zach.

"I don't know what I would have done without you the last few days," said Virgil.

Audrey had dragged Zach along and Marg had practically taken over for Virgil. Arranging the funeral, orchestrating the people who would bring food afterward, setting up times for people to sit with Doris, making sure that Virgil was eating and sleeping. Marg and Audrey were becoming fast friends and Zach liked Marg too. He called her Mama because she told him her real name was Mama Cass. Zach had no idea what she was talking about, but he thought she was funny.

Audrey gave Virgil a funny look. "Richard and I have been talking. I'm going back to school."

Virgil smiled. "Let me guess . . . to be a shrink?"

She laughed. "No. I'm going to study horticulture."

"That's perfect for you," he said, patting Zach on the head. "This boy needs some nurturing."

She glanced at Zach and nodded.

"Thank you again, for everything. And I don't want any of you to be strangers from now on," said Virgil, shaking hands all around. "You need a lift, Cooder?"

"Walkin'."

Virgil chuckled. "Of course."

"What about the other boy?" said Audrey.

"The one on the table we don't know yet, but we think we've identified one of the older . . . you know," said Virgil.

"Bodies," said Zach.

Virgil nodded. "It was Timmy Merrill. Apparently he had some talent that interested Tara. It was my friend Mac that took him. God knows how many others he kidnapped for her." Who better to find new victims for Tara's research than a private investigator? Mac had contacts everywhere. But that was for the troopers to handle. Virgil had given them all the information he had and backed off. He just didn't have the heart for that one.

"It wasn't his fault," said Audrey, touching Virgil's arm.

"I keep telling myself that. I want to forget what he did."

Audrey sighed, shaking her head. "Don't," she said. "Remember the good things about your friend, instead. Babs told me to always remember the good times."

Virgil smiled. "She was a nice lady. I'm sorry I didn't get to know her better."

"She was another one that Tara missed."

Virgil frowned. "She might have missed Babs's talents. But Babs had the misfortune of working closely enough with her to get dragged into Tara's web. The best I can figure is that sometime while she was working at Perkins, Babs stumbled across Tara's lab, and Tara hit her up with her drugs and hypnosis, never knowing that she was throwing away one of her best subjects until it was too late. If that hadn't happened and Babs hadn't dragged me into this, maybe the whole thing would never have unraveled. Or worse. Maybe it would have come undone just enough to get your family killed."

"Babs thought everything happened for a reason," said Audrey, matching Virgil's frown. "Now she's dead."

"It's over, Audrey. Babs is at peace. I know it. Go home, love your family, and get better. If you need anything, ever, you just call me. And you stop by and say hi, you hear?"

"Sure," said Audrey. But she watched his face, reading something there. "What?" she said.

Virgil shook his head. "I was just wondering . . . Why'd she do it? It doesn't make sense to me. Why did she want to enhance people's abilities so much she was willing to kill them to do it?"

Audrey frowned. "I don't believe that's what she wanted."

"But she said . . ."

"I know what she said. But what she wanted was what she got. Tara always got what she wanted."

"You mean a pile of corpses?" said Virgil, glancing quickly at Zach who was ignoring the conversation, shadowboxing with Cooder.

Audrey nodded. "A pile of dead adepts. Tara couldn't stand the fact that they had powers that she didn't."

Virgil shook his head, stopping to pat Zach on the shoulder by way of saying good-bye.

Virgil slipped the cruiser into gear and let the car drive itself. But he knew where it was heading and he wasn't at all surprised to see a truck sitting where he usually parked the cruiser. He put on his hat, closed the car door quietly and climbed the hill, trying not to disturb Tom Merrill. But Tom knew he was coming. Virgil could see it in the way his shoulders straightened. Tom didn't turn to speak though, and Virgil didn't intrude on his privacy. He knew what it was like to be caught crying.

Tom spoke without turning, choking out some of his words. "I know you come up here a lot yourself, Virg. I've seen you. I never stopped while you were here. It didn't seem right. I mean, I didn't want you to feel like I knew. Like I blamed you or anything."

"I know, Tom."

"The troopers just called me today and told me they found Timmy in the basement up there in Perkins."

"Yes. I'm sorry."

"So it was the Beals woman that took him. The woman in the papers."

"Yes."

"And she tortured him."

"We don't know that, Tom."

"No," he said. "No. That's right. It might not have happened like that. Right?"

"Right."

Tom took a long deep breath. "I'm going to have him buried right here. Beside his mother. Think he'd like that?"

"I think he'd like that a lot."

Virgil stared at the dark splotches of shadows in the trees, where specters had always waited for him. Today the shadows were empty. A whippoorwill called in the distance and a light breeze stirred the grass. The woods seemed alive. Timmy wasn't waiting anymore. He wasn't haunting this place, hoping for someone to find him so he could rest.

Tom turned and Virgil glanced away, not wanting to embarrass him. But Tom stopped right in front of him. "Do you think there's a hereafter?"

"Yes."

"You mean it? Rosie always talked about it, but she was more of a churchgoer than I am. You really believe when we die we go to a better place?"

Virgil took a long time answering. Not because he didn't know what to say, but because he wanted his voice to carry all the conviction he felt. He stared deeply into Tom Merrill's tear-stained eyes and nodded gravely. "Yes, Tom. I *know* we go to a better place. Doris and my little sister are waiting for me. Rosie and Timmy are waiting for you."

He thought of the séance with Babs and suddenly he was absolutely sure that now Timmy could move on out of that dark, fearful place.

Tom bit his lip, nodded, and squeezed Virgil's shoulder in passing.

"Just seems like so long to wait," he said.

"Yes," said Virgil, bowing his head in front of Rosie's gravestone. "It seems like a long, long time."

ABOUT THE AUTHOR

Chandler McGrew lives in Bethel, Maine, and has four women in his life—Rene, Keni, Mandi, and Charli—all of whom wish it to be known that he is either their husband or father. Chandler is proud to hold the rank of Shodan in Kyokushin Karate, and is now studying Aikido. He is the author of the suspense novel, *Cold Heart,* and other soon-to-be published thrillers. Chandler can be reached at www.chandlermcgrew.com.

TURN THE PAGE FOR A LOOK AT

Chandler McGrew's gripping new thriller

THE DARKENING

Restless waifs with empty arms
Whispered chants and leather charms
Herald dark and wayward things
Finalizing ever afterings.

—*Night Land* by Cooder Reese
from *Dead Reckonings*

Lucy

LUCY DEVEREAU SPENT HER DAYS WORMING information out of people she didn't believe, searching for men and women she didn't like, for clients she tried to feel a connection with but most times could not. She existed in a constant state of tension, waiting for some unseen ax to fall, some bullet to burst through the wall of her foggy past, and blow a giant hole in her head.

That night she'd lain in bed past midnight, trying to remember why she'd watched the cable news for the past six hours. The stories were all the same, Palestinian Muslims murdering Jews, Irish Protestants murdering Irish Catholics. When sleep finally took her, she tossed and turned, dreaming of a giant blind man with rotting teeth, who chased her down a darkened street, screaming at the top of his lungs that he was God, and he had the answers.

At two A.M. men broke through Lucy's front and back doors at the same time, the noise of the battering devices blasting through her dreams like thunder. Booted feet slapping her hardwood floors echoed down the hall. She'd barely had time to reach for her robe, when bright lights blinded her and she was whipped around and forced facedown into a mattress. Powerful hands jerked her arms behind her, binding them with something thin and constricting. A gag that tasted like a balled sock was shoved into her mouth, so her first scream was little more than a plaintiff moan. The lights went out as a cloth sack slipped over her head, tightening around her throat. Two of her silent assailants lifted her from the bed, dragging her toward the door, where she collided with a third.

Before she knew it, she was thrown into a vehicle out front. The engine roared to life and she was pressed back into the seat, and in no time at all the car had made so many turns she was impossibly lost. Just when she was certain she was going to die from asphyxiation, rough hands untied the bag and slipped it off. She blinked and sniffled. A giant of a man on the seat beside her regarded her with eagle eyes. He wore a coal-black jumpsuit with gun belt and a large knife in a scabbard. His thick red mustache made him look like a pirate, and Lucy thought that that might be just what he was.

"You going to struggle anymore?" His voice sounded like gravel bouncing around in a blender.

She shook her head. Anything to breathe again.

He jerked the gag over the top of her head, ripping out a handful of hair along with it. She bit her lip, glancing at the cloth in his hands. It was a sock.

"We on time?" said the man, glancing at the driver.

The driver nodded.

"What do you want with me?" asked Lucy.

"The Boss wants to see you," said the man beside her, smiling.

"Who?"

"Never mind," said the big man, glancing around nervously.

Maybe it was a case of mistaken identity.

"My name is Lucy Devereau," she said. "I live at Forty-two Mayfield Lane. I'm a private investigator—"

"We know all that."

"I don't understand. I just find people's real parents."

"and I told you we know all that stuff."

She shook her head. "Then why—"

"Are you stupid, or what? I told you we're taking you to see the Boss, and you don't want to disappoint the Boss. Do you, Frank?"

The driver glanced over his shoulder, smiling like a wolf and shaking his head. "I can guarantee that," he said. His voice was just as raspy as the first man's. Lucy wondered if they were on some kind of drug that affected their larynxes.

"Whoever the Boss is, I don't want to meet him," she said.

The passenger in the front seat frowned. "You don't have any choice, lady. Or, at least, you wouldn't *like* the other choices."

The road outside was country lane, open rolling fields lit only by moonlight. The eyes of the man beside her danced from window to window like flies in a bottle. He reached across the seat and tapped the driver on the shoulder.

"Pull over," he said.

The car slowed and Lucy's heart slowed with it. In the distance she could see the faint lights of a farmhouse. She leaned forward a millimeter and noticed a bright screen on the dash between the driver and passenger. Words scrolled along the bottom, but they seemed to be in some foreign script.

"We got company," said the man beside her, opening his door. He stepped outside and then leaned back into the car. "Get out."

She shook her head. Why get her *out* of the car now, in this deserted place?

"Get out," he said. "I mean now!"

The driver and his partner slipped out of the car with a fluid grace surprising in such monstrous men. Her door jerked open, and she was dragged onto the shoulder. She struggled, but her hands were still bound tightly behind her back, and the men's grips on her arms was as hard as steel manacles.

"Shove her under the car," said the big man.

Ed and passenger complied. Maybe they weren't going to kill her after all, but apparently no one cared if she was scraped or bruised. She twisted her head enough to stare back down the road, but no one seemed to be coming that way, and she hadn't noticed any oncoming headlights either.

"I'll do anything you want," she gasped.

All three men laughed.

"What?" said Ed, glaring at her. "You think we want you? If we did, we'd have had you already."

"No, you wouldn't," she whispered, sensing the lie.

Silence from above.

In the narrow slit between the back bumper and the road, headlights suddenly appeared like a double white dawn. The trunk lid slammed shut and Lucy heard what she thought was a rifle bolt clacking into place. Ed crouched beside the rear tire, and craning her neck, she saw Frank's or Passenger's feet on the other side.

"Take them out," said Ed.

The headlights grew brighter, and now she could hear the car approaching. Ed fired the rifle. Then Frank and Passenger opened up, and suddenly Lucy noticed lights approaching from the other direction. She thought she heard the tinny sound of bullets striking the car around her, the whine of ricochets bouncing off the asphalt. But that might have been only her imagination. She began to worm her way out from under the car.

Passenger was prone in the ditch, firing a rifle at the car that had stopped two hundred yards up the road. The big guy had his back to her, firing in the other direction. She rolled as quietly as possible down the incline, coming to rest on her side in the bottom of the ditch, gasping for air.

"Fuck!" shouted the big man. He was waving at Passenger and shouting for him to get her as she stumbled toward the barbed-wire fence.

Passenger took two lumbering steps toward her and fell flat on his face, blood oozing from his forehead and chest like bubbles in hot spaghetti sauce. Now Lucy *could* hear the bullets whizzing around her, and she dropped to the ground again, pressing her body into the dry grass, trying to belly-crawl under the sagging lower strand of wire as Ed cursed and crouched beside the car again.

"Get her, Frank!" he screamed over the tumult. "She's getting away!"

"Get her yourself!" shouted Frank, pumping out round after round. The night was alive with muzzle flashes.

A barb caught on her plastic bindings, and as she shifted and twisted, the rusted metal sliced into her wrist. She cursed under her breath but kept shoving herself along with her bare feet until she was clear, struggling to her knees, stumbling to her feet, heading toward the dark shape of the copse of trees in the distance, running like she had never run before, her heart pounding, lungs stretching to bursting, afraid to glance over her shoulder lest Ed be there and drag her back to the car.

Behind her she heard someone shouting, but she had reached the trees before she realized that the voice calling her name didn't sound like gravel at all.

Dylan

DYLAN BARNES HAD JUST AWAKENED NAKED in the foyer of his house with that weird sense of dislocation he got every time it happened. Now he moved stealthily into the living room. The barest golden moonlight stroked the floor. Deathly silence surrounded him. It was the silence that had awakened him to begin with. He'd been sleepwalking again. And like every time before, when he'd awakened, he'd known he was not alone.

Someone or some thing was in the house with him.

He centered himself, concentrating on that space in his head where the air from both nostrils came together. He could feel every drop of perspiration on his body, smell it in the air. Tuning his ears to the night, he finally discovered sounds in the silence. He could hear the light breeze outside *whoosh*ing around and through the eaves, the faint call of an owl, the refrigerator humming in the kitchen. A sudden noise behind him stilled his breathing, but it was just a creak in the old house.

He was standing *zenkutsu dachi*—his left leg extended in front of him, knee bent, his right leg behind—as he performed a slow, controlled *gedan bari*. His left fist now protected his groin and left side, his right was chambered, tucked in close beneath his right underarm.

Dylan's fingers were long and delicate, but his knuckles were permanently swollen from years of practice on the hand boards, and the knife edge of his palm was a line of callouses, as were the balls and heels of both feet. At five foot eight, one hundred eighty pounds, Dylan Barnes was as close to being a perfect kyokushin karate machine as one was likely to find in the state of Maine, especially in a town the size of Needland.

He flipped on the light and searched the room as he had every other room in the cottage. There was no one behind the sofa or his recliner, no one hiding behind the drapes. He noticed for the thousandth time that the room needed a good cleaning, but so did the whole house. Magazines littered the floor, and he didn't want to look into the coffee cup on the bookshelf beside him. Realizing he was now spotlighted through the window, he flipped the light off again.

He was headed back down the hallway to his bedroom, when the hair on the back of his neck stood on end. A wisp of air slithered between his bare legs, foul and dank, a breath squeezed out of the lungs of a corpse. With a brief buzzing sound like a short in the wiring, all the lights went out.

He spun, flowing automatically into *kumite dachi*—the fighting stance—his hands swirling in the fanlike stow block. He was blind, but his other senses were peaked. He tried to place an assailant's position by the movement of air currents, listening so intently, he thought he could hear cockroaches crawling in the walls. He sniffed, catching a hint of the odor again, fetid and rank, with an almost mechanical tinge to it. He had the sudden image in his head of rotting machines, but what kind of machine did that?

His pupils adjusted slowly to the moonlight. There were ominous shadows in the hallway, but he put a name to them one by one. The bookshelf along the right wall. The phone table opposite it. The open door to the attic.

Why was that door open?

The attic was nothing but bare joists and extremely dusty, blown-in insulation. He had been up there only one time in the eight years he and Ronnie had owned the house.

There was a rusted sliding latch on the cheap panel door, and it was always locked. He slid slowly around the bookshelf, his hands still stow-blocked, ready to swing in any direction like swords. His center was tensed, but the rest of his body was relaxed, fluid.

The gift.

The thought was in and out of his head so fast, he barely had time to realize it had happened. It seemed so irrelevant to whatever was happening that he wrote it off as just one more bit of evidence of his growing instability.

By the time he reached the door to the attic he was microscopically readjusting his stance with each step, and his hands with each movement. He knew he could put his hand through the plaster beside him, crush the old wooden lath beneath, and quite possibly break the two-by-four stud beyond. But he could just as easily direct that power at a moving target, a temple, a knee, or a throat. He stepped into the doorway and stared up into the pitch-black stairwell. His mind screamed at him to close the door, slam the latch back into place, run down the hallway, out the front door. Just keep on running.

Instead, he placed his foot on the first step.

Shadows gripped his leg as though he had stepped into a deep pool of black liquid. There was a strange chill to it, something beyond the temperature of the darkness alone. He kept climbing, his left arm above him, *jodan uke,* protecting his head. His hands stayed open, *shuto,* so he could attack with the knife edge or grapple with an opponent.

As he raised his head slowly above the level of the ceiling joists, he prayed that whatever had happened to the downstairs lights hadn't affected the wiring in the attic. The house was ancient. Maybe it was just one blown fuse. Somewhere above him hung the pull chain for the single attic fixture. He circled his arm around but felt nothing. He would have to go up another step or two in order to reach it. His hand was shaking, and he breathed deeply, forcing it to stop. Finally his fingers found the light cord and he tugged. The light flashed on and—for just an instant—the darkness seemed unwilling to die, as though it were not being overwhelmed by the electrical light, but instead was slinking away like a wounded animal.

He turned slowly on the top step, sweat tickling the notch between his buttocks. He eyed every corner, every nook.

Slowly the sense of presence receded, the emptiness mocking him. He stepped carefully across the bare joists, searching for anything that might have awakened him, that might have caused the smell. There were rat droppings on the insulation, and he made a note to buy poison, but there was nowhere for anyone to hide. The house was empty except for him. Still, he backed down the stairs, and he left the light on.

In the hallway he slammed the door, ramming the bolt into place with a finality he didn't feel. His fingers wouldn't seem to leave the latch, as though there were some clue embedded in its ancient paint-encrusted steel that he could decipher if just given time. Finally he stumbled exhausted back to bed, lying atop the sheets, staring at the ceiling.

Just sleepwalking and a nightmare to boot. That was normal enough.

Only it wasn't normal.

Normal people didn't go to bed in one room and wake up in another. Normal people didn't imagine spooks in their house all the time, and *he* had been imagining them for almost two years now. He wondered how in the world he'd made it through the past months without being locked up.

He sighed. Karate, of course. After Ronnie's death he'd concentrated completely on his small dojo in Needland, working out there for as many as fourteen hours a day. Training students. Instructing his assistant, Amy, in the finer points of the art, since she was preparing for her nidan test, her second-degree black belt.

But it wasn't just the presence that kept him awake nights. It was the dreams as well. The dreams that he could never quite remember, although he knew they were about Ronnie. And now between the sleepwalking and the dreams, he was getting terribly close to losing his mind.

Satan

THE LITTLE MAN WAS BARELY FIVE and a half feet tall, with a broad chest and narrow hips, and his limp was more than just pronounced. It was a swinging gait with a wild leg that barreled around beside him, causing him to half turn with each step, his shoulders moving stiffly, his gray eyes fierce. His face beneath the snarl had the rough, weathered skin of a seaman, or a ditchdigger. He looked to be forty, maybe even fifty, but the limp made him seem older. His knee-length coat was a new camel hair, the belt swung loose at his waist, and his hands were jammed deeply into the pockets. The temperature hung well below freezing and snow had started to fall.

He saw only three people from the time he turned the corner off Elm until he reached the next crossing at Willow. Everyone in Manchester, New Hampshire, was either at work at three o'clock or else safely ensconced in their warm living rooms, behind high brick or stone facades, and mullioned windows with heavy drapes.

As he neared the house with a bright blue door and tightly drawn shades, he slowed, glancing into the empty garage. He nodded to himself as he hobbled up the drive, slipping through the gate into the backyard. The homeowner always used the front entrance, but the rear walk was kept shoveled.

He cursed, gripping the iron railing on the back stoop tightly, throwing himself up each granite step. Fumbling in his coat pocket, he withdrew what appeared to be a brass cigarette case. When he opened it, a number of sharp, wiry-looking tools bristled from it, and he inserted one into the lock. As he jiggled the pick, he began to hum "The Battle Hymn of the Republic" under his breath. Finally he twisted the knob, and leaned against the door, coaxing it open silently.

Closing the door behind him, he stalked into the kitchen, shaking some of the cold out of his bones with a stiff, shivering motion. He found the downstairs bath and the living room before locating the small bedroom that had been converted into an office. Two tall bookshelves framed a narrow window that was half blocked by a computer monitor, keyboard, and stacks of computer manuals. He dropped into the chair, and reaching down to the tower case, booted up the computer. Tapping his fingers absently on the table, he watched intently as the machine went through its setup routine. He flipped idly from program to program, file to file.

"Mmm," he muttered between the last two verses of the song. His eyes raced back and forth across the screen, and he frowned, nodding to himself. He clicked the mouse several times, switching programs again, his frown darkening as graphic images suddenly popped up on the color monitor. One in particular caught his attention, and he stared at it for some time, shaking his head.

He removed a mini CD from his pocket and placed it in the drive drawer. Then he keyed the machine to run E:install. The computer chirped contentedly as it loaded the program, and he felt a pang of sympathy for the machine, watching it performing a lobotomy on itself. But the machine had one more service to perform.

When the installation was complete, the computer gave a satisfied little peep, and he removed the disk from the drive. He slid down to the floor, groaning as he set his neck into a more comfortable position before pulling the computer out from under the table. Then he used a small battery-powered screwdriver to expertly remove the cover.

He placed his hand on the case to dispel any static, and then found one of the auxiliary power supply lines. Reaching into yet another pocket, he removed a box the size of a deck of cards and screwed it into an open bay beside the hard disk. He plugged the power feed into a matching slot in the black box and replaced the cover on the case. Then he very carefully slid the machine back into its original location and turned it off.

Wiping any surface he might have touched, he passed back through the house the way he had come. Then—with one last quick glance around the kitchen—he exited the house, stopping at the gate to make certain no one was on the street or peering out of neighboring windows. Then he hobbled quickly back to Elm, where he climbed into his old Ford van and waited.

At twenty-five minutes after three Gregor Oskand passed the van without giving it a second glance, turning onto his home street in a mindless rage. His office manager—a woman he loathed even more than he loathed every other woman—had reprimanded him for being lazy and late, and she had done it in front of the entire staff. He couldn't storm out of the office because his current chances for other employment were nil, so he had seethed all day, until he was finally able to slip out at a quarter to five.

By the time he pulled into his driveway his anger was slowly rechanneling itself. Instead of imagining his office manager bent over a table with her pants down, he now envisioned a very young boy, and the heat in his belly had started to drift lower. He tossed his overcoat onto a chair as he headed for his office. Across the living room he noticed a wet spot on the floor, staining the salmon-colored carpet. He waddled straight to the dark area, feeling his erection wither. His knees shook as he listened for movement inside the house.

"Is someone here?" he croaked, hating the sound of his squeaky voice.

It might be snow he'd tracked in yesterday, but because he was fastidious about the house, that wasn't likely. He squatted down on his enormous haunches and touched the spot. It felt cool but not cold, and he wondered what temperature it would be if it were, in fact, from the day before.

He hurried to the kitchen and chose a large razor-sharp butcher knife from his chef's rack. He was certain he could never stab anyone, not even in self-defense, but hopefully, it would scare the hell out of an intruder.

There was no one in the bath. Ditto for the office, the upstairs closets, and bedrooms. When he lowered himself ponderously to the floor, inspected beneath his bed, and found no one there, he breathed a sigh of relief. He fought his jellylike three-hundred-pound frame back to an erect position and caught his breath. It must have been old snow after all.

The tension washed out of him, and suddenly he remembered what he had been doing before he saw the spot. He stroked himself as he descended the stairs slowly, imagining his collection of photos. He sat down at the console, one hand on the power button, the other still on his crotch, and clicked on the machine. As the computer hummed, Gregor closed his eyes, counting the seconds. When he reopened his eyes, he was surprised to find not his familiar screen saver, but text in a very large font, running the width of the screen. He read it slowly, goose bumps crawling up his arms.

REAP THE WHIRLWIND, ASSHOLE, read the monitor. The message was signed *Satan*.

Gregor didn't feel the blast that separated his torso from his lower body or the compression that shoved his skull so far into the plasterboard wall, the coroner had to pry it out with a loose board. He didn't see the left bookshelf disintegrate into toothpicks and paper snow, or his monitor launch itself across the neighbor's yard and into their bedroom window.

And he certainly didn't hear an old Ford van crank up two blocks away.